HOT P[illegible]SOR

IONA ROSE

Hot Professor

Publisher: Some Books

ISBN: 978-1-913990-88-6

AUTHOR'S NOTE

Hey there!

Thank you for choosing my book. I sure hope that you love it. I'd hate to part ways once you're done though. So how about we stay in touch?

My newsletter is a great way to discover more about me and my books. Where you'll find frequent exclusive give-aways, sneak previews of new releases and be first to see new cover reveals.

And as a HUGE thank you for joining, you'll receive a FREE book on me!

With love,

Iona

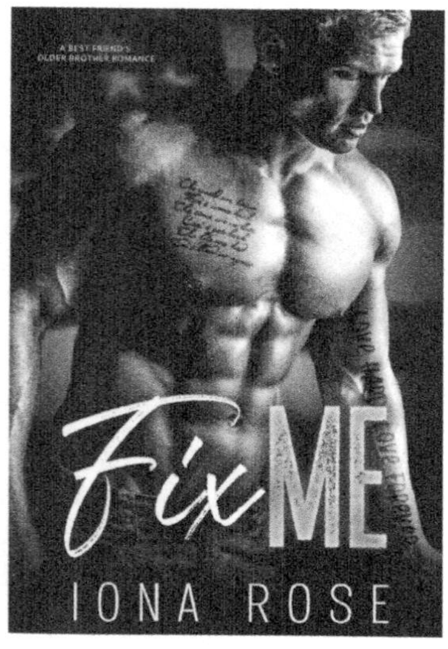

Get Your FREE Book Here:

https://dl.bookfunnel.com/v9yit8b3f7

PART 1

1

PAMELA

"Want to come to class with me?"

I didn't bother responding. But then as my mind turned my roommate's invitation over and over, and my concentration waned from the show I was watching, my interest began to grow.

I sat up on the couch I had been sprawled on for the past two days and see her leaning on the counter and scrolling through her phone, a spoon of cereal lifting to her mouth.

"Why would you invite me to your class?" I asked.

Meredith looked at me and shrugged.

"It's not the first time I've invited you. Since you're going through an existential crisis perhaps accept it, and come along? Who knows, you might get inspired by something? Plus, there's Professor Bach. I make it a point not to drool over him like everyone else but it's our final year and for once I would like to be silly."

"'What's silly about drooling over a hot professor?" I asked, and she rolled her eyes at me.

I smiled.

"Is he really that hot?"

Her attention returned to her phone. "You've asked me this question at least a hundred times since freshman year. And yet you've never bothered to check him out."

"I've been busy," I said and sunk back on the couch.

"Of course, with a major that you're still not sure you should pursue."

"Shut up," I said. "I'm figuring it out."

"All that incurred debt..."

At this, I frowned, and she caught the dark scowl on my face. "I'm sorry," she apologized, her smile sheepish. "But I do think you should come out with me. You've been cooped up in here for too long. At least meet me after class. We can go to lunch or something."

Her suggestion once again sounded good, but I still felt too lazy to get up.

A few minutes later, I heard the clattering of her keys as she came over to the living room and began to dig through the armchair.

"What are you looking for?" I asked.

"My lipstick," she said. "I'm sure it fell in here last night."

I returned my attention to my show. She soon found the tube and stopped to look at the TV.

"How many times have you rewatched Sex and the City?" she asked.

"A hundred?" I replied groggily.

"It can't be that good," she said.

"It's not," I replied. "It's comfortable and relatable."

"Come to class with me," she groaned. "Your stench is all over the couch."

"I bought the couch," I said.

"No, you didn't. We *found* the couch. You only bought the fabric for the overhaul. Why am I even having this conversation right now? I'm already late. All the seats must have been taken by now."

"People come early to his class?"

"All the girls always want the front seats so that he can notice them so of course they're there way ahead of time and fighting for them. It's pathetic I tell you."

I looked at her and was curious once again. "What exactly is the class about?" I asked.

"Data Structures and Algorithms."

"Ugh," I said, and she laughed.

"I'm leaving."

"What kind of algorithms?" I called after her. "Like the one Instagram uses to frustrate all the influencers?"

She laughed again and was soon by the door. "Come by and find out."

"I can slip in through the back door?" I asked, and she beamed.

"You can. Let me know if you'll be there and I'll save you a seat. Darryl said that he was probably not going to make it but just in case he does, he'll be seated by me."

"Of course," I said, and she blushed.

"Who knows? You might meet someone just like Darryl too."

I scoffed. "Someone like Darryl? You mean a nerd I've ignored all through my years in college but then found a ridiculously good kisser during a drunken night out?"

At her silence, I looked up from the couch wondering if she had left, but instead saw her standing at the doorway and watching me.

"Complete the story," she said with a straight face, and I couldn't hold my amusement.

"What?"

"Complete the fucking story. I'm late."

"You're aggravating," I said.

"Fine, I'll complete it then. This ridiculously good kisser now went on to be the very best possible lover to ever exist and now I think I'm in love."

I was amused, but at the last part of that sentence my eyes widened in surprise. "What?"

With a knowing smile, she turned around and pushed the door open.

"Meredith!" I shot up.

"Come to class," she yelled. "I'll tell you what you want to know at lunch."

She banged the door shut and I was once again left alone to my existential crisis.

Five minutes later, the episode I'd been watching came to an end and rather than switch to the next, I stopped and looked around. All the blinds had been pulled shut by me much to Meredith's complaints, but she had soon submitted to my desire for a dark and cozy apartment rather than a bright and uncomfortable one. It occurred to me then that it had been almost three days since I had last seen the sun, and a day and a half since I had taken a shower. Plus, my entire spine was beginning to ache. All of this I finally accepted was the perfect nudging to indeed get off the couch.

With a sigh, I moved my feet to the floor, my hair all over my face and eventually managed to pull myself up.

About ten minutes later, and as the warm stream drenched my head and soothed the ache in my muscles, I couldn't help but feel somewhat relaxed.

I still didn't think I had the energy to step out of the house until my own classes the following day, so I took things by the minute until my hair was blown dry. And then

I had absolutely no reason to stop myself from going to lunch with Meredith.

I pulled on some baggy light blue jeans, a clean white t-shirt, converses, and slung a tote bag over my shoulder. It wasn't the most attractive of outfits, but I was comfortable, and would be back in no time so I pushed the concern away.

In no time, I was out of the apartment and headed towards Meredith's computer science department. She hadn't been bluffing, as I soon found, because the class was indeed packed to the brim and it was a Monday morning. I was so struck that for the first few minutes all I did was peep through the door until a few students who were arriving late forced me to move away. I texted Meredith then and thankfully she had a seat waiting for me by her side.

I wasn't ultimately glad however because although she wasn't in the front row, her row was still close enough that it would be impossible to hide that I was sneaking in after the lecture was already thirty minutes underway.

I was surprised that the professor was even letting this happen, so I kept my head down and held my breath until I was safely seated.

Excitement flashed in Meredith's eyes at my arrival, and then she leaned over and whispered in my ear.

"How's our famed hottie?" she asked, however the professor in front was the last thing on my mind.

"I need your charger," I said as I pulled my phone out of my bag.

The next minute consisted of my fumbling to plug the charger underneath my seat, but then suddenly I heard Meredith speaking by my side.

Everything she said and out loud for that matter sounded like gibberish, so I looked up, wondering what the hell was going on.

It was then that I realized that the eyes of the entire class were on us. Well, except those in the front row as their attention was solely on the professor in front who had on a pair of dark rimmed glasses.

He also had hair falling in thick effortless waves down the sides of his face, and his hands in his pockets giving off the air of reckless sophistication.

My breath caught for a moment, but then when I realized that Meredith was still talking, I leaned slightly away from her and subtly held a hand to the side of my face to hide. I was for sure going to kill her after this for not even warning me.

Soon enough she was done, and he began to respond once again. I heard the words... advanced methods of algorithm analysis... time and space complexity classes and NP-completeness... but I might as well have been hearing Persian.

Meredith however had that proud look on her face that I was so familiar with, for when she had impressed even herself and I couldn't help but jab her side.

"You sure it's Daryl you're infatuated with?" I asked and she jabbed me right back.

"Shh."

With a sigh, I slouched even further into the seat and watched the front since there was nothing else to do in the meantime.

The professor was indeed something to look at I guess, especially since he was quite stylish.

He had on a white dress shirt, tucked into a pair of black straight jeans with a pair of loafers on his feet. It was simple but for some reason, perhaps it was the way in which the clothes hung off his tall frame, the elegance he exuded seemed fitting for a runway.

I wondered what his name was because as I stared longer, I couldn't help but realize that he looked somewhat familiar.

Maybe I was wrong, but the longer I stared and tried to convince myself otherwise the more my scowl deepened.

I needed to take a closer look at him, I realized.

"What?" I heard Meredith ask.

I turned to see the question in her eyes, and only then did it occur to me that I must have spoken my thoughts out loud.

"I want a closer look," I told her. "Of him."

Her brows shot up. "Now you want to act like the thirsty ones up in front?"

Shaking my head, I rolled my eyes at her and returned my attention to him.

"*You* were the thirsty one just now, 'Miss I need to answer a question so that all the attention including the hot professors can be on me.' Would it have killed you to know the answer and not share it?"

"Actually, it would have," she replied. "Plus, I'm not thirsty. I have Darryl."

I rolled my eyes. "What if he had recognized that I wasn't from his class.?"

"I'm sure he already has," she said, and alarm struck me.

"What?"

"He won't call you out. He is the only professor I'm certain in this entire school that never bothers with decorum, yet he gets it more than anyone else. None of the girls want to offend him so their attention on him and his work is always rapt, while the boys I guess don't want to offend the girls for being rowdy, so they keep their lips zipped."

I sighed again. "So, no one is paying attention because he knows his beans?"

"Oh, he knows more than his beans. He is the second half of a partnership that runs a unicorn company that provides cyber security protection for the biggest companies in the world."

Once again, gibberish, which spurred a headache that was beginning to throb in the side of my head.

"What are you saying? He runs a company that sells unicorns?"

A snort of laughter escaped her, which seemed to distract the entire hall for a few seconds and truly the glares we received were quite troublesome.

My gaze was instantly on the professor, wondering if he too had been distracted, and my heart jumped as I realized that he was staring straight at me.

He was speaking, calmly, unhurriedly but for once, his gaze wasn't lazily scanning across the room. Instead, it was on me, most definitely not on Meredith. However, since it didn't make sense as to why this would be the case beyond the possibility that perhaps he had realized that I wasn't one of his students, I was tempted to look behind to see if there was someone else in particular that had caught his eye.

"You're an idiot," she said, and I couldn't help my smile. He looked away.

"If he has such a successful business, then why does he work as a professor?" I asked.

"Who knows?" she shrugged. "Perhaps he doesn't like running a business. I've heard his partner is the one at the helm of things, but he owns about 65% of it. Perhaps he brought the funding? Or he's the brains?"

"Where would a professor get that much money from?" I asked and she shrugged.

"Maybe his family is wealthy."

"Maybe," I said, and once again truly wished I could go

forward to take a closer look at him.

I watched him through to the end of the class and could feel my heart lurch from time to time when he looked at me.

Eventually, the class was dismissed and just as expected all the birds flocked to the front. I sighed and turned to Meredith.

"Where are we going for lunch?"

She however was preoccupied with her phone, the widest smile spreading across her face.

"Um," she lifted her head, and I could see just how flushed she was.

"You can choose anywhere you want, I'll even pay," she said and in her tone I knew there was a catch.

I sighed again. "And in return?"

"You keep yourself busy for forty-five minutes to an hour until I join you."

"Meredith," I groaned, and she put her hands together in a plea.

"Darryl's waiting outside."

"Of course he is."

"I'll be back in no time. We'll be quick."

"Ew," I said. "Now I'll have to deal with that stupid smile you wear afterwards for the entire afternoon. You know what, forget this I'm going home."

"Oh c'mon," she complained as I grabbed onto my bag, and began to head up the stairs.

Suddenly however, I heard someone call her name.

"Miss Scott," the call rang out and we both turned.

At first, I wasn't sure who it was, but then he held out his hand in a gesture for her to come over and the confusion was cleared up.

"Yikes," she said and finally rose to her feet.

"You think he's going to scold you for bringing a stranger

to his class?"

"Who knows?" she said. "But I suspect more that it might have to do with my project."

"Come with?" she asked, and I shook my head.

"Oh no, I can't be among the thirsty ones."

"Stop," she said, and I rolled my eyes.

"Fine."

We were soon on our way, and as we approached, I couldn't really tell what had spurred my decision. I'd thought I'd be able to just leave but there was something about him that made me almost desperately want to take a closer look at him.

My curiosity however soon waned when we were forced to wait. He had his eyes on us from time to time, but I couldn't even see clearly enough through the number of students waiting for an audience with him.

Eventually he moved away from one and began to gather his things, but the request for another conversation kept coming, causing an exhausted look to come over his face.

"Ah so he's not some immortal," I said dryly, and Meredith snickered.

However, a gnawing feeling began to hack my insides, as I was finally able to see him a bit more clearly. I stared and stared until finally he called us over. His gaze was on Meredith and my heart began racing in my chest.

"I'll be quick," she said, indicating that I was to wait for her, however I soon found that I was already moving forward, my eyes wide.

I couldn't believe it.

Or perhaps this was some kind of trick my mind was playing on me. His gaze once again met mine and perhaps at my expression, he too stopped to watch me.

"Gideon?" I called the moment I arrived.

Meredith was appalled. "Professor Bach," she quickly corrected under her breath. He turned his attention to her, and they began their conversation, however I couldn't help but stop him mid-sentence.

"You're Gideon Bach! Aren't you?" I asked in shock. Suddenly it was as though I was set ablaze from the inside out.

I couldn't believe it, and instantly bounded over till the distance was almost entirely closed between us.

"I'm Pamela," I pointed to my chest, nearly jumping with excitement.

"Do you remember? Pamela Fraser? We used to live right next door to each other."

I could tell that the entire auditorium had suddenly gone quiet, and all incessant chatter had stopped as everyone was now paying attention.

He looked at me, his expression neutral and void of emotion. And then his next words hit me like a truck.

"I'm sorry, but I don't know you. Miss Scott?" he called, and Meredith went with him leaving me with my mouth agape and doubting my sanity. I could do nothing but watch them, in particular him, as they conversed. Meredith's gaze was now full of curiosity as she had no doubt been taken aback by what I had blurted. She would look at me from time to time, however I eventually couldn't look away. Neither could I leave without making him realize that we truly knew each other. He had matured so much and left so many years ago when I was still so young. I'd kept him in my memories since then but couldn't believe just how much of it had blurred. But now, I was seeing him in the flesh once again and even if I got everything else wrong it was impossible to get his name wrong, right?"

I noted the moment Meredith began to finish up with

him, so I hurriedly rushed over before another group of students took our place. They both looked at me once again somewhat startled at my sudden intrusion.

"Our house caught fire," I said to him.

"Pam!" Meredith exclaimed.

"I'm serious," I told her. "Not our apartment. My home back in Anaheim. You used to live in Anaheim, right? You rescued me? About nine years ago."

His devastatingly handsome face looked at me as though I had just announced that I crashed rockets for no reason.

"My apologies, again," he said unhurriedly. "But I don't know what you're talking about."

I had never been more confused, and for a few seconds began to wonder if the entire accident had mentally damaged him in some way. But then if it had, how was he a professor?

He had always been incredibly smart. The smartest boy I had ever known. At the time I had even believed he was the smartest in the entire world and with all he was up to so long after, I couldn't say that I had been wrong.

He was doing so incredibly well but then he couldn't recognize me. How was this possible? Tears misted my eyes.

"I've searched for you," I told him. 'For a very long time. And everywhere." My voice softened. "You really don't remember.?"

He was quiet now, and as it seemed, so was everyone else.

With an aggrieved sigh, I gave up and started to head out. "Meredith, I'll be waiting outside," I said and there was no objection whatsoever. From anyone.

I leaned against the wall when I got out, confounded at how there was absolutely no recognition on his face whatsoever for me. He might have as well been staring at a blank wall, while I on the other hand recalled almost everything about him down to his mother, Angela.

A light bulb came on over my head then as it occurred to me that perhaps I should have brought up his mother. Maybe that would have caught his attention because there was absolutely no way he could write this off as coincidence.

I turned around then and pushed the auditorium's door open, eager to head to him, but I was stopped by the person I almost ran into.

"No," Meredith said, her hand flattening on my chest.

"Oh," I staggered backwards. "You're done."

"Yes, and so are you. We're leaving."

I panicked. "No, I need to talk to him." I tried to move her out of the way. "I know his mother."

However, she wouldn't let me.

"No Pam," she said. "I don't know what that was earlier on, but it was so embarrassing. How could you pretend to know him?"

I paused then, my gaze on her incredulous.

"What? You thought I was faking it?"

She smiled, but at the complete lack of amusement on my face it soon faltered.

"W-weren't you?"

I couldn't believe her. "Why the hell would you think that?"

"Well, it isn't uncommon. Most of the girls do everything to try and-"

"And you thought I'd be one of them?"

Her lips parted but no words escaped.

My gaze lifted once more to the door and the moment I saw that he was heading out through the opposite end of the auditorium, I felt my insides deflate but I couldn't call out to him.

2

GIDEON

I sighed on my return to my office.

Her memory was impeccable. But then I guess if your home was nearly burned to the ground while you were asleep in it, it wouldn't be too hard to recall the person that rescued you from it even years down the line.

Seeing her come into that class had brought the kind of shock to me that I hadn't experienced in so long. I was well aware of her presence in the college even though up till now, our paths had thankfully never crossed. I hadn't particularly gone out of my way to ensure this but, and as I had hoped, it had worked out as such. She wasn't someone that I particularly wanted to keep in mind, so I'd long made the decision to react the way that I did to her.

She was no doubt confused, and due to the awkwardness, I hoped that she would accept things as they were, and not attempt to reconnect with me again or try to convince me that we once knew each other.

This was exactly what I wanted, but as I settled back into my chair and thought of her, I felt anything but happy.

She'd since changed from the awkward eleven-year-old that had had the biggest crush on me.

Back then, I'd been about to turn nineteen and was endeared by the little girl next door I'd known forever but was suddenly turning red and shy every single time she saw me.

I'd loved her company in the past because she'd been outspoken and free spirited, and I couldn't help but wonder if she was still that way.

I'd caught sight of her in various scenarios around campus, and in most of them she had the brightest of smiles on her face.

But not recently.

In the past year I'd seen her about twice, once in the library and the second time by the corner of a food truck, eating and just staring off at nothing. I noticed the same gaze in most of the senior students especially as their final year loomed so there was no cause for concern. However, in that particular moment when she had looked so lost, I'd wished I could go up to her for a chat, I'd wondered if she would even be able to remember me.

And today, I got my answer.

She most definitely did, and a part of me I had to at the very least admit, was glad.

She was gorgeous.

In her earlier years she'd been adorable to me and was sort of the little sister I'd have loved to have had, but now... she took care with her appearance. Not so much that every outfit was clinging to her skin but fitting enough to showcase her striking figure.

Today, she had on a pair of high waisted khaki shorts with a dark V-neck shirt tucked in. Simple but elegant and it had been quite the distraction for me in class.

It was truly a shame I pretended not to know her, because I wished I could as the adult version of her seemed quite interesting. Suddenly, there was a knock on the door, and it instantly brought me out of my thoughts. I realized I had been flipping through a folder and was now seated behind my desk. All things I had done automatically whilst my mind had been preoccupied with her.

"Come in," I groaned as I turned my computer back on, eager to tackle my remaining work for the day.

It was Oscar, and I was glad for the reprieve.

"There's a student here to see you," he said.

I frowned because we had long discussed how these matters were to be handled in the past.

"I tried to turn her away but she's insisting. She also mentioned the two of you used to live right next door to each other and that she just saw you today after nine years for the first time and that you're expecting her."

At this I stopped.

"She said that I'm expecting her?"

"Yes, that you couldn't act too familiar with her because of all the students that were around at the time."

I understood now why he had been unable to simply send her away.

"What should I do?" he asked.

"Send her away," I replied. "I am not receiving any visitors."

He seemed relieved at my streamlined response.

"Alright sir," he said and exited the office.

3

PAMELA

Once again, I was struck.

"What?"

"Please come back another time. The professor is extremely swamped and will remain so for the rest of the day."

The door was then shut in my face, and I was left to lick my wounds alone in the corridor.

The plan after class had been to head to the deli to wait for Meredith, but then I couldn't put my encounter with him out of my mind. And so, I had found my way all the way across the campus in search of him. His office was easy to find, but then all I got was his snooty secretary's reply that every single person, especially like me that just simply showed up, had been turned away.

However, I'd managed to convince myself that he'd acted that way because there were people around, because and otherwise, how could he not recognize me? I hadn't changed that much, had I?

Once again, I glanced at the door he had shut in my face and things started to become clearer to me. Maybe I wasn't imagining things. I could recall back then that even before the fire, he had begun to severely withdraw. He hadn't changed schools and although he had gotten busier since it was his final year, I hadn't expected just how coldly he would treat me. The fire had happened, and we had to move away. And that had been the last of us.

It was obvious to me now that he too had thought the same, and now so many years later, I was the only one who had forgotten.

With a scowl at the door once again, I turned and went on my way.

My mood was dark, sourer than it had been all month and it was something that no outing could resolve so I decided to just head home.

I texted Meredith to cancel our lunch plans, giving some excuse, and despite her protest, stood my ground and made my way back to our apartment.

Once back I called my mom for some casual chit chat, but before I could come around to asking about the family that we used to live next door to, Meredith came bounding through my bedroom door. "I'll call you back."

"You canceled on me? I've been looking forward to that lunch all week."

I frowned at the intrusion. "All week? We made the plans today."

"Exactly. That's how much I really wanted to go to 'The Corner' today."

I watched as she lowered to my bed, and then her expression began to soften as she took in mine.

I turned away and started idly scrolling through my computer at my desk.

"You're a hundred percent certain he's the one, aren't you?"

I didn't respond.

"And a thousand percent sure that he's pretending not to know you?"

Once again, I didn't respond, as I pondered on the matter over and over again. She rose to her feet and exited the room and soon enough and thankfully I was left alone.

She soon however returned, and before I could ask her to leave, I noted the two slices of tiramisu she had brought on two plates. I stared at the dessert and felt my sourness begin to dissipate.

So, I took it, knowing now that I couldn't kick her out.

We ate in silence, and then about halfway through, she spoke up.

"So, how are we going to get him to admit that he knows you?"

I look up, taken aback by her words.

"We?"

"There's obviously a serious reason why he's acting like a stranger isn't there? I mean who acts that way? It's not as though you intend on throwing yourself at him. You were childhood friends."

"Well, I wasn't exactly a child..." I corrected.

"Well teenage friends then."

"I was eleven," I responded.

"Fine then. Teenagers?"

"He was a teen."

"What the fuck Pam," she cursed dryly, a forkful of tiramisu in her mouth and it was amusing to say the least.

She gave me a forgiving look, and then she lowered her gaze to continue eating. I sighed.

"We weren't exactly friends," I said quietly. "But he was friendly for quite a while."

It was a little while later before she spoke again. "You

want to just forget about him too and move on?"

"I wish I could, but I just want to know, you know? Why?"

"You can't always know everything."

"In this case I want to."

"And it has nothing to do with him being extremely attractive?"

At her mention of this I scowled at her. "He was hot when he was younger too."

"And you let that slip away. I'm sensing a pattern here."

"Stop," I half-complained, albeit amused.

And then I sighed again.

"You mentioned earlier that he saved you from a fire. You were serious about that weren't you?"

"Of course I was," I replied. "Why would I joke about that?"

"What happened?"

I thought back to the scenario, and the scare of my life that I had gotten from it.

"It ruined my parent's finances, that's for sure. Plus, my dad's business started taking the strangest hits. It was the toughest time of our lives."

I went silent again, so she nudged me with her knee. "The fire?"

I shrugged. "I was asleep which made it a hundred times scarier. It was just me and Gideon's mother that were in the house."

"Gideon's mother?" she asked.

"That's the professor's first name."

"I know," she gave me a look. "My exclamation is for your mention of his mother. Why was she at your house?"

I shrugged. "I can't even remember. But it was one of those friendly neighborhood calls. Maybe she was delivering some wine over or something. My parents used to exchange wine with his parents in that way."

"And your mom?"

"She wasn't home. I think she was still at work at the time or something. It was a weekday, and she had a night shift at the hospital."

"Hmm," she said. "So, then what happened?"

Fear gripped my chest as I recalled the smoke and haze... and heat.

"I woke up coughing. I didn't even understand that anything was wrong and was too lazy to get up, so I just kept coughing until I realized that it wasn't subsiding. That's when I smelled the smoke and realized what was happening. "

"Is that why you never sleep deeply?"

"Maybe," I replied. "For about five years after that I had chronic insomnia and almost couldn't sleep at all. Anyway, I heard shattering, everything was breaking. For a while I thought I was in a dream because no one came to get me. There was no fire in my room, but I could see the glow from beneath the door and the heat seemed to be charring my skin. What's worse is that my window didn't face the front of the house so even when I screamed and tried to break the window so that I could at least put my head out to breathe, it didn't work. The glass was so hot. I think I grabbed a shoe or something and started to scream and pound on it. And that's when I saw him... or rather he saw me. His room's window was opposite mine. One moment it was dark and the next the lights had come on and he was standing in front of it."

"I don't think I'll ever forget the horrified look that came to his face when he realized I was still there. He ran out of the house but by then I think I was already collapsing on the floor. Everything after that was a blur. He carried me on his back and then found our way out. My dad was so horrified at how I could have been so easily forgotten... that even now he always checks for me whenever he leaves or returns to the house."

"Wow," she muttered, her tone barely audible but her attention rapt. "That must have been horrifying."

"It was," I said. "I was so thankful to him, especially because he sustained some burns. I wonder now if the scars ever left. I heard that the front door had been in flames when he'd run in, and his mother had nearly collapsed from screaming. He had to get me out at all costs and... I wanted to repay him back somehow. But after that he became so cold and withdrawn. I never heard from or saw him again... until today."

Meredith set her finished plate down on my desk. "I think I get it now," she said. "No wonder you were so shocked to see him and hurt when he acted as though he didn't know you."

I grew silent again. "I wonder if he hates me?"

"Why would he hate you?" She asked.

I shrugged. "Maybe the trauma of the whole situation? Maybe he hasn't recovered from it and of course since I was the cause-"

"You weren't the cause," she said, her tone stern. "Did you start the fire?"

"No," I shook my head.

"Exactly. But how did it start though?"

"No one knows. There was too little evidence by the time the fire was put out.

She nodded then and reached out to pat my shoulder.

"I think you should just forget about him," she said and although it took a while, I eventually nodded in agreement.

4

GIDEON

I couldn't believe I was seeing her in my class again. And in the second row for that matter possibly to ensure that I didn't miss her.

At this point, I truly couldn't understand what she wanted from me beyond admitting that we were once acquainted, and I couldn't understand why that was so important.

This was the third time in two weeks I was seeing her here, and it was beginning to grate on my nerves. I no longer looked at her and thankfully she didn't come up to me after the classes ended, but still, I was becoming so conscious of her presence that I imagined I would be seeing her everywhere anytime I stepped out.

The thing though was that she always seemed to disappear after the class was over which made me wonder if she was trying to simply appear around me as much as was possible in order to jostle my memory.

It seemed comical to me but became far from amusing when I noticed my mood somewhat going sour on the days when I noticed that she wasn't in the class, either hiding in a corner or directly in front.

Whenever she was present on the contrary, I would feel nothing or perhaps it was the case that I had just been forcing myself to feel nothing all along.

And this was the exact case this late Friday afternoon. I didn't mind feeling nothing I realized because my shoulders slumped when I became aware of her absence. The upside was that it made me a little less patient and unfriendly, and the students were always able to sense this and not barrage me as usual with the most bizarre questions.

I had a meeting scheduled for later with Michael, so I immediately got going. It was at a Thai restaurant in the city's downtown but since I arrived early, I brought out the files he had sent over earlier in the week for me to sign.

Afterwards, I reviewed reports and called the waiter over to refill my glass of wine. Just as he went away however someone suddenly slid into the vacant seat across from me.

I looked up, startled and expecting it to be Michael, but instead I met the student that I hadn't been able to get out of my mind since the moment she had barged in two weeks earlier.

I watched her, the slight heaving of her chest as she tried to catch her breath.

"What are you doing here?" I asked, as she finally settled in.

"Hi," she gave me a wide, bright smile and although I got ready to rebuke her for possibly following me all the way here, that glint in her gaze made me stop, rendering me unable to look away.

"Finally," she said. "We're off campus. Now I can speak to you."

"Says who?" I asked, my tone hostile even though I did my very best to control myself.

At this she stopped, and there was no way that I could miss the note of hurt on her face. She glared at me, and I glared back.

"You know who I am don't you?" she asked.

I sighed. "Why wouldn't I?"

"Then why would you say you didn't?" she asked, chest heaving again.

"What good will admitting it be?" I asked. "You're part of a past that I want to leave behind. Am I not entitled to that?"

She continued staring. "Alright," she said, and tried to work up a smile. It was quite painful to watch. "I understand. I just... I understand."

She rose to her feet. "Good talk," she said and then left.

My hands started to tighten again into fists, but they soon relaxed and loosened as soon as Michael eventually arrived.

"I was held up by traffic," he apologized. "I'm sorry,"

I heard him and thought to respond but I was too distracted by thoughts of her and just how dejected she had seemed as she had walked out of the restaurant.

"Eat first?" he asked, "and then we move this to the office?"

I stared at him, my finger tracing patterns on the surface of the table. I wanted to look around the restaurant to see if she had indeed left, and the need to was gnawing at me like an illness.

But I refused to.

"No," I replied. "I think we can round up here. Our major agenda is to review the candidates for the new R&D director position, right?"

"Yes," he replied, and lifted his hand to call out to the

waiter. "The almighty dilemma. Derek is more talented than Susan but he's a pompous prick. If this were a normal business organization then this decision would be a no brainer but since in ours, skill trumps all... I don't know."

I picked up the menu and began to peruse through, glad to have my mind preoccupied with something else except her.

"Skill can be gained," I told him and just like that a memory was instantly triggered.

Of nights with her at my family's kitchen table as I tried to help her work through her math assignment. She was terrible at math, always was and had been on the cusp of giving up before my mother had suggested that her father bring her over so that I could assist.

I recalled being patient with her and her being so apologetic till eventually she had quit altogether on her own. I hadn't pushed her, but I couldn't help my smile now as I recalled how she had returned to me a few weeks later, excited that she had managed to teach herself the basics.

"I felt like I was wasting your time," she said. "But I have a good foundation now so I think we can build on that?"

"Skill indeed can be gained," Michael said. "When they can learn from the best and that's you- their boss. Any thoughts on this?"

I sighed and focused on giving my order to the waiter.

After he left and with her in mind all I could say was, "I have a lot on my plate."

"Quarry is your priority," he reminded me. "And as you've just agreed, ours is a company that thrives on skill. Need I remind you that that's not exactly my strong point."

"Teaching is what keeps me informed," I told him. "And that in turn keeps the company alive."

He smiled. "Alright, but don't you have any vacation time

coming up? I've been proposing the idea of launching a semiannual seminar for the employees. We're growing incredibly fast and we need to be at the top of our game."

I considered this as my gaze went to the drinks menu.

"Why not annually?" I asked.

"Wow," he leaned back against his chair, a fork in hand. "I thought you'd push for it to be quarterly?"

"And why would I do that?"

"How about triennially?" he asked then and I shook my head. "No, they'll get lazy."

"And depend solely on your education? You're right."

"Plus, I want a competition," I asked.

"What do you mean?"

"Those who attend need to earn it. I'll prepare a foundational test for it and only those who meet the cut off mark will be allowed to attend. Obviously, these are the people that will also be up for promotions."

He pondered on it for a moment longer and then nodded. "I like it. But the dilemma with Susan and Derek remains."

"Postpone it," I replied. "Some things just need time to sort themselves out."

"Alright," he said. "I'll keep them both under close observation.

~

THE MEETING soon came to an end, and I headed home. However, on my way my words to Pam kept running through my mind over and over again. There it was... that guilty feeling of just how dismissive I had been to her back then and in the present.

I'd managed to convince myself back then that truly,

with time my antagonism towards her would perhaps dissipate but as I had found now it wasn't the case.

She didn't deserve this, though.

She was a victim just as I was.

And so, I pulled out my phone and worked my way into the student's portal. It didn't take too long, but soon enough I was able to pull up Meredith's address. It was my guess that they lived together, but even if they didn't then I would at least be able to get directions to her home from her.

Soon enough, I arrived at the apartment that wasn't too far off the campus and headed up to the third floor. There I stood before their door and wondered once again if I was making a terrible mistake.

I probably was but I also knew myself enough to understand that I would once again be carrying the weight of my unfair treatment of her on my shoulders.

So, I knocked on the door even though it was quite late, about a half hour to midnight and an answer soon came. However, it wasn't her voice, and at the relief that followed I began to suspect that perhaps I was more emotionally affected by her than I had realized.

"It's the history between you two," I told myself and then the door was pulled open.

It was Meredith I met, with a toothbrush in her mouth. She however instantly froze the moment she saw me, her eyes wide with shock.

I sighed and peeped a bit into the sizable apartment.

"Does Pamela live with you?" I asked, and she instantly began to nod her head. Then she pulled the toothbrush out of mouth and covered her mouth with her hand.

"I'll go get her," she mumbled, at least that was what I assumed I heard and then she was bounding away. I was left in the hallway, the door wide opened and wondered if it would be impolite to see myself in.

I was concerned that it would be rude since I hadn't been invited in yet, but when a door opened down the corridor, I changed my mind. The last thing I needed was word going around that I was paying a student a personal visit at their home. And word around the campus always spread like wildfire. So, I walked in and shut the door behind me.

Their apartment was bright which was an immediate eye sore for me. Everywhere I looked there were colors and though it wasn't particularly messy it wasn't all thoroughly organized either. I looked down at the entrance and could see a book rack right by it along with a few shoes. I was about to look away however when the book bag caught my attention. It was so familiar that I instantly began to try to recall where I had seen it before.

I was so preoccupied with it that I didn't even realize that she had come out of her room.

"Gideon," she called her voice small.

I lifted my gaze then to meet hers. She looked somehow just like she had when we were younger. Her face was scrubbed clean of makeup, her hair piled high up on her hair and falling in messy tendrils all around her face. Her body however was different. She had on shorts, and an oversized t-shirt but none of it was enough to hide the appeal of her wonderful figure. My gaze went to the fullness of her breasts as it pressed against the white fabric, and then down her long, slim legs. I couldn't help but sigh then as it dawned on me that even when younger, I had always had the appreciation for just how beautiful she was. She had truly grown up wonderfully.

Though she remained quite emotional and troublesome.

"Gideon?" she called again, and my attention returned to the present.

I nudged my chin towards the bag on the ground. "Why does this look familiar?"

She cleared her throat, her hands going shyly behind her. "Um... it's uh- "

I cocked my head wondering why it was so difficult for her to speak.

"It was yours," she said. "In high school.

My eyebrows shot up. "I gave it to you?"

A guilty look came over her face.

"Kind of," she said, and I lifted my gaze to think, recalling that back then it was more like I remembered searching for it and just being unable to find it for the life of me.

Shaking my head, the ghost of a smile curved the corners of my lips and when I lifted my gaze to hers, I could see something akin to wonder in her eyes.

"Can I come in?" I asked and she slightly jumped.

"Of course, I'm so sorry. I just left you standing there."

"It's alright," I said and headed straight to the couch. She quickly hurried over and then began to move away the piles of blankets and pillows on it. "Sorry it's a bit messy," she said, and I shook my head. "It's fine."

She then straightened, her hands once again going behind her.

"Can I have some water?' I asked and she jumped once again. I sighed.

"Sure of course. We have beer too in case... you'd prefer that."

"I would actually," I replied, and she quickly headed over to the kitchen.

In no time she was coming over with two cans of

Budweiser in hand and handed one over to me. Then she headed over to the armchair on the opposite end and took her seat. I took a sip and immediately got to why I was here.

"I just wanted you to know," I said to her, "that I don't have any hard feelings towards you. I know I've been quite dismissive in the past, and I don't want that to be the concluding narrative between us."

She nodded again, and I took another sip of my beer, eager to finish it quickly so that I could be on my way.

"Does this mean that we can at least be cordial to each other?"

I paused and didn't know how to respond to her without explaining to her in explicit detail why exactly I would prefer that we kept our distance from each other.

"A hello once in a while is fine," I said. "But it would be best to also maintain a distance between us. It wouldn't be good for unnecessary rumors to be spread and those are quite easy to happen."

"Rumors?" she said.

I met her gaze.

Lowering her head, she drained her can and then got up. I sipped on mine and watched as she headed over to the refrigerator to get another. She opened it right there and drained nearly half of it before coming back.

"You'll be graduating next year, right?" I asked and she nodded.

"That's great," I said, and only realized then how it sounded after the words had left my mouth.

She scoffed. "Great because you won't have to run into me again?"

I frowned and rose to my feet.

"It's late," I said. "It's time to head home."

I drained my drink and then set it on the coffee table.

Then without waiting for her I turned around and began to head towards the door.

"Gideon," she called but I didn't stop. "I'm sorry," she said just as I arrived at the door. I turned around then for just one more look at her.

"You don't have to be sorry for anything," I said.

The seconds stretched out between us.

"Can I hug you?" she asked, and I was a bit taken aback by the request.

"You used to let me hug you all the time when we were younger."

I recalled it. I had always acted sullen about it, with my arms remaining by my sides, but I had never objected to it. She had always felt warm, comfortable, and as I thought of this, it occurred to me I couldn't recall the last time I had hugged someone as innocently. Especially not my mother. It truly had been so long.

"Sure." I said before I could stop myself. Her eyes widened slightly in surprise.

She moved forward towards me then, slowly, cautiously until she was standing right before me. My heart rate began to pick up, especially when she lifted her head so that our eyes could meet. I noticed her scent... sweet and clean, like peaches, and the warmth that was radiating from her skin so powerfully. Her hair was all over the place, and I wished so badly that I could tenderly brush it away from her face. But I was torn because I liked it just as it was, and the way it softened her face.

She leaned up on the tip of her toes then and set her hands on my shoulders and my gaze couldn't help but go to them. And then they were circling around me. I heard her laugh and wondered why, but she soon explained.

"You're tall, sir," she said. "And I think I'm still probably the same height I was ten years ago. Lean down a little and help me out?"

At this I smiled and complied.

We stayed that way, and she didn't let go, her face resting against the side of mine, and the flood of warmth into my chest seemed to intensify.

I couldn't stop myself then. My arms left my side to circle around her waist, slowly and hesitantly until I was able to convince myself that there was no harm to this. We were old acquaintances, and it had been quite a while.

At this, she grew even more comfortable and seemed to settle into my embrace. I received the full weight of her body and couldn't help but shut my eyes. Holding her in this way... felt different. Not entirely as though I just had a female in my arms, but as though I was embracing a truly deep friend.

I didn't want to move away. I had to and so I slowly began to, but she seemed to sense this and tightened her hold on me.

"Just for a little longer," she pleaded softly, her voice in my ear. "I know you'll never let this happen again."

I wanted to resist, but eventually had to give in when I realized that she was probably right, so we remained that way for a few more seconds, until eventually she spoke softly again.

"Have you known all along that I attended school here?" she asked, and my entire body tensed.

I truly didn't know how to respond to this because on one hand I had been aware, and I didn't expect that mentioning this would allow our already strained interactions to continue with any cordiality.

She sensed my hesitation and then began to pull away. And not till I saw the slight crease between her brows did I realize that I was somewhat holding on. I immediately let go and she stepped away.

"Should I take your silence to mean that you knew?" she asked, and I held her gaze.

"I've seen you around," I admitted, and although her face remained expressionless, I could see her complexion pale.

"Alright," she said, and managed to work up a smile to the corner of her lips.

I had expected that it wouldn't bother me, but it currently didn't feel that way at all.

She took a step away from me, and then another and I couldn't help but watch her feet. Eventually they stopped and thankfully, this rung the alarm through me that it was time to leave.

So, with one last look at her, I turned around and took my leave. Soon the door was shut behind me and I found that I felt relieved. That we hadn't said any goodbyes to each other. There had been no words exchanged, and it just made me feel as though this was one chapter in the book between us that was definitely not closed. I'd come here with the intent of closing it, but she most probably didn't have such an intention and I didn't know how it made me feel.

I pondered on it as I returned to my car, and although it took quite the effort, I was eventually able to get my mind off her.

5

PAMELA

I was suddenly fuming.

From the moment he shut the door to go on his way, I had remained rooted to that spot in the entrance, somewhat confused about how I felt. I was disappointed at first, and then I began to go through the entire spectrum of emotions as sadness soon overcame me, and then my current annoyance.

"Pam?" I heard Meredith's voice then and was forced to turn around.

I saw that she was in the hall and had her head peeking from the edge of the wall. "He left, right?" she asked, eyes going to the shut bathroom door at the opposite end of the room. I nodded, took one glance at the door and then headed back to the fridge to grab yet another beer for myself. Then without a word, I started to head back to my room. I knew that she would come along to interrogate me so I reclined on my bed, phone in one hand and can in the other.

Soon her knock came, and when I didn't respond, the handle to my door was pulled down.

"Hey," she said softly, eyes darting around the room. I was somewhat amused.

"You know you've been here at least a thousand times before at this point, right??" I asked and her smile was sheepish. She soon came in, a can of Budweiser in hand and it reminded me of him. I stared at the can and all I could see was how he had seemed so intimidating on the couch.

Thinking back, I realized now that he had always seemed that way, and I had been so filled with awe and reverence but now, I had to ponder on if he was even worth it.

"What is it?" she asked as she shut the door behind her. "I thought you'd be over the moon that he visited. I still can't believe it. I had to pinch myself a bit when I saw him at the door."

I took another sip of my beer while she took a seat by my desk.

"What did he want?" she asked.

I looked at her and couldn't help but feel somewhat embarrassed and it just made me even more angry.

"He came to apologize," I replied. "For being so stand-offish and dismissive of me."

At this her mouth fell open. "He came to apologize?"

"Yeah," I replied.

"Okay," she said when she saw that I wasn't willing to say any more. Then she got to her feet. I watched her leave, wishing I could talk to her about this, but the words just seemed unable to come out of my mouth. Her hand closed around the handle, and I watched, but then at the last moment she turned around to glance at me.

"You're upset," she said. "And I need to know why. Please tell me?"

At this I sighed and nodded, and she came back but this time around sat by my bedside.

"In addition to apologizing, he also hoped that we could keep our distance from each other."

"What?" she said. "Why?"

"I have no idea. He mentioned something about rumors."

"Oh," she said. "I get that. I guess."

Another bout of silence ensued. And then she spoke again "I mean I get that but how would that happen unless you both were found in a compromising situation? I mean... the girls throw themselves at him all day, but he's never paid any attention to any of them. Well, he did once. A professor we had last year. She was beyond gorgeous though, so it was completely understandable."

"Maybe that's the problem then," I muttered under my breath, but she heard me.

"What do you mean?"

"Maybe the problem is that I'm not gorgeous enough?"

At this she smiled, a soft affectionate look on her face. "And why would this be a problem? You're not interested in him, are you?"

My attention perked up. I also couldn't bring myself to say the lie so shamelessly, I simply gave her an incredulous look and turned away.

She laughed.

"So, you do like him. I mean, accepting that fact makes everything else make sense because if I were you, I don't think I'd ever be hooked up on a past acquaintance that seems hell bent on pretending as though he doesn't know me in the present."

"He was kind to me," I groaned, and she gave me a bored look.

"Sure."

"He saved my life?"

At this she was forced to stop. "Alright, that makes sense. I forgot. Anyway, I have some thoughts on how you can resolve this or at least try to."

"What are they?" I asked.

"This one applies though if you're romantically interested in him."

My mouth instantly snapped shut. "Are you?" she asked, and I could see her lips twitching.

"Okay time to leave," I said and drained my can. Afterwards, I grabbed her arm, trying to pull her up along with me, but she refused to budge.

"I'm serious Pam," she said. "Incredibly serious. Just hear me out at least?"

I wanted to but didn't want to openly admit it so I kept pulling her along with me until eventually she arrived at the door. However, with her body to it, she kept the door jammed so I couldn't move her.

"Meredith," I complained, and she forced my gaze to hers.

"Admit it and I'll help you."

"What help could you possibly give me?"

"I got things going between myself and Darryl, didn't I?"

"Correction, the hook-ups all over campus between you two got things going between you and Darryl."

"And who do you think initiated it?" she asked, and I stopped. Then my eyes widened. I hadn't ever asked her about this before.

My head cocked. "How did things get started between you and Darryl? I can't believe I never asked."

"Same reason you didn't know Professor Bach has been

a professor here for four years when every single other girl is aware and can't shut up about him. Except me of course."

"Four years?" my eyes widened.

"Yep four. You're not curious about other people's business and it's fine. I like that."

"But you're my friend."

"I was going to tell you about it, but you had a pending test or something, so we postponed it till later. You knew we were together and that's what was important to you. You're somewhat of a baseline consumer of information. You only have the patience for 'need to know'."

At this I couldn't help a smile. "Alright," I conceded. "What's your idea?"

"Just do what Darryl did," she said. "He kissed me."

I stiffened yet again, waiting for the rest of her sentence but it never came.

"That's it?" I asked.

"Yup."

A frown. "I thought you said you were the one that initiated things."

"You think the kiss just came out of nowhere? I had probably teased him so much that at that point he was so sexually frustrated with being in my presence that he couldn't hold himself back any longer."

I cocked a brow.

"How did you do it?"

She puffed out her chest., "We need snacks for this," she said. "And more beer."

I rolled my eyes.

"What snacks?"

"Pizza? Chicken?

"Those are not snacks," I said dryly.

"Do you want my input or not?" she sassed, and I sighed again.

"Fine. I'll order in. And I'm guessing I'm the one paying for these."

Her scoff was of amusement.

"What a question," she said and headed over to my bed.

6

GIDEON

I was sure I wasn't the one being called out to when I heard my name.

Everyone in this part of my life all referred to me as Professor Bach, and very few even knew my first name. However, when the call persisted, I had to finally consider that perhaps I was the one and that it was some old acquaintance, however unlikely. I didn't slow down, but instead turned for a glance backwards and that was when I saw her.

At first, I wasn't sure who it was because she was bent over with her hands on her knees for support, and her head hanging low.

I immediately suspected who it was and turned back around. I considered stopping for a moment but there was truly no need to, so I kept going. I didn't hear the call again but thoughts of her now flooded my mind when it had been previously blank, and it was aggravating to say the least. About another twenty minutes later, I found a bench.

I was truly reluctant to stop but I needed the rest anyway and... I refused to admit the rest to myself.

It wasn't because I wanted to see her in any way, but

because it was so damn early and lonely and perhaps, she had been calling out to me because she needed help.

I couldn't believe it though, that just barely a week after what I had hoped would be our last confrontation at her apartment, I was running into her on this trail.

It just made me wonder now how in hell it had been so easy for our paths not to cross in the past when she had no idea of my existence here.

I sipped from my water bottle, and waited, my gaze glancing from time to time at my watch. I needed just a little while longer to complete my route, but as I looked towards the trail I was coming from, there was still no sign of her or anyone else for that matter, I was forced to rise to my feet.

I kept telling myself that I didn't care, but I had only run a few steps in my original direction when I cursed under my breath and turned back around.

"Just run back to the starting point and then head home," I tried to console myself. I considered doing another lap, but this would be impossible as I had to go into the city for a seminar at the company.

I searched for her as I ran, looking everywhere so that I could ensure that she was fine until eventually and from a distance, I found the still figure lying collapsed on a bench.

Her front was facing up to the sky, her arm dangling to the ground, and her entire frame just splayed out in complete exhaustion. Or perhaps she had fainted? I approached cautiously, but soon crossed the latter consideration out when I heard the low but endless whining and groans emanating from her lips.

I arrived just a short distance away from her, and it was then that I was able to hear the curses that also accompanied the moans.

"Fucking asshole," I heard her whine, and had a very good feeling she was referring to me.

Shaking my head, I pulled out my bottle and lifted my head for a sip, but there was no way to erase the appreciation that my mind had registered for her body.

She was slim, always had been but now, I couldn't help but clearly see just how much curvier she had become. And then there were her breasts which were much fuller than I had expected and straining against the pale green fabric.

My libido was instantly stirred which didn't surprise me but instead increased my annoyance. It had been quite the while since I'd felt such an intense level of attraction to a woman, and the last one that had happened had been so brief and exhausting that I'd instantly regretted even getting into it from the beginning. The result was a stretched-out relationship that I had no time, patience or interest in and thus the end had been unsavory.

The thing however with Pam was that a part of me remembered my attraction and affection for her from our past, and so it wasn't strange to me that I could feel this way from time to time for her. But since it was something that I had absolutely no interest in acting on, it felt like an annoyance.

As I intended, the water from the bottle began to drop on her face and coupled with what I was certain was her eventual awareness of my presence when she quieted down, her eyes eventually came open.

It took a few seconds for her wonder to dissipate and then she was jumping to her feet.

"Oh my God," she gasped, a hand to her chest.

I finished with my drink, my gaze on her, but then she kept stumbling backwards.

Only the alarm in her eyes alerted me to the fact that she was going to fall.

Immediately, I lunged forward, throwing the bottle aside and caught her just in time.

She still slipped, since I only had a grip on her arm with her legs sliding down. Thankfully though she was able to hold onto the bench which was the only thing that kept her from dangling from my hold like a rag doll.

"Oh my God," she muttered under her breath, and I shook my head. Then I managed to pull her up and of course she held onto me to stabilize herself. She was so close... much too close but I forced myself to remain patient to be certain that she was stable before letting go. Through it all, what I could see was the top of her head as she was no doubt filled with embarrassment so the second that she could, she was turning away from me and going on her way without even a second glance. I watched her go, my eyes on the gorgeous frame of her body and once again had to sit down. Then she stopped suddenly and called out to me. "I'll replace your bottle, I'm sorry."

I watched her, and after checking the time decided that it was time for me to be heading back. So, I followed her closely enough but then she went out of view because she started to run.

I kept walking, as my thoughts went to my later appointments in the day, until suddenly I heard a small cry. I couldn't see her and wondered if she had stumbled once again. It seemed likely and I couldn't help but sigh.

Once again, I tried to put her out of my mind but then something began to gnaw at me, keeping me worried. I began to run again and in no time rounded the trail to find that she was upright and walking slowly, but I could see that there was something off about her posture. I hurried over, and when I got to her side grabbed her hand to stop her when I saw that she was increasing her awkward steps even faster to avoid me, although for the life of me I couldn't figure out why.

"Ow!" she cried out, and when I stopped, I could instantly see the pain etched on her face and the tears in her eyes.

I was instantly alarmed. "What's wrong?"

"I'm fine," she muttered, and tried to pull her arm away.

"I'm fine."

I forced her then to stop and face me, but since I couldn't hold onto her arm for some reason I held onto her sides.

"Pamela," I called until she was forced to look at me, the ghost of a smile on her face.

"I'm fine, truly," she said. "It's just a little sprain.

I frowned. "A sprain? Where? Is it from when you stumbled earlier on?" I asked and her head started to lower once again.

"I'm fine," she said. "I'll just put some ice on it when I get home."

I looked at her clothes and when I saw that it was stained with some dust, I suspected that she had fallen afterwards.

That slight shout I had heard came to mind, and at the dust in her hair I knew she truly had fallen.

I lowered my tone. "Talk to me," I said, and although she remained reluctant, her face turned away, she eventually gave in.

"I think I need to go to the hospital."

"What happened?"

"I fell," she said. "Hard. That step there."

I sighed as I looked at it, and then returned my gaze to her.

"Where does it hurt?"

"I think I sprained my arm," she replied, and I completely understood now. I pulled my phone out of my pocket. "I'll call an ambulance," I said, and she immediately stopped me.

"No, I'm not going to the hospital. I changed my mind. I hate hospitals."

I recalled instantly that this was true.

"If you leave the arm the way it is right now, it might never heal right. Plus, I don't know just how severe the sprain is.

"No," she said and tried once again to move out of my hold. I was forced to let her go so that she wouldn't hurt herself even further.

I considered just calling for the ambulance anyway but then I remembered just how stubborn she was and that she would most likely refuse it if I insisted.

I continued to walk behind her as I tried to think of how to resolve this.

She continued going until eventually, we were at the end of the path and back out in the open park. There were a few more people around, and as I watched her begin to wander off, I couldn't help but go over to ask.

"Where's your car?" I asked.

"Over there," she replied and then somehow worked up a smile, but I could see the sweat beaded across her forehead and the tightness of her jaw. She was in so much pain and was doing so much to hide it.

"How are you going to take care of it when you get home?" I asked.

"I'll put some ice on it," she replied. "I'll be fine."

"Ice might not be enough," I said. "Do you have compression bandages?"

"Yeah... I'll use those."

"You won't be able to do it on your own. Is your roommate around to help you?"

At this she hesitated, but of course soon nodded. "She is."

I knew instantly that it was a lie.

"What if she can't do it properly?" I asked, and then she stopped, a frown coming across her face.

"You know what Gideon, please back off. You don't really care so stop acting like you do. I'll be fine. I'll take care of myself."

I glared at her as she walked away. "Then why were you calling out to me in the first place?"

"I'm sorry," she paused with a smile. "I forgot that we're meant to be strangers. My bad."

And she continued on her way. My temper flared but I tried all I could to keep it at bay so that I could react the way that I wanted to. I headed over to her and held onto her good arm.

"Gideon!" she complained and tried to release my hold, but I wouldn't budge.

"Gideon!" She called again, and angrily I turned to glare at her.

She met my gaze, her hand once again against my chest but whether it was to hold me at bay or for support, I had no clue. The look I gave her however was enough because she gave up and came with me.

After we got into my car, I instantly began to drive to my apartment.

"Where are we going?" she asked, but I didn't respond.

"Don't take me to the hospital Gideon. You know how things were with my mom before that fire. I hate hospitals."

I knew exactly what she was talking about and sighed.

"Do you really have compression bandages at home?" I asked and she went quiet.

I shook my head.

"Do you even have a first aid kit?"

It was a little while later before she spoke again. "I have pain killers," she said, and I shook my head again.

Soon we arrived at my apartment which was in a complex close enough to the university.

I went around the car to help her out and although she allowed me, she didn't exactly look too comfortable about it. I wanted to let her go but I couldn't bring myself to as I led her to the elevator. We got in and were then on our way up.

7

PAMELA

I was certain that I had never felt as shitty as I currently did about myself.

This had not been the plan at all but then here I was, in abject pain and so overwhelmed with shame that I felt myself melting from it.

In my heart I cursed Meredith, but then I couldn't completely blame her because falling and spraining my arm had not been the plan at all.

Her simple suggestion had been to appear in places where he frequently visited, and rumor had it that he had been spotted running along this trail multiple times per week.

I didn't have the energy to try my luck by just heading to the trail hoping to run into him and neither was I willing to exercise so I'd simply waited at the park early enough to catch him upon arrival.

I'd been unlucky the previous Saturday and Wednesday but this time around, I had arrived early enough and seen him. That was already enough to make me feel embarrassed but then as Meredith had pointed out, I was going after someone that I'd had in my heart for so long. Up till now I'd put effort into every other thing I wanted, so what was the shame in doing the same for this one? Her argument made sense, but my feelings were not at all aligned.

I was also upset at him because who freaking ran that fast and for so long. At the point I knew I was going to lose sight of him despite all my efforts to keep up I had then called out and everything had gone downhill from there.

But then here I was in his apartment, which I was certain I might have never ever been able to visit otherwise so to an extent reduced my embarrassment.

I was also so surprised by the way he had acted. Perhaps I was wrong, but I didn't think that he would have done the same to any other careless fake runner with a sprained arm.

I knew him fairly well and he wasn't that considerate, even on purpose.

But with me however, I could feel the grip of his care as he led me towards his living room.

The view blinded me, all tall windows and luxurious furnishings, and for the first time I truly began to believe Meredith's claim that he was one of the owners of that unicorn company.

Vision on Wilshire was a complex I had only looked at from afar and wondered what it would feel like to live in and wake up to the views of the city each morning. I knew now and it was so breathtaking, that for a moment I forgot I was in pain.

After ensuring that I was settled comfortably on his couch he disappeared without a word, and I sighed again.

This somehow seemed to be progress, but it didn't feel like it was helping my case in any way whatsoever. I didn't even think I deserved to have one anymore given how much embarrassment I was currently soaked in. Surely, he would prefer someone more sophisticated and with their shit together and not someone that could barely exercise without spraining an arm.

My gaze turned to the limb, and I couldn't help but notice just how much it was swelling.

I really needed ice but was forced to wait for him. Soon enough he arrived with an ice pack, and a towel, strolling briskly but somehow seemingly unhurried.

That was the thing about Gideon, no matter the torment and mayhem around, he almost always seemed to be in control and from time to time I couldn't help but wonder if this was how he truly felt inside or if it was all just a mask. He finally returned, and although I couldn't quite meet his gaze I did manage to look up. He was watching, probably trying to work out something so I waited.

"You need to be horizontal," he said, and my eyes widened.

Before I could process what he was saying any further, he was turning around and going on his way. "Come with me," he said, and I was forced then to rise alone to my feet.

I went with him, through the living area consisting of a magnificent kitchen and a huge dining room. And then we moved into the coziest carpeted room with even more magnificent views of the city coupled with the glass wall on the opposite end, and it felt like walking into a dream. The throbbing pain in my arm however quickly took dominance once again and reminded me of where I was and why.

"Don't touch it," he said, and only then did I look up to see that he had stopped by a door to glance back at me. I put my hand down and went with him.

"Lie down," he said, and I wondered if it was alright to be adhering to everything he was saying. Didn't it make me appear too weak? Without much of a choice I sat and then managed to lie on the bed and then he sat by me.

Then he began to gently inspect the arm and he was so damn close that I had to concentrate on breathing. He was gentle, so the pain didn't overwhelm me enough to cry out, but then his slightly damp hair and the way it fell onto his face, his blue gaze now more searing and intense than ever given his increased level of concentration, and then his body, made it quite a feat.

He had on shorts and a dark tee that stretched out across his incredibly taut chest. He had a magnificent body, and at the memory of how it had felt having it pressed against me, how his hardness had cushioned my softness, I couldn't help but sigh.

I truly wanted him, I realized, and as the days passed by it seemed as though this yearning just seemed to double. I couldn't get him out of my mind, and so suddenly all the memories from the years past, all seemed to be flooding back.

"Ow," I couldn't help but wince as he pressed a sore spot, and then our eyes met. The world seemed to stop in that moment as his mask fell and I could see the concern and worry in his eyes. Warmth filled me as I watched him, and then before I could stop myself my hand lifted. It was going to cradle the side of his face for some consolation of some sort, but then just as quickly as it had come, the spell was broken, and I was left with a hand hanging awkwardly in midair. He looked at it. "What's wrong?" he asked.

My lips parted then to explain, and truly I wondered what sort of excuse I was going to give to really what should have been the obvious fact that I had wanted to touch him.

Thankfully and for once, I was glad that he didn't dwell

as his attention returned to my injured arm. He placed a light towel over it and then the ice.

I shut my eyes and tried to convince myself to relax. It was too difficult especially as I imagined that his gaze would be on mine, and I didn't want to be oblivious of it if that were indeed the case.

"How does it feel?" he asked, his voice soft and careful.

I stared at him, wondering how this was the same person that had previously been so cold and dismissive to me. At my lack of response, he looked up to meet my gaze and my heart fluttered.

And at that moment, I had a decision to make. I quickly went through it in my mind before once again the moment was lost. Leaning up on my good arm, which made him confused I slanted my head however before my lips could meet his. He caught on and leaned away.

I froze on the spot, a sudden feeling convincing me that I was on the verge of dying.

He frowned at me. "What are you doing?"

My throat closed up and then suddenly I had to get out of there. I threw the towel and ice pack aside, and then began to move down the bed. It took everything inside of me to hold my emotions together, but I did the best I could.

"Pam," he called but I didn't respond.

"Pamela!"

"I need to leave," I managed to croak out as I began to move down the bed to the door. But then he grabbed my arm and stopped. Unluckily for me it was the bad arm, so I cried out, doubling at the pain.

"Fuck!" He cursed out and then released me.

"Pam," he complained, while my eyes squeezed shut as I tried to contain the pain. Eventually it subsided so I managed to straighten the arm and a hand and then I was leaving.

"I have something to get to," I managed to say, and thankfully he let me go.

This however seemed to hurt even more, and my only prayer became that I would be completely out of his hair before all the hurt let loose.

I reached his heavy front doors, but turning the handle became a challenge because the pain seemed to have also transferred to the other arm.

I felt his presence then, and my heart jumped so hard in my chest that it took my breath away. I wanted to ask for help but couldn't bring myself to. I kept trying, until suddenly he was by my side. I watched his hand go to the lock and then he twisted it shut.

Surprised, I turned to him with widened eyes, and then he was closer to me than he'd ever been before.

"What's wrong with you?" he asked.

"I just want to leave?"

"Because I didn't kiss you?" Something hard and sharp stabbed into my gut.

"I wasn't trying to kiss you," I said and realized then that he was forcing me backwards with his approach.

"Stop," I said, but he ignored me until eventually my back connected with the wall.

"If you weren't trying to kiss me then what were you trying to do?" he asked, and I was forced then to find the courage to look into his eyes.

I shut mine. "Please, just let me go."

"I'll kiss you," he said. "If that's what you want. But you have to stay and get your treatment. Do you want your arm to be ruined? You won't go to the hospital and yet you don't want to be treated here. When did you become so difficult to deal with?"

Tears filled my eyes. "Why are you yelling?" I asked. "It almost sounds like you care."

"Shut up," he said, and then his hand went under my chin to lift my head up. There was no warming or second to prepare for what was coming, so all I could do was take what was offered. At first, and as his warmth and scent overwhelmed my senses, I was unable to register exactly what was happening. But then as my shock began to clear, and what was truly happening registered, I began to melt. Thankfully, I was leaning against the wall, so I was able to get the support I needed. His kiss was soft, but there was nothing shy about it. He sucked softly on my lips... the bottom and then the top, and then his tongue was sliding into my mouth. I was powerless to resist any of it, a deep sigh emanating from me as the kiss seemed to seep into my system and awaken every single cell of my body.

"Gideon," I cried out as desire, poignant and intense, began to coil in the pit of my stomach.

He didn't hold back, and it surprised me more than anything because it didn't feel as though he was just doing this to oblige me. The kiss went on and on until I cried into his mouth needing to catch my breath. He broke the kiss then but didn't pull away and I had never felt more overwhelmed. My eyes came open, gazing into his with shock and something akin to wonder.

"You got your kiss," he said.

And I could do nothing but try to swallow the lump in my throat, however, this seemed to be the hardest thing in the world to do.

He moved away from me and instantly, I felt the loss in the weight of his body against mine.

I looked up at him then and saw the stern look in his eyes, but for once it didn't upset me. On the contrary, it made my heart flutter once again. He then turned around and began to head back to the bedroom, and I had no choice but to get myself together and follow him.

I found I truly needed support, because it felt as though my legs had turned to jelly. Eventually I managed to move but I held onto the walls where I could and took slow steps as I returned to the bedroom.

8

GIDEON

I had no idea what to do with her or how to talk her out of whatever interest she now had in me. I couldn't be mean to her, but at the same time I couldn't accept her. Yet underneath it all I couldn't deny the raging attraction I was beginning to feel for her.

It was a dangerous game, one that I could feel myself already losing. I couldn't even return to my bedroom after that shared kiss. Instead, I had to go into the guest bedroom in order to catch my breath. Frustrated, I leaned against the door, my eyes shut as I ran through the events of the morning up till this moment through my mind.

Could I really not have ignored her? I had to ask myself. Because if I had just left her to take care of herself like she had been doing all these years, then perhaps none of these complications would be arising. That was the aggravating thing about history, I couldn't help but think. It kept you attached when it was the last thing you wanted.

But still, I had to at least fix her up to an extent and get her home. Since I had started this then I had to finish it and then swear myself off her. I returned to get another ice pack, and then returned to my bedroom. I met her lying and waiting, and the hit to my groin was painful to say the least. She looked so soft and vulnerable, when I knew she was anything but and it made the desire to take her rev within me. And then there was the way she was looking at me.

She always wore her emotions on her face, and I couldn't help but wonder now just how much trouble it had gotten her into.

With a sigh, I settled back on the bed and placed the ice properly on her arm and this time around she complied without a single complaint.

"Twenty minutes," I said, and then rose to my feet. I went to the storage room to retrieve the bandages and then I went into the kitchen considering that she would need something to eat. However, I didn't want to take things too far by making her breakfast, which I had to recall now that she had made me make for her several times in the past even though she had come over solely for tutorship from me. At the time, it hadn't been a big deal, and had been somewhat amusing to me plus I immensely enjoyed the delight that was on her face whenever I made her meals. French toast was her favorite, and every time she took a bite of it, she squealed and did a little dance and it had flooded me with joy.

Wow, I had to say to myself now as all these reminders came back. It had been absolutely nothing to me then but now, and with the light of the future, it made sense to me why I had always been somewhat guarded with her.

Keeping my distance had truly been the best route, and I had to get back on to it as soon as possible. I found some cereal, raisins and almond granola which I was well aware that she liked. She'd never liked anything overly sweet which

I had appreciated back then, so currently it would do. There was also the fact that it took minimal effort to put together, so I wouldn't feel any guilt for not feeding her. Also, it was a way for her energy to be sucked out so she would fall right to sleep as this way, I could monitor her and keep her here for a bit longer without having to resort to drugging her. She wasn't lactose intolerant, but milk did make her extremely fatigued and sleepy as we had found after a very long time of her being unable to stay awake during tutoring lessons.

At the time she had called it boredom until I had run out of cereal and then she couldn't have fallen asleep mid lesson if I had paid her.

I got all this together and then I was returning to the bedroom, with a bed tray.

"Sit up," I told her when I got in, and she did as told. I could see the slight wince of pain on her face.

"Do you need any help?" I asked and she shook her head. Eventually she was in the position I wanted her in, so I set the tray where it needed to be.

"Can you feed yourself?" I asked and just then, the meeting I had planned at the company came to mind. I was momentarily stumped because I had forgotten all about it and so I had to leave afterwards to make the call that I would not be attending.

"Thanks for breakfast," she said, her voice small. "I'm sorry to be a bother."

"Are you?" I asked, and she looked at me as she stirred the liquid contents of the bowl with her spoon.

"Am I what?" she asked.

"Are you sorry to be a bother?" I repeated.

Perhaps it was the sternness of my expression as was usually the case, but suddenly she couldn't control her amusement. She immediately lowered her head, but I caught the smile that she was trying to hide.

Shaking my head, I stood up to leave but then she spoke.

"I'm not," she said. "By the way," and I truly didn't need to ask what she was referring to, but I did anyway.

"You're not what?" I asked.

"Sorry," she turned to face me. "To be a bother."

I looked at her, and then I exited the room and shut the door behind me.

My call with Michael didn't go well at all.

"You can't cancel," he said. "Unless you just found out you have a tumor that paralyzes you, you can't cancel. I'm coming over there right now to pick you up myself."

I sighed as I leaned against the kitchen counter and stared at the door down the hallway holding the current bane of my existence.

"What has come up is... unavoidable," I told him.

"Nothing except death is unavoidable."

"Michael."

"I'm not kidding. Your visit has been scheduled for months. It's a Saturday and yet more than half of the company is here just waiting for you."

"What?" I was surprised to hear this. "Why?"

"You're like Santa," he said. "At this point, most of the staff don't even think you really exist. Like you're the myth that no one can shake. You think they'd miss a chance to see you?"

"Well now I definitely don't want to come. You understand that I have to be low key right? That was our agreement when we settled on this."

"This is no fault of mine. You're great at what you do, the best in the entire world. Most of these people idolize you and even take lower salaries just to be able to work here, so you're coming today. I'm on my way right now."

"Don't bother," I groaned, a deep frown digging between my brows.

"Don't bother why?" he asked.

"Just... fine. I'll be there."

"That's the spirit," he said.

"But I'll be late."

"I'll let them know," he said unhappily.

I looked at the door down the hall once again, and truly wondered what I was going to do with her.

9

PAMELA

"You're what?"

"Incapacitated."

"What?"

"I hurt myself."

"How?"

"Long story. I'll tell you later." My gaze went to the door, and then I lowered my voice. "Actually, I'll just tell you right now. I ran into him and-"

"Oh my God!" Meredith interrupted. "Finally!"

I smiled. "Anyway, I fell and sprained my arm so now I'm at his house icing it."

She went silent for a few seconds, so much so I had to check if the call was still connected.

"Meredith," I called.

"I'm just trying to process this," she said. "None of this was the plan."

"I know right, but it worked out," I recalled the kiss. "Kind of."

"Kind of?"

"I'll let you know the rest when I get home. He might

overhear me or something. His apartment is huge, but I don't trust any walls."

"Where does he live?"

"Vision on Wilshire," I said and heard her sharp gasp.

"I know. I think he's on the topmost floor even."

"Away from the people who stay away from the peasants. Boss behavior. I like him even more."

This amused me.

"I bet he's wealthy enough to buy that building," she said. "He's probably only living there because he wants to be close to the university. And that's one thing I don't get so if this goes anywhere then please ask him... for a friend, why the hell he's teaching when he could be simply hacking companies and demanding millions in compensation."

"What? That's what his company does?"

"Somewhat or maybe? I don't know. But I would if I was them. He's so good that he can infiltrate anywhere and have them at his mercy. He'll never run out of business. I suspect though he goes the more honest route and lets the companies come to him. His reputation though is more than enough to bring him much more business than he can handle. Anyway, enough about his pockets, there are more urgent issues at hand. Beyond icing your broken arm-"

"Sprained," I corrected.

"Yeah, sprained." And then she paused. "Wouldn't it have been better to have broken it? Then you can spend a little while there."

I pulled away to look at the phone. "Wow," I said, and could hear her giggle. "I might like him, but it hasn't reached the stage of self-harm."

"So, you didn't fall on purpose?"

"Who falls on purpose?"

I could almost see her shrug. "You never know. You've been pretty desperate about this whole situation."

"Desperate?" I repeated.

"Dare to disagree?"

My lips parted to do just that, but I immediately shut them, I had no arguments to make whatsoever.

"Anyway, desperate is good. It'll make you determined to go after what you want."

At her words, I remained silent, and she soon caught on. "Did I say something out of line?" her tone lowered.

"When don't you say things out of line?" I asked.

"I'm sorry, I didn't mean you were desperate in a bad way I just..."

"I am desperate," I told her, a depth of me that I hadn't paid too much attention to revealing itself. Suddenly, I had to concentrate on breathing.

"He's been in my heart and mind for so long, Meredith," I said. "He saved me from a fire. Everyone told him it was too late to go back in, but he still came after me. I could have died but he protected me with all his heart. It landed him in the hospital afterwards. After we moved, I was devastated. He cut off all contact with me without any explanation, and for the longest time... up till now I was convinced that I'd never see him again and it made me sad Meredith. Now that I have a chance to reconnect with him, or perhaps I don't even have the chance, I am desperate to make one. I can't let him slip away again... so easily and trust me, he's great at that. The best really."

I heard the smile in her voice. "You're right," she said. "The best."

"Alright I'll take this more seriously and help you. Picture me cracking my knuckles."

The image came to my mind, and I couldn't help but shake my head.

"Is there a way to get physical in any way?" she asked. "It doesn't have to be anything too scandalous, but even getting your hands to touch might mean something?"

I hesitated at what I wanted to relay, but eventually I was forced to spill it out. I was here with him which I was well aware was a miracle in and of itself. Who knew when next I'd have this kind of chance again?

"I kissed him," I said, and heard her gasp.

"What?"

"Actually, he kissed me, but I tried… first."

"Okay there's more to this story," she said. "How did it happen?"

My gaze went to the door. "I'll tell you when I get home, for now we need to find a way to make some sort of plan again for when he can see me. Otherwise, he'll go back to pretending I don't exist."

"Hm," she said in thought. "The only route I can think of is you getting him to somehow go all the way? How was the kiss? Did he seem affected?"

I thought back to that moment and much to my disappointment, realized that I was so overtaken by my own enjoyment of it that I had failed to notice his.

"I- uh… I think so?" I replied.

"Well, if he was then you've got a good chance."

I considered this. "I don't think I can though…" I said. "Go all the way with him. We have indeed known each other for the majority of our lives but as of now, he's still somewhat a stranger. I'm just worried it'll cast me in a negative light no matter the way it unfolds."

She agreed. "Alright, let's just let things flow as naturally as possible then but…"

"But what?" I asked.

"What if you spend all this time waiting and building a friendship and maybe even a relationship, only for you to find out that he's bad in bed?"

My mouth fell open, part amusement and part astonishment. "... or something?" She sheepishly added.

I tried my best to control my amusement. "Meredith," I called, and lowered my tone even further.

"Do you really think it's possible for someone like him?"

"No?" she replied, "but anything is possible."

I could hear her amusement too, and once again the air was lightened.

"I know a solely physical relationship is not your goal with him, but it could kickstart things especially with how standoffish yet caring he seems to be. I mean, he didn't have to help you today. He could have just called you an ambulance or something, if he wanted to appear compassionate. Plus, I've known him for years and trust me he's not the kind. He keeps to himself and his work and pays no attention to anything else."

"Just like Darryl?" I asked and she laughed.

"Yeah, I guess so. I was so oblivious to him for so long and I'm so glad he kissed me out of that blindness. Because of how nerdy he was, I'd only just seen him as pleasant to look at or be around, and that was how three years went by. He told me he got frustrated and just decided to go for it but..."

"But what?"

"He said he only did so because at that point he was prepared to lose me. In case I was horrified and never spoke to him again, and it would be alright because he had already pined for long enough and needed to somehow make himself move on. And so, I ask you the same question. Are you prepared to lose him if you keep pushing forward like this? Or do you prefer to pine for a bit and steal whatever you can in bits and pieces before going for the whole thing?"

I considered her question, deeply considered it because it made sense to me, however I couldn't get myself to make a decision at that moment.

"I'll think about it," I told her, and the call came to an end.

10

GIDEON

Applying the bandages, thankfully, was a breeze. Holding onto her as carefully as I could yet still seeing her wince was not. She tried to hide it, bit into her lower lip and I could do nothing but be thankful that her eyes were shut so I wouldn't be caught in the act of watching her.

Soon enough, we were done, and I rose to my feet.

"Rest here for a bit," I told her. "I have to leave for an appointment, but I'll send a driver to pick up your car and take it to your apartment. Then he'll come and drive you home."

At all of this and all she did was look at me as though trying to process it all enough to respond. I didn't linger, although I was curious as to what was currently going through her mind.

I headed towards the door to take my leave, and she didn't stop me.

After heading to my bathroom for a quick change of clothes, I grabbed my jacket and keys and was soon back out to the living room. I was surprised however to meet her by my piano.

She was still oblivious to my presence, and I waited, knowing what she was going to do.

I shifted back into the shadow of the hall without meaning to, so when she looked up to check for my presence, she saw no one. Then she pressed a finger down on one of the keys and it resounded across the apartment.

My head fell then as a smile pulled at the corners of my lips. Especially when I saw her immediately move away from it, shocked by the noise. What the fuck did she think was going to happen?

Soon enough, I was able to get myself back together but when I returned to the living room and saw the guilty look on her face, I had to struggle all over again for control.

I didn't say a word and instead headed straight to the coffee pot to pour myself the cup that I had brewed earlier.

I took a sip, enjoying the kick and fragrance, and for a moment even forgetting that she was here.

"You still have your guitar?" her voice suddenly rang out across the room. I wanted to turn around for yet another glance at her, but I had caught on by then with what was happening, and I had no desire to comply with the yearnings that were stirring in my mind, so I replied without a turn.

"I don't," I replied.

"You switched to piano then. I guess it fits you better?"

I couldn't help then but turn to her, the mug in hand as I took a sip. I watched as she caressed the polished wood, and then she lifted her eyes to meet mine.

"How so?"

She gazed at me and then she shrugged, her eyes

returning to the piano. "It's bigger," she said, and I couldn't help but cock my head at this.

She straightened. "I mean... it feels a bit broodier. Guitars are quite carefree, and you were never that. At least I didn't think you were."

I continued to watch her and had to admit that her assessment was quite accurate. Soon enough though, I had to leave so I placed the mug in the sink and grabbed my jacket.

"Don't lift anything with your arm, and when you go home be sure to rest. Try to be immobile till tonight at least so that you can give it a chance to heal properly."

I didn't hear her response to this, and as I arrived at the front door to pull it open thought about giving her one last look. However, I knew that she would be staring back at me and the last thing I needed were those huge, guileful eyes to haunt me for the rest of my day.

So, I walked out of the apartment and slammed it shut.

THE COMPANY'S lobby somehow looked much bigger than the last time I'd been here, which made me notice that there had been slight changes to it. It was nice whatever they did, but I would have liked for a report of it to have been sent over.

Michael and a group of executives came scurrying over to me at the entrance, their voices loud and full of excitement. I slipped my hand into my pocket to wait as they caught their breaths, and in that time lifted my gaze to the void up above.

"You're welcome, Gideon," Michael tapped me on the shoulder, and then made a gesture with his hand for me to follow them forward. “You're an hour late,” he said with gritted teeth so the others wouldn’t hear.

“I told you I was going to be,” I said as we walked into the elevator. The other men however were stopped from joining us.

“We’ll meet upstairs and then I’ll introduce you.”

He didn’t need to, however, because I could easily recognize the Marketing Vice President, Brandon Lake, and Joshua Vance the Human Resource manager. It was just the last man. Although he looked familiar, I couldn’t quite place.

“He’s Morgan’s secretary,” Michael explained, referring to our CFO.

I nodded just as the doors slid shut, and we were left alone.

“Care to share what held you up?” he asked, and my mind immediately went to the woman I had left in my home.

It hadn’t felt strange or uncomfortable to leave her there, but rather what I was concerned about was that she wasn't going to manage that sprained arm in a way that ensured that it would heal right. She’d never been able to sit still for long enough so I was worried that she would just keep bumping into it.

“Gideon,” I heard my name then and turned to Michael.

“Itinerary,” he said, and I accepted it, quickly perusing through. The topics and format were straight forward enough.

We soon arrived on the seminar floor and then the double doors were pushed open. Within were what had to be at least two hundred employees seated and listening to the MC up on stage. However, all their eyes turned to me, and for the first time I wondered if my appearance was alright. I wasn't too casually dressed, but I wasn't as formally dressed as most of them either.

Eventually, I was led down the aisle and directly to the platform, and then seated with the other executives. They started to rise to greet me as I was announced with excited cheers, but I waved them back down and gave each a firm handshake instead. Then I took my seat as did Michael and the seminar began.

I COULDN'T REMEMBER the last time I'd been in a bar. I was with Michael and a few others from the company and as they spoke, I listened but through it all it was clear to me that my mind and interest wasn't there.

I wasn't one for the nightlife scene, but occasionally it was usually quite enjoyable. But currently, all I could think about was Pamela. I was aware that she had been long dropped off back at her apartment, much sooner than I'd hoped, which made me wonder if my expectation that milk would make her drowsy was a quirk in the past that she was no longer susceptible to.

It made me begin to wonder just how much of my current understanding of her was accurate. She seemed the same, but then I couldn't help but get curious. For instance, she had once told me that her dream was to be a veterinarian, but I was well aware now that her major was Business Administration which had nothing to do with that.

It made me wonder what had changed her mind and now what her plans for the future were.

"Gideon?"

I turned at the call and picked up my tumbler of scotch. "Everything alright?" Michael asked and I gave a nod.

"I feel as though the longer you remain a professor, the more distant and disinterested you get from the business scene."

"I think you're right," Mark agreed. "To be honest we were all certain you'd get bored with teaching within a year. But you've continued to be so occupied with it. "

"It's rewarding," I replied as I set my glass back down.

"The monotony isn't boring?" he asked.

"It's not exactly monotonous, is it? The students are different every year, and so are the projects."

"What about the curriculum?"

"I have free rein to update and adjust it as I see fit. It was one of the stipulations I presented before I even accepted the position in the first place."

"And so far, there's been no friction?" Michael asked.

"Of course, there has been," I smiled, and a round of laughter went round the table.

"Let me guess you never argued back. You kept silent and it brought them running back to you with full acceptance."

I smiled at this.

"Being there and teaching keeps me curious, which in turn keeps their department and students well informed. It's not about the money. I told them from the very start so the moment they drive me into silence they know that whatever the fight is about no longer interests me."

At this Michael shook his head with admiration in his eyes. "I'm so happy about the scheduled seminars for the employees," he said and at this I sighed since my schedule seemed to be getting tighter.

Pretty soon, it was time to call it a night simply because I wanted a chance to maybe check up on her before I headed home. The men were disappointed, but there was no convincing me to stay behind even for myself. The thought came to me over and over again that she was a grown woman and could take care of herself, but still I drove all the way until I got to the building with her apartment.

I didn't head up but tried my best to see up into her window. The lights were on which meant that they weren't asleep, and it made me even more curious as to what she was up to.

Eventually though and when I decided that she was fine, I won against the urge to head up to check. I went home and tried to put it all out of my mind. The next week however and for the first time, I was distracted during a lecture as my gaze kept going to her roommate. Both of their seats were empty which made me worried and concerned until half away through the class her roommate surfaced. She snuck in through the back door and although normally I wouldn't have paid any attention to it, today I was able to notice most of the students.

I ended the class early, which was unusual but there were no complaints.

Her friend instantly began to take her leave, but I immediately called her over and managed to get rid of the cluster of students around me.

She looked nervous, which made me worried if it had something to do with Pamela.

"Oh no, no," she said to me, her smile sheepish. "Pam is fine."

"Her arm?" I asked.

"Better. It still hurts but she's taking things easy. Well as easy as is possible for her," she said.

At this I frowned. "What do you mean?"

She hesitated, but at my expression which I hoped

relayed the message that wouldn't accept a tight lip from her, she spoke.

"She went to work," she sighed. "I told her to take the day off or a few even, but she said that they'd dock her pay and that she might even lose the job, so she went in anyway."

At this I couldn't help but frown.

"What job?" I asked.

Her friend's gaze lifted to mine and once again she hesitated in speaking.

"It's a bistro just off the campus grounds. She's a waitress there."

At my frown, her friend's words faltered while my annoyance surged.

As a waitress, there was no way that she wouldn't be asked to use her hands to lift something or the other. Or perhaps even someone would pull on her.

"She promised me that she would take it easy," her friend said and to this I just shook my head. "Thank you, Miss Scott."

With a nod, she started to take her leave while I convinced myself once again that it should be none of my concern.

However, just before she exited the auditorium, I couldn't help but call out to her.

She returned, once again looking quite nervous and flustered which I didn't understand.

"What's the name of the bistro?" I asked and for quite a while she appeared stumped.

I waited, and soon enough her response came.

"Flourish," she replied, and I nodded.

"Thank you."

11

PAMELA

"I don't know whether to tell you to get out of there, or... congratulations?"

"What?" I asked as I noted down a special request for a vegetarian order before passing it on.

"Professor Bach," she said. "He interrogated me in class on your whereabouts."

I stopped, certain that I heard her wrong.

"Pamela," she called when I had gone silent for too long.

"He asked about me?" I eventually managed to say; however, my voice was quite small.

"Yeah," she replied. "And he seemed quite upset that you had gone to work despite your injury."

"Upset?" I picked up the phone and turned away. I was a bit confused by her words but nevertheless, a smile was tugging at the corner of my lips.

Meredith heard it. "You're pleased, aren't you? You better not be because it seems as though he's going over there to draw blood."

At this I scoffed.

"You don't believe he will?" she asked.

"For him to," I replied. "He has to actually care. This bistro is located outside campus. Why the hell would he come all that way?"

"Why wouldn't he?" she asked. "Are you just trying to talk the possibilities down because you don't want to get your hopes up?"

I didn't know how to respond to that, so I simply ended the call. "I'll talk to you later," I said and returned the phone to my pocket.

For a few seconds after, all I could feel was a tingling running through me. I didn't want to revel in it, but I couldn't help it. After I'd left his apartment, I had pondered on things over and over again and couldn't truly find a way in which he could meet up with me except one of us went out of their way. I had already done that several times, but I didn't think that he would fall for that again since I was certain that he was already suspicious from the first time.

It had occurred to me that perhaps he would remain concerned about my arm and probably check up on me, but as time had passed and no visit or phone call had come, I finally realized just how unfeasible that was.

It had probably occurred to him later that perhaps he had overreacted with concern for me. It was just a sprained arm, not an incurable disease. So now and as Meredith was suggesting that perhaps he truly had concern, I didn't know what to think or feel. It seemed too unreal.

I hadn't given up on him yet but... I had taken a few steps back hoping that perhaps the universe or karma would step in for me. So perhaps it was this?

I stopped and tried to catch my breath.

For the rest of my shift, I was on alert. It would be going on till late evening which was the bistro's closing time and it worried me because that was the period that usually got quite busy.

I tried my best to look for him until eventually, we had about forty-five minutes till the end of the shift, and he'd still not shown up.

I was disappointed but tried to talk myself out of being so after all it had all been a speculation anyway.

"I'll be right back," I told Mark at the cashier as I took off my apron. "Bathroom."

"Alright," he said, and I was on my way.

By the time I returned, a slight commotion had started. Confused, I headed to the counter, and it was then that I overheard them.

Something about someone being particularly handsome, and at the words my heart gave a slight jump. I looked at both girls whispering in a corner and then followed their gazes over to a dimly lit corner of the restaurant.

Still however, the eyes of the man staring directly at me were impossible to miss.

I froze, and not until Angela came up to me was I able to recover from the shock. I was so excited and surprised that I couldn't think straight but still, her equally excited words managed to make sense to me.

"Sarah's going to attend to him," she said. "And she's going to try to get his number."

We both turned to watch the colleague that was heading over to him, a little sway that was unmistakable in her hips, and I couldn't help but frown.

"She's so lucky he's in her station," Angela sighed. "Unfortunate for the both of us."

She turned to me then and met the scowl on my face. This amused her and so she began to pat my shoulder.

"Don't look so sour," she said. "She's promised that if he rejects her then we'll both get our shot."

I looked at her, incredulous and then I dropped my apron once again.

"Bathroom," I said and walked out, and it took everything inside me not to check to see if he was watching. "Pam," Angela called after me. "Pam!"

"I'll be right back," I said and truly headed to the bathroom. There I thought to call Meredith, but I was unsure of who could be in the adjoining stall because I hadn't checked. So, I quickly texted her.

"You might have been right, and he is here to see me but everyone else is interested."

At this she went silent for a few moments and then she reacted.

"So?"

I sighed and slipped the phone back in my pocket as I headed into a stall. Another text from her soon came.

"He came to see you. Please focus on this and forget everything else."

"He couldn't even sit in my station." I texted back and then her call came.

"Are you serious? What's the actual problem here?"

I sighed then and tried my best to keep my voice down as well as look out for any entrances into the bathroom. "I don't know."

"You're jealous?" she asked, and I had to consider this.

"Sarah is beautiful."

"And so are all the other girls from my department. You didn't see him making a fuss over the fact that they're working despite their broken arm and then heading over to take care of them." I sighed at her words.

"*Sprained* arm."

"Whatever. Plus, you're beautiful too."

I shook my head then and let it hang. "I sound so insecure. I have no idea what's going on."

"He's a catch," she said. "And you really like him. He's there for you so please get out of the bathroom and be in sight at least so you can catch him ogling you."

"How do you know I'm in the bathroom?"

"Where else would you be having such a conversation? I'm sure someone has already heard you," she said and my heart shook. I immediately rose to my feet and only after checking the stalls, did I return to the restaurant.

However as soon as I arrived, I was forced to come to a stop.

"Are you back?" she called, but I couldn't respond. "Pam?"

"He just gave his number out. To Sarah."

She went quiet and so I added. "I told you she was gorgeous."

"Well... I've never seen him do that before. Just how beautiful is she? Send me a picture?"

Pulling the phone away from my ear, I gave it an incredulous look and then told her I'd call her back later.

Afterwards I headed back to the counter and just then a group of three guys came in quite loudly and excitedly. With a sigh, I put my apron back on, picked up my notepad and was on my way.

They took forever to give their orders, and then afterwards told me to hold on because they would be expecting their girlfriends soon. I sighed and looked at them. I reminded them that we had only thirty minutes till closing and they assured me that they would be out of there by then.

I returned to the counter and the gathering of both girls and even Brian. He soon left them and came over to me.

"I didn't know girls could be so excited about a guy's handwriting before," he said and shook his head.

I didn't respond.

"I don't think it's just his writing or looks though that they're so excited about. "

I was a bit surprised by what he was saying, but then I followed his line of vision and through the high windows of the bistro was able to see the sleek Mercedes he had come in. At this my eyebrows shot up. "You understand now, right?" he said, and I couldn't help my smile. "I don't blame you for being jealous. I would be too."

"What?" I frowned at his words, and then looked over to the girls who gave me a strange and amused look.

"He's not here to see them," I said, and Brian got curious.

"What do you mean?"

I rolled my eyes and saw that my table was still expecting their party. I walked out from the counter and headed over to *his* table. At my approach, my heart was thumping so hard in my chest that it felt as though I was going to pass out.

Suddenly, I could feel my heart begin to ache uncontrollably and right then I wished with all my heart that I could turn back. But it was too late. His eyes locked on mine and then to my added panic, he looked away and brought his cup of wine to his lips. I soon arrived by his side and stopped, and not till I knocked on his table did he respond.

"Hey," I said, and his blue gorgeous eyes rested on me. "What are you doing here?"

He looked at me and then his eyes went to my arm.

But he didn't say a word. I considered turning around to look at my colleagues but didn't dare.

"I heard you're giving out your phone number?" I smiled. "Care to share it with me too?"

Once again, he didn't respond so I added. "If I had it you wouldn't have had to come all the way to check up on me. I could have just told you over the phone that I was fine."

He set his cup down and then with a shake of his head that made me feel worse than I could have ever imagined was possible, he rose to his feet. I stepped away and then watched as he began to head over to the bathroom.

I stared after him and then I turned around to head over to my counter. The two girls immediately hurried over to me.

"What did you do?" Sarah asked, eyes flashing.

"Yeah Pam, he seemed pissed." Angela added.

"I've known him since I was four," I groaned. "Leave me alone."

"Oh," she said. They both came after me. "What's his name then?"

"He didn't tell you?" I asked.

"No, he only wrote down his number."

At this I sighed, checked my table to see that they were still not complete and then I headed towards the hallway leading to the bathroom where he had disappeared into.

It was quiet which was to be expected, so I stood against the wall opposite the door and waited. I heard the rush of water into the sink and then pretty soon, the door was pulled open. He came out and stopped in his tracks but didn't look surprised to see me.

I looked at him, and he did the same to me.

"I'm sorry," I apologized. "That was out of line."

"What was?" he asked, and my brows furrowed.

"You can give your phone number out to whomever you wish I just...

"You just what?" he asked.

"I... it seems as though I'm the only one you're not interested in."

He frowned, and I couldn't help but feel panicked like I was crossing yet another line that should never have been crossed. But I already felt too embarrassed to care. Might as well say what's on my mind and close this chapter.

"I told them I've known you since I was four," I said to him. "For absolutely no reason. Actually... it was out of desperation to explain my neurosis. It seems now to be the norm when I get around you."

He still didn't speak.

"Anyway, I just... I'm sorry. I'm sure I've made you uncomfortable. I surely have made myself uncomfortable, so just... forget I exist, I guess, like the plan was from the beginning."

"I'll remember you fondly and I hope you'll-" I stopped.

"Actually, I hope nothing," I said. And then I turned around to take my leave. He however suddenly caught my arm and the pain that ensued instantly struck my entire body.

"Ow," I cried out, my eyes agape in shock at him.

"You came to work when your arm still hurts this bad?" he asked.

"Let go," I said, and he did. He then sighed and looked so sadly at me that it made my heart ache.

"I'm fine," I told him. "It's fine. It'll get better, I can't afford to just stay home."

Shaking his head, he started to leave but I stopped him.

"C-can I ask for something?" I asked.

His brows rose and I knew then to speak.

"C-can you suspend the fact that we knew each other and just... give me what I want?"

"What do you want?" he asked.

I gave him a look, appalled that he was going to force me to say it out loud.

"You know what I'm talking about."

"I do not," he said, and I looked nervously towards the door. At any point now one of my coworkers was sure to come in or perhaps even a customer, so I went towards him and gathered my courage. There was no point once again in retreat. It was too late.

My hand rested against his chest and his gaze went down to it.

"You gave her your number, right? If you want her then... there's no reason why you would want me too?"

I couldn't believe the words that were coming out of my mouth, and so I was convinced that I must have lost my mind somehow along the way.

"I didn't want her," he said.

"What?"

"I didn't want her, and I didn't give her my phone number."

"Then what was the note you wrote down for her?"

"She told me it was some sort of bet and that if I wasn't going to write a number down then it would be okay to just jot down anything to save face."

"And you did?"

"She was going to be serving my food," he replied calmly. "What was the harm in it?"

"That doesn't sound like you."

"Pamela," he called, his tone short. "You don't know me. And you don't know everything. I wish you'd understand this."

I could do nothing but stare at him.

Until I threw caution to the wind and once again

pressed forward. I kissed him and although it was so unfortunately brief since I was worried that he would push me away, it sent my heart fluttering. I pulled away, my tongue licking his taste on my lips and met him watching him.

I started to move away then but to my surprise, his arm came around my waist and then I was stumbling back towards him. He slanted his head, and his scent overwhelmed me,

It didn't take much to get my lips open and then I could taste him. Thoroughly and properly and un-rushed.

"Gideon," I whimpered, quite surprised at the fervency with which he took my lips. I relished the way he sucked on my bottom lip, and then his tongue, warm and sweet, was sliding into my mouth.

Desire surged in the pit of my stomach, and I couldn't help but grab onto him, hard.

Thankfully, the kiss broke off so that I could catch my breath, but I was unable to pull my eyes open.

"I can only give you one night," he said. "Nothing more. Can you accept that?" My eyes shot open. I looked at him and then the pain of his hold registered.

I saw the seriousness of his words and felt quite sad.

"Okay," I said and was surprised as the words came out of my mouth.

His eyes seemed to darken, and then he let me go.

"You know where I live don't you?" he asked, and once again my heart thumped hard in my chest.

"No," I told him. "There's no need to take it to your home. "Let's find somewhere around here... to get it over with."

I wondered at my words, and although I couldn't believe how crass they were I also didn't think that I would be able to bear being in his home and not take this as more than it should be.

He looked at me and I could tell that he too was surprised at my refusal and subsequent suggestion.

"Your arm is in a bad state," he said. "You need to be comfortable."

"I know," I said, and had no other ideas of how to counter this. He straightened and moved away from me. My good hand went towards the wall because my body now felt drained of strength. I didn't trust that it would be enough to hold me up when he finally let go.

I looked into his eyes and held my breath.

"Then I refuse," he said. "You know where to find me if you change your mind." And with that, he turned around and walked away. All I could do was stare after him and even though I was somewhat disappointed I didn't think that I was surprised. What I suspected most was that I would have been truly disappointed if he had agreed to my nonsensical suggestion.

12

GIDEON

I waited outside the bistro, my gaze on the entrance as I was unable to leave.

I wasn't surprised at her offer, but I was surprised that she had agreed to mine.

I knew she wanted something more, but I couldn't give it and I needed to find a way to cut off any hope she might have.

A simple rejection hadn't worked so far, so perhaps this would be the best way.

I hoped that she would take it because after today, I truly doubted that it would still be on the table. The sadness in her eyes was what had prompted me to even agree to this in the first place, but in the light of day I was sure to come to my senses and recall that she didn't deserve this. She wasn't the one that committed the offense and caused my antagonism toward her.

However, I had to admit now that she had gotten under my skin... just as I seemed to have gotten under hers.

I had come here in search of her against reason, and as I

had gone in to take a seat, I finally admitted to myself just how affected that I had become by her. Wanting her had grown from a gentle nudging to a gnawing itch that I was unable to ignore.

Soon she came out and I watched as she sat in her car. There were two opposite directions from the bistro and one of them led to my home while the other led to hers.

I truly hoped that she would go home, because then it would give the two of us the chance to come to our senses.

However, and to my disappointment, she started her car and drove in the direction of my apartment.

I did the same and pulled down the windows, hoping the breeze from the night air would bring me to my senses.

We arrived at my apartment, and I couldn't remember ever feeling more turned on. I watched as she parked her car and remained in it, and I knew then that she had spotted me. So, I pushed the door open and began to stroll over to her side. I was going to head past her car but then just before I did, I found myself coming to a stop. I took a deep breath and then turned. I could see her eyes, wide eyed and anxious as she stared up at me. I lowered till we were at eye level and then spoke.

"Go home," I said, and a frown came over her face.

"You're changing your mind, after I've already driven here?"

I didn't respond, so she simply stared up at me.

"No," she said, and I shut my eyes.

Then I straightened and moved away. She got out of the car, her purse slung over her shoulder. She gave me a hard look and then she locked the door and was heading in.

She waited for me at the door and for a second, I continued thinking about ditching her altogether.

I couldn't help but admit to myself that perhaps I was the one who was afraid this would do nothing to soothe the need I felt for her.

Perhaps I would instead become hooked, and unable to control myself and at the end of the day I would end up hurting the last person that I wanted to hurt.

With a sigh, I unlocked the door, and headed in. She shut it behind her as I switched the light on, and the apartment was bathed in warm gorgeous light.

"Water?" I asked, however before I could go any further, I felt her hand wrap around my elbow. I stilled, careful not to make any abrupt movements because of her injured arm.

She then began to pull it up my arm and my breath caught in my throat. I looked at her and then she shrugged the strap of her bag off. It fell to the ground and my gaze lowered to her lips.

I wanted a moment to taste them like nothing else, so I no longer held back.

With my hand curving around her waist, I slanted my head and once again my lips were latched onto hers. She moaned in response, and the small breathless sound sent my heart banging against my chest.

I had kissed quite a number of women thus far, but there was something about this moment with her that meant so much to me and I couldn't understand it. Perhaps it was because of my already existing affection for her but with this, there was no end goal. I wanted to revel in and relish every moment of this exchange with her. I pressed her even harder against me and it wasn't long before all my inhibitions went out of the window. Both arms went around her waist and her warmth and scent engulfed me. I slid my tongue even deeper into her mouth, her name repeating over and over in my mind. She met my decadent strokes with as much fervor, but I couldn't get enough of her. Eventually I pulled away, worried that I was hurting her because of the way my entire frame was pressing against hers.

Immediately I missed the weight of her breasts as they rested against my chest and more than anything needed all of her against me.

This time around I was the one to take her hand, and the smile I could feel from her eyes was all I needed to convince myself that there was no hesitation on her part.

I led her down the hall, not bothering to turn the lights on. Eerily enough this felt too much to me like making love, which was already against what this night was meant to represent. However, I couldn't be brash or rough with her on account of her injury, so all I could do was succumb to the pace that I found things. It put me on edge as there was nothing I hated more than being out of control, but then I guess I had discovered one and that was having her hurt in any way.

Which was an irony given the terms of our current agreement.

Soon we arrived at my door, and I vowed to keep every thought contrary to or in protest of the time we were about to have, as far away as possible. The moment the door was shut behind us, I let go of her hand and began to undo the buttons of my shirt as I headed over to the bed.

"Do you need any help?" I asked when I noticed her watching me and instantly, she shook her head.

"I'm fine," she said.

She too had a button-down shirt which she began to undo. She lowered her gaze to the buttons, so I was able to watch as she fumbled with them, her cheeks flushing red.

I couldn't believe she was now turning shy as the reality

of it all was beginning to dawn on her, but I also knew that she would indeed have some difficulty due to her sprain hence why she went extremely slowly. The moment I flung my shirt aside, I started to head back to her.

She seemed startled at my arrival but didn't say any words of complaint when I held onto her lapels and took over. Instead, she watched me, and I could almost hear the rapid pounding of her heart. Or perhaps it was mine. I couldn't tell. I undid the buttons all the way to the bottom and then pulled the fabric away from her shoulders. It went down her arms, and then the creamy smooth skin of her chest was exposed to me. I gazed at the beautiful swells of her breasts, encased in a dark lacy bra that allowed bits of skin to peek through. I grew even harder as I stared down at them, wanting more than anything to lower my lips to taste them. I managed to hold back however but couldn't look away.

"Do you need any help with your jeans?" I asked.

She looked down at it and shook her head, but I chose instead to lower until I squatted. This brought my face at eye level to her abdomen, and I didn't miss her slight gasp.

It would have been amusing if I wasn't so hard that I could feel a headache coming on. My hand went to the band of her jeans and at the brush of my hands against the warmth of her skin I could feel her quiver.

I kept going, the buttons slipping out of their holes and then I was tugging them down her thighs.

They fell to her feet, exposing the matching lace underwear she had on. I leaned forward then, unable to stop myself and placed a kiss on the skin just above the band. She held onto me, her breathing harsh and when my tongue slipped out to graze across her skin, I felt her quiver.

The air was charged with so much tension and anticipation that I could feel the weight of it. I could no longer wait anymore so I rose to my feet.

"Hold on to me," I said and before she could understand what I meant, my arms had gone around her thighs. I lifted her off her feet and she giggled in surprise. I could feel a smile tugging at the corners of my lips but managed to contain it since I would be facing her soon. I laid her on the bed as gently as I could and then held onto the sides of her thighs. I urged her legs apart and then I was reaching for that core in between that I hadn't been able to put out of my mind.

Her hand grabbed my hair, trying to urge me away but before she could stop me my mouth was parting and closing around her dampness through the material.

"Ahh," she moaned louder than she had so far, and I could feel the rush of the added intimacy go all the way up to my brain.

I needed all the access that I could get so I pulled the lace aside and then my tongue was sliding into her wetness.

I reveled in her scent as I licked through her folds, and she cried out in response. She writhed and whimpered so hard across the bed that I was tempted to pause but then she called out my name, and I was spurred to continue even further. I spread her thighs even further open and with my fingers pulling at the lace managed to rip the scrap of material off her sex.

Instantly she was exposed to me, and I reached forward to feast on her the way I wanted to. My lips closed around her clit and then I was sucking so hard that I felt her cries resound across the room. Her grip on my hair hardened but I didn't relent with my pressure, the pad of my tongue giving her a hard lick from the base to the tip.

I then speared her with the tip but needed to reach even

deeper, so I leaned away and allowed my middle finger to take over.

It slid into her and her back arched slightly off the bed.

"Gid- Gideon," she shuddered.

My finger thrusted in and out of her, coaxing her open even wider and then another finger joined. I positioned myself over her, my arm curving underneath her waist and then I resumed my thrusting. At first my pace was slow, but as I watched her... the way her mouth hung open and how her cries intensified, I wanted to see her even further unraveled. I increased my pace until there was no longer a traceable rhythm. She almost bounded out of my hold then but at her wince of pain as she tried to stop me, I relented.

"Ow," she whimpered, one hand going to hold the other.

"You okay?" I asked and she nodded, until she was able to catch her breath.

"I'm fine," she said. "I'm fine."

I was swept with the uncontrollable urge to kiss her, so I reached forward and my mouth was once again melded to hers.

She melted in my hold, and I could feel her immediately begin to relax once again.

I loved all the breathy sounds she made... of wonder... of excitement... they made me tingle all over. I lost myself in the kiss reveling in the kind of connection that I couldn't recall ever feeling with anyone else.

I wasn't surprised at all, but unfortunately it just made me tense up even further until I had to pull away.

I hid my face in her neck as I wasn't certain that whatever expression I had on wouldn't expose the vulnerability I was feeling.

"Stay still," I whispered into her ear. "You'll hurt your arm otherwise."

It took a few seconds but eventually, I was able to sense the obedient nods of her head. I almost smiled because when it came to her it was indeed a rarity to be so agreeable. Soon enough I moved, positioning myself properly above her then and although I didn't expect it her eyes came open and we stared right into each other's eyes.

13

PAMELA

In those few seconds my heart stopped.

For the first time he was looking at me in a way that I had always hoped for, and I couldn't believe the circumstance surrounding the moment it was happening in. I'd thought that I would be too shy and that I would hesitate, however from the moment he kissed me, it was as though all of my inhibitions had melted along with the heat he had caused in me. I felt like my entire body was burning up.

He was being extremely gentle with me, and I knew that it was due to the sprain in my arm. I loved it, however given my suspicion that this would be our only time together I couldn't help but wish that I was in tip top shape so I could be as active as I wanted to be. Now and just as I suspected, all I would be able to do was receive and it didn't make me happy.

He leaned down once again to kiss me, and at the weight of his rock-hard body on mine, I couldn't help but reach out to hold onto him with my good arm.

"Pamela," he called, and I nearly sighed at the sweet sound of my name on his lips.

"I want to hold you," I told him. "It's my good arm." I urged him further until he had his weight on me since he was holding most of it in his arms.

He somewhat succumbed and I couldn't help my smile. Our eyes met once again and then I couldn't hold back. With my arm around his shoulder, I kissed him... deeply and couldn't get enough of the way his tongue stroked mine in the most delicious way.

He soon broke away once again, and I seemed to sink into his bed as he began to trace the kisses down the skin of my neck. He took his time, going slowly and carefully and it added to the magic of the thrill and sweetness that I couldn't quite put into words.

I gasped slightly when he reached the skin that covered my pulse and could feel goosebumps breaking out across my skin as the tip of his tongue traced down all the way to the base of my collar bone.

He kissed me there deep and wet and at the moist feel of his tongue, I couldn't help but push my head back into the pillow.

He began to trace the kisses lower and soon arrived at my breasts. I loved the way his lips circled my nipples, and the way he flicked his tongue around them. It tightened my core even further, and when he applied the right pressure and sucked on them, I felt myself cry out.

My hand found its way to his ass and although it was disappointing to find that he still had his pants on, I was still able to grab onto him. However, I needed him fully naked before me. I needed to feel all of him, but I also couldn't bear for him to stop what he was doing. I was so torn and overwhelmed all at the same time at the feeling of my breasts in his hands as he kneaded them delicately, wonderfully, and then sucked on the hardened peaks.

I needed him now more than anything and I relayed as much.

"You can take your time later," I told him. "I can't wait anymore."

I could hear his smile, and then he once again came up and kissed me. "Patience," he said, and I shuddered all over. Soon he was tracing the kisses down my belly and soon arrived at the sensitive part just above my panties. He had already ripped them apart earlier, the lace hanging loose and never had I been so glad that the room was dim. It wasn't completely dark like I think I would have preferred, but it was just lit enough to keep me comfortable. It pained me though that we wouldn't get the chance to become even more comfortable with each other so that we could both make the explorations that we wanted without any hesitations.

He took the rest of the material off, and then once again his mouth was on me.

I cried out until he had me writhing once again on the bed but just as I reached the edge however, he moved away, and I lamented at the loss.

"Gideon," I called out, but the complaint died in my throat when I saw the look in his eyes and realized that he was finally, completely undressing. I watched him and even considered looking away, but I couldn't bring myself to. Especially after I took in the solid build of his gorgeous body. My mouth watered as I took in the ridges and slopes of his abs, and then I couldn't look away from the light smattering of hair that trickled down his abs, disappearing underneath his briefs. The jeans were pushed down to his feet and then his hands hooked into the band of his briefs.

I held my breath and couldn't believe I was seeing him in this way, when so many other people had coveted the same.

Most especially I *had,* from the days I hadn't even known what I was asking for, but I couldn't remember a time when I didn't want to be as intimate as possible with him. The briefs were pulled down and his hardened cock was exposed. I gazed at it, nearly shocked out of my mind at the extent of his arousal. It was so hard that it curved upwards, laying nearly vertically against his stomach, and had to be the most wonderful girth and length I had ever seen. Not that I had seen many and truly I was never much impressed, but with him I couldn't look away.

"You can't be real," I said under my breath and although he heard me, he was thankfully not able to make out my exact words.

"What?" he asked softly, and I shook my head. But then what I truly wanted to say occurred to me.

"I want you in my mouth," I said, and could see the smile on his face.

"Maybe-" he began but then he stopped. I watched as every trace of amusement left his face and didn't need to ask what he had been about to say.

He walked away and I shut my eyes.

"Are you alright?" he asked when he returned, and I knew that he was really asking if I wanted to continue.

"I'm fine," I said to him and met his gaze head on, and it was then I saw the packet in his hand. He tore it open, and I watched, my sex pulsing with need as I saw him work it onto his length. He was so attractive that I could barely think straight, and by the time he returned to the bed and to me my legs were open in fevered anticipation.

His hand closed around my ankle, and the strength of

his grip evoked a wonderful sense of danger that sent chills coursing up my spine, but then his lips connected with my skin and once again I was overtaken with the need to simply bask and revel in him. He kissed his way up my calves and my inner thighs until I was all but pleading with him to give me the release he had worked up over and over again in me.

He kissed my sex the moment he arrived at the juncture of my thighs and then he positioned himself above me.

I looked into his eyes, cradling his face and then I leaned into kiss him,

He took advantage of my preoccupation, and then began to nudge into my opening.

I could feel the thick head as it nestled between my dampness, and then he was sliding into me and filling me up. It was exquisite and so was he, my mouth parted in barely contained bliss as I urged him on until he reached the hilt.

He let out a low groan, his eyes tightening, and I was in wonder because it was the first time I was certain that I had seen the reins of his control and composure loosen.

It was much too brief though, and I was quite certain he noticed and chose to hide. He settled his face in the crook of my neck as we both tried to catch our breaths.

"You alright?" he asked me once again and my throat began to close up with emotion at just how thoughtful he was. I nodded and then he began to move.

I could no longer keep my eyes open, so I closed them and gave in completely to the emotions and pleasure he was wringing out of me. The base of my stomach wound tighter and tighter as his thrusts increased and so did mine, more than eager to meet his.

He kissed me everywhere and with one good arm, I held

onto him for dear life reciprocating the kisses in any which way that I could.

He went even faster, railing me so intensely that I felt my eyes begin to roll into my sockets. The noises resounding across the room were a mix of our harsh breathing, the sounds of flesh hitting flesh along with a slight scent of musk.

I tried with all my might to keep my eyes open, to watch him, but then his thrust hit a particularly favored spot, and I began to writhe underneath like a child.

"*Baby*," he rasped out, and for a few seconds I was certain that I had heard wrong. It plagued me for a few minutes, wrenching the most intense of sensations out of me. My hand moved everywhere to touch him, my nails scraping down his back as he pounded into me even harder until I reached my peak.

I tried to hold on for as long as possible, but then his equally strained groan of release merged with mine and I felt it all in my core.

My limbs went numb, the crazed tingles followed, and I lost coherence. I could hear my agonized moan as it flowed out of my lips and felt the out-of-control grind of my hips to meet his as we milked every bit of pleasure possible from our joining. In the end, I found myself kissing all over his face, mumbling words that I couldn't decipher. He cradled the side of my face and then he kissed me, one last, perfect time and I sunk into overwhelming bliss.

14

GIDEON

I didn't want to move away from her, but I couldn't hold most of my weight in my arms anymore as my limbs had been drained of strength.

I began to pull out, regretfully but I kept my face in her hair and breathed in her scent before we were eventually separated. I collapsed beside her on the bed, my eyes barely seeing the ceiling and tried to catch my breath.

"*Fuck*," I cursed and then turned to look at her. Her eyes were shut and her chest heavily rising and falling and her hair sticking to her face. Her skin was flushed, her breasts perked up and her frame bathed in the most beautiful golden glow. I found myself leaning over, and by the time she felt my presence and opened her eyes it was too late for me to retreat so I kissed her once again deeply and slowly, and then pulled away when the racing of my heart became too much for me to control.

Afterwards she had the most beautiful and exhausted smile on her face, and I could feel my insides melt.

"Rest," I told her, and she seemed surprised by this.

“I uh...” she was eventually able to respond. “I don’t want to intrude. I could drive home.”

I thought of the correct response to give to this beyond what I wanted to which was that she could stay here for as long as she could possibly want.

However, our agreement for the night came to mind, and I couldn’t help but lament at my words and choice. But then again in this moment of weakness I was glad for them because it made things between us quite simple and reminded me of what the outcome of this was supposed to be.

My fears had come true, I wouldn’t be able to get enough of her but then if she left now... then perhaps the effects of her presence and our connection could be dulled and then our planned withdrawal afterwards from each other would be a success.

I made a choice and did the hardest thing I was certain I ever had.

I got up from the bed and gave a response.

“Sure,” I said, and could feel the room go eerily quiet. I knew then that her breath was caught, and guilt slammed into me like a boulder. But I couldn’t relent, so before she could spot any faltering in my detached demeanor or expression, I walked out of the room and escaped to the bathroom.

I felt like a coward and hoped with all my heart that she wouldn’t think I was worth the hurt. There was no future for us together and I had been so adamant about it for so long that I didn’t know how to think otherwise. This was however one of the greatest nights and experiences of my life and I planned to cherish it with all my heart.

In the bathroom, I cleaned up but forewent taking a shower. I wanted to still have her scent and warmth all over me, and when I exited my room and returned to the bedroom, I knew I had made the right choice.

Because she was gone. She had gathered up her clothes and left without a word and it was the least of what I deserved.

Dejected and exhausted all at once, and yet still high on the buzz that was her, I collapsed onto the side of the bed she had laid on and let the strains and exhaustion of the day take me away.

15

PAMELA

I had one more question for him I realized, but it only occurred to me and solidified in my heart on my drive home. Afterwards I tried to forget about it as well as our relations thus far and that… night.

But then it was all I could think about.

We'd had an agreement that it would only be this one night, and in the nights that followed when I'd woken up sweating and panting and so turned on, I had taken care of myself, I realized that it had been a senseless agreement. At least on my part because that one night just made me want him even more. I wondered if it was the same for him and if he, just like me, was regretting the terms of the agreement.

I would find out, I decided amongst other things, so I put my hesitation and shame aside and headed over to his office.

Once again, his secretary stopped me, feigning absolutely no recollection of me and remaining adamant that Professor Bach had given the orders not to accept any visitors that didn't have an appointment.

I was discouraged then and with no other choice but to

turn away, however at the last moment he received a call and gave me a peculiar look.

"You're Miss-"

"Fraser," I responded to his question.

"Miss Fraser," he said, and I held my breath. Eventually the phone call came to an end, and I was ushered in.

I loved his office. It wasn't as bright as his home, but there was something about the polished glistening wood and silk upholstered furniture that made it seem so picturesque and cozy. And then there he was, seated at his desk, and he had never looked more grand.

"Hi," I replied and then he offered me a seat. "I just wanted to ask you a question?"

"You don't want to take a seat?" he asked, and it was then that I allowed myself to look at him. I was already so nervous that all my focus was on speaking as calmly as possible, but those precautions went out the window as all I could do was stare at him. I couldn't believe I had had him in my arms.

My gaze went to his dark hair, which was gorgeous, and I could remember how my hands had sunk within and grabbed onto it.

Then there was the fitting and alluring broadness of his shoulders, encased in a simple white t-shirt underneath and a dark blazer. It was so simple. A sigh seeped out of me as I realized that I could truly just stare at him forever.

"Pamela," he called again, and I came to my senses.

I shook my head to clear it and resolved to keep my gaze solely on his face rather than think about all the things that I didn't get to do to him in one night.

"I wanted to ask you about the fire," I said. "Is it related to why you don't want anything to do with me right now? Or am I just not good enough for you?"

He looked at me, and since the words were already out, I proceeded to make my point. "I thought about things and the only thing that seems to make sense now is that the college prevents any personal relationships between students and professors, but I'll be graduating in a year anyways so... is this truly enough to stop you? I mean... if you didn't care about me at all back then then why did you risk so much to save me from a fire that could have severely hurt you?"

After this, I had nothing more to say so I stopped talking and watched how he dropped the pen that had been in his hand and with a sigh leaned back into his chair.

"Pamela, we had an agreement," he said. "That we would cut off all contact with each other after one night."

I sighed and looked at him. "I know," I replied. "But I'm asking you why you saved me?"

"I don't hate you," he said. "So why wouldn't I?"

"It sure sounds like you do now," I said. "Like you regret it."

"I don't," he replies.

"But you didn't save me because you were overly fond of me either did you?"

"No, I didn't," he replied.

"So, it was all in my head?"

"I don't know what was in your head," he said, "but I do know what was in mine and it was simply the fact that I didn't want any weight on my conscience."

I frowned at his words. "What does that mean? You weren't the one that started the fire. It happened in our house, not yours."

He looked at me and then he straightened and returned his gaze to his desk.

"I have to get back to work," he said, and I sighed.

"Alright, fine, goodbye," I said, and this time around I didn't dare linger. I could feel the grief already rising like bile in my throat and my entire body was brimming with the need to let it. However, I had refused to from that night, because even though I wanted more, and he simply didn't and grieving over that would be senseless. It didn't mean that I was less, it was just simply that it wasn't meant to be between us.

That night however, had convinced me otherwise because I couldn't believe it was possible to feel all the things he'd made me feel, and like an addict I craved for more, but I had to accept what was, gather my pride and dignity and keep moving.

I left the office and went on my way.

16

GIDEON

Three Weeks Later

I could feel the side glances that Michael was giving to me, as we descended the elevator down to the administrative floors where the interviews would be held. I tried my best to ignore him but when the elevators paused briefly and a few more staff came in and he refused to look away, I lost my patience.

At my scowl, he simply smiled and only when the elevator was emptied again did he explain.

"I truly want to understand why you're participating in the intern interviews this year. You don't even participate in senior executive interviews."

My response was simple. "I have a few students applying."

"You're not going to be partial, are you?"

I debated whether to tell the truth on this, but thankfully before I could we finally arrived. The elevator dinged, the doors opened, and we both stepped out.

"Gideon," Michael groaned, and I smiled.

"I just have two candidates I want to take a closer look at," I said. "They don't test well at all, but they always outperform when it comes to practical projects. I just want to make sure we don't miss out on them in case they don't do well on the test."

"Alright then," he says, and we went into the room. The applicants who had completed their exams began to come through and I let the questioning go to the other staff present. It was only when I had something specific to inquire about that I stepped in, but otherwise, I was focused more on listening to the candidate's responses and going through their submitted information.

It was in the process of this that I ran into Meredith's application and was truly surprised seeing it.

A little while later, she walked in and thankfully was professional enough to not seek out my attention. I listened to her responses carefully and allowed the final decisions to go to Michael, but I was impressed. Soon the interviews came to an end, and it made me wonder if her roommate had also applied for any of the administrative positions.

We went for lunch at the company's cafeteria and when I brought this up to Michael, he once again seemed surprised.

"You have a candidate too for the administration department?"

"I don't have any candidates," I replied. "I'm just curious. We only interviewed the engineers."

"I can get you a list," he says. "And have Liam discuss his assessment and choices with you."

I thought about it but then decided that I didn't want to be involved.

"It's fine,' I said and brushed the concern away. Whether and if she applied should no longer be my concern, and neither was whether she got in or not. I had done all I could to put her out of my mind over the last few weeks and thus far, I had been fairly successful, mostly due to taking much more than was advised onto my plate.

But then at night and when I laid in bed, it didn't take much for her moans, scent and sweet expressions to come to mind.

Seeking my release on most nights was the only way that I could find sleep, but I did wonder for how long I would be able to keep this up.

17

PAMELA

"How was your interview?"

After waiting at the entrance to the cafeteria for over ten minutes, I wasn't too happy to see Meredith as she bounded happily towards me.

"You're late," I said, but she threw her hands around me in apology.

"I'm sorry, they took longer with the interviews than anticipated. How was yours?"

I shrugged then and we both began to head in.

"You don't sound very enthusiastic," she said, and I sighed, not yet ready to tell her that I didn't get in.

"When have I been? You're the one who forced me into this otherwise why would I be applying for a job at Gideon's company?"

"Professor Bach," she corrected. "And truly, it's a great company to intern for. The pay is great and trust me even if you choose not to return here after graduation the prestige of having it on your resume is priceless."

"Okay," I groaned as we headed towards an empty table.

Just when we arrived however, we both came to a stop.

For a long moment there were no words, and then Meredith stepped in. “Professor Bach... Mr. Faust.”

His friend held out his hand to accept Meredith’s handshake, while he took a quick glance at me and then returned to his meal.

“You know Professor Bach,” his friend asked, and Meredith nodded excitedly. “I do.”

“She’s one of my students,” he said, and I couldn’t believe just how sad I felt as I looked at him.

He was dashing, to say the least, and even though I hadn’t been able to get him out of my mind over the past several weeks, it was nothing compared to seeing him in this moment and recalling all those nights where I forced myself to sleep with a damp face. We’d never even officially been together, but it’d felt like I had lost someone I’d known and cherished all my life.

“Did you both participate in the interviews?” his friend asked, and Meredith smiled. I turned to see Gideon’s reaction but found that he was already preoccupied with draining the glass of water that had been sent to his table.

“We did, Sir,” Meredith replied excitedly.

“And how was it?”

“All up to you,” she replied, and he smiled.

“What about you Miss-”

“Fraser,” I said and took the hand he offered.

“It was fine,” I lied, not wanting to get into explaining.

“What position?”

“Channel sales,” I replied.

“And your Major?”

“Business administration,” I said, and he nodded, satisfied.

My gaze went to Gideon’s then and I watched him

looking at me quite unashamedly. Soon we headed over to our table a few away from them, and finally took our seats.

"Jeesh, I can't believe we just ran into the top two executives."

"They interviewed you?" I asked.

"Just Professor Bach. I mean he didn't exactly interview me, but he was in the room. It was nerve-racking because he didn't say a word and simply just listened. He didn't even ask any questions."

"That should bode well for you," I said.

"I hope so," she replied. "I mean I'm not asking for any preferential treatment, but he should know to apply one to his beloved student. I'm sorry for saying this Pamela but never have I wished more than now that you both were on good terms. You couldn't have waited three weeks later to break up?"

"We never dated," I said as we got up to go pick up our meals.

"Oh yeah... right," her tone was sheepish as she followed behind.

I didn't look his way, throughout the rest of the lunch, and by the end of it, when they finally stood up to leave, I couldn't believe just how easy it was not to. For a second, I felt his gaze on me and since I didn't care enough to check, they went on their way and that was that.

A few days later however I was attending a class and struggling to stay awake when I received a text to my phone.

"You didn't pass the written test?"

My heart lurched into my throat.

I was already well aware of this as I hadn't gone on to the interview, but I wondered why he was contacting me about it.

I didn't respond but then later and just as the class was wrapping up, I received another.

"Can you come to my office?"

I truly didn't want to, but then again this was Gideon. I continued with the rest of my day, but eventually, my curiosity got the better of me. I got to his door and this time around I was immediately ushered in by Oscar. I met Gideon standing and looking out his window as he responded to a call. He however turned around at my entrance and gestured me towards one of his sofas.

"Michael, I'll call you back," he said and then turned to face me.

"How are you, Pamela?"

I shrugged.

"Can I get you anything to drink?" he asked, and I looked at his gorgeous face.

I felt bitter, especially as I took in his dark gray slacks and light blue dress shirt, folded at the elbows. It was as though every time I saw him somehow, he appeared even more handsome. But I wasn't ready to fall down this ghastly hole once again as I was already struggling to claw my way out of the last one.

"No need." I replied. "What did you want to talk to me about?"

He studied me. "I hope you don't suspect that I had anything to do with your test not making the mark."

It took a few seconds for me to process this, and afterwards, I was somewhat offended. "Why would you have had something to do with it? Wasn't it computerized?"

He smiled. "It was, and I didn't. I was a bit surprised though that you were interested in joining us."

"I wasn't," I replied. "Meredith talked me into it. But why would you be surprised though that I would want to join your company? It's immensely reputable and there are positions for those of my major."

He didn't respond quickly enough so I immediately shot out an accusation. "Is it that you also don't think I'm good enough to work for your company? Or did you think I was applying because of you?"

He was calm as he replied, despite my attempt to make him nervous.

"None of those things. It was just unexpected."

"That's it?" I asked and he nodded.

"That's it."

"Alright, since that's cleared up, I'll be leaving," I rose to my feet.

"Would you like to try again?" he asked, much to my surprise.

"There's a second round of interviews and tests going on next weekend. I'd like you to try again."

"Isn't that against the rules?"

"It's my company," he said. "I can bend the rules however I want."

"Wouldn't that be unfair to the other candidates?"

"How would it be unfair? I'm not giving you the answers to the test, I'm just inviting you to try again."

"What if word gets out of it and all the others that failed want a retest?"

"Then I'll organize a retest."

At this I was stumped. "Just to get me to try again?"

He nodded and anger surged in me.

"Why?" I asked.

"It's a great job and the starting pay is good. I don't think you'd get that anywhere else right now, and the skills you'll pick up from here will be invaluable."

I grew frustrated, "Why do you care if I get a better offer

somewhere else? I thought we were done. That you didn't want anything to do with me."

He grew silent. "I told you this before Pamela, I don't hate you. I have no hard feelings whatsoever towards you and if I can help you to move forward and ahead, then why shouldn't I?"

"So why won't you sleep with me again?" The words blurted out of my mouth before I could stop them. He looked at me and then sighed.

"I want to," he said, and my eyes slightly widened. "And that's the truth, but you're not just any girl to me. And since I don't want to be in a relationship, it's inevitable that just being physical without the intention to take things further will hurt you. I don't want that, Pamela. I don't want to see you hurt."

At his last statement, all the anger and frustration I'd held in over the last few weeks all seemed to surge to the surface, and I couldn't stand to be in his presence any longer. I turned away and stormed towards the door.

"Pamela," he called but I didn't respond.

However, just as I pulled the door open, it slammed shut.

"What are you doing? I asked, as I spun around to face him.

Without thinking I placed both hands on his chest to push him away. He staggered backwards, however his hand locked around my wrists at the last moment, so I was forced to move with him.

"Gideon," I complained once again but this time, his arms went around my waist to hold his body to mine.

"Gideon," I complained but he held on and wouldn't respond until I met his gaze.

"This is inappropriate," I told him.

"I'll let you go," he said. "If you don't storm out. There's no need to. Above all else I want things to be amicable between us."

I looked at him then and finally understood. "So, you want to reject me but yet bypass all the hard feelings?" I asked. He stared at me, and I knew that was the truth. At this I didn't know how to feel. On one hand, I was touched by his concern but on the other I was so aggrieved by his distance that I never wanted anything to do with him.

But then here we were locked in each other's arms.

I leaned forward then but he warned me.

"Pamela."

I didn't give the warning any attention. I slanted my head, my lips reaching for his but once again he pulled away. He staggered backward with me along with him and I used the chance to pull my wrist out of his grip. I caught this head in both of my hands and then kissed him.

His lips parted automatically for me, and although it was brief, I could immediately taste him. My lips swept across his, eager and ravenous and then my tongue slid into his mouth. The sensual strokes that ensued sent dizzying sparks of pleasure through my body, and it was only afterwards that I felt him still trying to pull away. I let him go then and met his eyes widened with surprise, or perhaps something more akin to amazement inside them.

"Pamela!" he spat, and I smirked.

His hand however closed viciously around my arm.

"Ow," I complained, and he immediately let go.

"Are you alright?" he asked. "It still hurts?"

I listened to his words, soft and kind, saw the concern in his eyes and wondered how I could have thought that he loathed me and wanted absolutely nothing to do with me. I let my purse drop to the floor, and then I kissed him again.

He held the back of my neck, his large hands easily closing around the petite column of my neck as he tried to pull away, but I didn't budge. Not till I had gotten my fix.

I soon did, and once again pulled away but this time there was a taunting smile on my face.

"Pamela!" he complained

"Oh, shut up," I said and grabbed onto his hair. "Fuck me," I told him, as I rose on the tips of my toes, ignored his scowl and kissed him. "No hard feelings."

In that moment, something dangerous boiled in his gaze and I wanted to be consumed by it whole. When he lowered and I felt my legs completely lift off the ground I had no complaints whatsoever.

He carried me over to his desk, and then pushed off whatever was on it to deposit me on it. I heard the flutter of documents as they were flung away and the dull thud of ceramic as it landed on the floor, but I didn't care, especially because he didn't seem to. With his glare on me, he began to undo the buckle of his belt and I didn't need to do much because I had on a skirt. But then I recalled how it had felt to have his mouth and hands on my breasts from that night and I wanted it all over again, so I pulled my t-shirt over my head and flung it aside, leaving me in just my bra.

He moved away and I mourned the loss of his presence, but then I heard the quiet call behind the door.

"Sir? Sir?" Gideon pulled the door slightly open, mouthed off some instructions and then shut it. Then he locked it from inside and returned to me.

I unhooked my bra by the time he reached me, but before I could pull it down my arms his mouth was already on the swell of my breast. He suckled across the soft creamy mounds, and I felt the sting and sweetness all the way to my core.

I held onto his head as he moved to the hardened peaks of my nipples and the moment his lips locked on them my head fell back. I tried to control my tone because even though the door was locked, this was still far from a safe zone. Relations between us were prohibited and getting caught would instantly lead to losses. I knew he loved being here even if he didn't have to be and I didn't want to take that away from him, plus I needed to be and didn't care to be kicked out, so I bit onto my lip and tried to restrain myself. The sounds however from his feasting were anything but controlled and it was like fuel doused on my libido.

I soon pulled him away because I couldn't get enough of kissing him. More than anything, it made me feel so connected to him and when he indeed wrapped his arms around me and kissed me so deeply that my back arched backwards, I felt my throat close thickly with emotion.

By this point, he'd kissed me several times before but this one was very unlike the others. Currently he kissed me as though I meant so much to him and as though he had missed me terribly. So much so that when we broke apart, I could only look at him, dazed.

He didn't look away, and instead returned to unbuttoning his pants. I couldn't stop staring at him.

I couldn't say it all, but I felt it all... and all over again my pain at being separated from him over the past several weeks began to make sense to me.

And I could see or at least hoped that it would be the same for him.

In no time his cock was out, hard and gorgeous and all over again I was struck with feral excitement.

I wanted to suck him off, I realized just like the last time.

"Gideon," I breathed, my hand wrapping around his girth in order to get him to pause.

"I want to..." I swallowed, my thumb stroking across the lush, damp head.

"Next time," he said, and my heart skipped several beats. At first, I was sure he had misspoken but when he held my gaze without looking away and then urged my legs apart, I knew he was very well aware of what he had said. *Next time.* He pulled my panties to the side and then he was stroking the rigid length up and down my sex.

"Ahh..." I moaned out loud, my eyes unable to remain open. He nudged into me, inclining me slightly back and my sex pulsed hungrily around him.

The ceiling above me blurred as the sensation of the silky smoothness of his cock grazing up my walls sent little tremors through me, and most importantly, was the satisfaction of being filled so perfectly. Gripping underneath my thighs, he immediately began to thrust in and out of me, his pace controlled at first but then a few seconds later and his hips were driving feverishly. I held on with a cry caught in the back of my throat.

I couldn't stop my whimpering and inaudible mumblings, so I buried my face in the crook of his shoulder as I tried my best to keep up with him.

He fucked me with an urgency that I felt to my very bones... reminiscent of our deprivation from each other.

I grabbed onto his ass, loving the strength I could feel in it as he drove me out of my mind.

He kissed my neck, temples, and lips and the warmth and sweetness of it all drove me dizzy with joy.

It didn't take long for us to come to completion, our desires for the other much too starved and brimming to be teased.

I was surprised by the volume of his shout when he came, considering how inconspicuous we were supposed to be. He didn't seem to be able to hold back and I loved every bit of it. I gave in too, our bodies melded as one and dampened with sweat.

The feel of him, solid and warm and desired made me feel as though I was on cloud nine. I didn't want it to end, ever, but it had to, however this time around and unlike the previous time a tiny flame of hope flickered in a corner of my heart.

There would be another time... hopefully like he had said, but just in case I clung onto him as hard as I possibly could, unwilling to let go. He kissed me once again and just like that all my fears and concerns were soothed away. As for the future, I pushed it far away and reveled in the unbelievable sweetness of our present.

PART 2

18

GIDEON

I hadn't smoked a cigarette in years, but as I held her in my arms, I wanted one. Once again, I didn't want to let go, but given where we were and the fact that remaining in this compromising position with her was beginning to excite me once again, I was forced to come to my senses.

I began to pull away and she let me go.

I looked down, and even though she immediately tried to close her legs, nothing could hide the aftermath of our joining. I watched it trickle down her thighs and when I looked at her once again, found that she couldn't quite meet my eyes.

I watched her gorgeous face, the tendrils of her hair framing her face, and couldn't stop myself from reaching out to brush it away.

This time I didn't hold back, and it made me wonder just what it bodes for us and our relationship.

I felt bothered, but as I examined my emotions a bit more closely, it didn't seem accurate to me that what the future held for us was the crux of my current trouble.

"I'll get you a washcloth," I said, and she gave a nod. I turned around to go on my way and it was when I arrived at the bathroom that it finally occurred to me. Shaking my head, I cleaned myself up, put my clothes back in order and then returned with a warm washcloth for her.

I found that she had gotten back on her feet, and had her back turned to me as she smoothed the creases of her outfit. By the side, I could see a couple of used tissues, and the moment she sensed my presence, she turned to face me.

"I'll be uh... leaving," she said, and I wondered where all her bravado from earlier had gone.

She tried to smile at me, but it didn't quite meet her eyes, however before she could walk away, I grabbed onto her arm and forced her to stop.

"You need to clean up properly," I said. "What's the use in feeling ashamed now?"

She pulled her arm away from my grip.

"Ashamed? Why the hell would I feel ashamed?" she asked, and at her indignation, she held my gaze head on. I couldn't help my smile then and the moment she saw it, a little confused frown came over her expression.

"C'mon," I said. "Don't take offense. Plus... I was too hasty. We weren't safe."

"It's fine," she said. "I'll take care of it."

At her words I couldn't help my curiosity. "Are you on the pill?" I asked, and as I waited for her response felt the most conflicted that I could remember feeling in a long time. On one hand, I wanted her to tell me that she wasn't sleeping with anyone else, and thus she didn't need it, but then on the other hand, I wanted to know that she was protecting herself.

She looked at me, and was about to respond without any

further thought, but then she stopped and cocked her head. "I don't think you need to know the answer to that," she said.

"I do," I groaned. However, she didn't agree.

"Don't worry," she said and then began to head towards the door. "I'm never going to come to you with any trouble."

I grabbed her arm once again to urge her towards me, but then she winced, and I immediately let go.

"Your arm still hurts?"

"You pulled hard," she said, and I immediately felt remorse.

"I'm sorry," I quickly apologized.

She looked at me and sighed.

"I don't expect any commitments from you after this, so you don't have to show concern. And moreover, I wanted this too. It was... fun."

At this I didn't know what to say, especially because we were both on the same page, but it suddenly didn't feel good at all. It never particularly had but now it felt more sour than it ever had before.

"Reapply for the position," I told her. "It'll be good for your resume."

"So, you've said," she said and then her gaze sort of lost focus as though she retreated deeply into her thoughts. "It sounds great, but I don't think it's what I want. As I move towards graduation next year, I've been thinking a lot about what I want to be involved in and Business Administration doesn't sound very appealing."

"So why did you choose it?" I asked.

"My dad had a business as you know," she replied. "Plus, the course's employment options are broad, and the pay can be really good. I also considered that it could somehow help me to run my own business in the future. And most importantly, I really didn't have a particular interest in anything else and that is my current dilemma. I thought I'd have found what I truly enjoyed by now and perhaps started a business related to it, but I haven't so far, so I'm focused on exploring myself a bit deeper.

"The internship program is only twelve weeks," I told her, wondering if she was under a different assumption that it ran for longer. "You could earn some money during that time and also have the chance to explore other areas that you might be interested in."

She paused, and I was certain that she was turning the idea over in her mind. My only hope was that I had made a good point or two that she could take with her and perhaps consider.

I escorted her the rest of the way to the door, and when she left, found that I had to lean against it to regain the strength that had timidly slipped out of my body with her presence.

Afterwards, I looked at the washcloth in my hand and then returned to the bathroom to dispose of it.

She was keeping me at a distance which I guessed was ideal, but after what had just happened between us, I had to ask myself once again if my reservations towards her because of her family were truly enough to keep us apart. I wanted her and that fact was truer now to me than any other thing.

With a sigh, I returned to my office and tried to get back to work, however, when I found that I couldn't concentrate, I pushed it aside and called my father.

As usual it took him a while to even notice that the phone was ringing, and by the time he did, it had already disconnected. I waited for a few seconds and then he called right back.

"Gideon," he called, and I smiled.

"It's been a while," I told him.

"What do you mean? Didn't we speak last week?"

"We're each other's family," I told him. "Shouldn't we make more of an effort to speak to each other more often?"

"Well, I don't have the time for that," he said. "And neither do you." He paused. "What's come over you today?"

I sighed. "Nothing," I replied. "I guess I've just been thinking about our family a lot more these days."

"Our family?" he asked.

"Yeah," I replied. "How's the restaurant doing?"

"Well. You're coming for the new branch opening at the end of the month, right?"

"Of course," I replied. "I'll be there."

"Alright," he said.

"Are you okay? How's your company?"

"Well."

"Still making millions?" he asked, and I smiled in response.

"I'm proud of you son," he said.

"Because I'm making millions?"

"Because you're stable. For a while there I was worried that you weren't going to be, especially with, you know... what happened with your mom."

"Yeah," I replied. "I took a lot of things quite hard then."

"Yes, you did," he said.

"I still feel the same now," I said. "About it,"

"Yeah, your mother told me. She said she keeps trying to reach out, but it's been impossible since she left. Are you going to ever change your mind? And let her in?"

"No," I said before he could go any further.

I heard my father sigh and was surprised at it.

"Would you?"

"We're friendly now, Gideon," he said. "And I wasn't

totally absent from blame. I was incredibly busy and neglected her in a lot of ways that I shouldn't have so I und-"

"Please stop," I told him. "I hate it when you defend her, and you always do this. Or rather she always talks you into this. She made you feel responsible, didn't she?"

"I am partly responsible."

"Stop giving her excuses," I gritted my teeth and he sighed.

"When you love someone," he said. "You need to be more lenient with them than anyone else."

I was taken aback by his words. "So... you love her?"

"No. But I did, truly, and it's not that easy to completely erase all those memories from someone's mind."

"Maybe this is the problem," I told him. "You're too lenient with her, you've always been."

I heard his sigh. "She caused a lot of damage to our family Gideon, and I can see its effect, especially on you. But time has passed and for my own peace of mind, I've decided to let go. She'll always be at arm's length, but I can take a call from her from time to time and truly, I wish her well."

I didn't speak, and my mind went to Pamela. "She's really missed you," he said to me. "It's been so long since you agreed to speak to her. Try? One of these days?"

I tried to process his words but just then there was a knock on the door.

"I have to get back to work," I told him, somewhat glad that the painful conversation had come to an end.

"Alright," he said.

"Speak soon. Hopefully not in another week," he said, and I could sense his smile.

"Later, Dad," I said and then the call came to an end.

I set the phone down and then picked up my office phone. "Oscar?" I called. "Did you just knock?"

"Yes sir," he replied. "There's someone here to see you."

"Who is it?" I asked, my nerves tensing. Surely it wasn't Pamela.

"Hannah Roule," he said, and I released a sigh of relief.

"Oh, send her in."

In no time, the door was pushed open, and I watched as the gorgeous woman walked into my office.

For a while I didn't know what to say as with a smile, she came over and then stood before my desk.

"Surprise," she held her arms out.

"Not really," I responded. "I think I already suspected it when you called earlier."

"That's impossible," she said as she pulled out a chair and took her seat.

"I only called to say a friendly hello."

"And when have you ever been friendly?"

At this she laughed, and as I heard the dulcet voice realized that I had somewhat missed her.

"You're applying for your old job here?" I asked. "Or just visiting?"

"Old job," she replied. "I called them, and they are willing to take me back."

"I wouldn't expect less," I told her. "You're brilliant."

She smiled. "Thank you but it's mostly thanks to Ferguson. He has the highest opinion of me though I didn't expect it to be so after I left so abruptly the last time, thanks to someone."

I smiled at the subtle accusation.

"I'm truly surprised that you're still here," she said. "I thought you'd have been tired of giving lectures by now."

"What's tiring about it?" I asked as I woke my desktop up. "I only do it a few times a week and it helps keep me sharp."

"You're ever so dedicated. I read about your company on Inc. congratulations are in order."

I smiled and gave a nod, "Thank you."

She studied me, and when I lifted my gaze to meet hers noticed for the first time that her hair was longer.

She noticed my gaze and held it in her hand, the long blonde strands sifting through her fingers.

"Yeah, most people cut their hair after they get dumped. I let mine grow even longer."

I sighed under my breath as I opened my emails. "You didn't get dumped," I said, and she smiled.

"I know, it was an 'amicable separation'. Still felt like getting dumped though."

I refused to respond, reaching my limit for emotional matters for the day and hoped that she would get up to leave.

"Oh," she later said. "Why are these on the floor?"

I looked and saw as she bent down to pick up a few papers and pencils. Then a key, and then she got up to bend even further so that she could reach underneath the desk.

"Yup... I thought I saw something shiny," she said and retrieved an award that I had gotten years prior. Then she looked around and noticed the slightly disarranged state of the desk. It was then that I remembered that I had pushed quite a lot of things off the desk in order to be with Pamela. When I had returned from the bathroom, I hadn't even realized that the place had been arranged and somewhat put back in place. It was obvious now that she had done it but missed some. My mind once again went to her.

"What happened?" she asked as she set the things back on the table and gave me a look. "A disgruntled student come in here and make a mess?"

"I made the mess," I told her. "I was searching for something."

"That doesn't sound like you," she said but I didn't know what to say in response "You're a stickler for putting things back exactly just like they were."

I smiled then and she cocked her head.

"You know I'm right."

"Okay," I said and thankfully she rose to her feet.

"I'll get out of your hair now. I know you don't like anyone staying too long."

Once again, my mind went to Pamela, and I couldn't imagine not wanting to be in her presence for as long as she wanted to be in mine. It had been that way in the past with us because I never felt her as a looming uncomfortable presence. She had just always been calming but interesting to have around.

Hannah started to walk away but then she stopped and turned around. "Would it be too early to invite you for a drink tonight?"

I considered it and my immediate response was a no. But then I thought of Pamela once again and the dilemma of our circumstances seemed solvable as an idea occurred to me.

"Sure," I said. "How about at Broke Birds."

She seemed surprised at this. "I was thinking of somewhere a bit fancier, in the city. That pub's mainly for the students."

"I know and I think I'd prefer that," I said, and she conceded.

"Alright. I'll pick you up at eight?"

This also made me smile.

"Meet me there at nine," I corrected, and with one last sly smile, she was on her way.

19

PAMELA

I was quite distraught as soon as I left the office.

I tried to collect my thoughts and emotions, but they seemed to be scattered all over the place.

I had just slept with Gideon again and I didn't know how to feel about it. I'd loved it... I'd loved it so much, and how connected I'd felt to him that it made me feel sad. I wished I could understand him and why he was so adamant that we not be together, and so when I returned home and despite how hard I tried I was unable to hold back my emotions. I went into my room, picked up my phone and did something that I hadn't done for quite a while. I called my mother and she answered.

"Hey," I said, and she replied in kind. "It's nice to hear from you. I sent you a message earlier in the week."

"I saw it," I replied.

"Okay," she said. "Everything alright?"

I tried my best once again to hold myself together, brushed my hair away from my shoulders and laid on my bed.

"I wanted to ask you a question," I said.

"Okay I'm listening."

"When dad just... left without any explanation, I know you felt horrible. But... was there really no way to change his mind, and to convince him to come back?"

She went silent, so I tried to say what I had in my heart for a long time but had never even bothered to voice. "I mean, I know at the time we were going through a lot as a family. Especially him with the business and how you two seemed to become distant overnight. Up till now, has he never told you that he regretted that?"

I heard her sigh. "It wasn't just because of the business that he left, Pamela," she said.

"You two were fighting a lot."

"Not really," I heard her smile. "We just stayed out of each other's way."

"And that's what I want to understand," I said. "It seemed to happen overnight, especially after that fire. What happened?"

I heard her sigh, and it was a long moment before she responded.

"Your father and I made the decision not to tell you this, but you're older now and I'm done playing martyr."

At her words, I immediately tensed up. "What do you mean?"

"Pamela, your dad cheated on me," she said, and my heart dropped.

"Wow," Meredith said as she lifted her glass of sangria to her lips.

"Yeah," I said as I munched on the bowl of almonds that had been delivered to us.

"That's a huge secret to keep from you for so long," she said and all I could do once again was nod.

"Yeah, she said she didn't want it to affect my perception of him."

"But you have a difficult relationship with your father. You both barely even talk. Keeping this from you didn't prevent that."

"No, but I guess either way he preferred to leave, as did my mother. But he didn't want me to see him in that light at such a young age. Now, I guess they can stomach it because I'm older."

"I guess so," she said, and I lifted my glass to my lips only to find it empty.

"I need another drink," I said and lifted my hand to the bartender.

"Um, sweetie, you've had three of those."

"Isn't that why we came here?" I asked

"We came here for a change of scenery and for you to be consoled responsibly. If you have any more, you're going to have the worst headache tomorrow and a bad day.

I didn't listen, so as the bartender came over, I ordered a refill of my cocktail.

I turned afterwards and could see Meredith staring wide eyed at a certain woman further down the counter from us.

"What's wrong? I asked and followed her line of vision. "Do you know her?"'

"She used to be our professor," she replied. "Last year."

"So, she's back?" I asked.

"Maybe," she replied. "I'll be glad to have her back because she was brilliant but..."

She turned to glance at me, and I saw the note of concern in her gaze.

"What is it?" I asked.

"She was Gideon's girlfriend."

Once again, my heart seemed to be slashed open for the hundredth time in the same day. Realizing how painful this felt, I lowered my gaze to retrieve my phone from my pocket and then began to scroll mindlessly through it. The last thing I wanted to hear about was him but I couldn't help but tell her. "I called my mom today because of him," I said with my gaze still on my screen. "I wanted to find out if there was ever any possibility that she could have gotten my father to stay and not leave... to work things out with her."

"What did she say?" Meredith asked.

"Well at the time I didn't realize that he had cheated. I had thought he'd been simply exhausted and frustrated and wanted a new start or something."

"Now I know that it wasn't as light as I imagined, their conflict I mean."

"And how does this relate to Gideon?" she asked.

"Well, he's been keeping his distance from me hasn't he, but... he seems unwilling to. As though deep inside he doesn't want to. But due to some circumstance that I have no clue about he has to. It just made me think of my mom and dad because there wasn't really a reason given when he left."

"But now that you've found out that there was?"

"Yeah," I replied. "I guess there's always a reason."

"Always," she replied.

We went silent for a while longer, but eventually I put my phone away and then looked up. I met Meredith watching me and was warmed by the concern in her eyes.

"Did your mom tell you? Who the woman was?"

"No," I replied. "And I don't want to know. I might just find her and murder her for breaking up my family."

She smiled and gave a nod, and then our gaze once again went around the bar.

And it was then that amidst the cluster of tables and chairs and in an incredibly small corner, was the current object of my frustration and obsession along with, as Meredith had earlier identified her, his previous girlfriend.

I couldn't breathe.

"That's his girlfriend, right?" I asked, knowing that Meredith had also spotted them.

"Yeah," she replied in a low voice. "Ex."

"Wow," I couldn't help but scoff. I stared at them while she turned to me. "Do you want to get out of here?"

It took me a while to respond.

"I guess I found the reason for his hesitation."

"Maybe not," she said, and I gave a bitter smile. I drained my drink then and got to my feet.

"I'm going over to say hi."

"No, you're not," she said and drained her drink. Then she rose to her feet, grabbed my purse, my arm and pulled me out with her from the bar.

That night, I couldn't sleep as I pondered about what the hell was truly going on, and the more I did the more hurt I felt.

I thought you were okay with him not being yours... I asked myself over and over again as I turned on my bed and shamefully drenched my pillow with tears.

Eventually, I couldn't bear to remain in the dark with my thoughts, so I got up and headed to the living room. I turned the television on, left the volume on mute so that it wouldn't disturb Meredith and then watched the colors and movements without it fully registering what was before me.

Eventually however I heard sounds and looked up just in time to see Meredith coming over with a blanket wrapped around her.

"Hey," she said, and I stopped to look at the giant mess that was her hair and her barely open eyes.

I reduced the screen's brightness. "I turned the volume down. Could you still hear it? Did I wake you?"

"It didn't," she said and then sat by my side. "You're not still thinking about them?" she asked, and I shook my head.

"You'd better not. They could have just been catching up. Exes do that all the time."

"I haven't caught up with James since we broke up."

"Well... I mean you guys... "

I turned as she struggled to groggily find an explanation. "We were the closest of friends. I even met you through him."

"Your breaking up with him was very painful."

"Exactly," I said. "Breakups should be so painful that exes never want to see each other again."

"She left," Meredith said to me.

"After they broke up, I presume. She's just now returning."

I shook my head and then she said. "Have you ever thought of getting back together with James? I mean, things weren't bad between you two, were they? You were just having a difficult time with your health and school and you both kind of drifted apart and 'took a break'."

"I don't know," I replied. "During such a hard time wasn't he the one I should have wanted to be with the most?"

"He tried his best to take care of you," she said, and I nodded. "I know. He was so considerate and helpful that it made me feel guilty."

"Why don't you try and give him a call?" she asked. "He

was quite the gem and I heard from the grapevine that he just got a new job at some engineering company so he's doing pretty well after graduating. You both might have some things to catch up about."

I thought of her suggestion and didn't know when I gave a nod.

20

GIDEON

I couldn't sleep.

Because there was something that I had seen in her eyes tonight that was haunting me.

But still, I didn't regret my decision to parade Hannah with me the way I had. I didn't have any intentions of getting back with her, but this was once again my last attempt to ensure that Pamela's and my paths never crossed again. She had seemed earlier on when she'd left my office to accept that nothing further would happen between us, but then I had been unable to push the worry out of my mind that this would not be the case. Funny enough I didn't think she would even be the one to once again initiate things. The person I suspected that was going to step out of line once again was myself. And so now as I thought things through, I realized that perhaps the whole show with taking Hannah to a bar that I was sure to spread the word around that we were back together, was more for my reminder to keep my distance than for Pamela's.

I truly had not expected that she would be there, and

once again as her forlorn eyes came to mind, I couldn't help but feel sad.

Perhaps I was taking things too far or perhaps I was even over assuming the depth of feelings she had for me. Maybe she didn't care at all and I told myself over and over again until I finally rose to my feet and headed to my study. My intention was to work. I focused on it for a few minutes until I realized what the work was about.

With her phone number in hand, I was able to send the link to her phone and expected that perhaps she would see it the following day. When the click notification came barely a few minutes later I wondered why she was still awake. I worked fast then and in no time was able to get the access that I needed. I felt bad about invading her messages, but I knew that I wouldn't rest until I was able to monitor her communications to be sure that she was alright. I found my way to her messages, but found nothing there, especially to her roommate Meredith. I stopped at the top two recent ones which also included one from her mom wishing her a goodnight.

Suddenly however, there was a new message, and I was able to access it.

It was to someone named James, and it was a simple hey.

I wondered who this was but just as I was about to do the insane thing and find out, I shut my desktop off, rose to my feet and returned to the kitchen for a glass of water.

I had stipulated a rule for myself a long time ago not to breach systems in this way, but then here I was reverting to my old habits.

At this point I really couldn't tell if she was bringing out the best of me or the worst. But what I could tell however and very clearly was that I was hard. And that I needed her in my arms for at least one more night. Maybe our first time and the second would never be enough to sate us. Maybe a whole night together where we could explore each other without any inhibitions and then be on our way would be best.

Her request to take me in her mouth came to mind and a low moan rumbled at the back of my throat.

It was something I was certain that I would have given anything in the current moment to have her do to me, however this was impossible.

I finished the drink, tossed the cup into the sink and was on my way to the bedroom. My body felt too overheated, and I knew that sleep would be impossible, so I instead headed straight to the shower. In there I did something that I couldn't remember the last time I had felt the urge to. I gripped my hardness and began to stroke as the heated stream coursed down on me. My pacing was slow but my grip was strong and not till I shut my eyes did I realize that I was picturing her warmth and scent all around me. I wished she was here with me, and at the frustrating thoughts, my pace increased. I felt a bit crazed but truly needed to be out of there and back to my sanity as quickly as possible.

I came with a strained groan, my entire body tingling at the effect but then afterwards and as I came back to earth, couldn't believe just how much the satisfaction felt short to even just merely kissing her.

It was just more than the release I had to accept. There was a fondness for her in the depths of my heart that I had hidden away a long time ago. But now, and somehow it was resurrected, and it was haunting me immensely.

I recalled her woes from the office earlier and wondered just how difficult a time she was having in trying to find the direction to go in a career after her graduation. No doubt this was a huge concern, and my only hope was that I wasn't adding to that stress. I wished that we could have dinner together and have a conversation about it, but I had so strained things between us that I wondered now if it would ever be easy for her to open up to me.

After the shower I went straight to bed, unwilling to dally any longer as it dawned on me that I could truly think about her all night and the time would fly past without me even realizing it.

I laid flat on my back, naked but with the covers over my midriff. My gaze was on the ceiling as I listened to the beating of my heart.

I then turned to my side and shut my eyes however it wasn't long before they came open once again. With a sigh, and a deep groan I reached for my phone and switched off my reasoning. Once again, I hacked my way into her cell phone.

It's only for a few seconds, I told myself. *This is just to ensure that she's alright.*

None of this made any sense to me but neither did her texting a man named James after midnight.

I had a dark suspicion in my mind about what this could be about, and if it was confirmed then it would be more than enough reason for my interest in her to completely fizzle out.

It was a little harder with my cell phone, but to return to my desk and desktop felt like the conscious effort would weigh too much on my conscience so I remained struggling with installations until once again I found my way in.

I looked and found that there were no further exchanges.

Instantly I felt stupid and somewhat deranged. I was about to throw the phone aside however when there was a response.

"Hey stranger," came the reply and I couldn't help my frown.

Her response was quite quick.

"Wow, I didn't think you'd reply. It's so late."

"Well, that shouldn't be the only reason you'd be worried that I wouldn't respond," he wrote back, and my understanding lessened.

"You're right," she wrote. "Ha-ha."

I could almost hear the awkward tone of her voice and couldn't have stopped myself from reading on if I had been paid.

"Is this your return from our break?" his question came. It took her more than a minute afterwards to respond.

"You never returned either."

"You called the break. You had to be the one to call it off."

"Sighs," she wrote. "I guess I'm looking for a way to loosen my conscience haunting me," she wrote, and I wondered what she meant. I could by this point put two and two together, but still, I didn't want to jump to any definitive conclusions.

"I'm just playing with you," he said. "I should have called and checked in. I knew you were having a difficult time then, I guess I just felt kind of hurt because it seemed that you couldn't lean on me."

She didn't respond after this.

I set the phone down, sighed and stared out the window. There was a slightly cool breeze coming into the room, but I could feel my body heating up once again. I was uncomfortable, immensely so, and only after a long while did I finally admit to myself that it was because I wanted to be someone that she could lean on. I wondered if she would trust me in that way… the way she obviously couldn't with whoever this dude was and probably everyone else.

Except Meredith, I considered. She seemed pretty close with her, and it made me wonder just how they had met. Perhaps as roommates? I sighed again, realizing just how curious I was about her, but I couldn't help but admit that I wanted to know everything about her but at the same time I wanted to keep her at a distance.

With one last sigh I picked up the phone once again and found updates to the message.

"I once had a close friend when I was younger that I could sort of speak freely with. And share everything with. But then one day he suddenly turned cold and shut me out. I guess this is the reason why I've found it hard to share my troubles easily with anyone. I prefer to just lean upon myself and fix things."

"Is that why you're texting me once again?" he asked. "You've fixed things?"

"Not really," she wrote, "but… I've missed you. It's been a while. We used to be incredibly close friends before we ever started dating and I truly miss that."

He didn't respond for a while longer and so she sent another message.

"I found one area in which you are at least at fault," she sent.

He replied. "And where is that?"

"I told you that dating would ruin our friendship and yet you insisted on it. I told you that I didn't think I was ready back then and needed to clarify a few things about myself and what I wanted to do in the future."

"Well, I thought we could do it together," he wrote. "I hoped we would do it together."

There was another long pause and then her message came.

"I'm sorry," she sent. "I'm out of excuses. I don't think it's possible for us to date anymore but I'd like to be friends with you again. We used to have the most fun together. You're busy now since you're not here anymore but we're still in the same city so whenever you have a free hour or so, please hit me up. We can have lunch. I'll even have sushi... for you."

At this his laughing emojis came.

"You hate sushi."

"Exactly," she said, and he sent laughing emojis once again. I was disgusted by him.

"How about tomorrow," he asked. "It's Friday night and I just happen to be going to the best sushi restaurant in town for dinner. Care to accompany me?"

"Oh wow," she wrote. "You were just casually going to eat sushi for dinner?"

"Maybe," he teased and something vile and bitter burned in the pit of my stomach.

"They must pay you in gold over at your new job?"

"That cannot be farther from the truth," he replied. "The cushy part I mean... the pay is alright. I can afford sushi on a Friday night once in a while."

"Can it afford sushi for two?" she asked, and I couldn't stand it anymore, so I threw the phone aside. Then I turned away to shut my eyes and tried to catch some sleep.

21

PAMELA

"I can't believe you're going on a date," Meredith said as she watched me check my outfit. I looked at her through the mirror, leaning against the door frame.

"Isn't it a good thing?" I asked as I straightened the creases in the pink dress.

"That dress is amazing," she said, and I couldn't help but smile.

"It's like Carrie's," I mentioned. "The only thing that's missing is the curly hair. I looked up and once again checked my slicked back hair in the mirror.

"Whose Carrie?" she asked, and I rolled my eyes. It took her a few seconds to get it while I searched for my perfume.

"Ah, Sex and the city. Right?"

I smiled as I sprayed, and she shook her head. Then she continued looking at me however the look in her eyes I could tell was somewhat worried.

"What is it?" I asked.

She started to speak but then hesitated.

"Nothing," she smiled.

"Don't do that," I said, and she sighed.

"I'm all for you getting your mind off Professor Bach, but I'm not exactly comfortable that you're using James to do it."

"You were the one that suggested getting in contact with him," I reminded her.

"Well, I thought it'd be a friendly chat," she said.

"Don't worry," I said as I cocked the bottle. "That's solely what it will be. Just a night out... with someone I won't talk to Gideon about."

As the words left my mouth, I recalled the previous night.

I had indeed mentioned him, however of course this wouldn't mean anything to James. I sighed and chose to keep this little bit of information to myself.

"Anyway, I hope you have fun, and be safe. If you get drunk, take an Uber or call me to come to pick you up."

"Don't worry, he'll ensure I get home safe," I said, and grabbed my purse. Afterwards I headed to the door, and she plopped herself down on the couch.

"No date with Darryl tonight?" I asked as I slipped into my white heeled sandals.

"No," she groaned. "He's busy with his thesis. He'll just ignore me if I go over there."

At this I smiled and was soon ready.

"Later," I called out, and heard her response just as the door shut behind me.

As I headed down the hallway and down the stairs. I couldn't help but note just how reluctant every fiber of my being was at this. Going out was the last thing I currently wanted to do, much less talk with James but I just wanted to break out of the rut I'd gotten myself into and it was truly too much trouble to do this with a stranger.

James is a safe choice, I told myself. A casual conversation with an ex should do me some good, just as Gideon was doing with his own ex. *Perhaps there was something magical about it that I had no clue of and would discover tonight.*

I got into my car and was well aware of how sarcastic and sullen my demeanor was, but I wasn't ready or willing to analyze it, so I just let it go and drove out of the complex.

James looked much better than I had expected, and for the first few minutes after our embrace, I couldn't help but find his slight nervousness in the way he couldn't quite meet my eyes endearing. He was dressed nicely and looked quite put together with a suit on, the tie slightly loosened at the collar and his hair pushed sleekly away from his face. He also had grown a very flattering layer of facial hair across his jaw, and I couldn't help but compliment him on how appealing and attractive it made him.

He seemed pleased by my flattery and the initial awkwardness between us began to dissipate. The conversation was easy, free, and fond. And mid-way through it I could feel myself become just a little bit more lighthearted.

However, one thing I noticed beyond the fact that I enjoyed his presence, was the fact that I didn't truly want to be in it for much longer. I think half an hour was the threshold for me and since I was noticing this now, it made me realize that we had drifted apart.

We had never really spent as much time together at a stretch when we were mere friends, so it began to dawn on me now as to why I became unwilling to remain in a relationship with him.

He was great, considerate, really organized... however, as I watched him talk about his job and coworkers, a particular ghost haunting my mind and thoughts that I had been able to keep at bay thus far seemed to be returning.

There was just no spark, I concluded and perhaps that was why I had been able to let him go. At the time I had felt guilty about it, but I just couldn't get my mind to disagree that he was better off as a friend to me than as a boyfriend.

Since I had called for this anyhow, I allowed him to take the lead for the rest of the evening and only when he wanted to leave did I nod and agree.

"This was great," he said, his eyes sparkling. "I'm so glad we could catch up."

"Me too," I told him now, feeling quite heavy all over again. Thankfully we soon rose to our feet and then we were outside waiting for our cars.

He turned to me, and I tensed up, hoping that he wouldn't be expecting more.

I sent him a smile and then looked away. Soon my car arrived, and he escorted me to my door till I was safely tucked in. "You okay to drive?" he asked, and I nodded.

"I only had a glass, I'm fine," I said, and he smiled.

"A glass of wine is usually quite enough to take you out."

"I guess," I said. "But that was back then. I'm stronger now."

"And more beautiful now," he said.

He leaned forward then, and my face turned to the side. I had tried my best not to, and to accept it but everything inside of me rioted. The kiss landed softly on my cheek, and I felt even worse. Once we pulled away, I almost couldn't meet his gaze.

"Tonight was great," he said, and I finally found the courage to look at him. "Let's take things slow... this time around," he said.

I smiled then and nodded. "It was great to see you again. Keep in touch."

"I most definitely will," he said and straightened.

With a tap on the roof of my car, I was cleared to drive away, and I did.

I turned on the radio, but eventually I couldn't deal with the noise from unfamiliar songs and suddenly couldn't stand to listen to the familiar ones, so I shut it off, rolled down the windows and reveled in the cool light breeze as it blew into my face. The moment I got to a stop light, I pulled my hair scrunchie away, releasing my bun and when I resumed driving, the wind blew right through my hair.

I sighed and hoped that it would clear my mind and heart, but it didn't seem to be the case at all.

Eventually my mind went to him.

Despite the slight chill, the moment my thoughts went to how it felt to be in his arms, my body began to heat up. I was hooked then and couldn't be pulled back to reason and it continued that way till somehow, I found myself parked by an intersection to his apartment complex.

Mine was in the opposite direction but I found myself unwilling to go towards it.

He wanted me, this much I was sure of so what could be the harm in going over there and demanding his touch and attention beyond the bruise to my pride and ego especially after the nonchalant way I had acted in his office earlier. But then what I truly wanted in this moment was to be consoled, and the thought of seeing his face and receiving this registered as the most important thing in my head. But I knew it was the wrong way to go so I quickly texted my voice of reason.

My hope was that she would reply immediately but when three whole minutes passed, and she hadn't picked up the phone I called her.

Just then however, her message came, and I ended the call.

"Was in the shower," she wrote. "And *what*?"

"Would it be that terrible an idea?"

"To stop at his apartment at this time of night? It's almost midnight Pam."

"So?' I asked and could almost hear her sigh, or perhaps it was me.

"I'm not in support," she replied. "Plus, do you think that your obsession with him might be due to the fact that you're kind of drifting recently concerning your career. Maybe this is a distraction?"

At this I smiled. "It would be nice if it was," I wrote. "I truly don't want to think that all of this is a result of my immense attraction to him. Can't I just take this as having fun?"

"Are you?" she asked. "Having fun, I mean."

"I could..." I responded. "If I went over there right now."

"Then go," she said. "I know more than anyone just how quickly things change so perhaps these moments are ones you might regret not seizing later. Plus, if you get there and he doesn't let you in like I assume, then come straight home."

"You're unkind," I typed back and her response soon came.

"I strongly disagree," was her quick reply.

I put the phone away, considered just returning home once again but at the immense resistance that seemed to grip me like a vice, I restarted my car and drove towards the opposite direction of home.

22

GIDEON

My obscene habit of peeping at her messages had ended the previous night.

Truly, I had woken the following morning with it already at the back of my mind, but then the evening came, and I couldn't help myself.

Most important of all was my crippling desire to see what she had worn for her date or perhaps was it a simple meetup? I had also seen the restaurant that he had picked for her, and it was quite mediocre. I wanted to take her and fly out to New York to Takeda's, where she would be able to taste the most authentic sushi that existed in the country. Or perhaps I could fly her to Japan myself. It wouldn't take much. A quick hire of a jet and we would be on our way,

However, since I had so blatantly rejected her, I could do none of these things.

Thus, I was forced to lose myself in studying the week's report from the company but all of that was until the next set of messages began to arrive. At first, I was able to ignore them but the moment it occurred to me that the date would have come to an end, and perhaps had gone well, I'd been nearly driven mad with the need to check if she went home with him.

Then I saw instead all that she was saying to Meredith and afterwards didn't know what to think.

Once again, my excitement returned but then along with it was immense worry. Pamela wasn't a woman that I could play carelessly with and her coming over here… there was no way in hell that I would be able to reject her or keep myself away from her.

I got up from my desk absentmindedly, and it was only when I found myself leaning against the kitchen counter and staring at the front door that I even realized where I was.

She would be here soon, judging by the message, and I had no idea what to do.

Just then my phone began to ring from the study, and I frowned, unwilling to return the call. When it occurred to me that Pamela was probably the one calling, I immediately moved.

I hurried over to retrieve it with my heart in my throat. Hastily and before it could disconnect, I picked up the phone and it almost slipped away from my hand.

"Hello," I said and for the first few seconds the line was quiet.

"Gideon," the soft voice came, and the first thing I felt was immense relief. Then I felt equally immense disappointment and truly couldn't figure out my emotions, so I took a seat and sighed.

"Are you alright?" Hannah asked. "Did you go running?"

I could indeed feel my heart racing and it was disturbing to say the least.

"No," I replied.

"Oh," she said. "I've started running by the way. Finally

got into the habit. Well, I kind of had to after putting on weight when my last relationship ended. I drowned myself in tubs of delicious ice cream. I only regret it a little."

I could barely process what she was saying so all I simply said was "Yeah."

"Yeah?" she repeated, and I was forced to pay attention.

"What?" I asked.

"You're not paying attention Gideon," she growled slightly. "Were you working?"

I was thinking then of how to respond and put an end to the call when my doorbell rang.

My heart caught in my throat.

I listened hard, sure that I had misheard however all I heard was Hannah speaking.

I couldn't make out her words. I waited and a few seconds later the doorbell rang again. I immediately rose to my feet.

Hannah's voice registered to me then.

"Goodnight Gideon," she said grudgingly, however the words came out of my mouth before I could stop them.

"Do you want to come over?" I asked and could hear her go quiet.

"Um..." she began a few seconds later, but then I was already heading out of the room as quietly as I could. I went over to the door, unhappy that the lights were on. She would no doubt know that I was home but ignoring her. But first I wanted to confirm that she was indeed the one at the door before inviting Hannah over.

I walked slowly as I listened to Hannah, and only when I arrived at the door, did I realize that she hadn't yet spoken. I looked through the peephole and it was then that she did.

"It's close to midnight," Hannah pointed out, and at first, I didn't understand why she was pointing this out but then as I looked at the lowered head of the woman before me, and how she kept looking to her left and right, I understood what Hannah was insinuating. I moved away from the door then just as the bell rang again, the sound piercing through me.

"Not for that," I told her. "I missed dinner. We could order something in?"

"You missed dinner," she laughed, and I wondered what was amusing about that. "Why invite me over when you could just have the midnight snack you're craving on your own?" At this I sighed and pulled the phone away from my ear to gaze at it.

I decided then to just face the woman at the door rather than to deal with the interrogation from this one.

"You know what, forget it," I said. "I'll talk to you later."

Before I could end the call, she stopped me. "I'll be right there," she said and ended it before I could refuse. I looked at the phone as a knock then sounded on the door. I looked at it and quickly sent a message to Hannah. "I'll order in so no need to stop on the way. It's too late."

"Alright," she texted back. "I'll be there in a few minutes." I put the phone away and with my heart in my throat headed over to the door.

23

PAMELA

I was going to turn around and leave. I gave myself the leeway to knock just one more time. It was obvious he was ignoring me because I could see the light on in his apartment. Or perhaps he had gone to bed and forgotten to turn it off. I didn't know what to think, but I did know how I felt, and it was sour, at the depths I was sinking due to my desire for him.

Gravely annoyed, I gave his door one last furious knock and of course there was no response, so I turned around then and started to storm away.

I had only gone a few steps however when I heard the door open. At first, I was certain that it was from some other apartment, but then I heard his voice, and my soul nearly left my body.

"You're leaving?" he said, and I couldn't believe he had responded. I stopped in my tracks and took a few seconds to wipe every emotion off of my face. Then I worked up what I hoped to pass for a bored look, when I turned around to face him.

He took my breath away, literally, and for the first few seconds all I could do was stare.

He was dressed simply… in what seemed to be dark joggers and a black t-shirt. These were casual home wear, but it seemed as though he was some cutout from a magazine. His hair was all over the place as though he had run his hand through it multiple times and I wanted more than anything else to smooth it with my hands.

He looked so relaxed and beautiful, that I felt my throat close up with emotion. It hadn't been the same way earlier on when I had met with James. With Gideon however, it felt like this moment was sacred.

"You answered," I managed to say but then my voice came out barely audible and somewhat cracked. Embarrassed, I cleared it and tried again.

"You responded," I said. "Surprising."

With a hard look at me, he turned around to head into the apartment and it took everything inside of me not to hurry along after him. I instead kept to a leisurely pace until I arrived at the open door to the gorgeous apartment. The first thing I took in was the north wall and its gorgeous downtown skyline. It was striking, better than a picture and for a few seconds I got lost in it.

"Lock the door, will you?" I heard his voice and turned to see him in the kitchen.

He jerked the refrigerator door open and pulled out a bottle of water.

And then he came over to me. I headed in, shutting the door behind me and looked down at the water he offered. I wondered why he thought that I needed it.

"You seem dehydrated," he said, and I accepted it. I opened it up and watched as he turned around once again, but this time he headed down the hallway. I watched him go and couldn't help but feel pleased that he wasn't acting all stiff and stuck-up in my presence. He actually seemed quite chill, as though he had been expecting me which I hadn't expected in the least.

It seemed suspicious, like the calm before the storm, so I couldn't exactly let my guard down.

At being left alone in the hallway I was forced to head down to the door he had disappeared into. He hadn't shut it so it seemed as though I was invited but he hadn't exactly extended an invitation so all I could do was stand by the door, trying my best not to look lost.

A simple peep in and I could see that it was a magnificent office with the most gorgeous woven rug I had ever seen in the middle. He was behind his desk with a desktop before him, his attention focused on it and for a moment I wanted to take a picture of him.

Perhaps this was why he wasn't particularly paying any attention to me. I had probably interrupted him in the middle of working and given his reputation, I didn't think that was a light matter at all.

I was more overjoyed than I could put into words at the fact that he wasn't out on some romantic date on a Friday night but was instead at home. Unlike me.

"Am I intruding?" I eventually had to ask when I became certain that he was capable of actually forgetting that I was even standing there. He didn't even bother to look up to respond.

"What do you think?" he said. "What are you doing here so late?"

Something seemed to occur to him then, so he looked up, his gaze was on me. He barely met my eyes but instead he seemed to take in my outfit all the way down to my toes.

I realized then how I was dressed, and it was clear what

it insinuated. It was either he concluded that I was just coming from a date or that I was dressed up because I was coming to see him and truly, I didn't particularly fancy any of those conclusions.

My lips parted then to explain but I didn't exactly know what to say in my defense, or if I was even supposed to have one.

He looked at me... a brief glance and then he returned his attention back to his computer.

What a bummer, I sighed, but I couldn't help but notice how excited I felt to just be here, in comparison to the last few hours of my evening. I sighed then and headed over to the bookshelf he had by the side. It was simple, filled with a few books and other items. There was a vintage airplane, and surprisingly a pair of handcuffs in a small glass showcase. My eyes widened at it.

I turned and met him still working but couldn't stop myself from calling his attention to it.

"What are these?"

He lifted his gaze albeit reluctantly and then it followed my pointed finger.

"Handcuffs," he replied as though he was slightly confused as to why I would be asking such a question.

"I mean, why do you have them here? And in a showcase for that matter."

His gaze lowered then and it was clear that he was not going to respond. I was offended but tried not to take it to heart. I however didn't mind offending him, so I lifted my phone and took a picture of it. Then I sent it over to Meredith.

"Have any idea what this could be?' I asked and lowered my hand. I couldn't help sneaking a glance at him to see if he had caught me in the act. It didn't seem that he had or if he had, he didn't seem to care. He must be really busy. I had to conclude and truly began to feel bored.

Perhaps causing some sort of ruckus would get his attention? I thought. Or perhaps it would only get me thrown out.

Meredith's message came in then.

"Oh my God! He's into BDSM?" she wrote, and my heart froze.

I read the message over and over again, and then was slightly startled because I heard him cough. The phone slipped from my hands because it seemed as though he had seen the message. I quickly picked it up and then like an idiot, found myself brushing the screen. Eventually I was able to collect my senses, so I stopped and quickly sent a response back to Meredith.

"You think so?"

"I wouldn't put it past him," she said.

I snuck another glance at him. "He doesn't look like the kind."

"How?" she asked dryly. "He's filthy rich, sinfully handsome and a genius that appears to be solely obsessed with his work. Honey, no one is that in love with their job. He's getting his excitement somewhere else, and I wouldn't put it past him to have it be as kinky and obscene as possible."

My eyes widened as I gazed at her message. I had to shut my mouth before he saw it hanging open.

"Jeesh, I'm turned on," she wrote. "Maybe I should be pursuing him along with you. Suddenly I'm seeing him in a better light."

I couldn't help my amusement. "Back off," I said and snuck another look at him. This time around I met his gaze head on.

I immediately looked away, clearing my throat, and to

my surprise he rose to his feet. I immediately began to back away without even realizing what I was doing.

I eventually stopped and although he too halted a healthy distance away, it felt as though he was right before me.

"When are you leaving?" he asked, and I didn't know what to say to that.

I cleared my throat then and looked away so that I could get my thoughts together.

"You haven't even asked me why I came over?"'

His arms folded across his chest. I tried my best to look away and not to notice just how broad his shoulders were.

"Hmm," I said. "I uh... I came to discuss what you mentioned the other day in your office.

His look on me darkened. "I thought our conclusion that day was that you had no interest."

I swore at him in my head. "Well, I thought further on it and I have some thoughts... and questions. "

"Let's hear it," he said, and I just stared outrightly at him.

24

GIDEON

I still couldn't believe how this night was going, but as I stared at her trying to come up with a reasonable sounding excuse for why she had barged into my home at midnight, I didn't think there was another thing I could have possibly enjoyed more. She looked gorgeous... and all over again I felt anger that she had dressed in this way for someone else. But then I considered the fact that at the end of it all she had sought me out and not gone home with him.

Now, I couldn't help but feel guilty at the invitation I had extended to Hannah to come over, however I couldn't regret it because given how we were right now, I imagined I was just a few seconds away from grabbing her and taking her right here against the shelf.

My gaze went to the handcuffs and what her friend had said concerning it, and I truly wanted to respond. But then that would be engaging and encouraging her, and it was the last thing I wanted to do. So, I kept my mouth shut and just watched her fumble.

"Umm, if I was to retake the test-" her hand ran through her hair.

God, I wanted to kiss her so badly I could feel my heart rate pick up, alerting me that I was mere minutes away from losing my mind. I stepped back, however, I wondered how that would help. I decided to just head into the kitchen and to stay as far away as possible from her. I wondered how I could get her to sleep and once again considered giving her milk. It hadn't seemed to work the last time which made me realize the mention of it would be prime conversation between us.

"Does milk still make you feel sleepy?" I asked assuming that she was behind me as I headed over to the fridge. At her silence I pulled the door open and retrieved a can of beer. I turned around then and turned to see her looking at me, somewhat dazed. It was then that I noticed that her bag was still hung across her shoulder. I hadn't even tried to make her feel at home, however it felt to me as though she felt quite comfortable at simply being in my presence.

"Umm, that's a weird question," she smiled. "And a quite sudden one too."

I felt my pulse go out of control in reaction to her smile and could do nothing but sigh and shake my head at how hopeless I was becoming.

"Why are you shaking your head?" she asked, and I could tell that she had interpreted it in a negative manner, because it had made her feel sullen. I however had no plans to correct it so I simply stared at her as I drank my beer.

"You're not going to offer me anything?" she asked.

"I didn't invite you over," I said to her, and she stared hard and directly at me. I felt sad. I truly didn't want to treat her this way and so I turned around and reached into the fridge to search for something that I could offer to her.

Suddenly, all the hair on my body seemed to stand upright and I was aware that she had rounded the counter and was now beside me.

I turned, startled and saw her hand close around the can that I had just set down. She lifted it, her gaze on mine and then it met her lips.

I didn't know what to say or do. Or how to react, so I remained in the spot and watched as she took a long drink from the can and then set it down.

"You don't mind if I drain this, do you?" she asked, and I scowled at her. I turned to continue my rummage through the fridge and settled on a bottle of water. I was certain she needed it after the night she had so far, and the alcohol I was certain was in her system. I set it before her as our gazes locked, and then I lifted the can back up to my lips.

I didn't miss the slight widening of her eyes at this, but before either of us could say anything further, there was a knock at the door.

My heart jumped, and as I watched her gaze turn to it, I began to wonder if it would be too late to call this off. She looked so soft and innocent as I watched her and truly the last thing I wanted was to hurt her any further.

"You should leave," I said after draining the can. I crushed it and then tossed it into the nearby trash can.

"You have a guest this late?" she asked, and I turned to see that she still hadn't moved from the spot.

"You're here late," I pointed out. "And I didn't invite you."

"But you invited this person? Whoever they are?" she had a smile playing at the corners of her lips, but I knew that it was far from genuine, or heartfelt.

With a sigh, I headed over to the door and when I looked through the peephole seeing that truly it was Hannah.

I pulled the door open and met her smile.

Her grin was wide as she lifted the pizza box in one hand and the wine box in the other.

"I came bearing gifts," she said, and I gave a nod.

I then stepped out of the way, and she came in

She however stopped in her tracks when she finally noticed the woman standing across the room and looking frozen.

I lowered my gaze then, feeling more remorse than I could have ever expected.

"Umm..." Hannah tried to pull off a smile.

"You have another guest?"

"She's leaving," I said and took the boxes from her. I headed over to the kitchen and kept my gaze on Pam. Her expression had turned bland, devoid of emotion, but I could see the clear hurt in her eyes.

I was compelled to add. "Why don't you come by the office on Monday so that we can continue our conversation?" I asked, and she continued to stare hard at me. And then she angled her head, a smile on her face.

"Sure," she said and then looked at the woman who had arrived by my side.

"It's too bad the food is only just getting here as I'm about to leave."

Hannah replied. "I can see you still have your purse on your shoulder. How long have you been here?"

"A few minutes," Pamela responded. "But then he never asked me to even sit. Terribly rude of him, isn't it?"

Hannah glanced at me, a weird frown coming across her features which sent the message that she was more confused by the scenario she was meeting than anything else and would like an explanation. I ignored her and went to retrieve plates for the pizza.

"Gideon isn't very... hospitable," Hannah said. "I apologize on his behalf."

"I know," Pam said. "He's been like that since I've known him. About fifteen years and counting."

I couldn't help but to stop and sigh, especially at the quiet that spread in the room.

I pressed the start button on the microwave, and it started to run.

"You've known him for fifteen years?"

"Yes," Pamela answered. "We used to be neighbors. He's practically the reason why I was able to graduate high school. Private tutoring lessons at his kitchen table."

"Oh," Hannah said, and I turned to look at Pamela.

She met my gaze head on.

"I'm... quite surprised by this. I don't think I've ever met someone from Gideon's past. Or even heard him talk about it at all."

"That's a bummer," was Pam's dry response.

"Anyway, goodnight, I guess," she said, and I was finally able to take an easy breath.

"Don't forget your pizza in the microwave Gideon," she said, and this caught my attention. I headed over to it and was sort of glad that it meant I wouldn't watch her leave.

Suddenly, Hannah spoke up once again. "Would you... like to stay? And perhaps have a slice or two with us?" I stopped in the process of retrieving plates. They both turned to me, and I couldn't help my scowl.

"It's just for a short while," Hannah softened her tone. "You don't share these things very often with me, so I'd love to hear them from someone else."

I started to reject the idea but then Pamela spoke, and hers surprised me even more.

"I'd love to," she said. "I am starved, and Gideon is the worst host."

With this she finally pushed the straps off her shoulder and pulled out one of the island bar stools.

She settled on it while Hannah came over to my side to ask for wine glasses.

She gave me a sheepish smile and then leaned in to whisper. "I know you're upset about this, but I'll find a way to make it up to you."

I wanted to retaliate and voice the reminder that she didn't have the right to invite someone to my home in such a casual manner, but then I reminded myself of the main purpose of the night and chose instead to focus on that.

Soon we were all seated at the island, ready to eat and I could have as well not existed.

"So... you're a student I suppose?" she asked.

"I am," I could hear Pamela's response.

"Must be nice," Hannah said. "To have someone in the faculty looking out for you."

"Who?" she asked and picked up another slice.

"Well, Gideon of course, since you're both on campus together."

At this Pamela laughed and I had to look at her. "This is the first time you're hearing of me, isn't it?" she asked. "But yet I've been here for three years. Doesn't that tell you that he is far from caring? Truly I would have graduated without him ever approaching me despite our history."

"Wow," Hannah said, giving me a peculiar look. "That's really... I don't even know what to say."

I did. "If you both keep talking about me like I'm not here, I'll ask you both to leave."

At this Pamela gasped. "Wow. See what I mean?"

Hannah laughed but I could sense the slight tension that

was now in her voice. "Alright, we'll stop," she said and then got up to retrieve the wine opener.

"I have red wine," she told Pamela. "However, it's dry. Gideon usually likes these kinds. What about you?"

"Anything's fine," Pamela responded.

"What about driving?" Hannah asked as she brought the bottle and glasses to set before us. "Will you call an Uber to take you home?"

"Umm," she began and at this, I lifted my gaze to look at her.

"I drove here. I think I'll be fine driving back. It's just this one glass. Hopefully."

She lifted it to her lips, and I couldn't help but frown. My lips moved to speak to reminder that this wasn't her first glass of the night, however I caught myself in time. There was no need to expose ourselves because there was absolutely no way that she would be leaving my house and driving home intoxicated.

"So," she said after she set the glass down, a loud clink as it made contact with the countertop resounding across the apartment.

"Are you two together?"

At this question and against my desire, I tensed, wondering what Hannah's response to this would be.

On one hand, I definitely didn't want her to claim that we were because it wasn't true, but then, on the other hand I also didn't want it to seem as though I was completely available to Pamela, otherwise inviting Hannah over here would be completely fruitless.

I could feel Hannah's gaze on me then, so I turned to face her head on, keeping my face expressionless. Perhaps it was the cold look in my eyes but thankfully she didn't claim that we were.

"That's a bit private," she said, and I returned my attention to my almost finished slice.

At this Pamela smiled. "I understand. It is private. I was just curious."

"It's alright," Hannah said, and the most awkward silence ensued.

Afterwards, we all ate our pizza slices quietly until eventually Pamela was done and to my surprise and disappointment she rose to her feet.

"I'll leave you both to it," she said and without waiting for any acknowledgment whatsoever from us, began to head towards the door.

I finished my slice, grabbed a wet towel to wipe my hands with and was on my way.

"You can't leave," I called after her just as she arrived at the foyer. "You had alcohol."

"Just a glass," she said.

"Still, you can't leave. Spend the night, I have a spare room."

"No," she replied. "I'd rather go home."

At this I briefly went quiet, wondering if I could really stand letting her go the way she wanted to.

I soon found out that I couldn't, so I tried again.

"I'll get you a cab and your car will be delivered to your apartment tomorrow."

She met my gaze then and smiled, dryly.

"No thank you," and then she pulled the door open and was on her way.

I had a choice to either go after her and prolong our connection to each other, or to let her leave as she wanted to and trust that she would be able to take care of herself like she had been able to thus far without my input.

A few seconds later, I made my decision and turned around to head back into the house.

Hannah was waiting for me at the counter, a glass to her lips.

"Interesting girl," she said but I was ready to call it a night.

"Yeah," I replied.

"You've really known her for so long?" she asked but I was no longer in the mood to speak. However, I didn't want to be rude to Hannah either so I tried to sit with her as we resumed eating, but then eventually couldn't take the prickling of my conscience any longer. I might not have invited her over, but I needed to make sure that she arrived home safely without any issues, so I immediately rose to my feet.

"I'm stepping out for a while," I told her. "You can make yourself at home or leave if you want to."

Without waiting for a response from her, I hurriedly grabbed my keys and was out the door.

I felt anxious, worried that perhaps too much time had passed, and I wouldn't be able to reach her. I headed straight in the direction of her apartment, keeping my eyes peeled open as much as I could so I wouldn't miss her. There was no sign of her so eventually I had no choice but to contact her friend Meredith.

She was incredibly surprised to hear from me, and for the first few moments seemed to be in disbelief that I was speaking to her.

"Can you help confirm her location for me Meredith?" I asked and at her agreement, I felt relief. The call came to an end, and soon enough I neared her apartment.

Meredith's call came just as I arrived, and I couldn't help but hold my breath as I responded.

"She just got home," she said, and I let out a heavy sigh in relief.

I continued to drive however until I arrived at her apartment complex and not till I saw her car parked before it did I completely feel assured enough to leave. I looked up at the windows, the apartment within it and then and for the last time, I contacted Meredith.

I sent her a message and it simply read. "I'd appreciate it if she wasn't aware that I came looking for her," I wrote.

I considered giving her yet another call to earnestly speak to her about this but decided against it. She and Pamela were quite close so there was nothing I could do to stop her if she wanted to relay that I had asked after her. So, I pulled out of the parking lot, and went on my way.

25

PAMELA

"I think I'm going to get another job."

At this point, I couldn't even remember what we had come to the mall for, yet here we were strolling through the endless parade of people and with no particular direction in mind.

Meredith stopped and looked up from her perusal of phone cases. "Um, you don't have time for that."

"Time or not I need one. Since I'm not sure about what I'm going to do after graduation, I need to have a healthy amount saved up. Imagine if I ever have to go to my mom to ask."

"Would that be too bad?"

"Yes," I said as the possibility formed in my head. "Absolutely."

"The cases are overpriced," she said as she finally moved away from the kiosk.

"Get it online," I said. "Why are we here again?"

"It's on the way home and we wanted to peruse some new lotions at Lush."

"Again, overpriced," I pointed out.

"Well, I might be having a very well-paid internship soon so I think I can afford it. I'll get you some bath bombs."

At the thought of where in particular would be awarding her this internship, I couldn't help but feel sullen all over again.

"Any updates about your professor and his gorgeous girlfriend?" I asked.

"No," Meredith responded. "And are you sure they're dating? After that night I've never seen them together."

I paid attention.

"So… there's a possibility that they might not be dating?"

"Who knows?" she said. "They're very low key. Or at least he is. The only reason we even found out the last time was because she was always showing up in places with him but now not so much. I don't think it's that easy for exes to get back together especially when the reason why they separated in the first place still persists."

"Do you know why they broke up?" I asked.

"Nope," she said.

I looked away then at the gorgeous gold shimmery dress on a display mannequin as we passed by a store, aware that her gaze was on me.

"It's been two weeks," she said. "How are you faring?"

"I'm fine," I groaned.

For a few moments she went silent, but then she eventually spoke. "I saw you this morning you know… when you were eating cereal. I think a tear dropped from your eye into the bowl. I would have called you out, but I was in a rush."

I ignored her.

"Dare to deny it?"

I slipped my hands into my pockets and looked away.

"You find yourself in tears from time to time as you think about the loss, don't you?" she asked.

I didn't know how to respond to this and neither did I plan to either, so I just looked ahead. However, a thought came to me, and I couldn't help but voice it out.

"This isn't really a loss though," I said. "It's not like I ever had him. I wasn't even given the chance."

Another long silence ensues between us as we head towards the store.

"I think that's what hurts the most."

"I know," she said and threw her arm around me even though I tried to shrug it off.

"Let's go to the food court," she said. "I think I want a burrito or something."

"Aren't we going to Lush?" I asked.

"It can wait," she said. "You need some comfort food and I'm starving."

And with this I was pulled along.

We stood in line for some burritos, and felt my phone vibrate with a message. My pulse slightly jumped and for quite a while I refused to check it.

This had somewhat become the norm for me because every time I did indeed check, hoping at the far back of my mind that it was him, I was gravely disappointed.

The phone then began to ring and I was certain it wasn't him because it was close to impossible that he would be calling. My gaze met Meredith's as I pulled the phone out to check who the caller was and was a bit surprised when I saw who it was. We hadn't really spoken after our date except a few hellos here and there, and I had tried my very best not to feel bad over it because not everything was meant to work out.

In order not to be further rude, I picked it up and responded.

"Hey James," I replied, and Meredith's eyes slightly widened.

"I see you," was his response and for a second, I was a bit startled. "What?'

"Look to the side," he said. "Towards the cotton candy kiosk."

I did and although it took a few more seconds I was finally able to spot him. He stopped, his phone pressed to his ear and his bag in hand. He waved at me, and I sent a wave back.

"Oh," he looks good," Meredith said as I tried my best to work up a smile.

With a sigh, I returned the phone to my pocket as he began to come over. Thankfully we placed our order before he did so when he arrived, I was ready for him.

"Hey," he gave me a hug and a quick kiss on the cheek, and I accepted it.

He did the same to Meredith and then we headed off to a table.

"You come to malls?" Meredith asked, amused and he smiled.

"I'm up for a promotion and I have an interview tomorrow. Just wanted something new and nice that fit."

"A suit?" she asked, and he shook his head. "Dress shirts."

"What did you get?"

He showed her the bag and she nodded in approval. "Light colors," she said. "Nice."

He nodded and she gave him a thumbs up.

He then turned to me but unfortunately my mind had already gone to a certain man that looked dangerous and sinfully good in a suit. It didn't seem to be too long since I had last seen him, yet it felt like forever.

"Pam, do you want to see the shirts?" Meredith asked, and I turned to her, perplexed. Amused she passed the bag over and I could feel his gaze on me as I looked within.

"They look really nice James," I said and turned just in time to see his smile.

It was nice and bright but nothing about it really made me want to reciprocate.

Afterwards, we continued with our food and a few random conversations until eventually Meredith rose to her feet.

"Darryl will be picking me up soon," she said. "So, I have to complete my shopping."

One look at her and I received the message that she didn't in any way want me to come with her since James was now present.

"Okay," I said.

"I'll get you your bath bombs," she said with a smile and then bid us goodbye.

I looked at James as I sipped from my drink and smiled. His entire gaze and focus were on me and although I wasn't usually uncomfortable with him, this didn't exactly make me feel thrilled to be under such close scrutiny. Except with Gideon, I imagined.

I didn't think I would ever not be happy with his focus on me.

"I thought I'd hear back from you," he eventually spoke, and I grew even more uncomfortable.

"I thought I'd hear back from you," I threw the question right back at him, and felt even worse.

"Alright," he laughed. "Let's call a truce."

He held out his hand and I shook it.

"Do you still have the part time job at the bistro?" he asked, and I nodded.

"You're going in tonight?"

"Yeah," I replied, and he looked disappointed.

"I thought we could have another night out together. How about I come over when you're done?"

I thought about it and realized this was one thing I didn't think I could manage for the day, so I immediately refused.

"No, I'm going to be so exhausted, and I have an assignment due that I have to do some reading on."

"There you go rejecting me again," he complained, and I sighed.

"I'm not rejecting you."

"Alright," he said. "I'll let you be. But we'll catch up over the phone?"

This, I thought on for a few seconds and realized that I was open to, so I nodded in agreement.

26

GIDEON

I couldn't believe I was here again.

It was the third time in the past few weeks but at least for the first time, I had managed to convince myself that it was because I was worried about her.

The first time, I'd simply wanted to see her leave for home at the end of her shift and I had, and she'd seemed fine.

The second time a few days later had been because I was on my way from the office and decided to stop by because it was time for her shift to end.

I had however waited until an hour after her shift... till the restaurant had closed for the night and had been unable to spot her.

It had me worried, but I had managed to convince myself that her wellbeing was no longer any part of my business and I had headed back home. That was four days ago. I had refused to spy into her messages any longer and I remained worried. I knew she was fine, as her roommate had been to classes and wouldn't have looked fine or attended if Pamela wasn't okay.

Now, I had to wonder how and why I was back here. There was no reason for it, but I was slowly beginning to once again ignore reason. I missed her more than I thought was ever possible and it was doing things to my focus and concentration that I loathed.

I waited out of sight in the parking lot as they closed for the night.

Just a glimpse… I told myself. Just a glimpse would be more than enough.

And soon enough I got it. She came out with a group of her coworkers and headed to her car. This was the norm but then tonight and even after she got in, she remained in it and in the dark. I wondered what was wrong and if she had some issues with the vehicle, but she hadn't even tried to start it.

I saw a light on from within and suspected that it was her phone. Her colleagues left and then it was just a few cars including ours in the lot. She hadn't spotted me, and I doubted that she would, so I decided to just wait until she was safely on her way because given how the lot had emptied out, I wasn't certain that it was entirely safe for her to be here. I watched her, and soon enough saw a car drive into the parking lot. The headlights flashed in my eyes and then headed over to park beside her. She remained in the car and then I saw the guy step out of his. He went over to her window, and I saw her smile at him. It pierced something sharp through my heart.

They spoke for a few minutes and then he pulled her door open.

She shook her head and tried to pull it back shut. He refused and stood in place. He kept pointing towards a direction and I could see the refusal in her eyes although she wore the politest of smiles. Her hand went to her forehead as though indicating that she wasn't feeling well, but still he stood there, and I grew furious.

My hand went to the handle of my door, but I stopped myself in time, so as not to overstep my bounds. Whoever this guy is, he's probably more welcome to her than I currently am. I just stayed put and continued to watch them and soon, it occurred to me that this was possibly the James guy that she had been texting.

I decided then that it was time to leave, but I wanted to wait before starting my car. I looked down for one moment to pick up my phone. When I looked back up, I saw that he had completely closed the distance between them and had her face in his hands. I frowned as I watched it, however when I saw her hand flailing as she tried to stop him, pushing him away, I couldn't bring myself to move. I was alarmed but still something in me hesitated, still slightly unsure that she needed me to intervene.

When he closed in on her again and her hands shot out to push him away, I threw the phone aside and got out of the car.

The door slammed violently shut behind me as I rolled up my sleeves and began to walk over to them. I got closer and could feel and better hear the desperation in her struggle.

"For fuck's sake James!" I heard her berate, and then she struck him across the face. He moved away with a hand to his cheek, and I saw the horror in her eyes.

"What the fuck is wrong with you?" she asked, and he yelled right back.

"Why do you keep leading me on?"

"I'm not leading you on?" she shouted back, but he never got another chance to say whatever he wanted to.

I lunged forward and grabbed him by the arm, slinging him away so hard that he rolled across the ground.

She screamed, a hand slapping across her mouth and it resounded across the empty parking lot.

I turned back to glance at her, and saw her eyes widened with shock.

I returned my attention to the bastard, watching how he struggled to get up, and fury, hot and blinding surged through me. I heard her call from behind but ignored it as I lunged at him and then had the front of his shirt in my grip.

"Who the fuck are you?" he yelled, but that was all he was able to say before my fist shot out and slammed into the side of his face.

"Gideon!" her shout finally pierced through, and it was then that I came to my senses.

All I could do was stare at him, bloodied and whimpering on the ground and it took everything in me to resist the urge to kick him.

I was finally able to because I knew that if I kept on going it would be even more difficult for me to stop.

Suddenly, I felt her hand around my arm and turned to see the horrified look on her face. She was looking at me as though she couldn't believe I was there, and then she turned to the man on the ground.

"What the hell is wrong with you?" she yelled and then went over to him to try to help him up.

"I'm sorry James," she apologized, but he pushed her away. As she fell on her ass, my entire body instantly moved to help her. But she pushed me away and watched until the man rose to his feet and gave me a cold hard glance.

"Professor Bach?" he seemed even more astounded despite the blood dripping from the corner of his lips.

"What is..." he looked between the both of us. "What the fuck is this? Why did you hit me?"

I couldn't quite place the man, but he did look quite familiar, so I reckoned that he had attended the university and been around.

Without a word, I turned around, aware now that she was okay, since she didn't feel scared of him at all. However, I was surprised at my reaction, so I headed back to my car. Without any further look at them or myself in the mirror for that matter, I started the car, put it in gear and drove away.

27

PAMELA

I was still so shocked at what had just happened that even when both men got into their cars and drove away, I still stood there, looking lost.

James had tried to force me to kiss him. It was wrong and violent, but I was certain that I could have handled it somehow. Gideon stepping in such a violent way had seemed to make everything worse.

Turning around, I got into my car, hoping to not bring any more attention to myself. In there, my head fell forward on the steering wheel as I tried to recall what just happened.

It had all happened way too fast.

In one moment, it had been James, in the next the two of them and then it was no one.

I thought of what to do and home was the first thing that came to my mind. Soon I arrived and met Meredith in the kitchen making dinner with an apron and shorts.

"We're having fettuccini tonight," she said. "Darryl made it for me last night at his apartment so I'm going to try to recreate it just the way he did for us."

I didn't respond and instead, headed straight to the couch to take a seat.

She soon realized that I was acting a bit strange.

"Pamela," she called out.

"Hm?" I turned a heavy gaze towards her.

"Are you alright?"

"James attacked me tonight," I started without thinking and her eyes widened in shock.

"What?"

"I mean he was just trying to kiss me but then, Gideon came out of nowhere and hit him."

At this she seemed even more stupefied.

"Okay you need to tell me every single detail of what you're talking about. She turned the stove off and headed towards me.

A few minutes later, she was aware of everything, and I wondered what she would say. It wasn't what I expected. "Thank Gideon, for being there for some reason."

My gaze shot up to hers. "What?

"He might get sued for it. You said James recognized Professor Bach, right?"

"Yes," I replied.

"Well unless by some miracle that makes James forget all that he has just gone through then he might sue his company. Not to mention the fact that he might report you both to the university and then you both would be kicked out."

"Wow," was all I could say. "You're all doom and gloom today, aren't you?"

"My advice ensures that you're fine and safe so this time I hope you will listen to me. Contact James now and ensure that he's fine so that he won't bear any grudge towards the both of you."

I looked at her blankly and she stared back.

"Hello," she said, waving a hand in front of my face. "Are you alright? Still in shock?"

"James was wrong," I said. "I told him not to come over even when we met at the food court. That I would be too tired to go out. He instead came at closing trying to convince me to go to a bar with him and when I refused, he tried to kiss me with force. That was wrong."

"You're right," she said.

"Gideon was right to step in the way he did. He doesn't know James so of course he was alarmed at what he was trying to do. I'm still somewhat calm now because I didn't suspect that James was trying to go further than a kiss but what if that had been his intention? He should be the one that's scared that I'll press charges. And he should be the one to call me and apologize."

She listened and then she nodded her head. "You're right."

Afterwards we sat in silence for a little while before she suddenly jumped up. "Oh my God I have a pie in the oven."

I turned to watch her in order to distract myself as she headed over to the oven in a hurry and grabbed the mitten.

"You're making pie too?" I asked. "What's the occasion?"

She was silent for a little while until she set the tray on the counter, and then she sent me a smile. "I got accepted today, at Professor Bach's company for the internship. Actually, it was yesterday but I didn't get the chance to tell you."

At this I scowled. "You didn't get the chance to tell me? We spent the evening at home. Why are you walking on eggshells around me concerning this? I never wanted to work there."

"I know," she said, "but with how things have been

recently, I just... wanted to keep any mention of him down to a minimum."

"That, I'm not in disagreement with," I said with a sigh and relaxed on the couch.

Another stretch of silence extended between us, and then she spoke up again.

"Where did he come from?"

It was the question of the century indeed, and one that I hadn't been able to keep from my mind for very long.

"Maybe I should ask him," I said.

"And check how he's doing," she added.

I lifted my gaze and it met hers across the room.

"So, I shouldn't just call?"

"What do you think?" she asked, and I sighed.

28

GIDEON

I was still fuming so much that it was only when I got into the shower that I realized that my knuckles were bloodied from my punch to his face.

They stung as the water touched them, and all I could do was stare at them. I evidently hit his teeth, cutting my knuckles. It was ignorable but then the scene returned to my mind, it made me even angrier.

I was going to find out who he was, and I wasn't going to let him go and that was my resolve. But then I couldn't help but feel confused about Pamela because it seemed as though she wasn't angry at him, and I couldn't understand how that could be.

Was she then perhaps truly attracted to him? My hands fisted at the thoughts and suddenly, I needed to breathe more easily, so I turned the water all the way cold.

I relived my fear at seeing her manhandled in that way, and by the time I stepped out of the shower I was in no way calmed.

I expected her to show up but at the same time there were many reasons to believe that she wouldn't so when the doorbell rang, I looked at it with some skepticism.

When I checked the time and saw that it was approaching midnight, I was certain that no one else would drop by so late at night, unannounced.

I headed straight to the front door to answer it and it was only when I was close that I noticed that I was still somewhat wet and covered by a long white towel. I thought of going to change but decided against it.

I didn't want her to think I was ignoring her, so I decided to let her in first and then head back to my room. She was indeed the one, looking wide eyed and vulnerable and it truly made my heart hurt just to see her.

I stepped back so that she could come in, and then she shut the door behind her. Without a word I turned around to head back to my room and she watched me go.

"Are you about to have a shower or did you just get out of one," she asked, and I stopped in my tracks.

I thought of whether to respond to her or not and eventually couldn't find a reason not to, so I turned around.

"I just got out. I want to change. I'll be right back."

"Hmm," she said looking disappointed.

"What is it?"

"I wanted to take a shower, "she said slowly. "But I was in such a hurry to get here... that I didn't take one."

At this I frowned and then I shook my head. What was the point in denying myself any longer? It was just prolonging the inevitable.

She held my gaze and then with a sigh, I took the towel off my hips and flung it at her. "Use this,' I said. "Don't keep me waiting."

I strolled back to the bathroom and couldn't believe how this night was unfolding.

I was already fully hard by the time I arrived, and the moment I got in, I turned on the water, adjusting the temperature. A few seconds later I could sense her presence and when I brushed the water out of my face I turned to see her with the towel wrapped around her body.

"Come in," I groaned and was sure I detected the shadow of a smile in the corner of her lips. Soon I felt the cool draft of air come in as she parted the glass door, and then she was by my side completely naked.

My earlier annoyance quickly transformed into excitement but with a dangerous edge. I looked at her, and although I wanted to scold her until all my annoyance was wrung out of me, I also wanted to take her in my arms and never let her go. To completely lose myself in her and ensure that she did the same with me. With her eyes still on me I pulled her underneath the water and drenched her with it. She shut her eyes, a slight whimper escaping her lips at the sudden stream.

"Hold still," I said quietly, and began to run my hands through her hair.

I reveled in the way the water softened the mass of her hair and couldn't help but gently stroke her scalp. "You sound angry at me," she said, her head leaning against my chest.

I was, but I wasn't exactly sure why because nothing that had happened had been her fault or perhaps, I was the one who I was actually angry with.

I squirted some shampoo onto my hands and then began to work it into her hair. I let the soap fall and soon it was coming down her forehead.

"Hey," she complained and then her hand hit against my chest.

For the first few seconds, and as the sting went through

me, I was a bit taken aback. And then I lowered my gaze to meet hers and could see the caution in her eyes as she hadn't expected to hit me that hard.

I sighed. "What? Do You think I'm going to hit you?" I asked and her face fell. She lowered her head then so I brushed the suds away so it wouldn't fall into her eyes and then lifted her head back up with a nudge of her chin.

"You have no idea how furious I am at what happened tonight."

"I have a good idea," she said.

"Why the hell did you-" I stopped reminding myself that this was not her fault. "Why would you let that kind of person around you? For any reason?"

"Up till now he's been fairly normal," she said, her voice small.

"He's never shown any previous signs of violence?"

"No more than you," she said, and my eyes widened. She instantly moved closer to me. "I'm sorry, I was kidding."

"When have I ever shown signs of violence toward you?"

"By rejecting me," she said. "Over and over again, but then somehow magically coming out of the bushes today to help me."

I glared at her.

"What were you doing there?" she asked.

"It's not yet your turn to interrogate me," I said but couldn't breathe as she completely closed the distance between us, and I realized that her chest and softness were pressed directly against me.

"Okay," she said, and I couldn't believe just how wanton she was acting.

I however wasn't ready to brush this under the carpet,

"Why were you not as alarmed as you should have been after the first time he grabbed you?" I asked.

At this she sighed, her arms hesitantly but eventually wrapping around me.

"The reason it appeared violent was because I didn't want to kiss him," she said. "And he wasn't expecting that. "We um... we used to date but then we... broke up a while ago. I guess he thought he could reignite the passion or whatever and get me to give in to it and that was why he persisted."

"Wasn't it painful?" I asked, "The way he grabbed you?"

"It was," she replied. "That was why I eventually reacted strongly to let him know that I wasn't having it."

"You didn't react strongly enough," I said and returned my attention to washing her hair.

"You shouldn't have rejected me," she said. "Then I wouldn't have even considered his advances at all."

"I'm not accepting you now either," I said and at this she stopped. So did I because I wasn't expecting the words to come out of my mouth in that way but as they did, I also realized that I meant this, and I couldn't take it back.

"I'm sorry," I apologized, but she was already turning around to leave.

I grabbed her and tried to get her to stay. And eventually when it didn't seem to be working, I held onto her face and connected my lips to hers.

She fought it, but eventually gave in and I immediately stopped when I realized that I was doing the same thing that I had wanted to break the other guy's neck for doing, and all in the same night. She smacked me on the shoulder, and I backed away.

"I'm sorry," I said, as she tried to catch her breath.

"What the hell is wrong with you males?"

"I'm sorry," I said again, disgusted by the fact that I could even be put in the same category, and my excuse was the same. I was sure that she wanted to kiss me.

"I'm sorry," I felt like I was on repeat and could no longer bear to face her.

"I'm truly sorry." I pulled the door open to exit the stall however, her hand closed around my wrist.

"You don't have to leave," she said, and I was surprised. I turned to face her.

"You still have to wash my hair. I'm tired."

I couldn't believe her. "How is this okay with you?" I asked.

She sighed. "Because unlike him, I want to kiss you. It's all I've been able to think about every minute of every day for the past few weeks, and I hate you for depriving me of that. So, I'm probably going to kiss you so hard that I bruise your lips, so take this as your forewarning. Either that or I'll try to bite your tongue off but..."

"But what?" I asked, the heat in her gaze nearly scorching me on the spot.

"I want it in my mouth. Your tongue I mean... and other parts of you." She lowered her hands and a gasp escaped me as she held my cock in her hands. It twitched at her touch, swelling even harder but I didn't know how that was possible. It was already erect against my stomach and was as hard as stone.

I didn't think anymore. I threw all my inhibitions out the window and shut the door behind me. Then I took her face in my hands once again, but this time even more gently, and I kissed her... with all my heart.

She received me, in a way that gave me no doubt whatsoever that she had me in her heart. Her lips parted and my tongue was sliding in. Her taste intoxicated me and at the realization of just what I had been deprived of for the last few weeks dawned on me, I felt all my resistance drain away from my body. I wanted to consume all that she was, and I wanted to protect her. To hold her so tightly that no one would ever be able to hurt or mistreat her like tonight again.

But then my conscience kicked me because as I kissed her even harder, I knew that I was doing the same. She was worth so much more than I would ever deserve and yet I couldn't keep away.

Quickly, I came to my senses and decided that I didn't want to go any further. And that she wasn't just someone to be used and discarded. No matter how much I wanted her.

I started to pull away, but she protested, alarmed, and her hands wrapped tightly around me.

"No," she shook her head, and I could see the hurt in her eyes. "You can't do this again."

"I know," I told her. "But... I'm not ready for more and I don't know when I'll be ready. I don't want to be to you what that guy was tonight."

At this, her arms finally began to loosen away from me, and I kept my gaze directly on her. And I knew then that I loved her. And as I stared at her even longer, it occurred to me that perhaps I had loved her all along. But my wounds from her family had kept it so suppressed that I had refused to even consider giving in.

Now and one more time I asked myself if I could give in, and if I could submit to a connection that I had treasured before I even knew how important it was.

I suspected that I could, but one thing held me back and it was the fact that I believed if I had been able to keep myself away from her in the past then I could do it once again. Sure, it was exciting and heated now, but what if when the harsh realities of life returned and all I could think about was the past and no longer the thrill of the present.

I could be away from her, but I couldn't hurt her, not the way I knew I would as the years rolled by. I stepped away and shook my head.

"Let's not go down this path," I told her. "There's no way that it is going to end well."

She seemed so confused that I wanted to apologize again, but instead I kept my cool. She watched me and then she seemed to take a deep breath and then release it.

"Gideon," she said. "I'm not in love with you. If you're hesitating because you think I am then it's not the case. I love sleeping with you. There's nothing like it and I don't want you to deprive me of it when I can clearly see that you want me just as much as I want you."

"So," she said. "Let's enter into some sort of agreement because the fact is that if we don't do this with each other, we will do it with other people. What's the point when it won't be as great? Or is this not the case with you?"

I didn't respond and she seemed to draw from this the conclusion that we were on the same page.

"I can do this," she said. "And at the end of it all, we'll go our separate ways. Unless of course, you care for me? More than you'd like to admit?"

I smiled then, my lips tilting slightly because of the intelligent way that she thought she was working around the rejection this time around. I reached for her once again and kissed her deeply.

"There are a lot of restrictions in our path, some I don't want to tell you about. And some you know of which is the fact that a professor cannot date a student."

At this she seemed to go still and then she frowned.

"You're giving me a headache. Can you make up your fucking mind?"

"I know," I said and leaned against her and pressed a kiss to her forehead. "I know what you're asking for, and what you're willing to accept but... I can't be that way with you. I've known you for too long and... I guess you got under my skin. I care about you, and I'd rather you'd be in a proper relationship with someone else than a solely physical one with me. You deserve the best of everything and truly I don't think that currently, I'm it."

"Ah," she said, her lips parting. "I see you've picked up the textbook way of how to dump someone and spare their feelings." I was a bit taken aback by what she was saying, but eventually came to understand it and could do nothing but smile.

"Date me first," she said. "For real and thoroughly. And then you can decide to break up with me but not before. I won't accept that."

A long silence dragged between us, and then I took in the state we were in with each other. Exposed and bare, and I knew that if there was ever to be a chance that I would be this way with someone in my life, it would be with her and no one else. And yet I didn't want to give it a chance. I had tackled numerous difficult things in my life and had managed thus far to overcome most of them, so why was it that I wasn't willing to try with her. The past between our families had hurt me, but I no longer felt the pain. Just the memories simply reminded me of my desire back then to keep away from them, but things had changed so perhaps... there was a chance.

She stepped towards me, and although I felt the urge to retreat I didn't. Instead, I held my ground until once again she had her arms around me and for the first time in her presence, I truly felt my heart racing. I let it be, didn't pull away or refuse to acknowledge the undeniable impact that she was having on me. The incident from earlier in the night came back to me and all once again I was furious.

For the second time tonight, I pulled her to me and kissed her.

It went as deep as possible, and I tried my best to let go and to give this a chance. It was the first time I'd ever considered doing this but then it made perfect sense to me that it would be with her and no one else.

Her kiss was just as fervent as mine, her tongue licking into my mouth with desperate passionate strokes that made my heart wrench with emotion. I could feel the feelings she had for me in the way she kissed me, and when she finally broke away and hid her face in the crook of my shoulder, I knew that she was trying to hide the tears that had filled her eyes.

I felt them a few seconds later as the wetness stained my skin, but when I tried to pull away so that I could wipe them away she held on and stopped me, shaking her head.

"Why?" I asked.

"Because you have to prove yourself," she said.

Her meaning was unclear to me, so she straightened but turned away, and not till she was back to normal did she turn back around to face me.

"You have to prove that you're worthy enough to see me cry and wipe away my tears. That's the privilege reserved for those who have decided to fight for me with everything they have. You're not one of those yet."

A smile managed to work itself to my lips because I knew she was right.

"Okay," I told her and turned the water back on. Then I

placed her under it, and she held onto me once again as the water washed us both.

"I might not be able to wipe them off now, but perhaps there are other ways I can make things better?" I asked, and her eyes sparkled with excitement.

"Like what?" she asked, barely able to catch her breath.

I lowered then, kissed the junction between her neck and shoulders and then I was tracing my lips along the blade of her collarbone and across her gorgeous breasts. I took them in my hands, molding and flicking my thumb across the nipples until her balance faltered and she was back against the wall of the shower.

"Gideon," her breathing came even faster, and of course not one to be outdone. I could feel the same effect come over me as she took my cock in her hands and began to stroke up and down the painfully erect length.

I kissed her once again, and then I lowered my hands, sliding down her gorgeous body. I loved everything about it I realized, as my lips kissed every bit of skin I could find along the way.

"Hold on," I told her, as I started to pull her legs a little further apart. I felt her hand fist in my hair and her entire frame became restless in anticipation.

However, there was nowhere she could go. Lowering my head, I licked from her belly button, licking and kissing down her skin till I reached the junction of her thighs.

"Gideon," her heated and sultry breathing filled the space and I held tightly onto her.

Firstly, I lapped her up, the warm sweet trickle of her pleasure instantly coating my tongue. I relished the taste, intoxicated with the fact that I was being this intimate with her.

She cried out, her soft electric sounds causing goosebumps to break out across my skin.

I dug in even deeper, extracting even more of her essence and then I licked through the damp folds of her cleft. I relished the sensation of her slight shivering around me, and by the time my lips closed around her clit, I had a smile on my face at her resulting moan. It was loud and uninhibited, and with the tightened grip on my hair, I knew she was letting loose as much as possible and not holding back, thanks to our new truce. It had an equally magical effect on me, in my head and heart, I was no longer just fucking a past acquaintance that I happened to desire so madly that I couldn't think straight, but I was with the woman I loved, and it made all the difference. I couldn't get enough of her and so I continued to suck and lap her up, greedily, feverishly until she was doing all that she could to get away from me. However, my grip around her thighs was too strong, and thus she couldn't get very far. When I eventually felt her begin to come however and lose a bit of her awareness, I loosened my grip on her and managed to rise to my feet so that she could find the support that she most definitely needed to help her contain the surge of pleasure through her body. Just as expected, she was bent over, barely able to lean against me as her release streamed down her thighs and her muscles tightened and spasmed.

I could see the strength was drained from her, but most importantly, I noted her need to connect so when she instantly tried to straighten despite her now limited strength, I allowed her to grab onto my face and give me what had to be one of the sweetest kisses that I had ever received from her. Afterwards, and for the longest time she couldn't open her eyes but all she could do was hold onto my face as she tried to catch her breath, her face filled with amazement.

Eventually her eyes opened... slowly, and I was certain that I was losing myself even further into their depths.

"That was amazing," she said, her eyes filling up with moisture.

I kissed her one more time and she complied, until suddenly, she was grabbing onto my hand a little harder than usual, and then she managed to turn me around till my back was against the wall.

"What is it?" I asked, and she gave me an utterly wicked smile. I knew then what she was about to do, and my heart lurched in my chest. I had been expecting it but given our newly admitted affection for each other I had no doubt that she would put as much love into it as she could muster.

She didn't let me down as she lowered to her knees, but still held onto me for support.

"I'm still recovering," she said, and I nodded in understanding. Her hands held onto the side of my hips and then she was kissing my cock. At first, I wanted to watch her but then as I felt her going even further and my body tingling in response I decided to let go altogether.

What I wanted now and beyond all else was to feel every single sensation of her hands and mouth on me, and to completely lose myself in it.

I relished the warmth of her touch as she took my cock in her hands, and then it was only a few seconds later before I felt her mouth closing around me. My eyes shot open because I realized that I wanted this image in my mind.

I looked down, and as I watched the girth disappear within, her gaze on mine, I once again felt my heart nearly collapse in my chest. At the whoosh of breath releasing through my lips I saw the smile on hers and then she closed her eyes and gave all her attention to my rod. I was already leaking, veins straining against the satiny smooth skin as she held it tightly between the roof of her mouth and tongue.

"Ah," I moaned, my head slightly falling back as she sucked me.

My skin was dampened with sweat, my hair clinging to my skin, and all of me felt weighty and somewhat tender. What I needed I realized then was this release, in the best way possible. And I looked forward to it.

She took me all the way to the back of her throat and then she pulled away, her hand curving around the base.

Her grip was at first gentle as she lifted her gaze back to mine. She then began to bob her head up and down my length, but then her pace heightened to an intensity that surprised even me and then her tongue was sliding between the slit.

I couldn't help yet another moan that rumbled in the back of my throat. She was relentless as she pumped me with her mouth, her fist settling into the most intoxicating rhythm. I needed to hold something then, as she seemed to go even faster, my little spurts of release seeping onto her tongue. She didn't let a single drop go to waste, licking and kissing along the engorged length, and I didn't think I'd ever felt as appreciated. She did it with all her heart as though it was the most beautiful delicacy in the world, and I was rendered speechless.

I was forced to grab onto the handle of the faucet to stabilize myself, as gradually I could feel the strength seeping out of my limbs. It had never been easy for any woman in the past to bring me this quickly to the edge, but with her I could feel and hear the roaring of my blood in my ears. My heart was racing harder and harder, pleasure infiltrating every nook and cranny of my system until my hand found its way to her hair. I held the mass atop her head as gently as I could, but then I couldn't tell just how out of control I was becoming with my own force, so I let her go.

"Slow down," I told her as I felt every bit of my control slipping. I wanted this to end because it was beginning to feel as though I couldn't contain the intensity, but then in the same vein my wish was that it would last forever.

I didn't want to come in her mouth, but she didn't seem to want to guard against this as she sucked me even harder, the slurpy sounds reverberating around the enclosed space. It was filthy and erotic, and it made my vision begin to flash. I tried to pull away when I felt the surge of my release, but she held on tightly to me, and so I had no choice but to spill into her mouth. I lost cognizance of everything else, the relief and pleasure so soul deep that for a few seconds I forgot where we were. But her name remained in my heart and thoughts and so accompanying my tortured, strained moans was her beautiful name.

"*Pamela*," I breathed, and realized that she was still yet to let me go. She continued to pump me until she had milked out every bit of ecstasy and left me completely drained of strength. Then she rose to her feet, and I felt her lips kissing along my jawline. All I could do was hold onto her... until finally I was ready to open my eyes.

All I could do was watch her... the soft smile on her face, the sparkle in her eyes and the innocence of her expression.

It was difficult in the current moment though to give the last title to her, but the hesitation cleared away as the girl that had glued herself to my hip many years prior came once again to mind.

Shaking my head, I lifted my hand and stroked the damp strands of her hair out of her face.

"Where did you learn that?" I asked, and her eyes

slightly widened. And then she blushed, and I couldn't remember ever enjoying watching someone as much.

"It should have been with you," she said, and my insides wrenched because she was absolutely right. I pulled her sassy self forward and sealed my lips against hers. She melted into me, her body going limp against mine and as a result, her arms wrapped around my waist to keep her standing on her own. It was not needed however because I soon lowered, curved my arms around her thighs and lifted her into the air.

She squealed lightly in excitement but soon resumed her beautiful assault on my lips. I turned until she was deposited gently against the wall and then I broke off the kiss. My head lowered once again to her gorgeous, full breasts, and I pulled her nipple into my mouth.

I sucked hard, my tongue flicking and stroking the aroused bud until I felt her back arching backwards. The softest of whimpers escaped her lips and they were like music to my ears.

With my sole focus on stroking and kissing every part of her that I could reach, it didn't take long before I was fully hard and ready to take her.

Grabbing my cock in one hand I stroked it through her sex, loving the sudden breathless gasps that followed and the complete submission to me that I could see in her eyes.

Her hands found their way to my hair as I began to slide into her, and I watched as the pleasure and joy of being stretched and penetrated so exquisitely came over her face.

"Faster," she said, and I was amused. When I refused to comply, her eyes opened and dazed, and her legs tightened around me. "Gideon," she complained and holding her gaze I finally gave in to what she wanted.

I pulled out slightly, her walls pulsing greedily around

me, and then I slammed back in, my cock going all the way to the hilt in her.

"*Ah*," she trembled in my arms, her head once again tilting backwards. I kissed her exposed neck, and then my grip on her thighs tightened as I began to slide out of her.

I thrust into her once again, my pacing slow and controlled until she couldn't remain still any longer. She began to writhe and grind her own hips into mine until eventually I could feel my control slipping. She called out my name over and over again with soft, affectionate whispers, and it did something to me to hear these from her. My rhythm became faster, and her voice became louder.

On my back I could feel the dig of her nails into my skin and the sting somehow served to turn me on even further.

I fucked her insistently, the force of my thrusts sending her ass hitting against the cool tiled wall again and again. The sounds drove me wild, and I completely submitted, knowing from the start that I wouldn't last long when I became sheathed in her heat.

My hips rammed harder and faster into her, and I could feel the articulation of my affection for her bubbling to the surface, which made me wonder just how she would react if I ever exposed it to her.

Would she use it to my disadvantage? I wondered or would she inform me that she felt the same and probably make me one of the happiest people alive.

I couldn't decide so I swallowed it back down and brought her to completion. She screamed out my name, shamelessly and without holding back for even a second and I adored her for it.

I watched as she fell apart in my arms, breathless and dazedly and it brought the sweetest rush surging through me. I continued however to fuck her, as I was still teetering on the edge but as I continued to watch her it was clear to me that it would be in no time.

When I came it was with a hoarse, deep groan that seemed to reverberate through my body. My release in her was warm and seemingly endless and it was only then that it occurred to me that I had once again been careless.

I was instantly worried, but thankfully I didn't forget to be caring and sensitive about it this time around.

I waited until my strength returned and then I kissed her.

"I was careless again," I told her. "But I haven't been with anyone since you."

She smiled, her hand lifting to brush my hair out of my face. "Neither have I," she said, and my heart jumped for joy.

However, these weren't all our concerns. "Are you on the pill?" I asked and she nodded.

"Yeah, don't worry about it," she said, but it occurred to me that I somewhat wished that she wasn't. Because perhaps if she got knocked up, then my mind would make the complete and unavoidable shift into sticking with her and working through my demons.

However, it wasn't right so I pushed it out of my mind but couldn't quite ignore my excitement at the thought. Soon enough, we had to move as we had remained in the same spot for way too long. We also had to complete our shower, so I leaned my forehead against hers to regain my strength and determination. Then I slid out of her.

She moaned weakly at the sensation, and I kissed her lips because I couldn't help my sadness too at the loss.

"You must be exhausted." I told her. "Bedtime."

"I can barely keep my eyes open," she said. "But let's finish our shower first. I'm all wet and sticky." Smiling, I slipped my hand between her thighs and could feel it all while hers closed around my wrist.

"I'm going to faint," she said, but I couldn't stop myself from stroking softly across her swollen clit and then sliding a finger into her.

"Gideon," she pleaded, voice growing breathless once again and I finally conceded. I brought her to the shower head, and after squirting what she would need onto a loofah, began to run it across her body as gently and thoroughly as I could. She watched me, the look in her eyes soft and sweet and it made my heart swell.

"If someone had told me that you'd be the one bathing me before bed tonight, I would have called them insane," she said, and I couldn't help my smile. I felt the same way.

Soon enough I was done but she took the loofah from my hands.

"Your turn," she said, and I laughed out loud.

"I already had a shower before you came, remember?" I asked, and her lips parted.

"Right, but still..." she coaxed, her hands running all over my torso flicking across my nipples and then going behind to grab my ass.

"Fuck that's taut," she said, and I shook my head at her.

"You just want an excuse to touch me all over, don't you?" I asked and her blush stained her cheeks a warm red.

"I want to lick you all over," she said.

"We'll do that in bed," I said and could see the feral excitement on her face.

We both rinsed off thoroughly and headed over to the sink. I grabbed a towel from the rack and lowered to begin with her legs. I dried her up till I got to her abdomen and couldn't resist placing a kiss right there on it. Afterwards, I rose to my feet, emotion overwhelming me, and then I had my tongue sliding into her mouth. She kissed me back with as much fervency, and I threw the towel aside.

"I'm not completely dried," she cried, but I didn't care.

I took her to my bed, laid her on it and was on her.

I kissed her for what seemed like forever with my cock edged between her thighs as she rocked against me. At first, we were able to simply revel in the sensations but much too quickly they became mind-numbing, and we had to make a decision.

"Go to bed, or one more?" I asked and she considered this.

"Go to bed," she said. "But wake me up with it."

At this I laughed and agreed to the request.

"Don't disappoint me," she said, and she turned to her side in order to spoon into me.

I promised her that I wouldn't.

29

PAMELA

Going to sleep in his arms was a dream but then waking up in them and feeling the warmth and assurance of his presence around me was pure bliss.

It was already past dawn when I awoke, and although the blinds of the room were drawn, I could see through it that the new day had arrived.

All the events from the previous night played in my head and I couldn't help now but be grateful to James. However, I still expected some guilt and reservations to plague me now in the light of the day and they didn't fail to come.

The most important being how Gideon would feel about us the following morning. Deciding to try... *together,* hadn't been a decision that had been easily arrived at. Plus, it had been charged with so many emotions from the night before. But now that we were calmer and reality was dawning on the two of us, I couldn't help but wonder how he would feel about it now.

I was happy though, with how he clung to me, his body

and scent so warm and sweet but then I remembered what I had asked him to wake me up to.

He had promised, but when I managed to look behind and saw the deep slumber he was still in, my heart softened.

It made me wonder if he had any problems whatsoever with sleeping because he looked as though it had been a long time since he'd fallen asleep this deeply.

I continued to bask in his arms until it occurred to me that I needed to pee, and that I had a class early this morning and so did he. I couldn't bring myself to move until eventually he sighed, and I slowly managed to turn around in his arms. His eyes were still shut but I could tell now that he was somewhat awake or at least partly coherent.

My hand reached out to stroke across the tip of his nose. He didn't respond, and I felt even worse for disturbing him, so I just began to pull away. He however stopped me, his arms coming around to pull me in even closer. I couldn't help my amusement while he buried his face in the crook of my shoulder and sniffed me.

"That's drug addict behavior," I said when he eventually pulled away.

"You are my drug," he said, his voice hoarse, and I could feel a swarm of butterflies run amok in my stomach. God he was handsome, and never more than in this vulnerable unguarded state did I understand the extent of it. He was borderline beautiful and when his eyes came open, my breath was completely stolen.

"I promised you something when you woke up this morning," he said as he stared at me, and I immediately recalled what it was. I smiled and then his hand began to move from underneath my waist and across my skin. Goose-bumps broke out across my body but more urgent was the need to use the bathroom, so I immediately jumped to my feet.

It was however a challenge for him to let me go.

"I'll be right back," I whined until eventually he did, and I was able to bound away, the covers trailing behind me. They were however too heavy, so I was forced to abandon them and throw them back on the bed and on him.

"Don't look," I said as I hurried naked across the room, but I was more than certain that he had his eyes on me.

I couldn't look at myself in the mirror when I arrived, but I didn't need to see that my cheeks were burning red. I was heated all over for all that we had done so far and how intimate we now were with each other.

With a sigh, I brushed my strangely dried hair out of my face and couldn't help but admit that I looked a bit of a mess. I immediately began to rummage through his things looking for how I would put myself together. I found a cotton ball and wiped away the smeared mascara under my eyes because of course there was no way he would have been able to wash that off slowly with shower gel. Afterwards I ran his brush through my hair, found an unopened toothbrush in a supplies drawer and couldn't help but marvel at how organized he was.

I completed my business on the toilet and then I found a robe and wrapped myself in it. It was however oversized so I could barely find my body, but I found it thankfully soothing.

"Pamela," I eventually heard him call out and it was clear to me then that I had spent too much time in here.

"Be right there," I said and pushed the robe off one shoulder to expose my slender, supple skin and a bit of cleavage. I arrived at the door and just as I had expected, watched him facing it and awaiting my appearance.

"You okay?" he asked and I nodded.

"Did you need anything that you couldn't find in there?"

I shook my head and began to head over to him.

Just before I arrived at the bed however, he began to sit up and I wondered why. He did so until his back was against the headboard and then he tapped his lap covered by the covers.

"Come over here," he said, and my breath caught in my throat.

"What?"

"I have to go to class soon but I'm a man of my word so come over here."

I didn't want to ask the details of what he intended to do, but I was certain it had something to do with riding him. The thought alone was near enough to drive me out of my mind with need.

I could barely speak as I climbed onto the bed, but then he reached out and untied the robe and once again I was completely exposed before him. I was incredibly shy, but it didn't take long for me to get used to him staring so blatantly and hungrily at my body.

"Astride," he said, and I did as he asked, my gaze on the unmistakable swell of his cock pressing against the fabric.

I started to lower when he caught me by the hips and pushed me forward until I had no chance but to flatten my hand on the walls for support.

"Gideon," I squealed, but that was all I got the chance to say before his mouth closed around my clit.

Pleasure struck me, causing me to arch my back.

I held onto the headboard for stability, however my arms couldn't help trembling as he held onto the side of my hips and kissed my folds. It was deep and indulgent, with absolutely no hesitation and red-hot pleasure pulsed through me as a result.

I almost didn't want any more, aware that by the time he was done I would be nothing but a weak shuddering mess, however I couldn't say no and yet I couldn't push him away.

I held on as tightly as I could, his name a constant prayer on the tip of my tongue. His tongue stroked hard across my engorged clit, and a deep moan of delight reverberated through me. I was in an awkward, unstable position and I couldn't care less. All I wanted was to feel myself on the brink and then falling into pure unadulterated bliss.

His hand moved from the side of my hips, and then his thumb was stroking against the bud. Unable to hold back any further, his name sounded from my lips but before I could even recover, he had two fingers nudging me open and then sliding in.

My sex rippled around the width of his warm fingers, the much-welcomed intrusion pushing me closer and closer to the edge of just where I wanted to be.

He finger fucked me with vigor, his fingers going deep and so rapidly that my back arched forcing my grip to loosen from around the wood. From my half cry and half moan, I soon found his fingers withdrawing from me.

His mouth replaced his hand and from then on, I couldn't remain still. His grip on the sides of my hips tightened to keep me in place but it didn't stop the writhing of my hips against his mouth and tongue. For a moment there I was sure that my awareness of everything else beside the overpowering ecstasy that wreaked through me as I fucked his face, and the sensations causing my eyes to roll back into my sockets were non-existent. I couldn't hold back or reduce my rocking as the pad of his tongue stroked and ate at my cunt.

I came faster than I probably ever had, and my cry resounded across the room. I was incapable of being completely aware of all that happened, much less muffling the sounds so I couldn't help but be grateful that he had such an apartment as this where you couldn't be heard by outsiders, unlike the one I was currently staying in with Meredith.

It was only by his help that I was able to get back down, and he ensured that I was laid softly down. I pulled him to me for a much-needed kiss and only the distant reminder that he had to get to work as well as me to class, led me to break away. It took a little while before I could pull my eyes open to meet his and when I did, I couldn't look away.

For a moment it all still felt like a dream as I couldn't quite believe we were together in this way. But still he felt real and solid in my arms, and I allowed myself to bask in the bliss and actuality of our current reality.

30

GIDEON

For the first time in a long time, I didn't want to get out of bed. Because doing so would entail that I would be away from her, and it was the last thing that I currently wanted. I watched as she hurried around the room, grabbing and pulling on her clothes and then she ran over one last time to give me a kiss.

I accepted it, reveling in her wonderful taste one last time before she was gone for the day.

"When's your class?" she asked.

"In an hour," I told her. "Or so."

At this she smiled.

"Alright, have a nice day?"

"I'm sorry I didn't make you breakfast," I said, and her smile widened even harder. "It's alright, I don't really eat breakfast anyway. I'll grab something at lunch."

"Are you working tonight?" I asked and her face slightly fell. "Unfortunately, yes. But... I'll see you after?" she asked shyly, and I kissed her in return.

"Of course. Keep in touch?" I asked and she kissed me one last time.

I watched her go and then a little while later finally found the will to get up.

I took a quick shower and was glad for once that I had my clothes laid out because as a result, I was able to quickly slip into a jacket and pressed pants and was on my way.

I received her text and couldn't help my smile at the update that she had arrived in class. She then sent me a picture and afterwards asked if this was too much. I didn't have a chance to reply then as I arrived cutting it quite close with my own class time. However, just before I began, I received one more picture from her and was slightly startled when I saw that it was me flipping through the notes on my laptop in my current attire. I lifted my gaze and the moment my eyes met her roommate's, I watched as she quickly lowered her head. I did the same to hide my smile, shaking my head at them both.

"Meredith says you look good," she had written, and I couldn't understand how such a simple statement, and one that I had heard so many times in the past, could come from her and mean so much to me.

It kept me in a great mood through the rest of class, and from time to time I couldn't help but stare at her friend. It was the closest thing I had to Pamela herself and I couldn't help it. But then when I realized that it was starting to gain attention as some of the students followed my gaze to hers, I focused all my attention then on the lecture.

Afterwards I tried my best to ignore Meredith, but she came over to me and I couldn't believe the excitement I felt at seeing her. Prior to now I'd never really had any feelings whatsoever concerning her, but now I truly took note, and even liked her. She was all smiles as she came to me, and I couldn't tell if it was because of what her roommate had told her about us or something else. I soon found out that the case was both.

"I've been accepted into your company, sir, for my internship, and I am so excited to begin." At this I smiled.

"You earned it. I hope you learn as much as you want to."

"I hope so too," she said. "Also, I wanted to ask if you came there regularly? I mean if you taught there as you do here?"

I shook my head. "Rarely, but there are a few programs in the works. Hopefully you'll be able to participate in them."

"Alright," she said and with her extremely bright expression I couldn't help but be equally as pleased. Afterwards I was finally able to reply to Pam's messages and I did so on my way to the office. Just as I arrived, I was forced to stop in my reception when I realized that she was there waiting.

I looked at Oscar to see his troubled and confused gaze at her presence, and I had no doubt she had somehow talked her way in against all odds.

"Sir," he began but I stopped him. "It's alright, you can let her in from now on and allow her to wait in my office."

I turned to see the mesmerizing smile on Pam's face and shaking my head, amused, and walked in. I had barely shut the door behind me when she was on me, her arms going around my shoulder. She kissed me deeply, her tongue sliding in with abandon as she sucked fervently on my lips.

At first, I was determined to cut it short but then as her taste once again overwhelmed me, I completely gave in and allowed her to have her way with me. In the end I was the one who chased her as she broke the kiss and loved the soft sound of her laughter as it filled the room.

She'd changed into a light blue sweater and pulled her

hair up. It made her look angelic, and my lips couldn't help but cover hers once again.

"Do you have another class?" I asked and she nodded.

"I do," she replied. "I would have skipped it, but I suspect that we'll be having a test, so I have to attend."

"And afterwards?"

"Work," she said. "And that's where I'll be until late tonight."

I nodded and could do nothing but watch her. I felt so much joy and contentment that for a moment it scared me. It all felt like a bubble that I expected to burst, and I wondered why. Perhaps it was because it was too good to be true or because I suspected that deep down I still had my reservations towards her and her family.

"What?" she asked, the tip of her nose stroking mine, and I shook my head.

"Nothing." I knew then what to do to dispel all my fears, so I slipped my hands into her hair and kissed her once again. Just then there was a knock on the door, and she immediately pulled away from me. I was reluctant to let her go but eventually had to. I couldn't take my eyes away from her as she adjusted her clothes and then came over to clean the lipstick off my lips.

"Okay, ready," she said, and I nodded.

"You're so quiet," she said, and I smiled.

"I'm used to being like that."

"That's true," she said.

"Come in," I said, and the door was pushed open. It was Oscar, but this time around he had someone behind him. I looked and found that it was Hannah.

She had a smile on her face but then the moment she noticed Pamela in the room I could see it slightly falter.

Oscar walked away then leaving the three of us together

and a heavy silence followed. And then as I expected Pamela reached out with a smile on her face. I watched as she waved and saw how Hannah not knowing what to make of her presence waved slowly back.

"You're here again," she said and then turned to me. "None of his students are seen with him this much."

"She's not my student," I said and both women turned to me.

The message was clear, and I could see Pamela look away to hide her smile.

"I guess you guys have rekindled your friendship from back then."

"Yeah," Pamela said. "He's suddenly been so nice. Anyway, I just stopped by to relay some information, but I'll be on my way now. Bye Gideon she said and picked up her purse.

"Bye Pam," I replied and try as I might, found myself unable to take my eyes away from her until she left the office.

After the door shut, I turned to Hannah then walked around my desk.

"What do you need?" I asked.

"Wow," she said. "That's a bit impolite."

I looked at her with an eyebrow raised.

"I know, I know, she said. "You're curt and that's your style but you weren't that way to her just now. Come to think of it, you weren't how you were just now to her when she visited your home the other night."

I didn't know what to say to this and neither did I care to respond to it, so I turned my desktop back on.

"Hannah," I groaned, and she held her hands up. "I know... I know, you don't indulge in idle talk. I'm here because I thought we could have lunch together. I'm craving a wrap from that Mexican place I told you about, so I was wondering if we could go together? My treat."

I considered this and refused because frankly, I didn't think I was in the mood.

"No, thank you," I said to her, "I'll pass. I have a lot of work to catch up on."

I didn't miss the hurt on her face.

I didn't want to coddle her because I saw nothing wrong with being unavailable to do as she wanted, even though we were friends, so my hope was that she would take it cordially. She didn't.

"There's something going on between you and her isn't there?" she asked. At this my gaze lifted to hers, the displeasure apparent on her face.

She continued. "It's against the rules," she said. "It could affect her, and you."

"Well, no one knows about it," I replied. "Except me and her and now you."

She smiled, the expression incredulous. "The walls have ears and eyes. You both could get caught."

"So, I shouldn't live my life?" I asked.

"Do you care about her?" she asked, and I refused to respond to her. So, she went on. "Because it doesn't seem like you do. I mean if you do then why would you allow something that could hurt her? And if she cared about you why-"

"Hannah," I stepped in. "Stop."

Her mouth snapped shut.

"You know how I feel about people commenting on my personal life. You're my friend, but please don't overstep your bounds."

She smiled bitterly. "Wow, so all that the other night was just for show? You were rejecting her weren't you, and you needed me for whatever reason to show that you were. So why did you suddenly accept her?"

"As you noted it is in our best interest to keep things as private as possible so the less you know the better."

She straightened then, squaring her shoulders and gave me another bright smile that didn't reach her eyes.

"Fine then. I guess... congratulations are in order, friend."

And with this she turned around and went on her way.

31

PAMELA

I didn't think it was possible for me to be happier than I am, but it turned out I was wrong. I was exhausted, the night wearing on quite slowly but then a little commotion began suddenly behind me. I looked to see what it was and was pointed towards the source of excitement.

"He came back," Sarah said, and my heart jumped into my throat.

Like the other girls, I turned and watched as the most handsome man I had ever laid eyes on strolled into the bistro and took his seat in the same hidden corner that he sat in the last time.

"You said you knew him, didn't you?" Angela came up to me. "Do you know why he came back?"

I lifted my gaze, a smile curving my lips

"Who knows?" I said and returned my gaze to the register. I was so excited that I could barely concentrate on what I had been doing. I didn't bother trying to catch his gaze because I was convinced that he wouldn't be trying to do the same either, at least not yet. Sarah went over since it was her section, and I made a note to inform him the next time around to sit in mine, although I was certain he always chose this seat because of the obscurity.

I kept working, acting as oblivious as possible even though every strand of hair on my body had acknowledged his presence and was aching to be in it.

Just then Sarah came up to me, and I was slightly startled at her sudden appearance.

She looked very far from happy, almost scowling at me, and truly it took little to guess what the reason for this was. "So, you truly do know him," she said, and my gaze went across the room. Finally, it met with his and my heart jumped into my throat. I cleared it and tried to speak. "Yeah, I do," I said, and she glared at me.

"He wants you. You can take care of my station till he leaves, and I'll take care of yours.

I was a bit surprised at the proposition, but I had no qualms with it, so I quickly went over. I saw as he watched the sway of my hips as I approached his gaze moving up my body and my cheeks couldn't help from burning.

"Stop," I said the moment I arrived, and his beautiful eyes connected with mine.

"Stop what?" he asked calmly, collectedly and the quiet of his voice turned me on so much that what I wanted most was for him to take me immediately. I however kept this reaction tamed and brought out my notepad.

"That's a nice apron," he told me, and I nodded my head absentmindedly.

"Maybe you should wear it and nothing else while I fuck you someday."

His voice was incredibly low, as not to be overheard by anyone but I felt such alarm that I had to turn around to check that no one else was behind us. There wasn't. As the bistro was finally winding down for the night.

"Gideon," I called, my eyes flashing wide, and loved the smile I saw on his face. It made me want to look back to see if anyone was seeing this apart from me. For some reason I wanted to protect the fact that I could see this side of him unlike everyone else. It was hard earned and for that I wanted to keep it solely mine. Him as solely mine.

I saw the other girls staring and grew curious.

"What did you tell Sarah to get her to let me take over her station and basically give you up?" I asked.

He took a sip of the glass of water that had been served. "I did her a favor the last time, by writing down a phone number. She owed me one."

At this I smiled. "You know she wanted your actual phone number, right?"

"Of course, I know," he said, as he set his glass down and ran his hand through his hair. I couldn't breathe as I watched the strands fall so fluidly down his temples framing his face in the most sensual way. My gaze lowered then to look at his brown corduroy jacket, the white shirt underneath and his slacks. He looked so simple and so dashing that once again I truly wondered how the hell it was possible that he wanted me. I started to take my seat then but quickly remembered where I was and rose back up. He was amused.

"You're getting off soon, right?"

"Yeah." I replied.

"Can you get off early?"

I once again glanced back at the girls behind me.

"Absolutely not. I'll be reported for sure since they know why."

"You guys aren't close?"

I shrugged. "It's not as easy to make friends and a true connection with people in the real world."

"I hear you," he said, and I finally remembered my notepad.

"So, what would you like?"

"Whatever's light. I plan to make you dinner at home anyway."

My heart stopped in my chest at the word, home. And to hide my delight, I lowered my gaze, my teeth biting my lips.

"Alright," I said, reminding myself once again that I was spending too much time in this one spot. "I recommend the Antipasto salad. Do you like sweet drinks? Or perhaps something with alcohol? But you'll be driving soon. Hm..."

"Just water is fine," he said, and I nodded, pleased.

"Has James contacted you today?" he asked, and I briefly froze.

My heart began to pound as I once again remembered the previous night. I could barely meet his eyes as the embarrassment from it all returned to hang as a cloud over my head

"No," I cleared my throat. At his silence I was forced to meet his gaze.

"If he does, let me know," he said. "Immediately."

"Okay," I nodded, and he looked away, but I could very clearly see the annoyance he still had in his eyes.

"I'll be back soon with your order," I told him, and he gave a nod. I could feel his eyes on my back as he watched me go and once again couldn't help but feel that dreadful feeling that perhaps I wasn't up to par with him. The guy was a billionaire for Pete's sake, and I was a lost college student with a psychotic ex.

I watched him as I worked silently, wondering if perhaps soon and once again he would wake up to realize that I was just not good enough for him.

With a sigh, I tried to keep my focus on my work especially as new customers came in and I was forced to attend to them. Soon enough his order was ready, so I took it to him.

"Thank you," he said, setting his phone aside and started to dig in.

"Looks good," he said, and I lingered. He took a bite and then raised his gaze to look at me, and somehow or perhaps it was clearly written on my face.

"What is it?" he asks.

I turned to give one last look at our audience all over the restaurant and had to voice my concerns.

"Relationships like ours... are not allowed." I began. "Last night... I didn't care. I wanted you at every cost."

"And now you don't?" he asked.

At first, I was startled by this, but when I saw the flicker of amusement in his eyes, it brought out a smile.

"I mean... we have to be careful. I would feel absolutely terrible if your job was put in jeopardy because of me."

He set his fork down and studied me. "Is that what you're concerned about?"

"Of course," I replied. "You don't have to teach, and the fact that you do just goes to show how much you enjoy it. You can't lose it. I wouldn't want you to."

"You're the one I'm more concerned about," he said. "Because as you mentioned I don't really need this job as it's more like a hobby than anything else. So yes, I have it in mind to be as careful as possible but solely for your sake."

"Alright," I said, my heart warmed. "So perhaps I shouldn't come to your office any longer. After all, I'm not even in your department so it's bound to raise questions."

"No," he immediately refused. "You can come as much as you want. We're family friends and have known each other for years. If anyone isn't satisfied with this explanation, then they can assume however they want. As long as they have no evidence and I will ensure not to give them any, then they have no solid ground to stand on."

This worried me as my mind once again went to James. No one else might have any evidence but he was now, or at the very least highly suspicious and the same went for his colleague Hannah.

It was as though he could read my mind because he immediately spoke to console me.

"Don't worry about them," he told me. "I will keep my eyes on the two of them. Just always make sure you contact me immediately if he does reach out to you and I want to hear and know everything he says."

"Alright," I replied and with the confidence in his tone I could once again feel completely assured and safe. I wanted once again to lean down to kiss him but at his caution about giving anyone any evidence, I managed to hold myself back. But I wanted to touch him by any means possible anyway, so I pushed a napkin to him and in the process ensured that my finger brushed against his hand. His gaze went to it and then back to my eyes and the heavy look of affection he gave me made my knees instantly go weak. I had to leave then before I did something truly stupid. So, with a deep shuddering sigh I went on my way.

Soon, the shift came to an end, and I could barely contain my excitement which was apparent to the other girls.

"You're making us too jealous and upset," they said as we changed, and I felt worried.

"We're family friends," I told them. "Not dating."

"What?" they asked. "We thought-"

I shook my head. "We're just close."

"I don't believe that," Sarah said. "I saw the puppy eyes

you both were giving each other. That is not how mere family friends look at each other."

"He has a girlfriend," I said. "A professor in his department. So how could I be dating him?'

"Oh," Sarah said but her countenance seemed to sink even more.

"How disappointing," she said, and it took everything in me to hide my pleasure.

I grabbed my bag and was soon on my way, wondering if he had left or if he was outside waiting for me. Just as I exited the restaurant, a call came to my phone that made me stop dead in my tracks. I looked at it for the longest time wondering whether to respond. I waited too long to decide, and the call disconnected. I couldn't help but look around the parking lot startled. I couldn't see him or his car. He was nowhere in sight, and it sent chills running down my spine.

His call came again and this time I didn't waste any time in responding to him, more than eager to find out what he wanted.

I answered, my heart in my throat.

At first, I was silent unwilling to say a word and then his laugh came through the receiver dry and cruel.

"I saw you both," he said. "So, you're an item?"

Breathing became difficult and my tone came out much smaller than I would have liked.

"What are you talking about?"

"Don't act dumb with me Pam," he said. "You are dumb but just... don't. Dating a professor is against the rules, so I'm sure you're well aware of the risks involved with you both fucking around campus. He doesn't have much to lose in case you don't know, he doesn't need that job, but you on the other hand..." he laughs.

"James," I called.

"Shut up," he said. "Shut up and just listen. You used me... you probably wanted to get his attention and dragged me into your sick game to make him jealous, didn't you?"

I was so struck by his statement that for the longest time I didn't know what to say.

"James, that's not the case."

He let me speak this time around, much to my surprise.

"So, what is the case then?" he asked.

"He's a family friend of mine. I've known him for years."

"Ah, so it's completely normal for a family friend to wait for you till the end of your shift and then attack your ex?"

"You tried to force yourself on me James," I pointed out, getting aggravated. "Why are you acting like a victim when you're the one that stepped out of line?"

"If you didn't want me to touch you then why the fuck did you contact me in the first place?" he asked.

To be friends, I wanted to say, but was certain that this would aggravate him even further, so I simply kept my mouth shut. And if I said that it was because I missed him then this was for sure to sound patronizing.

"James, let's just let this go and move on. I'm sorry about what happened but you were in the wrong too, so let's-"

"I'm not letting anything go. I need to be compensated in some way for my troubles and a broken nose, don't I? I couldn't even attend my interview because I looked so busted."

I didn't know what to say.

"Now you have two options, either I sue him and his company... he's a billionaire, isn't he? No doubt he has quite a few dollars lying around that I sure do need."

My heart instantly sank at his words, but I tried my best to keep my calm. "Would you like that?" he asked. "I promise you it's better than the second option. Or maybe I'll just request both, I mean why not?"

I tried to swallow past the lump forming in my throat, but it wouldn't go down. But eventually I was able to speak.

"What do you want?"

"You," he said. "I'm not naive enough to think that you'd look away from a billionaire for me. You are dumb but not to that extent." He laughed at the insult, and I tried to ignore it so I wouldn't lose control of my emotions. "Anyway, as I said, I need to be compensated for my time and I can't help but recall how much of a great lay you were. I want that again and I'm going to get it, that's if you want the two of you to remain a secret."

I could feel tears stinging my eyes however before I could respond the phone was suddenly snatched out of my hands.

I was so startled that my heart nearly flew out of my chest. My hand went to it as I tried to understand what was going on, and it was then that I saw who had snatched the phone away from me. It was Gideon. I immediately dove for him, worried that he wouldn't say something to further aggravate James but with one hand stretched outward he held me at bay.

"Gideon!" I called, but the stern look in his eyes made my lips snap shut.

"You know who I am don't you?" he says. "If you do, then you should know what I'm capable of. Contact her one more time and I'm promising you that your whole life will turn to ruins overnight. You know I can and will do this, and I never have to leave my desk for even a second. Be very careful."

After this he pulled the phone away from his ear and the call was disconnected. Then he stood still without moving as though trying to contain his anger.

I was so confused that for these few moments I too couldn't speak.

All I could do was stare at him, wondering what had happened and how he had known that James was the one calling. Perhaps it had been my face? He must have seen how horrified my expression was and instantly known. My head spun then, and not till I felt his presence and heard his voice did I look back up.

"Let's go home," he said and handed the phone over to me. And then without another word he started to head in the direction of his car.

I started to go to mine but then he stopped and looked at me.

"I'll drive you," he said. "I'll get someone to bring your car over before the morning."

I truly needed more than anything to be alone tonight, so that I could sort out my concerns and fears, however I couldn't say no to him, so I followed, just as he had asked.

32

GIDEON

It was an extremely quiet ride back home.

And through it all I could almost feel her withdrawal. I didn't know if it was because she had been so startled by the entire exchange, or if it solely had to do with me. I wasn't used to not getting the answers I needed since I could infiltrate anywhere that I needed to, but this time around it frustrated me that there was no way to guess what she was thinking in her mind.

I was furious that she could be so vulnerable, and that someone so detestable had once been in her life. It made me immensely unhappy. This was unreasonable, I was aware I couldn't blame her, and now he was the pebble in our shoe, and I wanted to crush him to pieces.

I didn't bother looking at her but from time to time, I could feel her gaze turning to me and then looking away. I wanted to comfort and console her, but I didn't know if I could hide my anger yet, so I took the time of the drive to calm down.

When we arrived at my apartment's garage, I turned the engine off but couldn't quite bring myself to just get out of the car without saying a word to her. It would no doubt send the message that I was annoyed with her and that was the last thing I wanted. So, I turned, and thankfully the underground was lit enough for me to clearly see her face.

It was void of expression, and this didn't make me happy when I knew that she was feeling so much more but trying her best to hide it.

It made me realize in this vulnerable state, I had made her feel anything but safe, and once again remorse overwhelmed me.

So, for once I decided to truly open my heart to her, and to share what I truly felt.

"I'm terrible at this," I said, and for the first few seconds she remained unresponsive. But then slowly, she turned to face me. She still didn't meet my gaze. She was far from timid as a person, so I understood her caution and hesitation and perhaps even shock at how the entire situation was developing. It was unpleasant and aggravating, and I didn't expect that she wouldn't feel equally as exasperated at it.

"Terrible at what?" she asked, her tone much lower than usual.

"Explaining myself... and why I'm reacting so strongly."

She smiled, and it surprised me. And this time around, our gazes met.

"What is it?" I asked and could feel the ice thawing in my heart as she tried but failed to control her smile.

"You're cute," she said, and at this I scowled.

"What?"

"Which do you think would make me feel better?" she asked. "That you remained seemingly unaffected, or that you lost your shit?"

I truly wasn't sure of the answer that she wanted, so I decided to say what I thought was best.

"Neither?"

She paused, her gaze lifting to the car's ceiling. "Hm..."

"Am I wrong?" I asked, and her smile this time around was more unrestrained.

"Not exactly. I just think the options I gave you were too narrow."

"What do you mean?" I asked.

"I prefer that you overreact. It won't exactly make me happy because I hate the matter concerning me is the reason why you're getting so upset, but... I love seeing how affected you are by me. I just... "

Her gaze lowered once again, and I looked to see that she was twiddling with her fingers. This was one habit that I could read clearly with her. She was holding back something that she truly wanted to say from the depths of her heart but couldn't.

So, I moved a bit closer to her and placed my hand softly on her shoulder. Gently she turned to me. "Don't hold back," I told her, hoping with these words she would understand what even I didn't know if I could freely express. "Let's try."

She smiled again, eyes slightly watering. "This all still feels like a trial to me, and I guess I just feel kind of helpless. I'm ready to do everything possible to convince you this is right... that *we* are right but with this whole situation springing up from out of the blue... it just... it just makes me feel as though nothing is in my control."

At her words I sighed, completely understanding her dilemma but then I leaned back into the chair because I wasn't exactly certain of how to console her.

A way however soon occurred to me. *The truth.*

"I don't want you to walk on eggshells around me, Pam," I told her. "When I conceded for us to try, it wasn't because I doubted my feelings for you or the extent of my desire to have you as solely mine. It's because as I told you, I want to make sure you get the best of me and I can give you all you deserve and more. With this... bastard right now, I'm not angry at you. I'm the one I'm upset at because I took so long to pay attention enough to what we have, to know to give in. If I hadn't then he wouldn't have even come into the picture."

She listened quietly, and then she turned to face me. "What do you mean by '*if you hadn't waited so long to give in then he wouldn't have been in the picture?*'"

At this I was slightly alarmed, but I couldn't quite pinpoint where I had gone wrong.

She explained. "You sound like you know he was a rebound. Well, at least a rebound in consideration."

I most definitely knew that, but then I wasn't exactly supposed to.

So, I simply diverted her attention.

"Was he? A rebound?" I asked. "How did you two get in contact again?"

At this she smiled and looked away shyly. "Before we started dating, we used to actually be quite close friends, so I guess I thought that if... I missed that connection, and it was something I wanted to have with you. I guess... after we parted ways... he came to mind, and I considered rekindling it."

I nodded in complete understanding, but then there was something else that I was curious about.

"Can I ask why you rejected him? Initially."

At this, tears pooled in her eyes again as she thought and then she turned to me. I cradled the side of her face, worried about her reaction.

"Because he's not you," she replied. "And I think that was

why I rejected him the first time we dated. I was bound to do that with everyone because they were not you. I hadn't seen you in so long but when I dated someone or even felt the mildest attraction to them, you would pop up in my mind. And I would wonder how you were and once again why we had drifted so far apart. At the time I didn't even think that it was possible for us to interact so intimately as we do now... but... you've always owned my-"

She stopped then, hesitating, and I didn't need to hear all the words to know exactly what she had been intending to say. A part of me was glad that she couldn't complete it because although I felt just as strongly as she did, I didn't think that I was ready to completely give myself over the way that I wanted to. I pulled her into my arms for an embrace trying somehow to let her know that I felt the same way, without yet proclaiming it with words.

I did however have one plea for her.

"Be patient with me," I said. "Please. I don't want to lose you, but there are some things I have to work on. So please... be patient with me. I want you to know that no matter what other curveballs are thrown in our way, you're in my heart. You've always been, and you forever will. So never doubt your importance to me."

I pulled away then to look into her beautiful eyes and caught the tear that slipped through a corner.

"Okay," she whispered, and I kissed her. Afterwards, we walked hand in hand as we headed up and back to the apartment.

33

PAMELA

I was in charge of dinner, even though he had promised that he would handle it.

I wanted to make him some fried rice because it had always been his favorite. In our younger years I had been the beneficiary of his brilliance in making it, but with how he had handled things between us and reassured me, I needed to do something to express just how much I adored him otherwise I was going to blurt it out. There was simply no other way I could keep this much emotion caged inside of me.

I tried to convince him to head upstairs to take a shower so that I could look at some recipes, and have the space to fumble around a bit, however he only disappeared for a moment to get some wine and then he returned to the island counter. He took his seat, poured himself a glass and then gave all his attention to me. It was what I had always wanted but now I couldn't help but wish that it wasn't the case.

"Do you need any help?" he asked, and I glanced back from my rummage through the refrigerator.

"I don't think you have any onions."

"I do," he said and rose to his feet. Then he came over to me and when I tried to get out of the way, he instead remained behind me and reached in. I couldn't breathe, but I couldn't get enough of his scent.

"It's diced already," he said, and retrieved the little jar that I had missed.

He handed it over and for the next few seconds after, all I could do was stare into his eyes, my blood roaring in my ears.

"Here," he tried to hand it to me once again and only then did I come back to my senses. Shaking his head, he moved away, amused, and I felt vindictive.

"You're a distraction," I told him as I took the onions to the stove. "If you keep being this way, I might mess this up."

"Being what way?" he asked, and although I knew he wasn't fishing for compliments because he simply wasn't the kind, I also didn't want to outrightly spell out to him the entrancing effect that he had on me.

"You know what," I said just as I was about to turn the stove off. "Let's go to bed. We can eat after."

"You're becoming a nymphomaniac," he said calmly as he lowered his gaze to peruse his phone.

My mouth fell open. "You're the cause of it!" I accused, and he smiled.

"I'll catch up on some work then," he said. "Since you're so uncomfortable with me watching you."

"I'm not uncom-"

"Carry on with your cooking," he interrupted with a drawl. "I'm starving."

Defeated, I sighed and faced my challenge.

After pouring some olive oil in the pan. I put the onions

in and then began to stir while sneaking glances at him from time to time.

I noted his concentration, which as the minutes passed by became quite intense which made me truly wonder about the caliber of man I was with. The world said that he was formidable in his field, but as I all but ceased to exist the moment he chose to focus on his phone, I couldn't help but wonder if I wasn't as in awe of him as I should be. I already pretty much admired him, but I didn't know or understand so much about his professional achievements.

As I reached for the can of tomato paste, I asked. "Are you really one of the best hackers in the world?"

At the question he smiled, which made me understand that his attention was still very much on me and in the room.

"I'm not," he replied.

"Is there a list?" I asked.

"Yeah," he replied.

"And are you at the top of it?"

He lifted his gaze then to me, something akin to mischief dancing in his eyes.

"Sometimes."

"So, you are the best?"

At this he sighed and returned his gaze to his phone.

"I've never competed with the others. So how does anyone know who is truly the best? I don't even know who they are. If anything, it's immensely problematic that I have been this exposed."

My ears perked up in attention at his words.

"Really? So, you weren't always this well known?"

"Of course not," he replied. "I was... '*apprehended*' a few years ago. I think it was when I turned twenty-three. The authorities were mad, and the company was willing to do everything to ensure that I rotted in jail, but the government needed me more."

My mouth fell open once again. I was so fascinated that for a few moments I forgot that I was supposed to be working on our dinner.

"Really? What did you help them with?"

"Cyber security. Basically, they wanted to ensure that guys like me couldn't get into their system so what better way to achieve that than to use a thief to catch a thief?"

"Yeah," I said, a smile bubbling across my lips, and I realized that I was probably with a myth of a person.

"Did you guys have any breaches or catch anyone?" I asked and he nodded. "Quite a few but nothing too big. Mine was high profile and thus my name was thrown around a lot. But I can't complain, especially since that was when I met Michael."

"That's your current business partner, right?' I asked. "At Quarry?"

"Yeah," he replied. "He had tried to start something with cyber security for so long but had failed. But after he met me and after my tenure with the government was wrapping up, we talked and decided to partner up."

"Interesting..." I said as I resumed my stirring. "You're not much older than me but you seem to have done so much... lived several lives. I feel so bad about myself."

He looked at me. "First of all, I am much older than you, almost a decade, plus I didn't go to college, so I have at least five years of solely working on my skills."

"Exactly," I complained. "I should have started a long time ago... found what I wanted to do. Now I just feel lost."

At this and to my surprise, he rose to his feet and came to stand by my side.

I ran my gaze up his towered height, and felt the

sweetest warmth flood my heart at the affectionate way he was looking at me. I couldn't look away.

"Should have and could have... and would haves are not helpful in any way. Everyone has their own path."

My lips began to tremble then as a smile tried to break through, however he couldn't understand what was so amusing about what he had just said.

"What is it?" he asked.

"Shoulda, coulda, woulda..." I explained, and of course he had no idea what I was talking about.

"It's a saying from Sex and the City."

"What is that?" he asked, and my eyes slightly widened.

"You don't know the show?"

"No, I don't," he said, and I set the spoon down.

"Oh my God, there is something I know that you don't," I celebrated, and he shook his head. It made me laugh.

"Anyway," I said. "I understand what you're saying. Different paths and all but it's hard not to feel like I've failed so miserably."

"Take your mind off those ridiculous assessments. That's society and its nonsensical routes. Only focus on what you want to do... on the dream in your heart. And if possible, try to enjoy it. That was what I did. I didn't try to be the best hacker in the world. I just enjoyed the craft so much that I put everything I had into discovering as much about it as I could. The setbacks, the successes... all of it. And that was how I got to where I am today. It's never a straight path and there are no set standards."

His words made me feel better, but I wasn't yet ready to brush all my concerns under the carpet.

"I understand what you're saying... but I'm worried that I might never find my passion like you have. That I'll just continue to drift aimlessly and end up as nothing."

He frowned, and at this I was forced to pay more attention. To my surprise, his hand reached out and he had the tip of my nose in his grip.

"Ow," I complained softly.

"Can there be passion without a vehicle?" he asked, but I didn't understand the question.

"Never say you're nothing," he continued. "You're wonderful just as you are... existing even is enough."

"It's not," I laughed, so endeared by him that it was hard to breathe.

"It is," he argued. "But I understand you and your need to find something that you truly enjoy otherwise the days become mundane."

"Well, not exactly," I said, my arms going around his waist. "I mean not anymore. I mean... I have you now... temporarily perhaps."

He smiled and I couldn't look away. And then his hand came to my cheek stroking softly.

"If you're actively trying to find your passion, then it's impossible to drift away. Unless you're sitting down and waiting for it to find you?"

I shook my head.

"Exactly... so try different things... anything... examine your heart and how it responds and then you will know. Might take a little bit more time but the process of the discovery should be just as fun or even more."

I continued to stare at him, letting the words sink in and then I nodded. "Okay."

He kissed me on the forehead, and it caused butterflies to run amok in my stomach.

Afterwards, I was forced to let him go so he could return to his stool.

My attention returned to cooking, however he kept speaking as soon as he took his seat.

"One way to examine things is to go back to when we were younger... what did you like then?"

I smiled "You mean besides acting coy and pestering you?"

He laughed. "Yes."

I thoroughly considered this question. The truth was that I had thought about it a couple of times in the past but had never really been able to come up with anything, so I decided to ask him.

"Do you have any ideas? About what I could possibly have had an interest in?"

He stopped and thought about it. "You used to love to paint... and make these cute little doodles in your notebook... and just about everything."

I recalled this and was incredibly amused.

"Yeah," I said. "I still do it from time to time but..."

"But what?" he asked.

"They're pretty childish, aren't they?"

"Says who?" he asked, and I shrugged. "Do some research on it," he continued. "I'm sure if you explored it more, maybe you'd find you could really do something with it. Plus, why would you think it was childish? You used to love it didn't you?"

I moved to retrieve some sliced carrots from the fridge and thought about the conversations about this I had with my mom in the past. "Before I got into college, I considered taking art classes, you know, getting into website development and such because it just felt so creative. But she was against it. She wanted me to go a safer route."

At this he smiled and lifted his gaze to mine. "There are no safe routes, Pamela. The tried-and-true ones only appear safe because they've been the most journeyed. But there's absolutely nothing safe about them. You can fail just as hard with something you don't want as you can with something you do want so... why not just do what you want? For instance..."

He pulled out a bill from his wallet and I was intrigued.

"Can't you make art on this with your doodles? You can frame it afterwards and I'm certain you can sell it to someone who would appreciate it. And through it all you've explored your creative side and had fun doing something you would have done for free anyway. My point is I want to see you begin to express every side of you."

I stopped then, emotion nearly choking me at his words. He was making it so damn difficult for me to keep from blurting out to him just how much I loved him.

"I have college debt," I said, more amused than anything else at the paradox between hope and reality.

"Then get a job," he said and returned his attention to his phone. "No one chases their dreams for free anyway."

At this I laughed out loud and focused on including the rest of the vegetables, then I came over to him and lowered.

He set his phone down and gave me all his attention. "I would have expected that you'd offer to wave a card and make all my problems go away?"

"Never," he said. "You get too spoiled easily. You need to sweat and struggle a bit, plus..." he leaned in to stare into my eyes.

"You'd never accept that."

At this I smiled and couldn't hold myself back from touching him. I threw my arms around him for a hug.

"You're absolutely right," I whispered to him. "And I'll figure it out but I'm just so glad I can talk to you so productively about this. You have no idea."

He rubbed my back and then pressed a soft kiss to my cheeks. “Me too,” he said. “I’m glad that you can share your concerns with me in this way.”

We pulled away from the other, and then gazed into each other’s eyes. I watched his gaze lower to my lips as mine did to his, and in no time, we were once again latched most intimately to the other.

His arms went around my waist and at the warm solid grip around my slender body, I felt my heart fluttering within my chest. He slipped his tongue into my mouth, the disturbance and aggravations from earlier in the night long pushed to the back of our minds. In its place was bliss... and a soul deep contentment that I couldn’t quite believe existed. But then with him it was the natural order of things, and I was far from surprised.

He was perfect, I realized as goosebumps broke out across my skin at the soul's deep connection to the one I was beginning to suspect was my soulmate.

I would take all his suggestions from tonight under heavy consideration and ensure that I did my very best to become someone that he too could be proud of.

I kissed him even more deeply, my hands cradling his face, so grateful that the person that belonged to me was one that made me want to be the very best that I could.

I would never be able to tell just how long the kiss went on for, but what I was certain of was that if not for the burning smell permeating the room and alarming us, we might not have stopped. I was the first to smell it, and immediately I jumped away in panic.

“Oh my God!” I hurried over to the stove, and when I grabbed the pot’s handle came away with a burned hand.

“Pamela!” I heard his concerned shout and couldn’t help my amusement.

"I'm fine," I told him, and this time around I grabbed a napkin. After turning off the stove I lifted the lid of the smoke infused pot to survey the damage and had to turn away and hide my nose in my sleeve.

It began to clear as he came over to me. We both looked at the burned pot along with the burned ingredients.

I felt disappointed, but far from unhappy even as a part of my mind registered that I should have been. I watched him shake his head at the scene, with not even a trace of annoyance on his face. I couldn't help my smile.

He sighed and then faced me.

"I was really looking forward to this."

I instantly felt remorse. "I know... I'm sorry. I'll make it for you again."

"We don't have any more vegetables," he said. "That was the last bag, I'm certain."

"What?"

I turned around and jerked his refrigerator open in disbelief. A few minutes after rummaging through it, I realized that he was correct.

At this I truly felt dejected, but then he retrieved his phone and unlocked it.

"I'm starving," he said. "I'll ensure a new batch of ingredients are available tomorrow so send me a list when you can later on, and I'll get what you need."

I watched him wondering what this meant until I realized he was ordering something.

"You still don't like seafood, right?" he asked, and I nodded until I realized that he couldn't see me. "I'll order something for us. It'll be here in minutes. What do you feel like?"

Excited and relieved, I instantly replied. "Chinese? Or maybe pizza?"

"Let's get both," he said.

This made my gaze peruse down his body and note once again how every inch of it was made of lean muscle with no traces of fat to be found. I was petite but not toned by any means, and so my mouth once again began to water at the delectable sight that he made.

"I guess you can say that since you can eat whatever it is that you want," I said, and he smiled.

"Yeah," he responded. "Working out is the price I have decided to pay for getting to eat whatever I want. And it's not too hefty a price so I'm satisfied."

"Do you have a gym here?" I asked and he nodded.

"I have a room for it at the end of the hall. They have a communal gym for the building downstairs though but sometimes things get quite hectic, so I don't even bother going down there. I just use the treadmill in the room, lift some weights, and move on with my day."

"Well, I look forward to joining you at one of your sessions."

"You kind of have though, haven't you?" he asked and I didn't quite know what to say.

"What do you mean?"

"Running?" he replied. "Falling and spraining your arm which, I am certain, was somehow purposely orchestrated. Or am I wrong?"

I sighed, shaking my head. "Gideon, I do like you to a scary degree, but I don't think I could ever intentionally hurt myself for your benefit or just to get your attention. During that run I was hoping to run into you but falling and spraining my arm was not part of the plan."

His eyes narrowed at me. "Sure," he said, and I smacked him on the shoulder.

Afterwards he placed the order while I settled down by

his side and sipped on his glass of wine. I looked around at the apartment and was once again impressed by the decor.

"Is this your only apartment in the state?" I asked.

"Just a second," he looked up from his phone after placing the order. I shut my eyes as his hand lifted and then he was stroking my hair behind my ears.

"No," he replied. "I have one downtown. Paid for."

"Oh," I replied and found the courage to stroke his hair back away from his temple. "You've done really well Gideon," I told him earnestly. "I'm so proud of you."

"Thank you," he said and leaned forward to kiss me. The taste of the wine mixed with his essence was intoxicating to say the least, and as the kiss went on and on, I found that I was losing myself in him. So much so that I started to lift from the stool just so I could take things even deeper, my hands sliding around the back of his neck.

I heard his slight chuckle and it made me smile, but he didn't resist until I subconsciously decided that I was going to take this even further. I leaned away to pull the tail of my shirt over my head, and then flung the fabric aside.

Instantly he held me, his face going between my breasts. I loved the way he breathed me in as though he couldn't quite get enough and as his lips connected with my flushed skin, I couldn't hold back the moan that escaped me.

"Gideon," I breathed and in no time, he had jerked my bra down and closed his lips around a nipple.

I held the back of his head, knowing of no other way to contain the pleasure that was pulsing through me.

His lips returned to mine, and at the thorough way his tongue stroked mine I felt the strength begin to drain out of my body.

"Think we have enough time before our delivery

arrives?" I heard him ask, his breath warm and sweet in my mouth.

"I don't know," I cradled his face and pulled away to look into his eyes. And just as I expected, I found the glint of mischief sparkling in them. He looked so calm, but I could also feel the heat and excitement in those eyes. "You're the one who lives here."

At this he turned away to look down at his phone and checked the time.

"Let's wait," he said. "And talk."

I couldn't help but feel a slight disappointment, but I was glad for every moment spent with him, so I wasn't disappointed for too long.

34

GIDEON

I watched the current light in her eyes, a vast contrast from the gloom that had been in them just a little while earlier. And this made me consider whether to bring up the gnawing issue that I truly wanted to resolve with her. I was sure this would be the best time, as the farther away from bedtime the better in case it upset her.

Whatever it had been, I was sure it was vile because of the way the expression on her face had changed. All the life had seemed to go out of her as she had listened, and it had made me see red. I couldn't remember ever feeling so angry and furious and all in all it made me realize just how protective I was becoming of her. Or perhaps I had always been this way because I could recall times in the past when her own parents had scolded her for staying too long over at my house, or having the poorest scores known to man in math. She had always sought refuge behind me and it had felt right... to everyone.

I watched her, very aware there was probably a ton of worry and concern weighing her down, most of which she wasn't sharing with me, I realized that I could no longer hold back.

"What did he say to you?" I asked, choosing to go straight to the crux of the matter rather than try to beat around the bush.

She stopped then, the smile on her face faltering and my glass halfway to her lips. She lowered her gaze from mine and tried once again to work up another smile.

"His ego was bruised," was her response. "And he's trying to find a way to save face. He's just being silly... really."

I was very unhappy with her response and didn't bother hiding my displeasure from my face.

"Open up to me, Pam," I told her. "Under normal circumstances I would have given you much more space and time to do this, but... this is a dire case. I don't want you to be in danger or to be frightened in any way and on the phone with him tonight, that was exactly how you had looked, and I hated every bit of it. So, share this with me... please?"

At my words she lowered her gaze again in thought.

"It's just so embarrassing," she said, trying to manage a laugh but it was to no avail. Instead, what I saw was the moisture in her eyes and the pain that she was trying her hardest to keep away from me.

I pulled her into my arms so that her face could rest on my shoulder, and she could be exactly how she wanted without the up-close scrutiny.

Her arms tightened around me, and although with each passing moment I grew even more impatient, increasingly angered by his attack on her I forced myself to wait and to resolve things at her own pace.

"He said he would bring a lawsuit against your company," she said, her voice croaked and low. "For assault and battery."

I scoffed and didn't comment but pulled away so that she could be encouraged to say more.

She however didn't say anymore and a part of me knew that the story wasn't complete.

"Is there anything else?" I asked and could feel her body stiffen against mine.

She started to shake her head, refusing to say anything out loud and I was certain then that she was hiding something.

"Pam," I called and a little while after she replied.

"There isn't. But I do want to know what you think. I've known him for a little while and truly I'm surprised by this behavior he's exhibiting. He has never really been so brazen or evil and it makes me unable to figure out if he means what he's saying or if he's just bluffing. What do you think?"

I looked into her eyes and the true worry within is unmistakable.

"It doesn't matter if he means it or if he's just bluffing, Pam," I said, hoping that the weight of my words would relieve the one on her shoulders.

"I have access to the best lawyers in the world and they'll crush him down in seconds. Remember he is the one at fault here, not you or me. In short, if he takes things too far, I'll push for a criminal charge."

At my words, I didn't miss her slight shudder.

I didn't know how I could further assure her. All I could do was leave things to time. Perhaps as the situation unfolded or dissolved, she would be able to see either way that there was nothing to be worried about.

~

THE NEXT DAY as I got ready for class, I received a peculiar visitor.

We didn't interact much as we generally tried to avoid each other's paths. Our goals and values were the same, but our methods differed, and so more times than not, a clash was unavoidable. We had always been able to remedy it, this time though and at his unannounced visit to my office I knew that whatever the contention was would not be as easy to resolve.

"Your class is at eleven right?" Our Head of Department, Patrick Sabre, asked, and I nodded. I gestured to one of the chairs before my table and with a nod, he took his seat. He adjusted the glasses sitting high on his nose as he looked around before finally sending me a smile. "I think I've only been here once," he said. "Before the renovations. I'm glad to see that you've utilized the space to your liking."

"Mmm," I responded, watching as he kept perusing the room. He soon noticed my gaze on him, and his smile curved even wider.

"You're curious why I'm suddenly paying a visit today?"

"Shouldn't I be?" I asked, and the smile on his face slightly faltered. Then he sighed.

"Alright," he said and sat up. "I'll get straight to the point. We treasure you a lot here Gideon. The students especially are beyond ecstatic to have you as their professor, so you might not believe this but the last thing I want is for you to encounter any difficulties with the university. Their system is tedious and bureaucratic and honestly a waste of time, so I truly hope that you won't have to be entangled with it."

So much for getting to the point. "What exactly are you referring to?" I asked.

"We received a lawsuit today, served to my receptionist,"

he said, and my chest tightened. “It accused you of assault and of having a relationship with a student?”

A cold shiver ran down my spine at his words. And it made me realize that I truly hadn’t expected him to go through with his bluff because he should know better right? Everyone usually knew better than to come against me and my company however it was clear now that he was much dumber than I thought.

At this, I sighed. “He’s right about the assault accusation. Last night he attacked a student outside of a bistro where she worked. They were ex-lovers, so he tried to kiss her but when she rejected him, he grew violent. I sent him to the ground but apparently, he didn’t learn the lesson that he needed to.”

The man watched me. “And what of the second accusation? That you are in a relationship with the girl in question?”

I replied simply. “I attacked him because he was behaving like a predator, and as for the girl in question, I’ve known her since she was a child. Does that count as having a relationship with her? I didn’t protect her because I’m in a relationship with her but because I feel responsible for her. Plus, I would have done the same for any other student, so this idiot’s claims are simply just a way to distract from his offense.”

Patrick stared long and hard at me and then he smiled.

“We’ll launch an investigation into this,” he said and rose to his feet. He stopped however before he left and met my gaze. “You’re invaluable to this department Gideon, so I can’t have any nuisance causing us any unnecessary losses. I also hope that you’ll do your part in handling him. And-” He paused.

“And what?” I asked.

"Just in case there is any truth to his accusation of your involvement with the student, I also hope that you'd take care of that. If not to you, it could be detrimental to her if the facts of it were further investigated and proven."

"Noted," I replied and with a tap on the chair, he turned and went on his way, I watched him and felt incredibly calm. I went back to work but as the day wore on, I couldn't help but acknowledge the fact that I was fuming.

It was rare for me to feel this extent of annoyance, and when I did it was even more difficult for me to feel any restraint in venting out my revenge. I tried to calm down as I thought of Pamela because this time around, it wasn't just my wellbeing that was at stake. Hers was too, and thus I needed to exercise every bit of caution that I could.

35

PAMELA

At the sudden, vicious knock at the door, I couldn't help but be startled.

I was preparing lunch, a new salad recipe that Meredith had learned from Darryl and so I was right by the door when the rude intrusion came. I glared at it, aware that it wouldn't be Meredith or Darryl knocking in such a manner and neither would it be Gideon. It only left one person in suspicion and instantly I felt cold. The knock came again, and I considered ignoring it but I knew that it would do nothing but make me worried for the remainder of the day.

After drying my hands, I went over and just as I arrived heard the call.

"Pamela," he sang and pounded hard on the door once again. "I know you're home. You don't have any classes today."

I frowned and truly wondered how I had never known he could be this problematic. He sure had hidden this insane and almost psychopathic part of him incredibly well during our years together. It truly terrified me because it just went to show how much no one really knew anyone.

My mind went to Gideon.

With a sigh and refusing to cower, I unlocked the door and met him head on. I stood by it, and even though he eventually forced his way in, I held it wide open and folded my arms across my chest.

"What do you want?" I asked, and he smiled.

"Wow, so cold. You weren't this way just a few days ago."

He took in my stance by the door, and then lifted the envelope he had in hand to the air.

"I brought a present," he said. "Don't you want to see what's in it?"

"Leave," I told him, realizing that I didn't have to listen to him to find out why he had stopped by. He was going to leave the envelope behind anyway.

He smiled. "You're not even going to offer me a glass of water?" I pulled my phone out of my pocket then and began to dial the cops. Before I could dial 911, I felt a painful smack as his hand connected with mine. The phone flew out of my hand and across the room to the floor and my mouth fell open in shock and horror.

"James!"

"You're incredibly rude Pamela, do you know that?" he asked. "I truly can't believe I was ever attracted to you."

"So why don't you stop?" I yelled at him. "Why don't you forget I ever existed? Why waste your time and embarrass yourself like this?"

"Because you took me for a joke," he said, and I couldn't believe him.

"You're acting this way because your ego was bruised? Why don't you look inwards and examine why you're so fragile that you can't even take a simple rejection? Why lash out at me?"

The sick, amused look on his face made goosebumps break out across my skin.

"I'm going to finish you," he said. "The both of you. But as I said you know how to stop this right?"

He flung the envelope, and it flew across the floor. And then with one last vicious look at me he stalked out of the door. It was a long time after he left before I was able to get my legs to work again.

I shut the door and tried my best to ignore the envelope on the floor. I didn't want to deal with it, at least not yet, so I returned to the kitchen. Soon, my salad was ready. As I stared down at the prepared bowl, it was no surprise to me that I didn't have a shred of appetite. I sighed and looked across the room, my gaze going to the envelope. I knew then that I could no longer procrastinate looking at it. I went over to pick it up and settled on the couch.

With shaky hands I opened it and began to read. It was a long while later before I looked up and it was only because I could feel a key being slotted into the door. I was certain of who it was, so I didn't feel any alarm. Instead, I felt relief, so I waited as she fumbled for a few more seconds and then the door was pushed open.

"Hey," Meredith greeted as she set the bags she had in hand on the floor. "Did you know that a new bakery opened next to the library? I checked it out and their pastries are pretty neat. I got you a honey and sweet potato muffin. It looks amaz-"

She stopped then as she finally took a good look at me. How I must have looked because she was instantly alarmed.

"Oh my God, are you okay?" she hurried over to me, but

I didn't want to react, so I simply managed to work up a smile.

"Gideon was at class today, wasn't he?" I asked and she nodded, her warm hands cradling my cheeks. "He was. Why? What's the matter?"

I sighed then and shook my head, not wanting to concern her. Her gaze went to the papers in my hand, and she stretched out her hand. I placed them on her palm and finally found the strength to get up so that I could get some water.

After I did, I didn't quite feel like sitting down so I searched through the refrigerator for a lemon and rosemary. Afterwards I took my time in cleaning them and began to slice. I watched as she read quietly, and by the time she was done the glass was refilled with water and I was lifting it to my lips.

Our gazes met then.

"He's a fucking asshole."

"He is," I agreed. I didn't like the sad expression that came over her face.

"I'm so sorry," she said, and I frowned, perplexed.

"About what?"

"I was the one that suggested you contact him."

"And you weren't wrong," I said. "You did it out of concern. Plus, it's best now that I know what kind of person he truly is, otherwise maybe I truly would have gone back to him in the future. As you rightly pointed out, he has never really shown how insane he is, and we got along quite well."

She sighed and leaned against the couch, so I grabbed onto the bag of pastries she'd bought and brought them over. After settling down on the couch, she immediately took my glass as I began to rummage through it.

"Red bean bun with walnuts?"

"It sounds delicious, doesn't it?"

I nodded and pulled out another. "Baguette and condensed milk?"

"Yup," she said, and I considered it. But then I chose the bun instead.

After ripping the packet open, I tore it in half and handed one over to her.

We took our bites and for the few minutes that followed, wallowed in our thoughts.

"Did anything seem off about Gideon in class today?" I asked, and she shook her head.

"Nothing out of the norm, but now that I think about it, he was a bit more withdrawn than usual. He didn't interact as much and as soon as class was done, he walked away, saying he had some appointment. I didn't need to speak to him, so I wasn't concerned."

"I'm sure he received the papers too."

"Of course," she said.

"He's probably worried about it," I said, but she didn't agree.

"I don't think so."

I looked at her. "Why?"

"Though he did seem withdrawn it looked as though it was because he was annoyed by something, not that he was worried."

I watched her and knew what she was getting at. She explained anyway. "My point is that you might see him as just a professor because he is within this premises, but he is formidable in the real world. This is nothing. It's like an ant trying to attack a lion. It's amusing if anything."

"Like David and Goliath?" I said, and she immediately jumped to agree.

"Yes!" she exclaimed, and I shook my head.

"David won," I reminded her, and she sighed.

"Really?" she said dryly.

There is always that small chance of being taken unaware and defeated. I don't brush anything away or carelessly dismiss threats no matter how inconsequential they might seem.

"And this is your problem. You should learn to have faith in him, but then again this is the first major attack that you both are facing together as a couple, so I don't blame you for being worried. Maybe with time and depending on how well he's able to handle this, your faith in him will grow?"

"I hope so," I said, and she smiled. She then pulled me into a hug that I was eager to get out of due to how suffocating it was. But then we both stopped the struggle when my phone suddenly began to ring.

My chest tightened because I didn't need to look down to see who it was. I thought of whether I was ready to receive the call, but when I realized that if I didn't it would worry him, I tried my hardest to speak with a light tone.

"Hey," I said, and since he was already usually calm on the phone anyway, I didn't feel any alarm when his response was delayed. He eventually spoke and the calm of his tone soothed me. However, I still felt on guard just in case there were any surprises lurking.

"How are you?" he asked, and I got up to head over to the window, clutching the phone against my ear.

"I'm great," I replied, unable to keep the smile from coming to my face.

"We haven't communicated today," he said, and I understood now why he seemed somewhat withdrawn.

"I know," I replied and tried my best to explain. "I arrived home pretty late this morning and just went straight to bed. Thankfully I didn't have any classes, well I had one, but I skipped it. I just got up a few hours ago but then-"

I stopped.

"But what?" he asked.

"I got carried away," I told him, and turned just in time to see the surprised look on Meredith's face.

"You won't tell him?" she mouthed, and I shook my head.

"Let's get away for the evening," he said. "How does dinner downtown sound?"

It sounded amazing, but just as I began to even consider attending, I stopped myself. It was a difficult decision, but I couldn't help but feel immense concern for him now. Everyone was convinced that he could very well handle this but my relationship with him meant too much to me and so anything that could potentially jeopardize it was unacceptable to me.

And with this I found the strength to refuse, even though all I truly wanted was to be in his arms.

"No," I replied. "I think it's best for us to keep a low profile right now. Plus, I have a neglected essay that needs to be submitted next week. I'm going to use the chance to get started on it. I hate writing essays."

For a moment I thought I could hear his smile but at his next words mine faltered.

"Have you heard from James?" he asked outrightly and I froze. I thought about how to respond to this and then gave a look to Meredith. I didn't want to lie to him, but I truly didn't know how best to handle this question.

"Pamela?" he called, and I knew then that I could no longer hide this from him.

"I have," I replied.

"He called you?"

"No," I said. "He came to the apartment."

"You opened the door?" he asked, and my eyes tightened shut.

36

GIDEON

After the day I had, I wouldn't have thought it would be possible for me to get any angrier than I currently felt. But it turned out, I could.

I couldn't believe that despite all the racket he was causing, he still had the audacity to go to her house, and she let him in. In no time I arrived at her door and couldn't help but inspect the security of her building. It was absent, with her door the only barrier between her and the sick bastard that was currently troubling us.

With a sigh, I knocked on the door trying my hardest to be as calm as possible.

Finally, the lock clicked open, and the door was opened to reveal her beautiful face. For the first few seconds all I could do was stare at her. She was like a breath of fresh air seemingly more than enough for me to be sustained by, but then at the sheepish expression she wore I was reminded of her earlier crime in the day.

"Hi," she said and before I could step in, she slid her arms around my waist and captured me in an embrace.

I could tell what she was doing, and a part of me wanted

to pull her away and keep her at arm's length so she would take my admonitions seriously. But then I couldn't help but consider just how stressful and even downright dangerous the encounter had been. I was unhappy that I hadn't been here to help her but then I couldn't fully blame myself for it.

"Why didn't you call me?" I asked. "The moment he knocked on your door, why would you open it instead of calling me first?"

She hesitated and I didn't force her immediate response. I did try though to understand why she had done what she had and for a moment a terrifying thought struck me. I didn't want to ask it... it was the last thing I wanted to fall from my lips but then I didn't know what else to think till this had at least been cleared up.

"You don't still have any feelings for him, do you?" I asked and could feel her immediately stiffen in my arms. She pulled away from me, and my heart pounded in my chest. Thankfully she didn't go too far away and instead looked into my eyes.

"What?" she asked, and I immediately took the chance to explain myself.

"I can't figure out why else you would still let him in."

At this she sighed, and she pulled me along with her to the couch. Then she spoke softly.

"He told me that he had something that he wanted to give me."

"And you believed him?"

"It was true," she replied. "He did have something to give me, and I couldn't not take it because it had to do with you. I needed to see how he was losing his mind and trying to attack you."

I looked at her and understood but still it couldn't drive away my annoyance.

"Pamela, you need to protect yourself first and I will do the rest. You need to stay away from him and don't let him into your space. You were alone at that time, weren't you? And yet you just let him come into your house?"

Her lips parted then to explain but then she shut them. I watched her and waited, needing to hear exactly what she had to say and refusing to let this be brushed under the rug.

She sighed. "I guess a part of me still thinks that he won't really harm me. Physically I mean."

I looked at her and could no longer stand to be there, so I got to my feet.

"I'll see you tomorrow," I said and made to leave but she stopped me.

"I'm sorry," she said. "I really am. I'll do better."

I still wanted to leave, but I could no longer bear to because no doubt she would be even more worried that I was unhappy with her.

"Okay," I said and brushed her hair behind her ears. "And I think you're right. I think we should keep a low profile for now until I resolve this but make sure to keep in touch and contact me."

I didn't wait for her response and started to go on my way once again, but she stopped me.

"We're keeping a low profile right now, aren't we?" she asked. "I mean, we don't have to be apart, just reduce our public meetups… for the time being."

I considered her request and couldn't bring myself to refuse it because the truth was I had thought and worried about her all day, and until I was able to convince my brain and heart that she was fine, I doubted my ability to get the rest I needed for the day. So, a little while longer with her I figured wouldn't hurt, and perhaps even being in her presence would help me calm down.

"Have you had dinner?" she asked, and I shook my head.

"Perfect, I can finally make you something and not burn the house down."

I smiled. "Is your roommate around?"

"Meredith? Yeah, she is but she's been banished to her room."

I smiled. "She doesn't have to be. Her company is fine. I'm the guest."

"No," she shook her head. "She's glad to give us some privacy and she has a lot of work to catch up on anyway. Plus, we only have to be here until I'm done with cooking. We can head to my room afterwards."

She made a face and then her eyes lowered.

"What is it?" I asked as I noted the flush on her cheeks.

"This must feel pretty weird to you right? And far from elegant. You have to eat in a shared kitchen and then scurry away to your college girlfr-" she stopped then, and without a word turned around to head to the kitchen.

I shook my head at her, very aware of what she had been about to say and understanding why she had stopped herself and scampered away. Sure, we had made the consensual decision to try together the previous night but no official titles as of yet, had been given out and no doubt she was cautious about jumping the gun.

I wanted to tell her that she was indeed my girlfriend, but I didn't know how to bring up such an assumptive conversation, so I decided to let time fix what it needed to with that.

I simply watched as she headed to the kitchen, the shirt she had on riding high on her ass and hips. I couldn't stop looking at the flattering shape of both as she went around the counter until unfortunately, they disappeared out of sight.

She got to work while I went back to mine, as there were quite a number of emails that I had ignored at work from the company and needed to review and send responses to before the following morning. From time to time, I looked up at the clatter of pans and the noise of the knife on the board as she prepared our dinner. Our gazes met quite often, and then she would smile, her eyes lowering in a blush.

Suddenly though I received a call from my lawyer Andrew McMillan, and I didn't want to take it in her presence so that I could ask all the questions that I needed answers to. So, I rose to my feet.

"I'll take this outside," I said but she stopped me.

"It's cold. Why don't you take it in my room if you need privacy?"

"Alright," I said.

"Down the hallway, the last bedroom on the right."

"Thanks," I said and was on my way.

"McMillan," I called, and the conversation began. I listened as he gave me updates of our investigations from the day and then I got into her bedroom.

It was warm, I had to admit and quite simple. There were very few knickknacks or pictures around and instead the space was filled with plants. The entire space was white with a beige finish, and it was quite similar to my minimalistic style I realized.

I sat on her bed as my eyes perused around.

"He has no case," McMillian said to me after he had gone through the faults in the lawsuit that had been served to me that morning. "Everything he is saying is based on speculation without any actual evidence. He'll be crushed in no time."

I had thought as much, and it was why I didn't understand why he was trying to start a battle that he was sure to lose.

"Look at the firm representing him," McMillian said. "Littler Mendelson. They're one of the top three major firms in the state."

I was surprised at this. "How can he manage to pay them?"

"Exactly, he can't," McMillian responded. "He probably approached them with your name and for sure any chance at being associated with or fighting and defeating you would most probably lead to great exposure. Thus, he was accepted. They probably promised him a hefty settlement with this, but my suspicion is that they want to weaken you as much as possible beforehand. Anyway, this will be handled quickly enough," he concluded. "So don't worry about it."

"Despite the odds not being in his favor, he's pretty insane to still be pursuing this isn't he?"

"Incredibly," he replied. "Or maybe not. Your company is worth over a billion and that makes you the light that every fly wants to buzz around. He's not stupid at all, just greedy. He found a thread and wants to follow it, hoping it leads him to some pot of gold. Don't worry, I'll make sure he follows it to the bottom of an empty well."

At this I laughed and rose to my feet. "You're only thirty-eight and yet you speak like you were born in a different century Andrew."

"Maybe? But I am obsessed with history," he said. "I've had to be in order to see ten steps ahead of the geezers."

I smiled. "You're great at what you do."

"Nothing compared to you," he said, and the call came to an end. I sighed then and once again looked around the room. Besides a pile of clothes draped across her chair everything else was organized but I couldn't help but notice she had no family mementos. No pictures of her parents but there was one on her windowsill of herself and Meredith at some carnival.

She looked happy and full of smiles, and I couldn't help but stare at it a bit longer.

Just then there was a knock on the door, so I turned around just as she came in.

"Hi," she said, and my gaze went down to the slightly oversized white t-shirt she had on. It looked like a man's, which made me wonder whose it was. I wished it was mine I realized, and for a moment considered pulling off the one I wore underneath and leaving it in her care.

It sounded crazy so I quickly pushed the thought aside and returned to my senses. The gnawing need however, for me to completely possess and protect her didn't go away. Instead and as I watched her head in, fragile and soft and oh so devastatingly beautiful, it only grew.

"You done with your call?" she asked and I nodded.

"Dinner's almost ready," she said. "I just came in to check up on you and to apologize. It's a bit messy."

At this I smiled and shook my head and then I began to head out of the bedroom. But then I stopped on the way and turned. Our gazes met and I couldn't hold back anymore.

"You're my girlfriend," I said to her. "And we're exclusive. That's our current status with each other."

For a moment, she seemed startled at the sudden declaration and then an electric joy came over her face.

"Umm," she said, her voice slightly trembling., "Sure. I mean... that's great. That's amazing. Thank you, I mean."

She was so flustered that I couldn't help but be amused. I lowered to press a soft kiss to her cheek. Leaving her bedroom, I went straight to the kitchen and when she arrived a few seconds later she was somewhat surprised to see me in it.

I looked at the chicken that was baking in the oven and was impressed.

"All seems good," I said.

"No fires," she pointed out and I smiled.

"Yet."

She whined at the gibe, her arm reaching out to strike mine, but I caught her wrist and pulled her to me. Her chest connected with mine and before I could stop myself my hand was digging into her hair to hold her head in place. Slanting my head I kissed her, needing the familiar and irresistible taste that was solely hers to once again flood me.

The effect was instant and her reception flattering as she completely gave in, crushing her body to mine and giving herself wholly to the kiss.

It was too easy to forget everything else beyond her in moments like this, so I discarded all my inhibitions and kissed her like I had wanted to since the start of the day. In the distance I heard a door creak open, but I didn't stop. Instead, I brought her with me to the counter till her back was pressed against it, and then I cradled her face in my hands to keep her head in place. My tongue stroked and licked along hers, the taste of her lips addictive and completely rendering me unaware of where we were. But that was until the sudden crash resounded across the apartment. We were startled apart and for the first few seconds after, all we could do was look at each other.

We looked towards the noise. We couldn't see anyone in the hall but the broken frame that had just dropped to the floor was clear in sight. She shook her head.

"We know it's you Meredith so why don't you just come out and say hello."

"Sorry about that," she apologized, and I brushed the courteousness away. Instead, I moved away from her and although unhappy at the lost contact, didn't want to appear too indecent before her friend. There was also the fact that I was her professor.

"Can I have some water?" I asked and Pamela nodded. Just then Meredith appeared and sent me a shy smile.

"Hi Professor Bach."

I returned the smile and gave a nod.

"Hello Miss Scott."

"You can call me Meredith," she said. "I mean here. I mean whenever you come here... when we're not in clas-" she stopped then and I didn't need to turn to see that her gaze had met Pamela's confused one.

"You can call me whatever you want," she said, turned around and scurried away.

I met Pamela's wide eyes and amused gaze and shared a little laugh with her.

"Wow," she said as she handed the bottle of water over. "Is this the effect you have on all your students?"

"She's just startled to see me here. It must be strange to see your professor at your home."

Pamela's arm went around my waist as I drank from the bottle. "What's strange is seeing someone so handsome in your home," she said. "Even I'm not totally used to it."

I screwed the cap back shut and lowered to kiss her, unable to hold myself back. It deepened once again and by the time we parted I was barely able to catch my breath.

"Fuck," I breathed as she pulled away giggling.

"You kiss me a lot," she said, her eyes sparkling and I was certain the same awed look was on my face.

"It's an ethereal experience," I said, and she blushed. I

started to lean down once again but her timer sounded, and she pulled away.

"I'm not burning a second meal before you even get to try it," she said, and I was forced then to let her go.

They didn't have an island counter in their home, so we had to eat in the living room. The dish of carbonara pasta, ham and chicken was spread out across the table and my mouth watered at the sight.

She handed me a plate which I took a forkful from, and through it all her gaze remained on me.

It was delicious, could have used a little bit more salt but I kept that opinion to myself.

"How is it?" she asked, and I gazed at her sitting on the floor.

"Wonderful," I replied, licking the corners of my lips and the beam of her smile shot straight through to my heart.

She took a bite herself and nodded. "Mmm, not bad."

Smiling, I took a sip of my wine and leaned comfortably into the chair.

"What do you usually watch when you eat?" she asked as she picked up the remote. "Or what sort of entertainment shows do you watch in general?"

"I don't usually watch shows or TV," I told her, and her head snapped back to mine, eyes widened.

I loved her expression and wanted her even closer to me, so I tapped the space by my side.

Excitedly she got up and came over to sit so close to me that she was almost on my lap. I encouraged it and lifted her leg fully to put it between mine. I instantly began to grow hard. My gaze remained on the fullness of her thigh and the creamy sheen of her skin, and I was immediately hungry for something else. I wished more than anything we were back in my apartment.

For the moment I settled for wiping the sauce stain at the corner of her lips while she continued with her questioning.

"You really don't watch any TV? What do you do for fun then?" I set my plate back on the table and put my attention on her, my hand rubbing up and down her exposed thigh. Her smile became knowing as she could no doubt feel the effect of what she was doing to me.

"Answer me," she said, her leg rubbing against my crotch. My breathing caught in my throat.

"I've always been quite occupied. And since I enjoy what I do, I've always just been eager to get as much of it done as I could."

"First of all, I envy you... and second, everyone still needs some form of escape," she said. "Like a hobby. What's yours?"

I lifted my gaze to think and watched as she lifted the glass of wine to her lips. Unable to resist the blood red liquid as it stained her lips I leaned forward and kissed her, the wine sliding into my mouth. She laughed, elated and then wiped the remaining stain off my lips. "I guess sports, occasionally I enjoy swimming, and I run a lot. Then I quite like visiting bars from time to time."

"Phew, you're human," she said, and I laughed.

"What kind of shows do you like anyway because I want to put one on now."

"I'll watch whatever you want," I told her.

She narrowed her gaze on me as she shifted, and it was incredibly obvious what she was doing.

"Stop," I said.

"I'm not doing anything," she said innocently, and my arm went around her. She tried to pull it off but when I refused to budge, she finally accepted it with a smile and focused on the meal and her show.

I watched it with her enjoying the moment as we both slowed down and just basked in each other's presence.

I thought of the looming troubles and tried my best to work out some way to keep us both safe until everything was completely resolved.

"Are you paying attention?' she asked, shaking me, and I returned my attention to the screen.

"Yeah," I replied.

"You don't want any more food?" she asked, and I shook my head. She set her plate down, took a sip of her wine and then gave the rest of it to me. Afterwards she set the glass down altogether and then she got up much to my disappointment. When she settled between my legs my heart jumped in excitement. I watched her, mesmerized as she pulled the blanket by the side over us and then began to pull her shorts down her legs. I was surprised, unsure of what she was doing until eventually her ass was against my crotch.

I kissed the side of her neck in encouragement, loving whatever she had intended to do. Her hand grabbed mine, and then she brought it to her abdomen before slowly slipping it into her underwear. I nearly groaned aloud. Now this was the kind of relaxation that I needed with her. I buried my face in her neck as I grabbed her mound and felt her body slightly tremble. Then my finger began to stroke the pulsing, swollen bud of her sex and she couldn't hold back her moan.

"We have to be quiet," she eventually managed to speak. "Otherwise, Meredith's going to kill me. But then again, she's been rude many times with Darryl in the past, so I guess I have at least one free pass to be naughty. "

I could barely process all she was saying, as what I wanted more than anything was to be completely sheathed in her heat.

I slid a finger into her, trying my best to keep my gaze on the screen just as she was and then began to slowly move it in and out of her. It was difficult not to chase the euphoric completion that I knew was available to the two of us, but it was also quite easy to just revel in the soft gasps that were escaping her lips.

I loved how she writhed as she tried to contain the pleasure that was taking control of her. I loved watching her eyes struggle to remain open and her tongue as it slipped out to lick across her soft peach lips. She was breathtaking. I slipped another finger inside of her and another moan tore from her throat.

I was amused, especially with the way she glared at me accusingly. But she couldn't even hold my gaze for much longer than a few seconds because I began to increase my pace in response.

Her hand shot out to close around my wrist, to get me to pause but I didn't. I finger fucked her as hard as I could, but the barrier of her panties made things less than graceful, so my second hand slipped in to pull the fabric away. I had all the access I needed then and with my thumb stroking against her clit, I drove her wild. She couldn't remain still and all I could do was watch her, mesmerized as she tried to get away but couldn't help but rock her hips to the rhythm of my thrusting.

"Gideon," she cried out and although I tried to catch her lips with mine so that I could muffle her sounds, she was too restless. Eventually she came and the sound, though still low, resounded across the room. My gaze went to the hall hoping that her roommate wouldn't suddenly appear and when my attention returned to Pamela, I found her eyes hazy with lust.

"Fuck," she said, and I kissed her.

I then pulled away, but she grabbed me and kissed me even harder. Then she rose to her feet.

"My legs are shaky," she said as she pulled me up along with her, and I could tell that she was holding on for dear life.

"We're not done," she said, and I had absolutely no complaints whatsoever.

She led me to her bedroom and the moment we got in she locked the door behind us.

I wondered if her single bed would contain us both, but when she pushed me down on it, I found that I didn't care because I was perfectly horizontal.

One leg hung off the bed and without waiting for any further instructions I began to take my pants off.

She had the dirtiest, naughtiest smile on her face as she pulled her shirt over her head and then her bra went with it, and I couldn't breathe. I wanted her breasts in my mouth so badly that I was barely able to make out the words to ask for it.

What completely screwed up my brain was when she began to touch herself. She was no longer shy with me, and I was enthralled. I watched as she took the heavy mounds in hand and began to plump them. They were gorgeous, the small pink peaks in the middle, hardened with arousal.

"I have a question," she said, her voice hoarse and sultry and it was like a spell over me, draining my strength but at the same time revitalizing me with a hunger that felt as though it would consume me whole if I didn't shove my cock into her in the next moment.

Still, I managed to exercise control, watching as her

hand began to slide down her abdomen all the way to her sex.

"Are you going to respond?" she asked.

Her hand covered her crotch, and I watched mesmerized, but then frustration struck me like a blow when she suddenly stopped. My gaze shot up to hers then and I met the amusement in her eyes. She laughed and the desire for vengeance competed greatly with my need.

"My question is about the handcuffs I found in your office," she said. "On the shelf?"

I wasn't surprised at all about the question because I knew she was eventually going to get around to asking about that. My mind went to the speculations that had passed between her and her friend, and I couldn't help but be amused once again.

Her middle finger slipped between her sex.

She began to rub and stroke, her lips parted and at the sheen that stained her skin, I couldn't help but swallow.

"Come here," I said, my vision flashing but she wouldn't comply.

"Not until I get my response."

"Then ask the damn question," I growled, and she laughed.

"What were the cuffs for?" she asked. "Earlier when I asked about hobbies, I thought perhaps you would mention them, but you didn't."

I smiled now, thoroughly entertained by her.

"Why are you curious?' I asked. "Is that what you're into?"

Her gaze was incredulous but then she parted her legs even further and slipped a finger inside herself. I couldn't bear it anymore so I lunged forward and before she could escape, I caught her around the waist. I brought her to me, and she squealed in excitement.

"Not concerned about your roommate anymore?" I asked and she hit me slightly on the chest.

"Of course I am. Shhh,"

Shaking my head, I pulled her roughly down to kiss me and she had no choice but to comply.

"I didn't get them for what you're suspecting," I said, and she could barely control her blush. "I'm not into BDSM," I told her. "Or rather I don't know if I am because I've never done it with anyone before. But if you have an interest then I'm at your service."

"Oh my God," she blushed. "Really?"

"Whatever you want," I said and saw the stars in her eyes.

She kissed me hard and hungrily and then pulled away.

"So, what were the handcuffs for then?" she asked.

"Long story," I said. "I'll tell you after we're done." She nodded then more than willing to solely concentrate on the play at hand.

My mind went to the sheen I had glimpsed on her finger, and I was ravenous.

"Get up," I said, and it was an inadequate warning before I gripped her by the waist and pulled her until she was poised over my face.

"Oh my God," she gasped. "Again?"

"You didn't like it?" I asked and her eyes nearly rolled into the back of her head.

"I loved it," she said and immediately lowered her cunt my lips. My tongue slid out and gave her a hard lick and she trembled above me.

"Oh God," she cried. "Meredith is going to kill me."

This was one aspect I wasn't willing to protect her from

so I ignored the danger and devoured her the way I had been thinking about since that morning.

She cried out, fucking her hips against my tongue and lips until eventually I needed her on my cock.

I couldn't take the longing anymore so in no time I pulled the rock-hard member out and then I was guiding her down to the base.

She was uninhibited, her moan ringing out across the room as she sheathed all of me. She only took a few moments to revel in the impalement before she was rocking against me, her hand against her stomach. She rode me hard, my name and profanities, many of which couldn't be actual words ringing from her lips.

She went fast and I laid back to watch her, fucking into her and unable to take my eyes off the euphoria on her face.

The pleasure streaking through me was mind numbing and the heat at our joining made every hair on my body stand at attention. I leaned up, needing to feel every inch of her against me and held onto her. My hand went behind to grab her ass and only then did her pace slightly slow. She collapsed into the crook of my neck, my name repeated over and over again while I drove into her.

I couldn't hold myself back, all the tension and worry I had felt from the start of the day seemed to culminate in this moment and find its release. I tried to remain quiet, aware that we were not alone in the house but when I felt her grip tightly onto me and my name escape in a scream for her lips, I lost control. I came so hard that my whole body shook, and for the moments afterwards I couldn't quite tell anything. Not where we were or who I was but through it all my arms only tightened around her.

"Pamela," I could hear myself gasp as I fought to contain the unbelievable pleasure that had left me incoherent.

She jerked and spasmed against me and then she kissed me, hard.

Afterwards I could no longer remain upright so we both collapsed onto the bed until eventually, my eyes were able to come open. But still, I couldn't quite see the ceiling as my vision remained hazy. My hand went to the back of her head as I needed to pet her, somehow knowing that it was what she needed too.

Once again, the words almost fell from my lips, the ultimate declaration of my heart for her but once again I didn't trust that I was ready. I vowed instead to show her in every way that I could that she was mine, and that I would protect her in a way that no one else could.

37

PAMELA

I fell asleep with him still inside of me, and when I awoke and saw that I was curved against him, I couldn't help but feel slightly disappointed. But when I realized he was now also completely naked, and our bare skin was glued against each other, my joy was restored.

I stretched and yawned like a well satisfied cat, pushing further into him even though there was no further possible space that could be closed between us. I loved the weight of his arm around me, the warmth of his skin and his decadent and luxurious scent.

I smelled like him I was certain, and it was a scent that I never wanted to be rid of.

I looked behind, wondering what the time was though it was still dark, and couldn't believe he had spent the night with me, at my apartment.

We had moved fast... much faster than I would have ever anticipated which made me suspect perhaps he was never truly reluctant. That perhaps and just as Meredith had said, there had been something holding him back that he just needed to work through. This made me curious as I thought back to our conversation. I couldn't quite figure out what it was no matter how hard I pondered the events that occurred that day.

I felt close to him now... more than I ever had in the past and it occurred to me that perhaps I could ask him? Things didn't feel so fragile anymore so perhaps this could be a step forward in pulling down whatever walls remained between us.

I sighed as I imagined what it would be like to have no barriers or reservations between us... to be immeasurably vulnerable. The prospect sounded unreal, and it was what I was certain I wanted more than anything. And with him... I truly thought it could be possible.

Just then he stirred behind me, and I was immediately alert. I thought he would get up in order to get ready to return to his apartment, when his arms tightened even further around me and pulled me tighter to him, I couldn't help my smile. He leaned into the space between my neck and shoulder to breathe me in and butterflies swarmed the pit of my stomach.

"Don't you need to be anywhere?" I asked, unable to keep the smile from my face even as I gazed at the wall.

"Are you kicking me out?" he asked, his voice groggy with sleep.

"Nooo," I replied, slightly alarmed until it occurred to me he was teasing me. I turned around till my face was right in front of his. He didn't open his eyes which was all well and good because I leaned forward to press kisses against his eyelids.

His eyes came open, the most striking and gorgeous blue, and it took my breath away.

"Do you have somewhere to be?" he asked, and I couldn't stop myself from brushing his hair out of his eyes.

I nodded. "Class, but much later."

"Same," he replied and slightly moved away to stretch.

When he returned, curling his arm around me to once again pull me close to him I found the courage then to ask.

"Last time..." I began. "I mean... generally speaking, was there a particular reason why you didn't want us to be together?"

At this question, I could feel his body go still and immediately began to evaluate my choices.

"I thought we discussed it," he said. "That I just wasn't ready to maintain a relationship at the time."

"I guess this is my question then. Was there a specific reason why?"

He watched me, his eyes seemingly boring into mine and for a little while I became uncomfortable.

But then he responded, and I was flooded with relief.

"I don't want to lie to you," he said. "So, for now I'll say yes, but I don't want you to hear it. At least not now."

My heart sank and I ran his words over and over in my mind. I realized there was some sort of hope.

I found the courage to ask again.

"So... in the future then?"

With a light laugh, he leaned forward and pressed a kiss against my cheek. "Maybe," he said and although it was a less than savory response, it was one I could deal with in the meantime.

I settled further into his embrace until daylight began to flood into the room. I could no longer deny it was time for the two of us to get up in order to prepare for our day.

He let me go, albeit reluctantly and I headed straight to the bathroom. I lifted my face to the warm stream, and it soothe away the slight exhaustion I still felt from the previous day.

I needed more time in bed, preferably with him as I couldn't recall ever enjoying my sleep as much as I just had with him. I felt safe and treasured and it was an exhilarating feeling to say the least.

Suddenly, there was a knock on the glass stall, and I was so startled that my heart nearly flew out of my chest.

The door was pulled open and what I saw was a nosy human with a nest of a bun piled on top of her head.

"What are you doing?" I complained and she gave me a sheepish smile.

"Is he still here?" she asked, as I grabbed for my shower gel.

"Of course he is," I replied and she smiled.

"I can't believe it. I just can't," she said. "No one would believe me if I told them this was actually happening, Professor Bach and his girlfriend spending the night in my apartment! I could sell this info. It would make me rich."

"You better not," I gritted my teeth, and she smiled back in response. I pushed her out of the way and returned to my shower.

When I returned to the bedroom, I saw it empty and slightly panicked. But as I listened and heard the soft clanging of utensils from the kitchen, I was certain that was where he was.

Initially and on my way from the bathroom, I had thought it was Meredith but as it turned out this wasn't the case.

I dressed in shorts and a black tee shirt despite my mind's urge to wear something a bit skimpier.

Next time, I managed to convince myself. *When we are alone and in his home.*

I was certain we had already somewhat disturbed Meredith through the night and although she didn't mention any complaints just yet, I couldn't help but wonder if I would receive an earful from her after he left.

I stood by the wall and snuck a peek at him before coming fully into sight. I wanted to see what he was up to. I saw him standing by the stove and could already smell the bacon in the air. It all smelled so yummy and for a moment I couldn't believe how excited I was about bacon.

He seemed to feel my gaze on him because he turned, and our gazes met. He smiled, and I watched as he returned his attention to the stove. In no time my arms were around him and his warmth and scent encapsulated me.

"You smell great," he said as I looked over at the sizzling bacon in the pan.

"So do you," I replied, and he laughed softly. "That can't be, I haven't showered yet."

"Would you like to?" I asked and he gave it a thought, then he shook his head.

"I'll just head home. It'll be a hassle since I don't have my things here."

"You're right," I said and rested my head against him. "I'm becoming quite clingy, aren't I?" I asked and he laughed.

"When haven't you been?"

I couldn't stop smiling.

"I ran into Meredith, and she said I could use these to make something quick for you to eat. I'll replace them later."

"Are you serious?" I asked and came around to give him a ludicrous look.

He smiled. "I would have ordered you something in gratitude for dinner last night, but it seemed like it would be too insincere. So, I hope this will be decent."

"It'll be fine. Besides burning bacon nothing else can go wrong with it," I said.

Just then there was a ding, and I turned to see the pieces of bread jumping up in the toaster."

"I'm trying to put a sandwich together," he said.

"Nice, I'll help you," I said and went to retrieve the slices. In no time we were standing beside each other and eating our meals.

"We should get stools or something for this space, shouldn't we?" I asked.

"You should," he nodded as he looked around.

"We just felt it would be a bit cramped. I'm sorry for making you stand."

"Stop apologizing," he said, and I smiled.

He looked towards the hall, and I watched him, knowing something was on his mind.

"What is it?" I asked.

"I made enough for Meredith too but she's not coming out. It feels as though we've trapped her solely in her bedroom. She must be feeling restricted."

"Maybe," I said. "She usually snacks a lot but trust me she's excited that you're here. I'll call her out. Maybe the more time she spends around you the more comfortable she'll be with you around here."

I pulled my phone out and called her.

"Jeesh, you couldn't text?" she asked. "Now he's going to be certain you reached me, and I rejected your offer."

"Are you going to reject the offer?"

"Is the phone on speaker?" she asked, and I shook my head.

"No."

"Yes, I am going to reject it because it's weird," she said. "I'm going to be seeing him in class in a few hours for Pete's sake. Although I would like to stare at him a bit longer with that messy morning hair. I've always wondered if he would look more devastating that way than when he was put together, and I guess I have my answer."

I laughed, my heart warm.

"Come on out. It's not weird."

"Well now that you've said that for him to hear I have no choice now do I?"

"You don't," I replied, unrepentant.

"Fine. And I am starving so I guess I could ask him for some tips on my project."

"No," I said. "That will be taking advantage of him. No professional or academic talk in the house."

She paused and then spat. "When did you become his mouthpiece? Shouldn't I get some perks from your dating him?"

She ended the call and I looked at the phone. In no time we heard the door open from down the hall and then she appeared looking more put together than I had ever seen her in the morning. She had let her hair down and brushed it perfectly, and she was wearing the decent pair of pajamas I had gotten her the year before as a Christmas present. Usually, it would be wrinkled and washed-out t-shirts and barely any underpants.

"Good morning," she said, and we both sent smiles to her.

"Your plate's in the microwave," Gideon said and she finally met his gaze. "Thank you... um Mr.-Professor Bach."

I laughed out loud then as she scurried in embarrassment over to the microwave.

"Just call me Gideon," he said, and she shook her head as she brought it over to the counter.

"No, that'll feel weird."

"You have to get used to it," I said, and she scowled at me.

"We can be casual at home," he said, and she eventually agreed.

"I'm sorry we don't have stools. This one here insisted that it'd make the kitchen cramped."

"That's understandable," he replied. "And this is fine."

I nudged him gently on the shoulder for siding with me and turned just in time to see her roll her eyes at my coyness.

"Meredith was saying that she'd want to ask you academic questions from time to time," I said, and she almost spit out the drink of coffee she had just taken.

"I was joking," she said.

I narrowed my eyes at her. "No, you weren't".

Gideon was amused. "That's alright, I'll help out as much as I can."

She seemed surprised, but immensely pleased. "I promise I won't be a nuisance," she said. "I'll only ask when I'm completely stumped and see no other way out."

"I'll be glad to help."

"Gosh," she said. "Others usually line up for your help and almost never get it. Thanks Pamela," she said and picked up her plate.

"Shouldn't I get a commission of sorts for making this access happen?" I asked.

"I helped you get hi-" she stopped just in time and instead snarled at me.

Then she returned to her bedroom.

"Sorry about that," I said, and he smiled.

"She's a good friend," he said. "She suits you."

I leaned my head against his shoulder and apologized once again for making him stand to have his meal.

Parting at the door was a significant ordeal as I couldn't

seem to let go of his lips. Eventually though he pulled away with a sigh and gave me a stern look. "I'll see you soon."

"Sure," I said and leaned forward for one more kiss, but he quickly moved out of the way. I smiled and watched him leave and then leaned against the shut door when he eventually disappeared out of sight. It took quite a lot for me to remain standing upright and not melt into a puddle on the floor as I tried to catch my breath.

And it was then that Meredith's *'tsk, tsk, tsk'* floated over to me. She was watching me, a cup of coffee in hand as she leaned against the wall.

"You're completely hopeless," she said, and I didn't even bother to argue. She was absolutely right.

38

GIDEON

For once it was difficult for me to concentrate.

Within me was a mix of emotions which in one moment was pure joy at how adorable I found her, and in the next moment complete annoyance at the troubles that were currently looming against her.

Right now, things seemed calm and uneventful, and it worried me, until eventually I was forced to rise to my feet and head to the window, wondering how I could handle this disturbance on my own. I wanted it immediately nipped in the bud, because there was no doubt it was troubling her as she went on with her day.

My mind went to the admonition from my lawyer from the previous night to not be too concerned but I couldn't help it. She meant too much to me.

The office phone began to ring so I returned to my desk to answer it.

"Miss Hannah is here to see you," Oscar said, and I took a moment to consider if I was in the mood to accept a visit. In the end I figured it would help temporarily get my mind off my concerns, so I allowed it. Moments later she walked in, her demeanor wasn't as pleasant as it usually was. Instead, she wore a complicated expression as she pulled out the chair before my desk and took her seat.

"I just heard something," she said. "That you're dating a student?"

At the outright statement, a dark scowl came across my face. She studied me.

"Where did you hear that from?" I asked.

"It's true, isn't it?" She asked. "And it's that girl, right? Your childhood friend?"

I didn't respond, my expression darkening at how she had ignored my question.

She sighed. "Wow, Gideon."

"Where did you hear that from?" I repeated.

"It's floating around," she said. "I heard you're under investigation for it and everyone is throwing speculations all over the place."

I lowered my gaze and picked up my phone.

"So..." she said. "Are you?"

I ignored her and rose to my feet. Moments later the department head Patrick, was on the line as I gazed out the window.

"You allowed the rumors of the complaint to leak out from your office?" I asked and for a few moments the line remained quiet.

"I didn't purposely release it if that's what you're asking," he said. "However, this is a public institution, so word is sure to get out. You can't hold me responsible for that."

"Of course," I said and ended the call.

"I guess it's true then," she said.

"You're still not going to tell me where you heard it from?"

I shot the question back at her and for a moment her

mask fell, and I could see the hurt on her face. It was easy to recognize because I had seen it once before after our relationship had come to an end.

She rose to her feet but didn't leave. Instead, she paused and with her face turned away, spoke.

"I don't want to tell you what to do, Gideon," she said. "You are more than capable of navigating your own affairs but… I guess this is concerning because of her. She's what? A junior? This might bring serious problems to her education, and she has just one more year to go. Don't you care about that?"

I didn't need to hear any more, so I returned to my chair to grab my jacket.

She knew then to take her leave while I grabbed my keys and immediately began to dial Michael. He immediately picked up.

"Is Susan in the office right now?" I asked and he seemed taken aback at the sudden inquiry.

"Um yeah… I mean I should hope so. I'll confirm for you. Why? Is everything okay?"

"I'll be there soon," I said. "Have her look into someone for me. James Caldwell. He graduated from my current department about two years ago. I'm not sure of where he currently works but I need her to find out immediately. I want to know everything possible about his current position."

"Alright," he said. "You got it."

The call came to an end and in no time I was on my way.

39

PAMELA

I was in the middle of a quite boring class on management ethics when the text message came to my phone. Thankfully, it was put on silent prior, but my heart still skipped when the device vibrated on my table. I expected to see that it was Gideon since I hadn't heard from him all day, but when I saw who it was, fear gripped my heart.

"Where are you?" it read.

I ignored the message and even considered switching the phone off but then I didn't want Gideon to be unable to reach me. For the rest of the class, I was more alert than usual, but I didn't hear a single thing the teacher said. Instead, I looked out the window, my heart racing hard as I wondered if James was on the premises.

I thought of where I could go to hide and decided that even my apartment wouldn't be safe enough for me. Soon the class came to an end and as I remained in my seat with my phone in hand, I had to make the hard decision on whether to contact Gideon.

He was sure to come to my aid, but I didn't want to

disrupt his day in that way since nothing particularly alarming had occurred yet.

I decided to just head to his apartment. I gathered my things and immediately placed a call to the bistro telling them I couldn't make my shift today. However just as it connected there was a bit of chaos at the entrance and my head shot up. James appeared at the door with smoke coming out of his ears as he searched around for me.

I almost crouched down right then but before I could, he spotted me and eventually began to head towards me. I looked down at my phone fumbling to dial Gideon's number but before I could even find it the phone was smacked out of my hands. It flew across the seats, and I looked at it in complete shock.

I couldn't believe what was happening, and as I looked around at the alarm and chaos that his actions had generated, I suddenly felt a surge of rage burn within me. I turned to glare at him, refusing to consider that there would be any valid or concrete reason for him to have acted this way with me and in such a public space.

"You got your boyfriend to tamper with my job?" he said, and for a few moments I couldn't understand what he was saying.

Pretty soon however I did, and it became clear as to why he was so furious. It still however didn't dampen my fury at his harassment.

"Why are you acting like this?" I asked. "If he tampered with your job then why are you harassing me and not him?"

He looked at me as though he couldn't believe my words, and at the mess of his hair and loosened tie I could tell whatever had gone wrong had gotten him crazed enough to rush all the way down here.

"You want me to completely ruin you, don't you?" he said. "The both of you. That's truly what you're pushing for."

I glared at him and felt absolutely disgusted. I couldn't believe I had once been associated with someone so small and I couldn't believe I was letting him control me now. I straightened my back.

"You know what? Do whatever the fuck you want to do and let's see who wins in the end. You want to ruin me, and you think I can't do the same to you? Or even worse? What exactly do you even have against me? That we're dating? Where's your proof? After all, I've known him since I was a child, and I can prove that. I can also fucking prove that the real reason you're so worked up is because you nearly molested me and are scared shitless that I'll expose it."

"What?" his eyes shot open. "You call asking for a mere kiss molestation?"

"Exactly," I said. "It could have been worse, and I am emotionally damaged and scarred from it. How can you prove any of this otherwise? After all there were only three of us there and no surveillance so how do you think the testimony of two over one will hold up in court?" I scoffed. "You're actually the one in hot water and yet you're trying to intimidate us?"

He snorted, his expression incredulous. "Pamela, I don't think you know who you're messing with."

At this both of my hands shot out and pushed at him causing him to stumble backwards and almost topple over the row of desks.

"You're the one who doesn't fucking know who you're dealing with. How dare you barge in here and harass me? You fucking loser!"

I was so furious I couldn't believe I had been so terrified of him from the get go. I grabbed my things, found my phone and sent him a deathly glare before storming out of the classroom. Along the way, a few acquaintances tried to get my attention, but I ignored them all.

James however was not done.

"Pamela, think about what you're doing right now," he called out. "If you both don't rectify the damage that you've done you best believe that everyone will know the truth."

"What truth?" I turned around to ask. "That you think I'm dating a professor?"

At my words the murmurings across the classroom seemed to heighten even further but I didn't care... not at the detriment at being so shamefully harassed by this piece of shit and even subjecting Gideon to it. I was so irate.

His expression was theatrical... one of absolute disbelief.

"Go ahead," I said to him. "But make sure to provide the proof. When you're not able to, I will destroy you for spreading such a baseless rumor."

I exited the classroom then, unaware of everything around me beyond my current and singular focus of just walking. My head was a mess of wonderings as to what Gideon had done that made James barge so furiously at me. When I arrived at my car, I hurried inside and only after the door had been locked was I able to take what seemed to be my first breath within the last few minutes. I almost couldn't believe all that had just happened, especially my outburst, but I guessed I was finally pushed to my limits.

My heart continued to race so hard that I had to turn the car on to roll down the windows. I took deep breaths, trying to bring myself under control and soon enough my clarity returned. I began to mentally assess the damage I had done and how I would be able to rectify it.

I had practically almost openly admitted I was indeed dating a professor but then again that could be refuted.

There would be rumors and that was unavoidable but those perhaps would eventually die down if I kept my distance from Gideon.

My heart wrenched with grief so hard that I couldn't help but rest my head against the steering wheel. I wanted to scream but that would draw even more attention that I couldn't currently stand so I tried my hardest to pull myself together.

It hurt because after so long of wanting to be with him, I finally was, and a stupid mistake made in a moment by contacting James was now threatening to ruin everything.

"Gideon," my heart thought of him, and more things became clear. James' accusation from earlier that his job had been tampered with. I needed to know exactly what he had been talking about.

There was only one way to find out, so I immediately retrieved my phone and placed a call to Gideon.

40

GIDEON

I decided to remain at the headquarters for the remainder of the day. I had to monitor James' response to our attack, and I didn't particularly want to return to the campus. I was so aggravated that someone so small could be such a huge thorn in my side, that it took quite a bit of effort to manage my temper.

There was no point in trying to completely cool it off because until this matter was resolved it would be impossible. Thankfully, I had overdue company matters to attend to and it sufficed in redirecting my attention.

I wanted to be alone as I worked, but all efforts to drive Michael out from my office over the last hour had proven futile. So, I had no other choice but to forge ahead with the report reviews on my desk while he sat on one of the chairs across from me and watched.

"Does your presence here have to do with the lawsuit that McMillan is currently handling for you?" he asked.

At first, his words didn't mean much to me but when it finally occurred to me what was wrong about them, I looked at him.

"He didn't reveal it to me," he rushed to explain. "It's just that... rumors go around like flies here you know. Plus, that secretary of his..."

Shaking my head, I returned my gaze to the document.

"I know," he said. "McMillan will never change him since he worked for his father for so long, but the geezer needs a zipper, doesn't he? He's great though. There's always something warm and baked on his desk for anyone that visits the office. He claims it's his wife that makes them, but we suspect his second favorite place is the kitchen. At this point most senior staff just make up excuses to go there, feigning legal enquiries that they could have just called to clarify."

I gave him a look at all the babbling, wondering why he was talking so much.

He once again explained himself. "I'm just trying to fill you in on how things are around here. You're only concerned with the major stuff but it's pretty fun if you stick around."

I remained silent.

"I guess you're not going to let me know what you had Susan handle for you earlier either then are you?"

I considered his request and realized I didn't particularly have any reason for keeping it from him. I just always preferred to keep my affairs private and the fact it wasn't currently added to my irritation with the day. Either way the beans had already been spilled so I decided to just reveal what I could since I didn't want him feeling as though I was deliberately shunning him.

I briefly explained the situation and he was quiet for so long that I had to look up to confirm that he was still present.

"You're dating someone?" was the first question he asked.

"Yeah," I replied, and his expression was one of abject shock. This amused me despite my bad mood, which made it impossible to concentrate so I couldn't help leaning backward and setting my pen down.

"There are only a few more hours till the end of the day and I'd really like to get these done by then. So can you please leave?"

"Absolutely not," he said, his tone rising, "You're fucking dating someone? So, you have like... a girlfriend. And she's your student!"

I sighed.

"In all the years I've known you I've never had you claim that you were dating someone. What the hell is going on?"

I knew exactly then what the cause of his surprise was.

"We've known each other since we were kids," I explained and understanding seemed to wash over him. He relaxed then but seemed to have a list of questions which he immediately began to spout off.

Thankfully, and before I was forced to respond, my phone began to ring. I checked who the caller was, grateful for the intrusion but when I saw it was the call I had been awaiting, I couldn't help but slightly tense up.

"You breached my company's servers?" the accusation came, and truly I wondered if he expected me to admit to anything especially over the phone.

"You have until midnight," I told him. "Withdraw the lawsuit and apologize to her for the trouble you have caused so far."

"And why the hell will I do that?"

"You don't have to," I said. "But I hope in exchange you're ready to watch every bit of your life fall to pieces."

The call was abruptly terminated, and it was only then that I recalled that Michael was still present in the office.

With a sigh, I tried to ignore his burgeoning curiosity but, in the end, it was no use. I was forced to explain fully and by the time I was done, his eyebrows were almost to his hairline. And then he began to laugh.

I didn't expect an applause in reaction from him, but this was particularly aggravating, and I let him know it.

"I'm sorry Gideon," he said, "but you've always been so averse to even dealing with people because of how low your tolerance is for things like this. However, you're not even blinking an eye when tackling this now because and for what has to be the first time, I'm certain, you're doing it because of someone you truly care about. I'm impressed, and I wholeheartedly support you, but it's all just fascinating to me."

I glanced at the clock on the wall and said to him, "You need to leave or else you'll have to wait till the start of next week to get these approvals."

He panicked at this. "Oh no, I almost had these sent over to you at the university. Please complete it today."

I gave him a look and finally conceding, he rose to his feet. But then he paused and said to me, his expression now somber, "I know you're truly unhappy about this otherwise you wouldn't have gone as far as-"

The phone began to ring but I didn't pick up, preferring instead to listen to what he had to say so he continued. "You wouldn't have asked Susan to infiltrate his company's systems."

"He needs to be taught a bitter lesson," I said, and this made Michael smile.

"You're already being quite lenient. I imagine you didn't even risk doing it yourself to avoid destroying the whole thing. At least Susan will only take your instructions and not go overboard."

I sighed and leaned back into the chair, my gaze once again going to the phone.

I picked it up as he left.

"Pamela," I called cautiously, but the line remained quiet. A few seconds later however she spoke.

"Where are you?"

I was instantly alert. "Did you try to look for me? I'm not on campus, I'm at the office downtown."

"I figured," she said, and I could hear something of a smile in her voice.

"What is it?" I asked, concerned.

"Would it be too dangerous if I came over?"

I immediately agreed. "Of course not, this is my turf."

"Yeah," she said. "I just don't want to be around here right now."

"I'll send a car over," I said but she refused.

"No need, I'd have to wait for it to get here and I want to leave now. Plus, traffic. I'll be there soon, okay?"

"Alright."

I ordered us both a salad while waiting since I wasn't certain about what she would like to eat and didn't want to keep her waiting for its arrival when the order was finally placed. I wished we could head home together but since she was already on her way, I chose to patiently wait, and it was excruciating.

The moment she arrived, she was cleared seamlessly through the doors and then escorted straight up to my floor.

I watched her through available surveillance and couldn't help but feel excited she was in a part of my life where I wasn't solely known as a professor.

I thought of how to meet her and considered waiting in

the office but since this would be her first time visiting me here as her boyfriend, I decided to go out to meet her so she would feel as welcome as possible.

No doubt word would spread as a result through the company, but at this point I didn't care.

My secretary Grace was quite startled to see me as I suddenly emerged from the office. Her gaze instantly went to the schedule on her computer and then back to me, looking more confused. And then a light bulb seemed to light up in her head because she suddenly lowered and grabbed the bag of food that I had asked her to order. "I was going to come in to hand this over after your meeting with Mr. Faust." she said. "I didn't know he left."

"That's alright," I replied just as I arrived at the door. I pulled it open and there she was... looking unsure.

My heart swelled in my chest as I took in her windblown hair, wide eyed expression, and how she generally looked awkward as hell... just as she always had.

I was also incredibly endeared at the huge relief that washed through her face as she saw me.

"I think I'm immensely underdressed," she said as she turned for a glance back at the other employees walking down the hallway and peeping at her from the reception. At my stern look at them they quickly tucked their heads back in while my hand circled around her wrist.

"Hey," I said, and she finally smiled, her eyes boring straight into mine.

"Hi, I hope I'm not intruding."

"You're not," I said and even though I hadn't planned to, found myself leaning down and pressing a light kiss to her lips. She seemed startled by this, but then her smile grew even wider, and I was certain that I had welcomed her in the best possible way.

"Hello, I'm Grace," my secretary greeted with a smile, and she returned the greeting in kind, her tone feathery soft.

"I'm Pamela."

I led her to the door, but Grace called out to me.

"Should I bring this in now, sir?" she asked, gesturing towards the salads and I nodded.

I pushed the door open but then Pamela stopped at the entrance.

I almost bumped into her but managed to catch myself in time. "What's wrong?" I asked and she turned around, wide eyed to stare at me.

"This is your office?"

I smiled then in understanding and strolled ahead towards my chair.

"Yeah. The second one."

"Oh my God," she said as she took in the wall length windows and the magnificent fiery red streak of the setting sun across the downtown skyline. "This looks unreal," she said. "And your company... takes up all the floors in this building?"

I nodded.

"All fifteen floors?"

"Seventeen," I said, and her mouth just hung open.

"Oh my God," she said, and then began to laugh.

I was confused.

"You're a billionaire... and I made you sleep in a tiny, creaky bed last night."

I was immensely amused at her antics.

"I enjoyed that creaky bed, and most importantly I enjoyed the woman that was in it with me. Come sit down. I ordered some salads since I wasn't sure what you wanted for dinner. You can place the order now for what you want so that it'll get to us in a little bit."

She smiled and began to head towards me, and I couldn't look away as her hand brushed across the top of one of the leather chairs before my desk.

"Luxurious," she said and started to take her seat, but then I saw mischief come into her eyes.

Instead, she simply set her purse down on the table, and then she came around. I pulled my chair out to give her all the space she wanted regardless of what she wanted to do.

She arrived and cocked her head as she looked at me affectionately.

"Can I sit on your desk?" she asked, and I nodded. "What about your lap?"

I laughed then and shook my head. "Inappropriate."

Still, she gave a small, adorable frown and then she turned around and proceeded to sit on my lap.

"I just want to see how it feels to sit here and rule the world," she said, and I shook my head. She hadn't changed at all with being naughty and I loved her for it.

She sat with her ass to my already hardening cock and then set her hands on the desk.

"Nice," she said and then turned to look at me.

"I'm rarely here though," I said, and she nodded.

"I still don't understand why you give all of this up to deal with annoying faculty and students."

"If I hadn't, I probably wouldn't have met you again," I said and felt her go still. Then she turned to look at me once again.

"Point made."

I smiled and couldn't help but circle my arms around her waist, pulling her in to inhale her delicious scent.

I remained that way as she continued to explore and

fiddle with the things on my desk until eventually, I heard her voice.

"Tough day?" she asked, and I smiled.

She moved a bit on my lap trying to get my attention, and at the sharp jolt of pleasure through my system I was instantly alert. I pulled my eyes open, slightly out of breath and with a frown ready for her.

When all I did was stare, she asked, "Want a kiss?" And my gaze lowered down to her lips.

I nodded and she slanted her head to meet mine.

Just as our lips connected there was a knock on the door. I was reluctant to stop but she immediately did, startled. And then before I could stop her, she was off my lap and arranging her outfit of slightly baggy jeans and an off the shoulder flowery top. She looked so simple, just like a student and I couldn't help my smile.

"Someone's at the door," she said, and I nodded. I glanced down at my hardened cock and quickly pressed down on it for some relief. She truly was my undoing. She also started to move away to go around the desk, but I stopped her just in time, once again grabbing onto her hand.

"Come in," I called out and Pamela's eyes widened at me.

"You're just standing by my side," I said. "What's the alarm for?"

Grace came in then with her usual, courteous smile on her face.

"Where do you want me to arrange it, sir?" she asked, and I pointed my chin towards the sitting area.

"Let's go," I got up, but Pamela's gaze went with alarm to my groin area. Her hand shot out to perhaps press it down and I quickly moved away before she could touch me. I was so amused I couldn't hold back my laughter.

"She'll see," she muttered to me, and I couldn't believe her.

"Touching will make it worse. Just get your mind off it. I'll be fine."

She followed me reluctantly, so I called out to Grace. "Just leave them on the table, no need to lay it out. There are beverages in the fridge too, so we'll sort it out ourselves. Right? I haven't checked."

She smiled. "Both alcoholic and non-alcoholic," she said.

"Alright, thank you." She took her leave, and I went over to Pamela.

"What do you want to eat?" I asked her as we settled down and she looked at me in surprise.

"What do you mean? Aren't we already eating?" she asked as she picked up the bowl of salad.

"You don't want more than this? I just got this for the interim."

"Oh, this is perfectly fine, but you can get more if you want," she said, her eyes lighting up and she lifted the salad bowl.

"Wow, avocados and sausages and sweet corn... no tomatoes."

She looked at me with a huge smile on her face. "You remembered I don't like tomatoes?"

"Of course," I said, and she suddenly leaned over and pressed a huge kiss to my cheek.

"You're the best," she said, and I almost couldn't contain the warmth that overwhelmed me.

We soon settled down into eating peacefully, and to my surprise we both remained silent as we retreated into our thoughts about the day.

A few minutes later, I retrieved a bottle of wine and realized regrettably that we should have had our meal at a better place.

"There's an outdoor setting on the rooftop," I told her as I opened the bottle of wine. "And the weather's not too bad. It would have been better for us to have our dinner there, no?"

She looked out at the now darkened sky and smiled.

"Will you be leaving anytime soon?" she asked, and I shook my head.

"What about you?"

"It's my day off," she said. "Well, I took the evening off, so I don't have to be at the restaurant today."

"Perfect," I said.

"But will it be empty?"

"Maybe not," I said, "But I'm sure the staff will know to give me some space when they see me there."

She considered this and then added. "Alright."

I got up and went to the door, however I met Grace packing up to leave for the day.

"Do you need any help, sir?" she asked.

"No, we just want to take our meals up to the rooftop. Have a lovely evening."

"Oh, I can help," she said. "You're almost never here so I'm more than glad to."

"Thank you," I smiled, and she came in.

Along with Pamela we gathered the bowls and glasses, and then headed one floor up to the roof.

The breeze was wonderful just as we had expected, and thankfully the space was empty. At least this was what I thought until we finally noticed a few employees by a corner smoking. They quickly hurried up to us when they noticed me, gave brief greetings and soon disappeared.

After they left, I watched as Pamela lifted a glass of wine to her lips.

"When was the last time you were here? They all seemed as though they were seeing a ghost when they spotted you."

I smiled. "I don't think I've spent an entire day here this year."

"Why do you love teaching so much?" she asked, and I shrugged. "I mean this is a much more glamorous gig."

"I keep telling everyone this, but no one seems to believe me," I replied. "I love the atmosphere as it stimulates curiosity and learning. I love computers and what they can do, and I want to have every bit of it under my control. But as I said I also don't mind sharing this knowledge plus, I'm not overly fond of the business side of things. So, for now, the university is a good enough place for me. Plus, that was where I was before Michael found me so most of this has been his effort in growing the company while I've been majorly focused on research. I like it that way."

She nodded and returned to her meal.

I watched her and could sense underneath things, a slight gloom to her demeanor. Plus given all that had happened I didn't expect that James hadn't yet contacted her, but still she was yet to mention it to me.

And so, I asked. "How was your day?"

41

PAMELA

I looked up at him as he asked the question, and for a moment I wasn't exactly sure of how to respond. I thought about this and kept on eating.

"It was okay," I replied, my heart which had been previously lightened by being in his presence was suddenly heavy all over again.

He gave me a soft, knowing look and suddenly tears rushed to my eyes. I didn't want to be as far as I currently was from him, so I rose to my feet and went over to his side. He welcomed me with open arms, and when I leaned against him to take a deep breath, he squeezed my hand and gave me a kiss on the forehead.

"What happened?" he asked.

I looked at him. "You tampered with his company?"

He smiled. "He has until midnight to set things right or else I'm leaking all of their data."

"Won't this affect you?" I asked and he smiled.

"Remember what I said about loving computers but ensuring they have no control whatsoever over me? Nothing is traceable back. Even my secretary doesn't know of it although there is someone in the company in charge of things. They won't be able to find me if they tried."

"But James knows."

"He has no proof. Nothing in this world works without proof. Proof is the truth, not hearsay."

I wanted to feel completely assured of what he was saying but it was so difficult because it concerned him, and the last thing I wanted in this world was for any harm whatsoever to come to him because of me.

"Don't worry," he told me. "I'm more capable than you think."

I smiled and wished we were back in the privacy of his office so I could kiss him the way I wanted to, but I was wary of surveillance cameras around.

"Did he come to you at campus today?" he asked, and I hesitated on whether to relay this information or not because it was sure to annoy him even more and perhaps cause him to take even more drastic actions against James.

However, after James's behavior today I couldn't help but wonder if being drastic was the way to go with him.

Eventually I decided not to hide anything from Gideon.

"He did," I said, and Gideon instantly sat up.

"What? When?"

"He came to my class and made a scene."

Silence.

"What did he say?"

I sighed. "I was the problem. He threatened to expose it all and I basically said, 'Expose what?' that you think I'm dating a professor? Go ahead and prove it."

"What?" he asked, his eyebrows shooting up, but he seemed more amused than anything else.

"I was enraged because I couldn't believe how much power I had given to such a small person by just acting afraid. Truly, what is the worst that could happen? Except of course you could get reprimanded."

I turned and looked at him, his words from earlier about how much he liked teaching returning to mind. "I'm so sorry," I said, my error dawning on me. "Oh my God."

"Sorry for what?" he asked.

"What if this badly affects you?"

"You need to stop worrying about me," he said. "I'm the one that should take care of you, it's not the other way round. "

"No," I couldn't help my smile. "We should both take care of each other."

He leaned forward then to kiss me, much to my surprise but I was so alarmed by it that I pulled away.

"Cameras," I complained, and he looked around at the dimly lit rooftop.

"Where?" he asked, and I was surprised at this.

"There are no cameras here?' I asked, and he held my gaze as though contemplating whether to lie to me or not. I pinched his arm and refused to let go.

"Don't lie to me," I gritted my teeth, and he captured my lips. This time around I couldn't have fought against the spell he instantly pulled me under if I had tried. His tongue stroked against mine, softly and unhurriedly at first and then I was completely lost. My arms curved around his shoulders while he deepened the kiss and sucked on my lips. My heart was instantly pounding in my chest threatening to jump out with excitement and a bit of adrenaline from all that had happened thus far.

I wanted to be close to him, in the way we had been the previous night, joined body and soul and it almost overwhelmed the intensity of emotion I had for him. Tears burned in my eyes as the desire to let him know exactly what he was to me and how I felt about him bubbled up my throat.

"Gideon," I called out, trying my best to put up all the fight within me to hold on and not to bare it all out because I didn't think he was ready yet. It was too soon.

He broke the kiss, and the soft smack that ensued made me shudder. I pulled my eyes open to meet his, aware that I could no longer hold back.

"I..." I began.

"Yeah?" he stroked my hair away from my face and behind my shoulder. His touch was so soft and so loving that it gave me the courage that I needed.

"I l-" I began but there was a sudden interruption. I didn't even realize how quiet the surroundings were, with the only noise, the hum and honks from the street way down below. But at the sudden ring of his phone, I was startled.

I pulled away from him, barely able to catch my breath and he looked amused. Then I watched as he retrieved his phone from his pocket and answered the call.

He listened for a bit, a frown on his face and then he sighed.

"Come alone, Susan," he said, but then there was another pause as he listened.

And then without a response he ended the call.

"We'll be briefly having some visitors," he said, and I was somewhat surprised.

"Visitors? Who?"

"Michael," he said. "My business partner. You met him before when you came for the internship interview."

"Oh yeah," I replied as my memory was juggled. "Yeah, you're right."

"He doesn't have any particular business with us, he's

just being nosy. Susan however does because she is in charge of the whole issue with James."

"Oh alright," I said, and just then the door leading to the rooftop was pushed open. A man and a woman emerged, but due to the dim lighting I couldn't see them properly until they were almost at our table. Michael, I immediately recognized. I met his gaze but when he stared long and hard and quite excitedly at me, I was forced to move my eyes to the woman standing by his side.

She reached out first with her hand for a handshake, and I took it. "Hello I'm Susan Dane. I'm the head of the Research and Development Department here."

Michael, who seemed to be of incredibly high spirits, also offered his hand and I accepted the handshake.

"We've met," he said. "Miss Fraser, right?" he asked, and I nodded.

I caught the woman then perusing my appearance and felt slightly embarrassed. Everyone was dressed so impeccably, but I perfectly embodied the image of a broke college student. I had never felt so out of place, and my gaze couldn't help once again but go to Gideon. My heart felt a bit heavy once again at all the trouble that had come since he had given in to me, and it made me wonder if I was even up to par with his standards.

A part of me, despite the fact that he had never outrightly mentioned or alluded to this, couldn't help but suspect this might have been the reason behind his refusal of me from the start.

My heart though, seemed to know better, because it pricked me with rebuke at thinking this way because Gideon thus far had shown me with absolute perfection the depth of his affection for me. He might not have outrightly declared it, but I could feel it in the way he looked at me, and his actions and currently the way he had slid his arm around me to ensure that I wasn't in any way uncomfortable.

He motioned for the woman to take a seat.

"Pamela," Michael started but quickly stopped himself.

"Excuse me, Miss Fraser, or can I call you Pamela? Gideon isn't giving me very warm looks at this request."

I turned and saw that Gideon wasn't in fact showing any emotion, so it was apparent to me that Michael was quite dramatic. This was alright, as he made the air a bit lighter since the other two by our sides were quite serious minded.

"Pamela is fine," I told him, and Gideon turned to me with a question in his gaze. "I'll feel more comfortable," I explained, and he nodded.

"Don't allow him to become too familiar with you though," he warned me. "Otherwise, he becomes the proverbial pest that you cannot get rid of."

I was amused, but when I noticed the serious gaze of the woman on me the smile immediately fell from my lips.

She quickly caught herself when she noticed this and moved her attention to her boss.

"What are the updates?" he asked, and she responded.

"We just got a message from them requesting a meeting so we can come to an agreement."

I watched as Gideon stared at her in consideration of this, and just like that the warmth was completely gone out of the space. I shivered slightly and he seemed to sense this because he turned to give me a worried glance.

I shook my head to assure him that I was fine, so as not to distract him and he returned his attention back to Susan.

"What is there to discuss?" he asked. "Were our stipulations not clear or simple enough? Our only request was that they immediately let go of James if he didn't give the response I wanted before midnight." He glanced down at his watch. "It's almost eight pm. Are they trying to test me?"

Once again, I felt a cold chill run down my spine.

"Um..." she looked down at the file that she had brought with her. "I think what they were trying to imply was their shock that you had been able to so easily breach their systems. It seems that they are interested in a collaboration of some sorts."

"Well, I'm not," he said but Michael's hand shot up.

"Actually..."

Gideon turned a stern look on him, and it quieted him down. I almost wanted to move away from him then, more tense than I had probably been all day. He seemed like a completely different person.

Perhaps it was because his arm moved away from my waist as he leaned forward to take the file from Susan. He perused through it while Michael's gaze connected with mine. He sent me a compassionate smile and I didn't know how to feel about it.

"Gideon," Michael called, his tone now back to being bold and assured. "You really don't want to consider any sort of collaboration with them?"

"How can that be when they don't even know who's attacking them."

Michael turned to Susan, and she explained. "It's all anonymous. But James must have told them."

"So?" Gideon asked. "Can they prove it?" He smiled, shaking his head. "How's your trail so far?" he asked Susan. "Are all tracks covered?"

"We're completely out of sight," she said, "that's under control."

He set the file down and turned to me. I met his gaze as his arm curved once again around my waist. It softened and slowly he began to feel quite familiar and approachable again. I also realized I was now so damn turned on it was becoming quite difficult to breathe.

Silence followed and as I looked at all present, I noticed that their gazes were all on Gideon's. It was obvious that they were waiting for some sort of a response from him.

He released a sigh then, seemingly not yet ready to speak, so Michael took over.

"Pamela, what do you study at the University?" he asked.

"Business Administration," I replied, and he nodded.

"That's great. We have a couple of positions open here for someone with your qualifications. I'll have to confirm with HR on the options available."

"Um..." I didn't know what to say to this.

"You attended the internship examination, right? Have you gotten your acceptance letter? What position did you apply for again?"

"Uh..." I began, but Gideon spoke up.

"Michael, she's here to rest right now. Can you please stop with the interrogation?"

"Jeesh," he straightened the excitement draining from his face. "Are you going to be this protective of her all the time? It's borderline offensive. Pamela can hold her own and choose not to answer her own questions. Pamela, I'm right, aren't I?"

I looked between the two of them and saw the annoyance on Gideon's face.

"You're putting her on the spot!"

My gaze went to Susan, and it was just in time to see her shaking her head in amusement.

"Get used to this Pamela."

I found a smile curving across my lips at this.

"I can answer my own questions, Gideon," I said. "I'm not too tired to speak."

"Exactly," Michael said, and I smiled at him.

Gideon however wore a look of betrayal on his face at me that I couldn't quite ignore.

"It's fine," I told him and turned to Michael.

"I wasn't accepted in that position but it's alright because I'm not certain that's the route I want to go. I still have a bit of time left in college so I'm going to use it to explore a variety of other things in order to hopefully, finally be able to know exactly what I want to do."

He considered this for a few moments and then nodded his head. "I understand. As they say, the best way to find what you want is to begin tasting and eliminating the things that you don't want."

I smiled. "It's not exactly the best way but it seems to be my only option now so I'm going to be diligent with it."

He nodded. "That's a great attitude."

"Thank you," I said, and he gave me a smile that somewhat felt more genuine than all the others prior.

I felt Gideon shift then, so my attention went to him. He leaned forward in thought and then he looked at Susan.

"Tell them that I'm making a change to my demand and they now have an hour left."

Her eyes shot open in surprise and so did mine.

Everyone stared at him, but no one objected.

"Let them know that if my demands are not met in the next hour more damage than what they're expecting will be made to every part of their organization."

42

GIDEON

Her mood completely changed after our two guests left with my instructions. I could tell that Michael wasn't quite pleased about it, but I was grateful he respected the fact this was an incredibly personal affair to me and so he didn't object to it.

Pamela, however, couldn't quite hide her worry.

I turned to watch as she lifted a glass to her lips, and even though she sent me a smile she couldn't quite hide the fact it was far from genuine.

I shook her slightly and she met my gaze.

"What is it?" I asked.

She thought for a moment and then said. "How much longer are you going to be here?"

I was a bit surprised at the question.

"Um... I could take you home right now if you're too exhausted. You know what, let's go home."

"No," she said. "I mean... since you've moved the deadline time to an hour, I imagine you'd like to be here to handle things?"

I told her the truth. "I would like that, but I can also control things from home."

She however refused. "There might be traffic and you might not even get there on time. So… I'll wait."

"Okay," I said, but couldn't ignore her nervousness. "Everything will be fine," I told her, and she nodded.

"I trust you I just… can't help but feel a bit of guilt for all of this."

I immediately tried to counter this, but she stopped me.

"I know… I know. I shouldn't feel bad about it but… I care about you deeply… and us, so I can't help but feel bad about it. I can make you a promise though that from now on I'll be much more careful. Although I already made a mess about the whole professor dating thing earlier in the day." she sighed.

"Pamela," I told her. "Just be free. Live freely and not cautiously with me. I would hate it if you felt stifled in any way. Attacks are normal, at least in my world and till now I've always handled them seamlessly. Whatever comes our way we'll tackle it together so don't ever hold back or be restrained because you're thinking on my behalf. Trust me, I'm more than capable."

She gave me that soft smile that always made me unable to look away from her.

"I know," she said. "I know." And then to my surprise, she leaned forward and threw her arms around me. I was a bit startled by the embrace, but I fully accepted it, and rested in her warmth and affection. But then she broke the spell when she whispered in my ear.

"I know how we can pass the next hour."

I leaned away, my head cocking slightly as I wondered what she had in mind.

She rose to her feet then, took the bottle of wine in one hand and then grabbed my hand with her other.

"Where are we going?" I asked, but she didn't respond. Instead, she laughed, mischievously and began to lead me back into the building.

Soon we arrived at my office and there, she returned to the sitting area to set the bottle down. Then she turned around and with her gaze on me, now sultrier than amused, she grabbed the bottom of her shirt and pulled it over her head.

My heart pounded against my chest as it became more than obvious to me what she had in mind. I took a glance at the clock on the wall and decided we had time, and even if we didn't there was no way I was going to say no to this. So, I headed over to the door to lock it and by the time I turned around she was pulling her bra down her arms. I felt my steps falter as I took in her huge, full breasts and instantly took my jacket off.

I flung it aside and with long strides was on her in no time.

"Is this a bad time?" she asked, just before I cradled her face and kissed her. It was a long time afterwards before she got her response.

"Absolutely not," I breathed and kissed her senseless once again. I could feel her softness pressed against me and at the reminder from the previous night of how it would feel to have our bodies pressed so intimately together, I could no longer bear to have the barrier of clothing between us. I moved to grab the tail of my shirt but was amused when I found that she was already pulling it out from my pants.

We shared a silent laugh just before she pulled it over my head, and then we were pressed against each other. Skin to skin, heat to heat, heart to heart. I kissed her once again and was so lost in it that not till I felt her hand grab the buckle of my pants did I realize we needed some sort of plan. Reluctantly, I broke away from her. She ran her tongue across my taste on her lips and looked around the office.

My gaze went to the couch, but then it went to the desk and my excitement grew. I couldn't decide.

She seemed to sense my dilemma then because with a hand curved around the side of my face, she turned my gaze to meet hers and relayed her exact desire.

"I want to be fucked," she said. "*Hard*. It's been a hell of a fucking day."

Amused, I lowered and with my hands around her thighs, lifted her. With a slight squeal, her legs wrapped around my waist, her arms around my shoulders and beyond all else I was just so glad to see her smile.

I took her with me to the desk and settled in the space between the two guest chairs.

She slightly pouted.

"I'd have loved to see the view," she softly complained as she glanced back. "Wait, can they see us?"

I smiled and shook my head. They can't see in. We can only see out."

She looked around the office. "And are there any cameras in here?"

"Of course not, that would be an invasion of privacy. Plus, if there were, would you think I'd let this happen?"

I captured her lips once again.

She pressed me even harder against her, the hardened peaks of her nipples rubbing against my chest and her crotch digging into mine. I leaned down to take her breasts into my mouth and she cradled my head for support, her head falling back as a soft moan escaped from her lips. The sweet sound relayed her complete submission to me and my total ownership of her body and heart and it made me feel weak. It was the most amazing feeling to know that someone so precious to me could offer herself so completely, and it made me even more enraged at the threats and troubles that the bastard had brought to her over the past few days.

I wanted to destroy him more than anything else, but then as she cradled me oh so gently and planted a kiss on my forehead, I couldn't help but soften once again. It was a hell of a picture. She hardened me and softened me all at once and made me feel things I hadn't even known where possible. She was mine and I was certain now a part of me had known about it all along. And now I needed to find a way to tear down the barriers I had put up for so long in order to completely accept this. I swore to myself I would try with everything I had inside me. Because she was worth it and because no one could ever love and care for her better than I could.

"Gideon," she called out, and the sound of my name from her lips was an aphrodisiac that heightened my desire to a dangerous level. I pulled away and held her face once more in my hands so she could see in my gaze what I felt for her, and what my mind was still too cowardly to say.

I was amused because the plan with setting her here on this surface was to fuck her hard and fast just as she had requested, and to give the both of us the most treasured release we both craved, but once again as our gazes met, I couldn't help but fall so hard, pulled under by a forced I couldn't quite understand.

She kissed me and my hands finally went to the buckle of my pants. I made quick work of getting it out of the way and then I moved my attention to her. She lifted in order to give me all the access I needed, and I pulled her jeans down along with her panties. I flung both away and then she was bare before me. This time around she was far from shy and was more than eager to open her thighs for me. I smiled, loving the haze of lust in her eyes and at the way her teeth bit down on her lower lip, I leaned forward and began to trace kisses down her soft torso. She tasted and smelled amazing but then I could no longer delay in getting to the exact spot I hadn't been able to get out of my mind all day. From time to time, the memory would come to mind and assault my concentration till all I could see was her.

The troubles that had followed had hijacked my attention but now that she was with me once again, I didn't hesitate.

My mouth closed at her pulsing wetness and a whimper sounded at the back of her throat.

"Fuck," she cursed, and the soft yet fiery note to it amused me.

She grabbed onto my head, spurring me even further and my tongue slipped out to devour her the way she wanted.

"Gideon," she cried out over and over again, and with her tightening grip I completely understood what her message was. She tried to pull me away as she moaned and writhed, rocking her sex against my lips with her legs closed solidly around me.

"I can't... oh God," she breathed.

I knew she was trying to alert me of her inability to control her tone and I completely understood. I straightened and she grabbed onto me, pulling me to her. My fingers however took over from my mouth, one finger slipping in carefully after the other and then she managed to pull her eyes open.

"Hold on," I whispered to her and all she could do was

shake her head. I began to thrust slowly at first and then my pace increased fervently. With an arm around her I held her in place and finger fucked her. She came within a minute, her release spilling out over my hand and her mouth closing around my shoulders as she tried to muffle her cry.

"*Fuck*," she cried, and held on so tightly to me that I could almost feel the pain of her hold. Regardless I embraced her, holding her equally as tightly as she recovered. Afterwards, I felt the moisture on her cheeks but when I tried to pull away to see it, she refused... shaking her head.

"I'm still not deserving?" I asked but she shook her head.

"You are. You are, it's just... it's embarrassing."

I couldn't help but laugh, my hand stroking the back of her head to calm her down.

"Ready for more?" I asked and felt her slightly shudder in my arms.

"How much time do we have?" she asked, and I met her gaze.

"Doesn't matter."

She smiled, her grin blinding as it spread across her face and there were words I knew I had to say aloud.

"You're the most beautiful woman in existence," I told her, and at first, she seemed shocked at my words. But then her smile grew impossibly wider, and her cheeks flushed red.

"Oh my god," she cried out, a hand over her mouth. "That's not true. That's not true at all."

"To me it is," I said as I ran the tip of my tongue across my bottom lip tasting her there.

She crushed her frame to mine and kissed me with every ounce of emotion she had in her. It went on for quite a while and I knew she was pouring out her heart to me and perhaps trying her best to express words that just like me, couldn't yet find the guts to express.

And in this moment, I wanted to do the same and to connect with her in the most intimate way I knew how. Grabbing the sides of her thighs, I pulled her even further towards me and then guided my cock towards her cleft. I stroked my flushed head through her damp folds and relished the intoxicating sound of her moan.

I slid into her, and her passage welcomed me hungrily. She was warm and oh so fucking sweet and all over again I temporarily lost myself in the bliss that she was.

I could no longer bear for any inch of space to remain between us, so I thrust the rest of the way in, and just in the manner she had requested.

Her nails dug into my skin as I reached the hilt of her and for a few moments, we both remained in that state, savoring the feel of complete and utter connection with each other. I held onto her tightly and she did the same to me, our lips joined and our hearts nearly beating as one. Soon I could feel the restless reminder of time come to me and so I began to move, aware we would probably soon be interrupted.

Her hands moved down to my biceps, gripping me hard in order to ensure she was stable, and then her hips were moving in perfect rhythm with mine. At first, we were somewhat calm with our rhythm, our gazes connected but then I began to lose control of my restraint and before I knew it, I had tilted her in just the right angle and was pounding my hips into hers. She did the same to meet the hardness of my thrusts and couldn't keep her reactions tamed.

I highly suspected we would be heard but I didn't care. Especially since it was after hours and truly there should be no one within the vicinity except my secretary and she had since clocked out for the day.

So, to any others that caught on, they were in the wrong and not us.

"Gideon... *harder*," she gasped, and I was almost amused. She was barely able to take the current intensity with which I was fucking her but since she asked, I held on even tighter and pummeled my cock more fervently into her. My balls were heavy with need, and I loved how with each thrust they connected with her sex. Suddenly, she reached down, her hand trying to touch them and in response I couldn't help but shudder. It had been an almost unconscious move I realized as I opened my eyes and met her barely able to keep hers open. I smiled and pummeled her even harder. This time around we were both driven to the edge simultaneously and held on tightly to each other as we reached the peak and lost ourselves together. I was fast learning that at moments like this, and with her, it was impossible to control my tone. In past relations it had never been a problem as this peak of ecstasy had been at most enjoyable, but with her I felt myself lose cognizance temporarily of everything beyond the feel of her in my arms. Heat surged up my body, nearly consuming me with her warmth and sweetness and I couldn't help but continue thrusting into her. She accommodated me, until I was somewhat sated... and could no longer go on. Until every ounce of pleasure had been milked out of my cock. Afterwards I collapsed against her shoulder but reveled in the feel of her legs as they wrapped around my waist.

In her arms I realized, was where I was meant to be, and I wanted to find a way to express it to her, but I soon found that I couldn't. And this time around it was because I was just too exhausted to, so, I just leaned against her, taking as much strength as I could so we could both continue peacefully with our evening.

Suddenly, there was a knock at the door and both of us were aggravatingly forced to come to.

"It's locked,' I reminded her at the panic on her face, and at this she was able to catch her breath. Then she collapsed once again against me but neither of us were able to afford this any longer, so I took the liberty of putting us both back in order. First, I ensured her legs were solidly on the ground and although it took a few movements to confirm she was stable, I was soon able to go across the room and gather our clothing.

Soon enough we were presentable and after one last kiss, I headed over to the door to open it. Just as expected I saw Susan waiting and saw the concerned look on her face.

"Is everything alright?" she asked, and I nodded.

"Everything's fine."

She looked skeptical but had no choice but to believe this.

I moved on to the crucial matter at hand.

"Has there been any response?" I asked and she nodded, a light smile curving the corners of her lips.

"McMillan just called and informed us James would be dropping the lawsuit. He is advocating we make him liable for damages. He said he's been trying to reach you but there was no response from your phone, so I hurried over."

I looked behind then and could see Pamela watching and waiting.

"I left it on silent," I responded. "I'll give him a call with my final decision."

"Alright," she said and then turned around to go on her way.

I shut the door and saw that Pamela was much closer to

me than I realized, the distance between us now only a few steps.

"Did you overhear it all?" I asked as I began to head towards her.

"Mmm," she nodded just as I reached her and embraced her. For a few moments after we were both silent as we basked in the pleasant news.

Until eventually she spoke.

"If it's possible, do not push for any compensation for damages. Settling it amicably would be fine. I don't want anything concerning James looming over my head in the future especially since he might not even have a job anymore."

"He better not," I couldn't help but snarl and this made her smile.

"Either way I want to be completely done with him. There's no way he would have come out of this unscathed."

"Alright," I said, but she kept her gaze on me, as though she couldn't believe I would adhere to this.

"Gideon," her voice softened, and I was amused.

"He needs to apologize to you."

"I really don't want to see him again. Ever."

"On his knees," I continued as though I hadn't heard her. She stopped then and gave the cutest pout to ever exist.

I couldn't help but to succumb.

"Let's go home," I said but then her eyes rolled sideways in thought.

"What is it?" I asked and she shook her head. Amused but too eager to leave and have her once again in my arms, I began to gather our things.

Soon we were in the car and on our way, with one of the designated company drivers in front to take us home when I noticed the looks she kept sneaking at me.

"What is it?" I grinned and she giggled.

"I want to ask for something else," she said.

"Go ahead," I replied, and she did.

"You still haven't told me the full story of the handcuffs in your study."

For a moment I was a bit taken aback by this because I had thought she already knew the answer to this.

I cocked my head in thought. "Didn't I explain this when you asked yesterday?"

"You touched lightly on it, but we never got to the explanation."

I smiled. "Really?"

"Yeah," she said, however I didn't say anything more on the subject. I wanted to see just how curious and insistent she could be on the matter, so I kept quiet on it until we arrived back at my apartment.

She kept sneaking looks at me and although they were endearing, they were also incredibly distracting.

"Stop," I told her.

"Tell me," she whined slightly as I entered the passcode for the door.

"I will," I said. "When the time is right."

"And when will that be?" With my hand on the small of her back, I pushed her gently into the apartment and she went willingly.

She however turned around and kept pestering me.

"Will it be today or tomorrow? Or next week? Or this month?"

"You know this is just making me want to drag things out even longer," I told her and at this she stopped. However, I was already on my way to the bedroom.

"What?" she asked, and I couldn't help but laugh. I needed a shower... in fact we both did so the moment I went to the bathroom, she came in with me. I immediately locked the door behind her.

"Hey!" she said but it was too late to escape. I grabbed her and heard her squeal, no longer restrained as her voice resounded through the entire bathroom.

"I'll tell you after our shower," I said but then I thought better of it.

"Let's take a bath instead. I'll get the jacuzzi going."

Her gaze turned to the glistening jacuzzi in the corner and just like that, I could instantly see her interest shift from the response she had been hounding me for.

43

PAMELA

I sincerely didn't think that I could feel better than this. I pondered on how and what exactly would make it feel better and there was just no answer. So, I concluded that by some chance, I had been granted heaven here on earth in advance of everyone else. And it had everything to do with the man whose arms I was currently floating and resting in.

My eyes were shut, the warmth and scent of the water encapsulating me, and the weight of Gideon's arms around my waist, both equally comforting and sensually stimulating.

We didn't speak and had been this way for the past few minutes, and I had absolutely no qualms whatsoever about it. I knew he needed to rest, and so did I and what better way than in each other's arms?

Soon enough though my mind came back awake and began to fill with questions.

"Do you have a jacuzzi like this in your apartment downtown?" I asked, wondering why we hadn't headed over there to spend the night.

"I do," he replied, his voice even deeper and more hoarse than usual. The lazy but unhurried tone was a near irresistible aphrodisiac all on its own. "It even has a pool."

I glanced behind to meet his drowsy gaze.

"Can I ask why we didn't head there tonight since we were in the area?"

He smiled, and then his eyes opened to meet mine.

"Here is closer to the campus. I didn't want you cutting your rest time short and worrying about traffic as a hindrance to getting back on time. Plus, I don't know where the key is."

My mouth fell open. "And now we get the true answer," I said, and he laughed.

"I have a spare with Grace but she'd long headed home, and mine is somewhere in the office back at campus, and I didn't think you'd appreciate us making a double trip to retrieve it and then returning."

I relaxed back against him, amused.

"Maybe not," I said, "but then maybe I would have? I don't know but interior spaces have always fascinated me. I especially love what you did with this apartment so I was curious to see how the one in the city would look."

"Huh," he said, and I reached to the side to grab the glass of champagne that he had poured out for us. On the side table, there were also candles with the sweetest scent and a box of macadamia chocolates that he had suddenly pulled out.

I took a sip of the exquisite drink and set it back down, my tongue *clucking* in disapproval as I wondered when I would ever begin to appreciate champagne. He heard this and leaned around to look at my expression, and then he laughed out loud, the sound though low but unmistakably unrestrained.

"Not to your liking?" he asked, and I shook my head.

"I prefer red wine."

"Understandable," he said, and I turned to glance at him, loving the sheen of sweat on his face.

"What about you?" I asked, and he lifted his gaze a bit to consider the question.

"Whiskey is my preference," he said. "But I can't exactly consume too much of it so I guess the next best thing would be red wine."

"Nice," I nodded, but couldn't help but wonder about the sophistication of our conversation. Or perhaps it was the norm? I mean, the last time I'd had a conversation like this with him it'd been about cereal. I wondered if he remembered, and as the full memory came to me, I turned to him with barely contained excitement on my face.

"Do you remember?" I asked and narrated the incident.

He thought about it, and at the slight raise of his brows it was clear to me he remembered. We shared a laugh as we recalled the argument which had been quite brief because back then, he had absolutely not wanted to engage in a trivial conversation with a middle schooler about what cereal was best. He'd chosen some granola cereal, claiming that he loved that it wasn't too sweet while I'd gone the opposite direction and chosen Coco Puffs.

I recalled now that his mom had come into the house during our debate and as always, greeted me warmly. He however hadn't responded to her, and I remembered wondering back then if they had a fight. These little details had initially slipped from my mind, but I was incredibly glad while we were reminiscing, they were easy to recall. I was curious now though and wondered if it would be too personal a question for me to ask him. Eventually, I decided against it and chose instead to inquire about the handcuffs, especially at the feel of his rock-hard cock against my back, was what I especially wanted to know the details of.

So, I turned once again to look at him. "It's time," I said, and he arched a brow.

"Time for what?" he asked as he reached out towards the box of chocolates.

"To tell me about the handcuffs. You said you'd do so after our bath."

"We're still having a bath," he said, and I frowned at him.

"Alright, I'll get out then."

I started to stand to make my way out, but his arm tightened around my waist, forcing me back in place on his lap, and as result water splashed out of the jacuzzi.

"Gideon!" I laughed, having no choice but to submit to his insistence in holding me in place.

After things had calmed down a bit he replied. "I already told you what it was for," he said, and I turned to him, confused.

"When?"

"Yesterday, when I was talking to you about my professional past."

"Oh," I said, knowing I was supposed to be recalling something but couldn't for the life of me discover what it was.

He soon lent me his assistance.

"I told you I was apprehended when I was younger," he said.

It took a few more seconds for me to process this, and after I did my mouth fell open.

"From when you worked with the government?"

"Yeah," he replied, and I felt quite silly because he had indeed mentioned it.

"Oh," I said. "*Oh.*"

He laughed and leaned forward to press a kiss to the side of my neck. "Let's rinse off properly in the shower and then head to the kitchen. I have some Magnolia tea and it does wonders in helping me relax. Maybe it'll do the same for you too so you can properly rest tonight." I was more than eager to comply.

He carefully led me out, and just as we arrived at the stall, I had another request.

"Will you wash my hair?" I asked. "I'll wash yours."

"Of course," he smiled.

A little while later, we were strolling out to the kitchen, now toweled dry but our hair still slightly damp. He was dressed simply in a pair of pajama bottoms riding quite low on his hips which I had absolutely no qualms about. While I was in what had to be the softest robe I had ever encountered.

It felt like a big hug and clouds all at once, and at the imprint of his initials on the front I couldn't help but feel slightly jealous. "So, this is what true luxury feels like?" I asked as I walked towards the counter. "Was this gifted to you? Do you have any more? And can I have one of them?" I shot off my questions and he smiled as he began to retrieve the tea from one of the cabinets.

"No, the designer that worked on this apartment had them custom made. No, not this apartment," he paused. "The one downtown. I just brought some of them here. In the apartment downtown a lot of things are branded with my initials. I didn't quite see the point, but she insisted so I gave her free rein to do as she pleased."

"Free rein?" I said as I took my seat before him. "She must have had a blast."

"I hope so," I replied. "I didn't interfere much, so she

pretty much had full control. My only request was that she keep the decor uncluttered and void of bright colors."

"Now I'm really excited," I said. "I can't wait to pay a visit."

I watched as he retrieved two cups and then began to make the tea. My gaze remained on his long slender fingers until eventually he brought something to my attention.

"You used to love looking at my mom's magazines back then," he said. "You'd always go straight to the living room when you came over and then bring some with you back to the counter. Do you remember?"

"Of course," I smiled.

"Were you interested in fashion?" he asked. "Was that why you were so interested in them back then?"

I immediately raised my hand to correct this. "No, no, not at all. I didn't care about the fashion, I just got them to look at the housing section. The internet was still new to me then, so I didn't know how to just search online for the pictures I wanted to see."

"So, you might have some true interest in interior decorating?" he asked, and I met his gaze.

With a smile, he set the tea down before me and I looked down to see the rich golden color.

It made me pause to think of his words as a light bulb had suddenly come on over my head.

"Have you never thought about this?" he asked, and I nodded.

"I have. I have noticed it but... but I'd have to work with clients and people, which I'm not quite fond of or have the patience for so I always immediately put it out of my mind."

"That doesn't have to be the division of the field that you participate in," he said. "I mean you're an artist, so why don't you apply your interest and skill and perhaps make tools for the designers to use and maybe decor items? You could start small, a little vase here and there? A lamp?"

"Stop," I said, and he complied.

My eyes were wide as I looked at him, the possibilities for what he was suggesting immediately swarming my mind. I considered his words for a few moments, and not till I heard him speak did I realize that he was now seated by my side, sipping from his own cup.

"Your tea will get cold," he said, and I finally returned my attention to the room.

"Your idea is wonderful," I told him, itching suddenly to be with a pen and paper of some sort.

"Thank you," he smiled, and I couldn't help but lean closer to him, "It truly is wonderful, there's so much to explore." I then looked towards the hall. "I need to get my phone and charge it. I can search for some information right now."

I rose to my feet and before he could stop me, was on my way back to the bedroom where we had earlier discarded our clothes.

44

GIDEON

I watched her leave and felt relief… and possibly even excitement for her.

I didn't think I had ever seen her so enthusiastic before, so I hoped she would be able to latch onto this idea and that it would interest her enough to run with it. It was a fantastic one in my opinion, and I couldn't wait to see what she would come up with to make it work.

Suddenly, my phone began to ring so I set the cup down so I could retrieve it from my pocket. I expected to see that it was Susan from the office but when Oscar's ID flashed on the screen, I frowned.

He had never ever called me so late, so I couldn't help but wonder if there was some sort of severe emergency.

I immediately picked up and rose to my feet.

"Oscar?" I asked, and his familiar voice soon floated over.

"I'm sorry to disturb you, sir," he said, and I brushed the courtesy away.

"There's no need. Why are you calling?"

"One of your students, Meredith Scott, called me a little while ago," he said.

"She mentioned Miss Fraser's name and said she was urgently trying to reach her but couldn't because her phone is off. She was wondering if I could get in contact with you so she could confirm she was alright. She also had some urgent news she needed to relay to her."

"I will take care of it Oscar. Thank you for calling," I said, ending the call more curious than ever as to why Meredith would have tried to reach us both so late at night. Perhaps she was worried about the whole issue with James? But then I wasn't even certain she was aware of it.

"Do you have a charger?" I heard the question from behind me and immediately turned towards her.

"Come with me," I said as I headed to my office and immediately found the needed charger. I took her phone and just as I plugged it in, I relayed the message.

"Call your roommate to confirm that all is well," I said. "She's trying to reach you."

"Oh," she said, slightly surprised by this information. "Sure."

She immediately began to do as requested so I exited the room to give her some privacy.

A few minutes later, I heard her as she ran to the bedroom.

"Oh my God!" I heard her say. I immediately got up and went after her and got to the bedroom just in time to see her searching for her clothes.

She immediately began to put them on, panicked and when I saw her face, I found her eyes were damp with tears.

"Pam, what's wrong?" I asked, immensely alarmed as the tears began to fall down her cheeks.

"My dad," she said. "My mom called earlier to tell me that he had a heart attack. He was rushed to the hospital. Oh my God," she stopped then as she looked around. "Where's my shirt?"

I immediately moved into action. I gave her one of my t-shirts, put one on myself and in no time was leading her straight to the foyer.

"I'll take you," I said as she put her shoes on. "What hospital was he admitted to?"

"Hoag Memorial," she said.

I grabbed her hand and led her with me out of the apartment.

In the car, she was quieter than she had ever been.

Her gaze was to the window, and her fists clenched on her lap. I didn't need to inquire as to just how tense and terrified she was. Her brain was probably moving at countless miles per hour, and I felt frustrated because I didn't exactly know what to say to console her.

"Do they know what's wrong with him yet?" I asked as softly as I could manage. "Is he still unconscious?"

It was a while before she responded to me. "They don't know yet and yes, he's still unconscious."

She released a shuddering breath and I wished I could pull her into my arms and assure her that things would be fine. However, I was certain what she needed more than anything was some quiet so she could process her feelings and thoughts.

The slight traffic we met on the road caused us to arrive a little later than we would have liked, but eventually we arrived at the hospital and were instantly directed to the room he had been placed in. Along the hall, I met a familiar figure and as we came closer, the person eventually turned.

"Pam," her mother called out and she let go of my hand. She immediately hurried over and began to speak, while I took my time in joining them, wanting to give them as much privacy as possible.

Her mother soon noticed me, and her eyes widened in surprise.

"Gideon?" she called, and I nodded. I sent her a smile and she reciprocated in kind.

We both turned then to watch Pamela as she headed over to the door and peeped through the glass.

"I'm going to head in to see him," she said, and walked in.

Her mother's attention returned to me. "You two met again?" she asked, and I could tell this was pleasing to her. "Wow, I would have never expected that."

I simply nodded, unaware of what to say and filled with concern for Pamela.

"Are you two dating?" her mother asked, and although I hesitated at first because I didn't know how Pam intended to relay the news, I also couldn't bring myself to lie or be elusive towards her mother.

"Yes ma'am, we are," I said, and her eyes seemed to widen even further.

"Oh my," she said. "How did you two meet again? Come sit down."

I followed her and then we took our seats. I trained my gaze on the door as I lightly recapped our meeting to her, and she was even more surprised to learn I taught at the university.

"You lecture?" she asked, and I wondered why she was able to ask these questions when her ex-husband was in a critical state. I supposed perhaps she didn't feel as affectionate towards him. I know I didn't. In fact, I downright loathed him and if it weren't for Pamela, I truly had no business being here.

She continued to ask more questions just as she always had, and I wondered then if she was interrogating me in this way because of the relationship I had admitted I was in with her daughter, or if it was because she was truly trying to find a way to take her mind off her worries for the time being. I eventually decided it was the latter and paid more attention in conversing with her.

"You own a cyber security company too?" she asked, and I nodded. "I'm part owner. My business partner runs it."

"Still," she said, smacking my arm. "You've done so well. I'm so proud of you. It's been like what, ten years since I last saw you? You're all grown up now."

It was a little strange hearing these kinds of endearments from her but for Pamela's sake I ensured to be as engaged as possible. She finally emerged and we both went quiet.

I immediately rose to my feet as she stood by the door, and then her eyes went to her mom.

"What's wrong with him?" she asked, and with a sigh her mom explained.

"They've run some tests so we'll be able to get detailed reports on him. Currently they've only been able to resuscitate and stabilize him. The doctor didn't tell me anything else, so we'll have to wait a bit longer."

Pamela continued to stare at her mother, and I had no idea what to do. It did look like she could use my support in standing at least, so I headed over to her. I hesitated but, eventually I touched her, my hand going around her arm and she finally looked up to stare at me.

It was as though she was seeing me for the first time and was trying to process everything. Eventually, I felt the exhaustion come into her and held her. She allowed herself to rest against me, and I led her back to the waiting room chairs.

Her mom watched us. I let Pamela rest in my arms and her eyes closed.

45

PAMELA

I didn't know when I fell asleep.

One moment I was being led by Gideon to sit down, and the next I woke with a start. It took a little while for my understanding of where I was to register, and as I pulled away to meet his kind eyes, I saw deep concern in them.

He sent me a smile while I looked around for my mother. "She has to go to work in the morning," he explained, and I nodded until I realized that he too needed to go to work, and me to class. However, these were the last things that I wanted to consider. Him however, I couldn't further inconvenience.

"You need to head home to rest," I told him. "You've had a long day."

"And so have you," he said. "Don't worry I'll wait here with you."

"Gideon," I called.

"I won't leave you here alone. So, it's either we go home together and come back in the morning, or we remain here and wait till then."

I sighed and looked once more towards the door. Then I turned to Gideon and knowing he truly wouldn't leave, rose to my feet. I needed to rest and there was nothing I could do until the next day, so I went along with him.

We headed straight to bed but as I laid in his arms, I found it was much more difficult to fall back asleep. I worried I was also keeping him awake so I tried to remain as still as possible. Soon enough, I could sense his even, relaxed breathing and was relieved he was finally resting.

As for me on the other hand, all I could do was think about my father and hope he would be okay. I felt a mix of emotions, fear at how critical this situation might turn out to be, and guilt at the fact I hadn't kept in touch with him recently. For as long as I could remember, I had kept him at arm's length, not considering a moment could come that threatened his presence and existence in the world. I was no longer close to him, but I wanted him to be healthy and happy and thus this was a nightmare to me. Life for me seemed to be one thing after another and once again, a different set of troubles weighed on my heart.

The next day, we received news of his condition from the doctor and for the longest time all I could do was stare at nothing.

"He'll need triple bypass surgery otherwise his heart will fail. Three coronary arteries are blocked, and this is severely restricting blood flow to his heart. It has to be scheduled immediately otherwise further complications may arise."

I had no choice but to turn to my mother by my side.

"Medications can't handle this?" she asked, and the doctor shook his head. "It's way beyond that now. His only option is open heart surgery."

"And um... and the cost?" she asked.

"Does he have insurance?" the doctor asked, and my

mom shot me a look. "He used to, but currently I don't think so. He hasn't been employed for a while."

My eyes widened at this as I turned to her, absolutely confused as to what I was hearing.

"We'll figure things out and get back to you," she said, and then we were once again left alone. I looked at my father on the bed, and all the tubes he was hooked to and considering the recent statements my mother had just made, his appearance made a little more sense.

He was scruffy, more unkept than I had ever seen him and thin. And I couldn't understand at what point along the years he had fallen to this state.

"This was why he never really pushed to see you," she said. "He wasn't doing too well himself. He struggled to find his feet after the businesses failed."

I sighed, and truly didn't know what to say.

Eventually I had to turn away, my ability to watch him in such a helpless state faltering.

"Let's go out for some fresh air," my mother said. "Grab a sandwich or something. There's a coffee shop across the street."

I didn't know when I agreed to this but not long after I found myself walking side by side with her as we headed over.

She placed our order, we took our seats and soon enough our food was delivered. I stared down at the club sandwich with blue cheese and mayo.

However, I had no appetite, so all I did was push it away and stare at the other people and families around.

She ate as she watched me and then spoke. "I'm a bit surprised," she said, and I looked at her.

"About what?"

"I didn't think you'd be this affected."

I couldn't help my frown. "What do you mean?"

"You've been... *angry* with him for a long time."

"I haven't been angry at him."

"Alright, dismissive then," she said, and I sighed. Needing something to do, I picked up my fork and pulled the meal towards me.

"I'm glad," she said.

"That he's not doing well?" I asked and gave her a dark look. She however shook her head somewhat amused.

"He hasn't been doing well for a long time, Pam. At first, I was glad," she smiled sadly. "But then I guess affection is a hard thing to completely get rid of all at once. He hurt me deeply especially with the divorce but... I don't want him to be so miserable. I couldn't possibly be happy about that because a small part of me always wondered if perhaps, our split wasn't totally his fault. If I had been a better wife, been more attentive... been *more* for him then I guess... maybe he wouldn't have looked at someone else and cheated."

I looked at her and my frown deepened. "You're trying to excuse what he did?"

"No, I'm not," she said. "But when you're part of a union, you can never actually just completely shuck all responsibility for its outcome because, whether you like it or not, your influence whether positive or negative was a part of it."

"Yeah," I said and reached for my bottle of water.

"I didn't want him to be happy because I wasn't, but I do want him to be at peace like I am. I don't think he ever quite found it. He always seemed haunted, dissatisfied, and I couldn't fix that for him. I had no idea how."

She smiled. "He was so ambitious when I met him but then nothing he ever did really worked out. I keep thinking that maybe the frustrations of so many failures eventually got to him, and he just needed a way out. I question myself if it was right that I had divorced him after he had cheated. Maybe if I had stayed just a little longer I would have been able to help him fi-"

"Mom," I interrupted her, and she lifted her gaze to meet mine. "Don't do that. There's no excuse for hurting you the way he did."

"I know but seeing him now..."

"What's happening to him now is unfortunate and painful but what happened to you back then too was unfortunate and painful. This family was all you had, and he was irresponsible with it. He tore it apart. That broke your heart. I'm hurt by what is happening to him now, but it doesn't excuse his past offense."

Her smile for me widened.

"I'm glad," she said. "To see that despite all of this, your affection for him remains."

"He didn't hurt me," I replied. "At least directly. I felt the pain of the separation, but he didn't directly hurt me. All I truly have of him are the fond memories. Of how attentive he was to me. He was a terrible husband, but I can't ignore the fact that he was a great father to me. And so, in the face of this.... how can I not be affected?"

"I understand," she said and reached out to place her hand on top of mine. She squeezed and I looked up at her, she was beyond exhausted.

"We'll figure this out," she said. "Somehow."

"How?" I asked. "Every minute that passes is one wasted and delayed. We need to sort it out now."

She sighed and pulled her hand away, then she continued with her meal. I continued with mine too and for the next few minutes neither of us spoke.

"I'll examine his finances," she said. "And see what we can uncover. I'm still his next of kin so this gives me adequate authority. I was a bit surprised to learn this. I would have thought he'd changed it to-" she stopped then and I looked up.

"Who is she?" I asked, and at the confusion that came on her face, I explained.

"I never asked who the woman he cheated on you with was."

"You don't know?" she asked, and I shook my head. But then her reaction put me on guard as though I was supposed to know so I couldn't help but narrow my gaze at her.

"Why?" I asked. "Is it someone we know?"

She stared at me and then she sighed.

"No," she shook her head.

"So..." I urged. "Who was she?"

She returned her attention to her food. "It doesn't matter," she said. "It was more than ten years ago."

I didn't push the matter, considering that even though so much time had passed this was probably still a difficult topic for her to address.

In the end, she resolved to see what she could do and promised to update me. I had a class to get to immediately after and so I quickly hurried over, although all my concentration was shot. I could do nothing but think about my father and Gideon. I hadn't heard from him since the day began but I figured he was extremely occupied so didn't bother reaching out to him. Afterwards, I headed home and made lunch but once again I didn't have any appetite and the stress was making me nauseated so in the end, I just headed straight to bed and fell asleep.

46

GIDEON

Meredith was in class.

My gaze couldn't help going to her from time to time.

It was so much that by the time the class came to an end she came over to me wearing a soft smile.

"She's doing okay," she said without me even asking. "She went to the hospital this morning and made it in time for her class. She's at home now, resting."

"Oh," I said.

She then placed an envelope down on the podium and my brows raised at it. She smiled at my reaction. "It's not a bribe," she said. "It's the key to our apartment. In case you wanted to go check up on her later."

I looked down at it and accepted it with gratitude.

"Thank you," I said, and she waived the courtesy away.

Afterwards, I was scheduled to head downtown to see to some company affairs, but I was left with no choice but to reschedule it for a later time so that I could head over to Pamela's. I went with some soup and bread, just in case she hadn't had the time to have lunch.

Thankfully, I was able to access the apartment as Meredith had facilitated.

It was deathly quiet when I walked in.

A little messier than usual, and completely void of the life that had been around the last time I was here.

I headed in, set the food down on the counter and went straight to her room.

She was lying in bed, fast asleep and with the covers almost all the way above her head. The angle she was in was awkward as though she was curled in a fetal position, and it made my heart hurt seeing her in this state. But at the same time, I didn't want to risk trying to make a change to it in case it woke her up since I didn't know how difficult it had been for her to fall asleep in the first place.

All I could do was sit on the armchair in the corner and watch her. She looked so peaceful, but I could only imagine how troubled she was by all of this. James' situation had just been settled and now this had cropped up and I wanted to take away all the strain it put on her. However, it felt like I was being tested or mocked, or even both.

Because since I had solved the earlier one with so much vigor, this was then sent which was much more complicated. I wanted to help her in any way that I could, but I truly hoped that it would not extend beyond her otherwise, I didn't know what my reaction would be. Perhaps I would be able to look away and do what was needed, but thus far I had never been able to and I couldn't help but feel as though we were both walking on thin ice although she didn't necessarily know it yet.

Suddenly, my phone began to ring, and I immediately pulled it out of my pocket. It was from Michael, but I didn't want to take it, so I immediately canceled the call and remained in place. I set the phone on silent but when the call came in once again, I had no choice but to leave the room in order to answer it.

"How's Pamela?" was the first question he asked, and I was a little taken aback by it.

"Why are you asking?" I asked and heard his smile.

"You are officially together, aren't you? So why shouldn't I ask. In a way she's almost like an extension of you now."

I thought about his words and a frown came over my face.

"I have a question for you," I said.

"Really? Go ahead."

"When you lo-" I tried again. "When you care about someone deeply, can it be excusable for you to not extend the same care towards their family?"

At this question he sucked in his breath.

"Absolutely not," he said. "You love someone and the crows on the roof of their house."

"What?"

"It's an idiom and it means you can't just love someone independent of whatever baggage they may have. You love them and you love everything that comes along with them, the good, bad and ugly. Or perhaps maybe *love* is extreme, but you have to tolerate and accommodate it."

At this I sighed, my mind going once again to the broken man I had seen earlier on that bed.

He had once been tall and haughty, confident and self-centered and now he looked so helpless it was as though his past self had been a mere figment of my imagination.

I once vowed to keep my hatred of him alive and to extract my pound of flesh wherever I could from him, but now I was in a relationship with his daughter, whom I was now quite certain I was head over heels in love with, I didn't quite know how to react.

"Gideon," Michael began to call then so I returned my attention to the call. We discussed what we could of the meeting I had blown off that afternoon, however suddenly I felt a presence in the kitchen.

Pamela was standing at the entrance.

She looked at me, her gaze somewhat expressionless and I could very clearly see just how much all of this was affecting her. She didn't seem outrightly worried, but her demeanor felt a bit cold, and for a moment it almost felt as though I was watching a stranger.

"Where's Meredith?" she asked, and I quickly ended the call with Michael.

"Hey," I greeted, and she nodded in response.

"How did you get the key?"

I knew she wasn't saying this curtly but really wanted to know where I had gotten the key from.

"She gave it to me in class," I told her. "In case I wanted to check up on you."

"Oh," she nodded and then her gaze went to the plastic bag on the table.

"You want some soup?" I asked. "It's a creamy tomato and there's some garlic bread to go along with it. It'll be soothing for you."

She seemed to contemplate this for a little while, and then she came forward till she was beside me at the counter.

I scooped out a serving for her in a bowl, and then took it over to the microwave to warm.

"Thank you," she said, and I didn't ask any further questions. I figured this was the safer route although I couldn't help but wonder if this would be weird. It couldn't be interpreted that I didn't care since I had brought food all the way to her.

I set the timer for the microwave and waited by it as the food heated up.

"My dad needs surgery," she said, and at the sudden announcement I was forced to pay attention.

"The doctor said he has blocked arteries and needs triple bypass surgery."

I turned to her, knowing my silence wouldn't suffice. But I found I still didn't know what to say.

She looked at me as though she realized this and didn't say a single word more of it afterwards.

"He'll be fine," I said. "Hopefully."'

I didn't ask for any further details and returned my attention to the soup. Finally, the timer sounded, and I retrieved the bowl.

I placed it on the waiting plate on the counter and carried them over to her.

She stared down at it, and then grabbed a spoon.

"Do you want to sit down?" I asked as she tasted it.

She turned to me, her tongue slipping out to lick across her lips and I couldn't help but watch it.

She shook her head in response and then took another spoonful. I wished I could kiss her, but I couldn't bring myself to. I had to hold back from her until this entire matter was resolved.

It was awkward remaining here in silence, but still I waited and watched her eat.

"You had to blow off work to come here, didn't you?" she asked. My plan had been to deny it but, in the end, I gave a nod and she seemed to be a bit surprised by this too. The ghost of a smile curved the corners of her lips and then she said, "Thank you and I'm sorry. I keep bringing hassles your way."

"Don't say that," I said and she nodded.

She took another spoonful and then returned her gaze to me. “Thank you for the soup,” she said. “It’s delicious. I’ll have the rest of it and go back to sleep.”

It was very clear that she was giving me permission to leave, and I took it. I too felt like I needed my space away from her, in order to get my thoughts together.

I had dreaded a situation like this coming up before we got together, and it had been one of the major reasons that had held me back.

I knew given the depth of my affection for her, and since she was mine then I wouldn’t be able to refuse helping in any way I could. Even though I didn’t want to.

Exhausted, I turned around, grabbed my keys and was soon on my way.

47

PAMELA

Something was wrong but I couldn't quite pinpoint what it was.

I watched him go, noticing how rigid he seemed and withdrawn and once again it brought me back to before he had agreed for us to be together. How he had seemed detached and unapproachable.

I sighed, wondering what the problem was and feeling a bit alone. This didn't at all feel like it had when James had been harassing me. Then he'd been warm and consoling, but although he was doing the same things now like bringing me food and ensuring I was okay, it still just felt different like there was a huge distance between us and he was a stranger. It wasn't something I wanted to expend my energy into anyway because there was always the possibility I was reading too much into what I was seeing, so I was able to convince myself to let it go.

I remained standing at the counter as I ate my meal, but I once again felt nauseous and couldn't understand why. Suddenly there was a knock on the door, and I turned to it, wondering who it was. I started to go around the counter but suddenly a wave of disgust hit me so hard I nearly retched. Instantly I headed over to the bathroom and thankfully was in time to lower to my knees before the toilet. I retched until eventually every bit of the food I had just eaten made its way out of my mouth. I was exhausted to my very bones, but still I was so surprised I immediately rose to my feet afterwards. Holding on tightly to the sink, I managed to rinse my mouth and then began to head back out.

"Pamela," I heard the call then and ran into Meredith as she came in with two filled grocery bags.

She looked at me, her expression immediately one of alarm as she took in my appearance.

"Are you alright?"

"Hmm," I replied. "Were you the one knocking?"

"Yeah," she replied. "My arms were full, and I wondered if you were with Gideon, so I wanted to announce my presence first in case there was anything untoward going on."

At this I smiled and headed over to her bags to see what she had gotten.

I found some fruits and instantly was in the mood for a pear so after helping her put them away, I took one and began to eat it. She watched me.

"I thought he'd stay longer. Did you drive him away?"

"I wish," I said, and she cocked her head in concern. "What do you mean?"

I wondered if there was any point in talking about this but due to my suspicion that I was probably reading more into it than was needed, I decided to share.

"He seems weird. I mean not weird, more like... not the norm. We've been pretty close over the last few days given this whole James debacle, and although I never expected it, I found out he could be quite doting when he's worried about me."

"He was weird in class today," she said. "Well not outrightly, but he just couldn't stop looking at me. I'm sure someone noticed. He does this a lot when he's thinking about you and apparently, I'm the next best thing."

I smiled. "Really?"

"Yup, I think at this point the rumors are going to start flying around that I have a thing with him. I wouldn't mind though, all the girls would die of jealousy."

"Please try to avoid that, if possible," I said. "He's just gone through the ordeal of a possible entanglement with a student, and I want him to have some peace. Perhaps that's even why he seemed so withdrawn today. His life has most definitely gotten much rowdier since I came around. Maybe he's even rethinking this relationship."

A heavy silence followed and when I turned to Meredith, I could see the scowl on her face.

"Can you have faith in people for once, and if not him then at least yourself? Why do you think it'll be so easy for him to make the decision to leave you? There's no one else like you and this is especially true for him, isn't it? Given your history."

"Yeah," I replied. "You're right, but I can't help but wonder why he seemed so withdrawn today. He didn't hug me or touch me and just delivered the food, said a few words and went on his way."

"Maybe he's busy and exhausted just like you are. He was at the hospital last night, wasn't he?"

"He was," I replied, and she gave me a look.

"You're right," I said. "I guess I'm just being sensitive. But then... he didn't really ask about my dad. I was the one who gave him the update and he didn't ask for any details. It was almost as though he didn't care."

At this she paid attention and took some moments to ponder on what I had just said.

"You're certain?" I smiled and took another bite into my pear.

"Of course, I am, and I'm not exaggerating this."

She sighed as she raked her hand through her hair.

"It's just one encounter," she concluded. "Perhaps he didn't want to bother you concerning it. After all these are just facts and he can get them from you some other time."

Something sad came over my face then and she didn't miss it.

"What is it?" She asked.

"I don't know," I replied. "I guess I was just hoping he'd offer to help. I mean... I wasn't going to take it... I mean... we actually kind of don't have the choice right now but to take it but I was kind of hoping he would offer and then... I don't know. He didn't ask if there was anything he could do like I had expected him to, especially with the huge looming bills and now, I can't bring it up, even if I wanted to."

"Do you want to bring it up?" she asked and again that horrid nausea came over me.

"My dad definitely can't afford the bills. My mother told me she would make some inquiries concerning it but from the look of things, we're going to have immense difficulties and I literally don't know what to do about it."

"Hmm," she said, and I felt a headache coming on so with a sigh, I turned around and returned to my room.

"Try to rest," she called after me, and I wondered how that would even be possible.

I checked the time as soon as I got into my bedroom and began to get ready for my late evening shift at the restaurant.

A FEW DAYS LATER, things seemed to have worsened even further.

I was at work and walking past the kitchen when my nose registered grease and garlic. In an instant I was running for the bathroom and managed to get there in time to retch into the toilet bowl.

I remained there because this time around, more food than I had anticipated came out. It was frustrating, confusing and disgusting and I couldn't understand what was happening and why my stomach was suddenly becoming so sensitive.

I couldn't afford to remain on my knees on the floor, so I immediately got to my feet. To my surprise, when I walked out of the stall, I saw Sarah standing by the sink, reapplying her lipstick. Our gazes meet in the mirror and instantly her eyebrows shoot up.

"That was you?"

"Yeah," I replied and began to rinse my mouth.

"Are you sick?' she asked. "Is it the flu?"

"I don't think so," I said as I shut the tap off and headed towards the paper towel dispenser.

She let out a laugh. "Maybe you're pregnant?"

I immediately stopped in my tracks.

So much so that I didn't even realize it until she started to leave but was startled to find me in the way.

Her gaze was of true concern and so was mine.

"Pam are you alright?" she asked and came around then to properly study me. "You really don't look good at all."

She reached out to touch the side of my face, but I pushed her hand away.

"I'm fine," I said and turned around to exit the bathroom.

I immediately returned to the counter as I tried to regain

my composure, but my heart seemed to be beating at an impossibly fast rate.

I didn't speak to anyone as I busied myself with taking the drink orders that had come up to the counter.

But then suddenly, Brian called out to me.

"A guest is at your station Pamela," he said, and my gaze lifted. I served the iced coffee to the customer and couldn't help but stare at the customer in question that had just come in. Our gazes met across the room and then she lifted her hand up to wave at me. With a sigh, I picked up my pencil and notepad and began to head over.

"Do you know her?" Brian asked, and I nodded in response.

"I do."

"Looking sharp," were the first words my mother said to me as soon as I arrived.

I pulled my pen out and glanced at the unopened menu on her table.

"What would you like to eat?"

"What do you recommend?" she asked. "You know what I like."

I cocked a brow at this. "You don't want to check the menu?"

"I'm exhausted," she said. "It's been a long day. Is it possible for you to sit with me for a few minutes?" she asked.

I looked behind at my colleagues at the counter, and then around at the bistro. Things weren't too busy but still I couldn't do that.

"No," I replied. "But I can stand and talk while you eat. I'll go place your order."

"Alright," she said, and I went on my way.

After placing her order, I waited a bit for it and in the

meantime returned to keeping myself busy at the counter. There was a lot to think about but still I managed to push it out of my mind for the time being.

Soon enough, her meal was ready, so I retrieved it and brought it over to her.

"BLT sandwich," I said, and she nodded in approval.

"No tomatoes," I added as she began to search, and she smiled again. "You do know me."

A concerned look however came over her face. "I really thought you could join me or perhaps I could head to your apartment and wait for you there instead? What time do you close here again?"

"No need," I told her. "Is what you have to say long?"

"Well, I would like to spend some time with you," she said, and I was tempted, but then I steeled my heart, exhaustion the barrier to any affection I could currently feel.

"Come by during the weekend," I told her. "The weekdays are impossible."

"Alright,' she said, "Have you gone to see your dad?"

"I was there for a few hours this afternoon before my shift," I said, and she nodded.

"The bills are racking up."

"Yeah," I said and didn't know what else to say. I suddenly truly needed to sit down.

"What's the update?" I asked and she pushed her tray away.

"After inspecting his assets, I found that he doesn't have very much at all. Not even enough to cover his current bills. He's renting where he currently stays and even his car is being paid for in installments, and he is behind on payment. So, I don't know what to do. I really don't. Unless I take out a loan on his behalf, but I don't know if I can do that for him. I'm not done paying for my current house, and I don't want to put myself in so much debt and stress when I'm not sure he would even appreciate it enough to pay me back. I don't even think I can get it and I definitely can't ask his mom because she doesn't have it. Plus, I'm trying my best to keep all of this away from her so she won't be worried. She's too old to handle it well."

My grandma came to mind then and I couldn't help but sigh.

Every possible window seemed to be closing in on us and we were running out of time. There was no way out and I had no idea who to turn to.

"We can't let him just..." I couldn't complete the sentence

"Of course not," she said. "But it seems that there's very little we can currently do."

I understood her words and finally took my seat. Then I buried my face between my arms. Not only did I feel nauseous, I also felt light headed and none of it came as a surprise anymore. With this degree of stress, I truly didn't understand how I would be able to manage and survive.

My mind once again went to Gideon but I couldn't fathom going to him for help.

We had remained in touch, and he had come over two more times, but things had been brief and cordial and I couldn't even remember the last time we had shared a proper heartfelt and passionate kiss and it was driving me crazy. Even in this moment, it caused tears to sting my eyes and I truly didn't know what to do.

I needed him, but at the same time I truly couldn't go to him. I wanted him to make the offer that I come to him, and I hated that he hadn't done so. My mind went to my phone as I toyed with the idea of calling to give him a piece of my mind, but I held myself back. Because he had done all he could. He checked up on me, he sent me food, we just weren't speaking as we should and it seemed as though he was the one making the sacrifice to give me as much space as I needed, but it didn't feel that way and I couldn't figure out why.

48

GIDEON

I stopped in front of the bistro.

It wasn't hard to instantly recognize the two of them by the window and for a little while as Pam stood and conversed with her mother, I saw the pained and concerned expressions across their faces and my heart wrenched. I could help them, but they hadn't asked. And I couldn't offer because I didn't want to help him.

And if perhaps they asked, I still didn't know what my response would be. But whatever it was, whatever feelings arose in me was what I was going to follow. But that moment hadn't come and so I had stayed away. To give them space, and for me to examine if I could let go enough to be there for the woman that I loved.

I watched the two of them and then Pamela took a seat and buried her face between her arms. I didn't think I could do anything but just wait for life to play out whichever way it wanted to.

I wanted to reach out my hand, but it seemed too heavy, and I didn't know how to lessen the weight. So, for the first time in months, I got back into my car and took a three-hour trip to Big Bear Lake.

I hoped the drive would clear my head, however as I arrived at the restaurant, I found I was just as muddled as I had been. I heard his boisterous laughter as I pushed the door open and since it was late evening, the crowd was already slowly gathering,

I immediately spotted him, through the display window behind the order counter. I sat in a far corner and watched as he interacted with his staff and delivered food until eventually one of them came over to me.

"What can I get you sir?" the young male waiter asked, and I looked at him.

"It's not on the menu," I said, "so I'll order it in. Tell your boss to join me."

The waiter had a confused expression at my words, but nevertheless he at least acknowledged my clear instruction and turned around to return to the kitchen. I pulled my phone out, wondering if there was anywhere around where I could find some fish tacos. However, after about five minutes of searching I still couldn't find it. I was about to give up when a man appeared before my table and spoke.

"It's not easy to find that around here," he said, and my heart shifted. There was warmth, sorrow and joy. I lifted my head and met the ocean blue gaze that I was perhaps more familiar with than any other I had come across thus far in my lifetime.

"Dad," I called and managed a smile.

His was even wider as his hand closed around my hand, and then he was pulling me up for a bear hug. I accepted it, needing the consolation more than I had realized even though on most days I had managed to convince myself I didn't need such affection any longer.

I accepted the hug, and it went on for longer than I would have liked. Regardless, I didn't complain and waited till he had gotten his fill. And when we finally parted I didn't miss the sheen of tears in his eyes.

I shook my head at him as he took a seat.

"You know we live just three hours away from each other, right? You wouldn't be so emotional every time you saw me if you just visited me more often."

"I've tried, several times," he said. "But the universe doesn't seem to want me to go to you. Something always comes up, some fire that I have to put out, some reservation I need to personally attend to, some meeting I had completely forgotten about. I'm barely managing to keep up."

"Why are you working so hard at this age," I asked him. "Isn't it time to rest?"

"Never," he exclaimed, his voice booming out across the room. "Will you rest, when you get to my age? I mean you've made all the money you could ever need right now, haven't you? So why don't you rest?"

I looked at him and I guess mine was a dry expression of defeat because he suddenly laughed aloud once again. He seemed happy… free, but I could recall a time when he had been anything but.

"So," he said. "I'm going to order you our stockyard top sirloin. It's new on the menu and you will love it. Trust me."

"Alright," I replied.

"You drove here or came with a driver?"

"Drove," I replied.

"So, you can't drink? Or you can spend the night at my place?"

"Let's start with a glass of wine," I told him. "I'll make my decision after that."

"Alright," he said and called that same waiter over. This time around the waiter had a larger and genuine smile for me and I tried my best to return it.

Soon he went on his way, and I was left alone with my dad once again. "I have to return to work soon," he said, and I nodded. He cocked his head and studied me. "Care to share why you suddenly came over?"

I smiled. "Can't a man come see his father for no reason?"

"Not you. You would have called beforehand if it was for no reason. This was an impulsive trip, wasn't it?" he asked. I watched him. "You have ten minutes, otherwise you have to wait another hour for me," he said.

I smiled then and nodded. Just then my glass of red wine was delivered, and I lifted the glass for a sip.

"Did you ever forgive mom?" I asked. "For cheating on you?"

At the question, the ease gradually seeped out from my father's face and in its place was a quite serious expression.

He then sighed. "This is the second time you're asking me questions along this line in this month alone," he said. "What's happening?"

My gaze lowered to the rich red liquid in my glass as I wondered about how to relay what I wanted to. I wasn't certain whether to be indirect or if it was better to just say exactly what was in my mind. I eventually decided to relay it the exact way it was because everything now hung in the balance.

If I made a mistake and took the wrong path and lost Pamela, I knew now I was going to regret it every single day for the rest of my life.

"I'm in love with Cecilia's daughter," I said. "Cecilia Fraser."

My dad went silent because of course he knew who that was and what this implied.

"I love her," I said, "and I think I have from the time we were kids. I never stopped. And now..."

"And now?" he urged at my pause.

"I don't know," I replied. "Because of what happened... because of what her father did with mom, of how they ruined both of our families, I've held back from her. I've ignored her and rejected her but now... she really needs me, and I don't want to turn my back on her. But, at the same time I don't want to help her father. I want to give her what she wants but at the same time I don't want to deprive myself of what I want. And that is for him to rot just the way that he is."

"Wow," my father said, and I lifted my gaze to his.

"I never knew you were this angry at them. I don't think I was ever this angry at them." He smiled but I didn't reciprocate, and he soon understood that absolutely no part of what I was saying was taken lightly.

He sighed.

"Have you spoken to her about this?"

I shot him an incredulous look. "How can I speak to her about this?"

"Communication does wonders," he said, and my frown deepened even further.

"How am I supposed to tell someone that I claim to love that I don't want to help her critically ill father because I'm still upset that he destroyed my family?"

My father looked at me.

"Love makes you do crazy things," he said, and I just couldn't understand him.

"What?"

"Love makes you do crazy, irrational things, doesn't it?"

he said. "Like help someone you loathe because he is the father of the woman you claim to love unless of course, you don't really love her so we shouldn't even be having this conversation."

I continued to watch him and didn't say a word.

"You know what to do," he said. "And you know what you can't do. You just can't accept them both and that's why you're here. I'm sorry but I don't have a different answer from what your heart is telling you, and you're in this dilemma because you truly love her. If you didn't, you'd stick to your guns and be ready to let your relationship go to ruins but that isn't what you want is it?"

Picking up the glass of wine, I drained it regretting that I hadn't ordered something stronger.

Our food was delivered then, and my gaze went to the plate of steak.

I had never had less of an appetite to eat than I currently did. My father however was beyond delighted, and began to dig in.

"This is the first meal I'm having since lunch," he lamented. "Too long."

I gave him an incredulous look which he laughed away.

"Please... I work out. I'm allowed to eat as many times as I want plus today has been a trying day. You're coming for our new restaurant opening right? It's next weekend."

"Dad, you keep repeating this. Of course, I'll be there. Why would I miss it?"

"Alright," he said and continued his meal.

I watched him, envying the pleasure with which he consumed his meal.

"I asked you if you ever forgave Mom?" I said, and he responded without looking at me.

"Forgiveness has nothing to do with your current

dilemma. And moreover, you don't forgive people for their sake but for yours."

He paused and stared directly at me. "Holding in grudges haunts you and not them so yes, I forgave her for my own peace of mind, because she had moved on with her life and there was no point in me drowning in self-pity for years after because of how angry I still was. And Gideon, I hope you can do the same. He might have destroyed the family you had back then, but not forgiving him might destroy the family that you could have in the future. Or do you not want to go that far with Cecilia's daughter. What's her name again?"

"Pamela," I said, and he nodded.

"I remember her. Extremely adorable and chatty. Clung to you and never left your side. I'm not at all surprised. You were always so fiercely protective of her while at the same time complaining about how much of a pest she was. I loved you two and the never-ending antics you stirred up."

"*She* stirred up," I corrected him. "I was just always the one tasked with setting things right".

"Of course, you were," he said. "You were older. Anyway, I have to return to work soon."

I gazed down at the meal again and decided to dig in.

We spoke of the finishing touches and changes he was making to his new branch, until eventually he was called back to the kitchen. I continued with my meal and my thoughts until eventually I was done and ready to head back. I went behind the counter and met him by one of the stoves as he prepared some shrimp. He beamed when he saw me, and after accepting greetings from the other staff in the vicinity, I focused my attention on him.

"I'm leaving," I said, and he nodded.

"Sorry I couldn't have the whole meal with you. You're

staying for the weekend after the opening?" he said, and I nodded in agreement. "Okay. I have a question for you, before you leave," he said.

"Sure."

"Were you ever mad at me for not always being around? For being so busy with work and then later with the restaurant?"

I didn't have an immediate response to this because a lot of conflicting thoughts and emotions were involved. Nevertheless, I told him the truth.

"Maybe," I said. "But I understood you and it made you happy. Working has always made you happy... this work at least and I saw a time when work didn't make you happy. So, I guess I just appreciated your good mood. You would come home and have so many new stories and... I couldn't fault you for that. Plus, if I wanted to spend more time with you then I knew exactly where you were, otherwise I was fine with occupying myself. I had my own things that I was exploring. Plus, it was through working here that I met Thomas. I might never have taken computers as seriously otherwise."

He smiled, but I could tell he was in quite a thoughtful mode and had a bit more to get off his chest.

"Your mother didn't see things that way," he said quietly, the usual smile on his face now gone and replaced with a heavy countenance. "She was glad I was doing fine but she on the other hand felt stuck in her own life and didn't know how to get out of it. She was a stay-at-home mom, but there weren't any more kids to take care of after you, plus you pretty much became a full-grown adult by ten years of age."

We shared a laugh at this.

"My point is, nothing excuses what they did but there are a lot more things to consider. And if you don't consider these you will forever be unable to forgive and let go. I could have been a better husband to her... been more attentive, and appreciative but I was so busy living the life she wanted while she felt as though she had been delegated to solely supporting and facilitating that. She had her own dreams when she was younger and had pushed all of that aside. Again, like I said I'm not making excuses for her, but there's a lot to consider so I guess that's the official response I'm giving to you. Consider things beyond the red target in the middle. It simply looks the biggest because it's the only thing you've chosen to focus on. Plus, have you ever considered that she would feel equally as furious to learn that her father cheated with your mother?"

At his words I stopped because I had never truly considered this.

He saw it in my eyes. "Exactly," he said. "Then you'd want her to be lenient right? Then you'd want her to accept you regardless. Or would you want her to hate you because of it?"

"I don't hate her."

"But you rejected her? Why put her father's sins on her? And by the way, you're doing it again. Putting her father's sins on her because how do you think she will ever be able to comfortably be with the man that refused to help her father?"

I glared at him, and he smiled. "Let it go. Set yourself free. Doing otherwise will haunt you possibly even more. You have a chance at your own family now. Start it with a clean plate. And as a reminder, mercy is not called mercy because someone deserves it. Do the right thing, and you'll mean more to her because of it."

I turned around then and walked to the door. My expression was sour, but I knew every word he had spoken to me was true.

"No hug?" he called out and I couldn't hold back my smile.

"Next weekend," I said and made my way out.

I looked forward to the drive ahead but at the same time, I also couldn't wait to see her. She would still be at the bistro so perhaps I could take her straight home. I wanted to at least see how she has been sleeping and help her, if possible, to get a good night of rest because I suspected that it hadn't been that way for a long time.

I soon arrived at the bistro just before it closed for the night, so I decided to wait outside in the car so I wouldn't interrupt her. In the meantime, I sent her a message.

49

PAMELA

I'm outside. Can I take you home when you're done?

The moment the message came in my heart began to race, and I didn't understand why. A message from Gideon should have brought me excitement and calm as was usual but now I just felt nervous. With a sigh, I put the phone away and got back to work because I didn't know what to do just yet. But there were only a few minutes left till closing, so I didn't feel too concerned about having him wait. As the time to meet up with him came closer and closer I became even more tense until eventually it was time to leave.

I hadn't responded to his message yet and it made me wonder if he had decided to leave. But when I got out of the restaurant with the strap of my purse slung across my shoulder and saw his sleek, dark Mercedes waiting for me in the same obscure spot by the trees he had previously parked in during his visits to me. I stopped and stared towards that direction knowing he had probably spotted me and was staring right back at me too.

A few minutes later and as I approached, I found that I was right.

I pulled the passenger door open and got in.

"Hey," he said, and I turned to look at his gorgeous face. My gaze lowered to his lips and then back to his eyes, and once again I didn't know how to feel. But it was clear to me that I would prefer to go home so I relayed exactly that.

"You'd rest better at home?" he asked, and I knew he was going to act the same way he had been acting for the past several days.

I nodded and soon enough, his response came.

"Okay."

Emotion surged up in my throat and as the tears started filling my eyes, I pulled the door's handle and tried to escape.

Quickly I found he had locked the doors.

I turned towards him in alarm and met his gaze head on.

"What's wrong?" he asked, and I managed a smile.

"What do you mean?"

He continued to watch me, and the smile fell off my face. I knew I had to make a decision about how we were to move forward with each other, but it couldn't be in this manner. I didn't know what to say or where to even start.

I sighed and leaned back against the seat.

I ran a couple of thoughts through in my head and then mentioned the one that sounded the simplest to me.

"You've seemed a bit distant the last few days, so I just wanted to give you space," I said.

I wanted him to counter this, hoped even that he would, but when a while passed and he didn't say a word to me, I was forced to turn to him.

His gaze was still on me.

"I've been distant?" he asked. "Is that the problem?"

I paused, wondering if he had caught on to me, but I couldn't be the first to bring it up because it would seem to me as though I was the one constantly stirring problems between us.

"Yeah," I replied, slightly disappointed with myself.

"How's your father doing?" he asked, and I shrugged.

"The same. Awaiting a surgery appointment."

"Alright," he said and then I heard the door lock click open. He was telling me that I could go, but now, I no longer wanted to.

I turned to look at him. His attention was no longer on me but was instead directed forward.

I mustered up my courage.

"I'm sorry to ask this, but could you help me out?" I paused then, unable to go any further because this had to be the hardest thing I had ever done.

"With what?" he asked, and I looked up wondering if I had heard him right. I was sure I had but it didn't make sense. He was smart, so surely, he knew exactly what I was talking about but then... he wanted me to spell it out? I had never been so confused.

"This is difficult for me," I said. "Incredibly."

He turned then and met my gaze. "It's even more difficult for me," he said and once again I was taken aback because I didn't understand what was happening. I didn't even know if we were talking about the same thing.

Thankfully he explained.

"I'm antagonistic towards your father Pamela," he said.

All I could do was stare, my eyes slightly widened. "Why?"

He paused but I knew that he was going to explain. He

would never have brought it up if he hadn't been planning on making things clear to me.

"He cheated with my mom. It ruined my family. And yours. I've hated him for a very long time and... I don't know, I just... " he stopped, but my blood had already run cold.

"What?" I asked, but he remained calm. "What are you talking about?"

"Why do you think your family moved away? Why do you think the relationship between your parents and mine was ruined?"

The tears that had previously gathered in my eyes began to roll down the corners.

"I didn't know," I said, and he nodded.

"I know."

"I didn't fucking know," I repeated, anger broiling inside of me. "Why did no one tell me? Does my mother know?"

"Of course she does."

"And how did you find out? They told you?"

"I walked in on them," he replied. "I'd come over to your house. I think I got something for you or maybe I was searching for something. Now that I think about it must have been my backpack."

I watched the smile come on his face and didn't think that I had ever seen something quite so bitter.

"It went on for a while. I confronted her about it because I couldn't take it anymore. I threatened to tell my dad but then I found out he already knew. And she had promised him she would stop but she didn't. I confronted your dad about it, and he told me to stay out of it. And that I knew nothing since I was a kid. I hate him for it. I might have known nothing but the one thing I knew was the pain that it brought to my father and to me. I also knew the hatred I now had for my mother, who before then was someone I loved so immensely. But because of what he was doing... of what they were doing, I couldn't even have a conversation with her without getting angry. I couldn't even be in the same room with her, and yet all he could say to me was that I knew nothing. That my pain wasn't valid because I was a kid."

I turned away from him and stared ahead at nothing, my eyes wide open with shock. A lot of things now concerning the distance and detachment I had sensed from him all began to make sense.

Now I truly didn't know what to think or feel or even say. All I could do was remain in place, frozen solid and unable to even bring myself to leave because I didn't know how to return if I did. I didn't even know if he would want me to or if I would even want to.

All of this became inconsequential when he said his next words.

"I set the house on fire," he said, and my heart stopped.

I was almost afraid to turn to look at him this time around, but I didn't have to because he continued.

"And I've never regretted it. If anything, I hated it didn't achieve what I wanted to and it just made me... towards you-" he stopped and tried once more to be coherent, because despite how calm his tone sounded his thoughts seemed to be in disarray.

"That was why I had to do anything to save you. I know now I cared about you then but at the time, I just didn't want any harm coming to you on my conscience, and that had to be one of the scariest moments of my life because at the time I thought it would. That I would be too late. The fire forced your family to move away at least and I was glad for that. However, I wanted every memory of that time and of my mom, and of what I had tried to do to be wiped away, and that was why our separation happened. And my resistance to you even after we met again."

I could feel him turn to me then, but I couldn't bring myself to meet his gaze... not yet, because I didn't know what I wanted him to see in my eyes.

"So, it's not that I don't care, you're going through such a hard time. It's just that... I really don't know how to overcome this. I'm trying to because I care about you... and I know you can't help but care about him."

A long silence passed between us, and I grew nauseous.

"Okay," I grabbed my bag and got out of the car, desperate to move away from him before the full force of it hit. I had barely gone a few steps when the vomit came spewing out of me. I immediately bent over, absolutely and completely miserable and from the distance heard the door to his car slam shut. Suddenly I didn't want to be around him and especially didn't want his help so I moved away before he could touch me.

"Don't," I said and when I looked up to meet his gaze, I could see the hurt my words had caused. "I'm sorry but... I need some time so... don't."

He respected my wishes and stayed away, and as I headed back to my car I understood why.

I needed to be away from him and to try my best to revert to a time and head space when I didn't crave him like I currently did. When I hadn't known what it meant to have him the way I had. To need him the way I wanted to.

"Let me call you a cab," he called out, his voice louder than I had ever heard it and I could hear the desperation in his voice.

I didn't respond and soon got to my car.

Eventually I arrived back home and immediately went

straight to my room. There I sat on my bed with a completely blank mind. I didn't even know what to think about but eventually, and as his words turned over and over again in my mind, I was soon a mess of emotions. I felt angry and resentful, but at the same time hurt and lost and I couldn't understand which emotion applied to which situation. And more importantly I didn't want to think about it because it would mean I would have to think about him and that in turn would ruin the only plan I had come up with to be able to navigate through and properly process the circumstances.

I got up, needing to keep my hands and mind busy, when I felt suddenly so overwhelmingly dizzy that the world seemed to tilt before me, I was forced to sit down, shocked and confused.

I hadn't had anything since lunch, and I didn't feel hungry. But perhaps my body didn't agree with that conclusion. Or perhaps something else was the problem? My mind went back to Sarah's comment from earlier at the bistro and fear gripped my heart.

It couldn't be.

I had exercised as much caution as was needed, so it definitely couldn't be, however as I examined the symptoms that had seemed to plague me from nowhere over the last few days, I found myself getting to my feet.

Meredith's periods were irregular and since she was pretty active with Darryl, she always had test kits in the house in order not to be hit with any surprises that came way too late and took options out of her hands.

I instantly began to sort through her toiletries and soon enough found the test. I grabbed it, headed over to the toilet and said a simple word.

"Please."

I didn't know what I was asking or praying for, but all I could say was please.

I did all that was needed and shut my eyes tight. However afterwards I found I couldn't look at it. Not now. Not till things with my father had been settled. The possibility of my suspicion was one circumstance that I wouldn't be able to currently manage as there was too much going on. So, I took it with me and returned to my room. Just then however, there was a noise at the entryway.

"I'm home," Meredith called out and I quickly pushed my door open. I returned the stick to the packet and kept it under my pillow.

And then because I couldn't bear to be in the same room with it, I got up and headed out.

She was in the kitchen and rummaging through the fridge, so I leaned against the wall and watched her. She turned around then and smiled as soon as she saw me. "Hey. Did you just get in? You're still dressed."

My gaze lowered down to my outfit.

"Yeah, I did," I said.

"Alright. What do you want for dinner? I want to order potato pizza. Do you want any?"

I didn't have any appetite for it or for anything for that matter, so I just shook my head. "No, I'll have some fruit."

"Alright," she said as she grabbed a bottle of juice for herself.

I watched her, all the while on the verge of tears but not wanting to even speak a word. Eventually and before she could notice I turned around without a word and returned to my room. I sat at my desk and began to pull out my study materials because that was what I needed to do in the meantime. I was so behind but I was in no mood whatsoever to catch up on school. For a moment I thought of Gideon and about the peace and consolation he could usually and effortlessly bring me but in the present that didn't seem to be the case at all. It didn't even seem to be possible, and I couldn't help but feel as though I had lost something incredibly valuable.

50

GIDEON

The next day, I didn't want to be anywhere around the campus, so I took a personal day, sent notes instead to my students and headed over to the office downtown.

At my arrival, I went straight to the R and D department. When Susan saw me, she was so startled that for the first few seconds she couldn't say a word.

"I decided to work from here today," I explained, and she nodded profusely.

I inquired about the project she was working on, and she soon collected herself enough to respond. She began to speak as we headed straight to one of the staff's desks and it was loaned to me for the day.

My plan was to completely drown myself in the hardest software complications I could find and spend every single moment trying to troubleshoot it. Barely twenty minutes had passed before Michael came in bearing gifts. Truly, I had expected the word of my sudden and unannounced arrival to meet him immediately, but as I saw the tray of sandwiches and coffee he brought in, I understood what had caused him the slight delay. I smiled despite my bad mood and shook my head as I returned my attention to the computer.

"Signed and delivered," he said to the amusement of the other staff, and I couldn't help but ask.

"When will you stop treating my visits to the office as events?"

"When you start coming in more often," he replied. "Come to think of it, we might be close because I think in this week alone you've come here more than you have in the last three months combined."

"Thank you," I said as I took the wheat bread, ham and cheese sandwich and began to unwrap it. He pulled a chair right next to me as I ate, simply watching me.

Eventually he spoke in a tone that was hopefully low enough for only the two of us to have heard.

"Is everything okay?" he asked, and for a few seconds I didn't respond. I considered whether to talk about what was currently plaguing my mind but, in the end, I decided I had nothing to say.

I was done with talking and what I realized I actually wanted was for someone else to do the talking. One person in particular. The moment I finished eating, I took a brief break from the department and left the premises.

I didn't think what I was doing was the best of ideas, but I was out of better ones, so I had no choice but to press on. Soon enough I arrived at the hospital and my only hope was that Pamela would not be there.

Thankfully she wasn't, and although it was a bit difficult, I was finally able to get the access I needed.

I didn't know exactly what I was going to say to him or what I wanted him to say to me, but the current trouble his state was bringing to my life was not something I wanted to deal with any further.

He was asleep when I walked in his room, which was disappointing, but I didn't intend to leave just yet, so I pulled a chair to his bedside and took a seat. Then I watched him.

He seemed so frail and feeble that for a moment I couldn't help but feel compassion for him, but then suddenly he came awake and opened his eyes and the moment instantly disappeared. Before me was the man that had forced me to grow up more quickly than I had wanted to. The man that had brought me to a point of despair and anger that I might have never had been able to recover from.

Everything could have been ruined for me if that fire had truly done what I had intended it to do. I would have been changed forever and in the worst of ways. And yet he had the guts to tell me that I knew nothing. Maybe that was true and maybe that was why I was here, so he could tell me exactly what I was meant to know if everything that I had been plagued with back then and still haunted me still today, were all 'nothing.'

It seemed to take him a little while to recognize me, and when he did, he was startled.

The surprise was evident on his face upon seeing me there, and I knew he hadn't been informed by anyone of my association with his daughter. I sighed, truly annoyed I was even here and giving him even a little bit of my time.

"Kid," he called and when I looked up found a genuine smile on his face. "Gideon, right?" he asked. "It's been a while. A very long while. Wow, you look great. What are you now? Thirty?"

I didn't respond to any of this, and instead my frown

deepened. It was then he probably noted perhaps this wasn't a courtesy visit.

My gaze went down to the tubes attached to his hand, and the machine monitoring his heartbeat and truly I hoped it would just stop. Or at the very least that I could do something to make it stop.

I sighed and knew where to start from.

"You're causing a lot of grief in my life," I told him, and he seemed taken aback by this.

"What?"

I lowered my head, my hand running through my hair.

"Truly, I should have gotten rid of you when I had the chance."

"What the-" he started but when I lifted my gaze to glare at him, he suddenly kept silent. He did try to sit up and lean away from me. I smiled, loving the true fear I saw in his eyes, but it wasn't what I truly wanted to see. And maybe I realized, that was why I still couldn't forgive him.

"Do you regret it?" I asked.

"Regret what?" he asked, and I grew annoyed. But still I forced myself to remain calm because that was the only way this meeting was going to unfold without any disastrous accidents.

"Ruining my family," I said. "Ruining yours."

He stared hard at me, and I could see something truly sad come over his face. He sighed and his gaze moved from me to the ceiling.

"Are you here to judge me again?" he asked.

"I'm here to check if you still feel no remorse."

At this he turned to me, his gaze incredulous.

"You still know nothing," he said, and I saw red. It took everything inside of me to keep from getting to my feet then and punching him dead. Somehow however and as Pamela came to mind, I was able to keep myself seated. My hands however tightened into fists while my nails dug into my palms and nearly brought blood. I didn't even bother speaking.

"Are you married?" He suddenly turned to me and asked.

I didn't respond.

"Do you have kids?" he asked. "More importantly do you have a kid as beautiful and kind as Pamela is?"

My heart skipped several beats and before I could stop myself, I bit out. "Don't say her name."

He smiled. "What? You hate her, too?"

He couldn't have been farther from the truth.

He released a heavy breath once again. "I just can't believe you're asking me the same question again, but I guess I have to clearly explain myself. What I felt then and feel now, is more than remorse. Sometimes I even think it surpasses regret. Nothing quite comes close to it or maybe it's a culmination of all three. I wish I hadn't made the choices that I did back then. There was no way it was going to end well, and I knew that. We were both aware of that yet at the time we'd both gotten to a point in our lives where we were void of feeling. Everything was dull. There was nothing to look forward to. It was all gray, and sometimes even outright black. The funny thing is I had felt that way from time to time in my youth but there'd always been hope at the end of the tunnel."

"But during that time... with your mom, all I could feel and see was despair, and it was eating away at my soul. It felt as though I was approaching an end that was going to completely destroy me and so I couldn't resist the spark of hope that came with my relations with your mom. For the first time in so long I saw colors and I didn't know how to turn away from it. Despair is a scary thing, it leaves you grabbing at anything within reach irrespective of reason because you *are* desperate to survive."

He turned to me then. "I hate I'm explaining this to you, but I think... you don't seem to be free. You still have that rage you had for me back then in your eyes and I can't imagine it's been easy carrying that in your heart. So, if you want me to tell you I felt remorse then my response is I felt much more than that. I feel more than that. But I've forgiven myself for it because at the time I truly felt like I was drowning. It was my fault I wasn't a strong enough person to find a better way to save myself at the time... instead I chose the easiest route and that was your mother."

"That affair made me feel like I had a second chance... that I was still alive and not withering away so now, even after I see that it left my entire life in such shambles that I was never able to pick up the pieces afterwards, I can't truly regret it with every fiber of my being. So, in a way, I am at peace with myself. At least now. I wasn't, for a *very* long time."

I looked at him and no words came to mind. Eventually I couldn't stand to be in his presence any longer and since I didn't want to speak either I simply got to my feet and turned around to leave.

"I hope you find peace," he called out to me in his frail voice. "For you and no one else. You were just a kid and you didn't do anything wrong. I truly hope the mistakes I made at that point in my life don't unfairly rob you of anything good in the present."

Tears stung my eyes at his words, but still I had nothing to say to him. As I started to leave someone appeared in the door. I froze in place and so did she.

I stared at her and as his words repeated in my mind, I

knew what I had to do. But still I wasn't ready to face her or anyone, so I instead continued on my way. She moved out of the way as I pushed the door open, and I didn't say a single word to her.

I walked down the hallway, exited the hospital and didn't look back.

51

PAMELA

I watched him walk away without a word and was truly afraid that my heart was going to break.

I could no longer so easily call out to him given my discovery the previous day and judging by the past and the reminder that he had never been the one to reach out to me first, the future seemed truly dark.

I understood his anger and hurt and even felt the same way, but as he disappeared around the corner and I turned my gaze to glance at the man that I still couldn't understand how I could still care so much for, it was clear to me whose side I would stand on. No matter what and until the end, otherwise, I wouldn't be able to live with myself.

As my gaze met my ailing father, I smiled, and warmth came into my heart. He still looked terrible but for once I was glad to see that his eyes were open.

"Hey Dad," I greeted, and his gaze remained on me. He didn't say a word but after staring at me for a little while, I felt his frail hand reaching out for mine. With a smile I took it, linked our hands together and sent him the sweetest softest smile I could muster.

"It's great to see you," he said, and I smiled even wider.

"It's great to see you too."

I took the seat that had just been vacated and looked fondly at him.

He watched me and I couldn't help but wonder what he and Gideon had spoken about. Everything in me wanted to know but I admonished myself not to ask because it didn't matter.

Currently all that mattered was that my father got better.

"Did you see Gideon on the way out?" he however suddenly asked. "The boy from next door?"

The question was sudden, but I soon regained my wits and responded. "I did."

"Do you speak to each other?"

"From time to time," I said, and reached forward to brush his hair out of his face.

He seemed to note that I didn't want to talk further about this, and the conversation switched to how I was doing at school.

A few minutes later, the door was pushed open, and my heart lurched into my throat. I didn't expect that he was the one that had returned but since it was a possibility, I couldn't help but be on guard because I didn't think I was ready to face him just yet.

"Hello," my mom's voice suddenly rang out and I was able to breathe easily. When I lifted my gaze to my father however I was startled again because I found him watching me.

He squeezed my hand in his and I sent him another smile before turning to my mother.

"I just came from the doctor's office," she said. I got up so that she could take a seat.

"Thank you darling," she said and looked at my father.

"You're awake," she said. "Finally."

He smiled and I watched as they shared a look.

In that moment more was spoken than I could ever comprehend so I turned away to give them the privacy they needed and found another chair to pull over.

"We can't wait any longer, so I've scheduled your surgery for tomorrow evening. It costs a soul, but I think we'll be able to work something out."

"I'll chip in with what I can, include what you can, and we can see how we'll go from there."

"I have some money saved up," he said, and both of our heads instantly perked up.

"It's not much, but it should make a dent in it."

"Oh," she said and shot a glance at me. "I wasn't able to find anything."

"Well, it's not kept in plain sight," he said, and we both smiled.

"How much?" I asked.

"About twenty-eight thousand," he said, and I was even more surprised at this.

"That's good," my mom said. "That's not bad at all. Coupled with my input we should be able to have at least half paid upfront."

He sighed then and we both listened.

"Never in a million years would I have thought I'd be using it to pay for medical bills."

"Well, that's life," she said. "I'll go speak to the doctor. I'll be right back."

I took my seat by his side and this time my smile wasn't forced. He stared softly at me.

"It was going to be your graduation present," he said, and I watched as tears filled his eyes.

"What?" I asked.

"I wanted you to use it as a down payment for a home or apartment. I was going to try and make it to fifty before you graduated."

Emotions flooded my chest.

"You were planning to buy my affection on my graduation day?" I asked and he laughed.

"Yeah," he said, and I couldn't help but shake my head.

"It's free." I told him. "You're my family. No matter what."

"I'll make sure to do better," he said. I nodded and lowered my head.

I couldn't hold the tears then from dropping from my eyes to the floor but the last thing I wanted was for him to see me this way.

"I'm sorry," he said. "I truly am."

"I know," I replied and quickly wiped the wetness from my face. Just then the door slid open once again and I turned back immediately to see that it was my mom.

"You're back so soon?" I asked and her eyes were wide with shock.

I instantly felt alarmed.

"What's wrong?" I asked as she headed towards us. She looked at my dad and then me.

"Your father's bill.... has been paid in full. Well, more like a credit card was deposited in his name and all charges are to be billed to it."

My heart stopped.

A thousand thoughts went through my head so much so that I couldn't even blink as I stared at my mom. She stared back at me and then began to smile as it dawned on us who was behind this. The only person who could be behind this.

"Did you know he was going to do this?" she asked, and I shook my head.

"No."

"Oh, maybe he wanted to impress you? How generous of him. I'll call him to express our gratitude."

"No," I replied. "Don't call him. I'll speak to him myself. I'd prefer we not take the payment, but I don't have the means right now to handle it. Neither do I want to put the strain on the both of you. So, we don't have a choice but to accept. However, we'll pay with what we have, take a bit from him and then pay him back. Agreed? I'll let him know this."

I rose to my feet then to exit the room, and even though my mom tried to stop me she eventually gave up when she noticed my expression and that I wasn't going to take my words back.

I exited the room and only when I got in the hall was I able to catch a deep breath. I inhaled deeply and then exhaled, and then the tears truly began to fall down my face. I headed straight to the bathroom, found an empty stall and bawled my eyes out.

Luckily, no one interrupted me, so I was able to express my frustration and annoyance at him. It felt as though he had just thrown the money at us and walked away, and I hated him immensely for it. I knew he wasn't happy doing it and perhaps was just doing it maybe for my sake or perhaps just his conscience. But I truly wished we could fully reject it.

My arms curved around my stomach, and I held on tightly, almost unable to contain just how confused and conflicted I felt. I couldn't remember ever feeling this way and to this extent in my life, and it truly terrified me because I had no clue what the future held.

Absolutely none whatsoever, but I had to be strong. And I promised myself that no matter what, I was going to be. I got my feet, wiped my face but just as I was washing my hands the door swung open.

I looked up and was unhappy to see it was my mom.

She instantly knew that something was wrong but the last thing I wanted to do was talk so I straightened and headed over to the dispenser to retrieve some paper towels. "I don't want to talk about it," I said, and she sighed.

"Can you at least tell me what's going on between you two? Please."

I stopped at the door and decided to give her an explanation once and for all. "He's still mad at dad and his mom for cheating."

"Okay," she said. "But he paid for his bill. That's kind of him."

"Sure," I rolled my eyes.

"So why do you want to return it?"

It took me a while, but I was finally able to find the strength to not only face it but to allow the words to fall from my lips.

"Because we're no longer together."

Hey eyes widened open.

"What? What happened?"

I definitely had no clue as to what to say so I ignored the question and walked away.

52

GIDEON

"It's been two weeks. Are you two really broken up?"

"If we haven't then why hasn't he contacted me?"

"Honestly it sounds like you two are kids again. And how is he to contact you when you sent a message returning his card and informing him that the part of his money used for your father's care would be paid promptly. Is that a way to show gratitude?"

"I told him thank you too."

"You said your contribution is appreciated. What the fuck is that?"

"Why the hell are you randomly interrogating me in the middle of the day?"

"Because I'm in his class and I can't take it anymore."

"Why? He doesn't look okay?"

"He looks perfectly fine, and so do you and I truly cannot understand how you both can go through so much effort to pretend when you're withering away inside. Just two weeks ago you were inseparable and suddenly now life is a bed of roses without each other?"

"Stop butting your nose in. Also, I have a favor to ask. Actually, it's a request."

"Rude but go on."

"Can you..."

"Yeah?"

"Can you accompany me somewhere this afternoon?"

"Where?"

"I'll send an address so just meet me there."

"I have an important test to study for tomorrow, you know. Darryl will be quizzing me from lunch onwards. So, unless it's a lung transplant, I can't make it."

"It's not a transplant but it's equally as important, if not more."

"What do you mean?"

"Here's the address."

"Is this... is this a family planning center?"

"?????"

"Pamela!"

"I just want to see how I feel about it. I'm considering my options."

"For Pete's sake why don't you just tell him?"

"Why do you keep saying this?"

"You're not the only one this affects."

"Are you serious right now? I'm not the only one this affects?"

"I'm sorry but I just believe he truly loves you and you both can resolve this separation between you two. I mean you haven't even properly talked so this might just be a prolonged silent treatment. Why consider such drastic actions?"

"You know what? Don't come. I'm sorry I asked."

"Pamela!""

"Pam!"

"I'm calling you!"

"Pick up!"

"My God don't you dare do anything stupid."

"Pick the hell up!"

"I'm going to hurt you when I see you."

"I'm on my way. Please don't do anything drastic."

"I'm calling Gideon!"

"Gosh you're aggravating!"

I STARED at the messages over and over again, and truly didn't know what to think about them.

All of these had been about two hours earlier during Meredith's class, after which I had left campus and headed straight to the company.

Currently I was in my office and was quite startled. It was true we had been somewhat 'separated' over the past two weeks and I had tried my best to ensure it didn't bother me. But it was fast becoming obvious to everyone around me that I was hanging on by a thread.

I was far from happy with her, but then at the same time I hadn't expected us to go so long without speaking. On the first day I was sure she would contact me but then that had passed, and then the next and then I had gotten the letter delivered to my office with the credit card attached.

It had been curt and formal, and I had immediately thrown it out.

I knew then how much she hated that she had to accept it, and I didn't feel like calling her in order to further aggravate matters, so I had kept my silence and distance. And now, this was the state we were in.

At Meredith's concerned gaze throughout class, I had no longer been able to help myself. I had even caught her contemplating afterwards whether to speak to me or not. Eventually she had come over, and everything she had wanted to say had been written on her face. But then she had worked up a far from genuine smile and then turned away with the excuse that she had just wanted to say hello.

My plan had been to ignore it but here I was, trying to figure out what was going on.

A call from Grace announced Michael and Susan's presence suddenly came and I had to accept it.

A few seconds later both walked in, Susan with reports in hand while Michael as usual came empty handed.

"You're here again, Gideon," he said. "Don't get me wrong I'm happy but your frequent visits these days are making you less of a myth."

I shook my head at him as I began to read through the messages once again on my computer.

"Are you trying to discourage me from coming to the office?" I asked.

"Of course not," he said as they both took their seats.

Susan was amused but I wasn't.

"I mean I am, but it's for the company's good."

I shot him a dark look while Susan pushed the reports over to me and began her briefing.

I listened as best as I could, but soon enough it occurred to me that I could ask her about the one question that was currently gnawing at my mind.

I looked up and met her gaze.

"Sorry to interrupt but can I ask you a question?"

She glanced at Michael somewhat surprised by this but soon smiled and nodded.

"Of course, sir."

"What's a family planning center and why would women suddenly go there?"

After the words left my mouth, the room remained so

silent that if a pin had dropped, I was certain that I would have heard it.

"A family planning center?" Michael repeated and I frowned at him.

Susan however seemed uncomfortable.

"Is this question too personal for you?" I asked and she shook her head.

"No, not at all,sir," she glanced at Michael and then sat up. "Um, there are a few reasons for a visit to the family planning clinic. Um… the most common one though has to do with pregnancies."

I went still.

She had been about to go on but when she saw whatever expression I had she stopped, unsure of whether to continue.

"Pregnancy?" I asked and could sense Michael sit upright.

"Yes. Women usually go there to have tests if they suspect they are pregnant or um…"

"Or what?" Michael asked when he saw her hesitate.

"Or when they want abortions," she said.

The room went quiet as their eyes then turned to me. I didn't need a genie to tell me what they were thinking because I was thinking the exact same thing.

I almost jumped to my feet then but managed to keep myself seated until they left at least.

"Is everything alright, Gideon?" Michael asked, genuine concern in his eyes and I nodded.

"I'm fine."

"There are a couple of other reasons," Susan went on and I knew that she was trying to break the ice. "Suspicion of STD's, routine checkups… and so on." She trailed off as I picked up my phone.

I immediately called Pamela for the first time in the last two weeks, no longer caring about the audience before me.

I placed the phone to my ear and turned around to concentrate on the call. The call went to voicemail at least twice before I turned back around to see that the two chairs before me were now emptied. I rose to my feet, copied the message from the texts and grabbed my keys.

In no time I was on my way, and although I tried not to panic, I was unable to stop calling all the way until eventually she picked up.

My heart slammed against my chest, but still I tried my best to keep as calm as possible.

"Pamela?" I called but there was no response.

And before I could say another word, the call was disconnected.

53

PAMELA

My eyes were wide open as I lifted my gaze from the phone.

He had called me.

Gideon had called me!

And I had stupidly picked up and then ended the call.

I had simply wanted to confirm that he was really the one that was calling and as my name had left his lips, it had been confirmed alright.

His deep, low voice had reverberated through me like a bell, and even when Meredith returned, I had still not collected myself.

What strange timing, was all I could think.

Because how was it that it was now of all times that he was calling me?

"Here," Meredith handed over one of the cups of water she had just gotten but then she noticed my stupor.

"Are you okay? What's wrong?"

I turned to her and then narrowed my eyes in suspicion.

"You didn't say anything to Gideon, did you?"

She frowned.

"I'm serious," I said, refusing to be intimidated by her.

"You're really getting on my nerves today, Pamela," she said, and I brought the cup to my lips for a sip.

"It's just weird," I said. "I mean why would he call me at this exact time?"

"He called you?" she asked, and I nodded.

"He didn't say anything though. Well, I didn't let him say anything. I was too startled, so I ended the call."

She sighed then and slumped into the chair.

"Maybe I should have called him. He seems to be the only one capable of talking any sense into you. Maybe that's why you're avoiding him."

I ignored her for a bit, but then as I stared at the other women waiting in line and around the clinic my heart grew heavy once again.

"I can't believe it," I muttered. "I can't believe I'm here."

"You better believe it, and deal with it properly," she said.

"It will disrupt everything," I said, and at my small voice she finally paid attention. I turned and saw that her expression had softened.

"He'll help you with it."

And to this I didn't know what to say. She reached forward then and took my hand in hers.

"We're here now," she said. "How do you feel?"

I thought about this and in mere seconds my eyes were soaked.

"Pamela," she leaned forward just in time and caught the tear before it could roll down one corner of my eye. The other one however came even faster and so I turned away just as it rolled down my cheek.

She gave me time and space to get myself together and eventually I was able to rein in my emotions. I dried my face with a tissue and lifted my gaze to the ceiling.

"I love him," I said. "Deeply."

"I know you do," she said.

"And so... I don't think I can do it. He or she will be a mini him. They'll probably be as brilliant or probably even more so. Definitely beautiful."

"Devastatingly so," Meredith added. "His father is already quite the problem."

This amused me, but it saddened me even more. "He'll be perfect, but the timing is all wrong. Terrible in fact."

"Maybe," she said. "But he'll be there to help you. He's able to help you."

"We aren't even on speaking terms," I said, and she didn't say anymore.

"This was not how I imagined things would go between us. He'll take responsibility I know he will but... I don't want him to choose to be with me because of this. I'd rather do it on my own if that's the case."

"I understand," she said and took the emptied cup from me.

I turned to her then, with my eyes puffy.

"I thought coming here would make things clearer for me but I feel even more conflicted."

She nodded, and I was more than grateful she was able to just listen to me.

"Thank you," I said and squeezed her hand even harder.

"You're welcome," she said and then gave me a tight hug. "Ready to go?"

She asked and I looked around one more time.

"I think I'll stay a while longer," I replied. "But you can leave if you want?"

"No, I'll stay. Let's leave together in another fifteen minutes?"

"Alright," I agreed.

Suddenly, my phone began to ring again. I didn't need to look down to see who it was but this time around I didn't want to reject the call because I truly wanted to know what he had to say.

I moved slightly away from Meredith so that I could concentrate and picked it up.

"Hello," I said, and his response was a question.

"Where are you?"

There was no way I could tell him where I was and neither was I obligated to answer the question, so I frowned.

"Why are you asking?"

"I'm at the family planning center. Where in the building are you? What are you planning to do? What's happening?"

At his words I felt as though I had been slammed against a boulder.

"What?" I sat up, my gaze darting around in alarm. "Y-you're here? How did you-? What?"

I turned to Meredith. "You told him!"

She seemed confused. "Told who what?"

I ended the call and rose to my feet.

"I can't believe you," I said and snatched my purse. Then I turned around and began to storm away. She soon came after me. "You can't believe what?" she asked, and I yelled at her once again.

"You told him! How could you!? When I haven't resolved it yet by myself. I haven't fucking made my decision."

She caught my arm then, forcing me to come to halt and to turn around to face her.

"I have no fucking idea what you're talking about. What are you talking about?"

"You told Gideon that I'm pregnant, didn't you?" I cried. "And that I'd be coming here today."

I was forced to come to a stop then in the middle of the parking lot as she jerked me around to face her.

"I would tell you," she said, her tone offended and insistent all at once. "If I had told him, I would tell you. I'm not hiding it from you. I've never hidden anything from you."

I caught the sincerity in her tone then and stopped. And I believed her because she was right. She wouldn't hide it from me.

"So... how did he... how did he find out then?"

Just then we heard a slight screech and turned around in alarm.

And there he was.

I immediately recognized his car. He stopped and through the windshield our gazes met.

"He's here," she said. "Right? That's Professor Bach's car, right?"

I sighed and turned to her. "Yeah," and then, "Go."

"Will you be alright?" she asked. "I'll wait in my car."

"Okay," I said, and she walked away. He took in the situation and then parked. Then he strolled over to my car.

My heart pounded so loudly against my chest that it became hard to breathe, as I couldn't help but deny this would be a pivotal moment between us.

I stared at him as he approached, my expression stoic but in some corner of my heart the sweet warmth I felt at his presence returned. It was as though my heart couldn't comprehend he was someone I currently wasn't on good terms with, and instead could only process his presence with excitement.

Dread, fear, and anger all rolled into one in the pit of my stomach. I was suddenly so still that I seriously doubted I could remain standing any longer.

He soon reached me, his beautiful eyes on mine.

He took in my appearance, his gaze going down my body and then lingering on my stomach. Then he turned to glance at the clinic we had just exited.

"What's happening?" he asked. "Is this what I think it is?"

I turned then without a word and headed over to my car.

He followed and as soon as I got in so did he.

The doors were shut, and a grave silence ensued.

Until eventually he spoke.

"Are you pregnant?" he asked.

I sighed and replied. "Yeah."

His gaze turned to me.

"How long have you known?"

"Since the last time we spoke," I replied.

Another stretch of silence followed.

"And you had no plans to tell me?"

"I haven't made any concrete plans. I'm still considering my options."

"Is that what you're doing here?" he said through gritted teeth. "Considering your options?"

I turned to stare at him and could see the rage and hurt boiling in his eyes.

"Yes," I replied, and he cocked his head in wonder at me.

"Were you planning to get rid of it? Without telling me?"

I sighed. "And what if I wanted to?" I asked. "It's my choice to make."

"No, it's not," he yelled, and I jumped. "It's fucking not. That's my child too."

To this I didn't know what to say.

"If you're going to keep yelling at me then please leave. I can't stand this right now, so I recommend you schedule a meeting for later. That way we can meet and speak when you're calmer."

He glared at me, and I turned my face in the opposite direction.

"Pamela," he called. "What's wrong with you? Why are you acting this way?"

I didn't know what to say, but one thing was for sure and that was the fact I wanted to know how he had found out about all of this. So, I turned to face him.

"How did you find out?" I asked. "How did you know to come here?"

His mouth parted to speak, but then he stopped and shut it, exasperated.

"Tell me," I insisted. "If you don't then I'm not saying a single word more."

He glared at me and then suddenly he got out of the car.

He slammed the door shut and I watched as he walked around the vehicle.

Then he was by my side and jerked the door open.

"Get out," he said, and my lips opened to refuse, however they wouldn't move.

"Get out," he said again, and I would never be able to understand why I submitted.

With an angry sigh, I did as he asked, and he held out his hand for my keys.

I placed them in his palm, and he locked the car. Then he began to walk away without a word, but I didn't follow him. I heard Meredith call out my name then.

"Pamela," she called, and I turned to look at her a few spaces down. "Is everything alright?" she asked. "Do you need my help?"

I considered the option and then turned to watch as he got into his car and slammed the door shut. I shook my head.

“No,” I replied. “I’m fine.”

And I believed it. Groaning aloud at how aggravating he was, I moved and headed over to his car. The passenger side door was already open, so I slid in without a word and slammed the door shut.

In no time, we were on our way.

54

GIDEON

I didn't think I had ever been more furious than I currently was.

I was so mad I couldn't say a single word to her so all I could do was drive on.

I went straight to the downtown apartment since it was the closest and the moment I parked in the underground garage, I got out and exited the car.

I didn't slam the door shut, although I was tempted to. But I was well aware of how stubborn she was and the last thing I needed was for her to close up and refuse to communicate or cooperate. She had done this several times in the past when we were younger, and nothing was ever able to convince her to speak to me.

At the end of the day, I would end up being the one to plead for forgiveness and in this case, I couldn't afford it.

I headed straight to the back entrance.. However, it was then I realized I needed her to be with me so she could gain access. With a sigh, I shut my eyes for a moment and glanced back at the car several rows down. I could partially see her and noted that she wasn't even looking at me. She was staring straight ahead, a furious scowl on her face and it took everything to resist the urge to pull my hair out.

I considered just texting her the code since the card was with me but then I doubted she would respond.

Aggravated, I turned around and began to calmly stroll back to the car. When I arrived, I went over to her side and even though she was aware I was there, she still didn't say a word.

I knocked on the window and after a few seconds she finally turned. She didn't look at me but eventually grabbed onto her purse. I stepped back so she could push the door open and then without a word she was heading in the direction I had just come from.

I shouldn't have softened but somehow, I did, endeared by her but thankfully it was only for a moment.

I unlocked the door without a word as soon as I arrived and thankfully, she waited for me to lead the way. In the elevators, we didn't say a word to each other and stood at opposite sides until eventually we arrived at the top floor.

In no time I was unlocking my door, and then shutting it behind her.

She stood in the huge foyer, her gaze on the tall vase of lilies on the table.

I stared at them too, realizing that I had never really paid attention to their presence but was grateful to my housekeeper for consistently replacing them. I started to head in, but it only took a few steps for me to realize she hadn't taken a single one further. I turned and this time around, met her gaze.

"I want to be out of here in ten minutes," she said as she folded her arms across her chest. "So, say what you gotta say."

I looked at her, and almost gave in but then I recalled

that she was just as affected by me as I was by her and so with a cold stare, I turned and continued on my way.

I walked carefully so I could listen, hoping with all my heart she wouldn't turn around to leave. If she did, it would make things extremely difficult for us to overcome this hurdle between us. I loved her but acting incessantly and endlessly spoiled was not a behavior that I was going to tolerate.

I arrived at the kitchen and headed straight to the fridge, and it was almost a minute later before I turned and saw she had arrived in the living room. She stood in the massive space almost three times the size of the one closer to the university and didn't look around. I knew she wanted to as she had previously expressed her immense desire to see it, but then given the current tension she refused.

My heart softened once again, so I decided to meet her halfway. Since she had come into the room, I was certain the message of part submission had been sent clearly between us. If she had turned around and left, the next conversation would have been severe and difficult.

This one however I was going to try to keep as civil as possible.

"Okay" I said and slammed the door shut as I turned to face her. Then I went straight to the point. "Were you really planning on getting rid of the baby?" My head spun even at the mention of it, as I couldn't understand how this was even real and that she had planned on keeping it away from me. "How long has it been since you found out? And were you truly planning on never letting me know about it?"

Granted, I hadn't expected to ask the questions all at once, but I couldn't calm myself down enough. I couldn't remember the last time I had been this jarred.

She frowned at me.

"How did *you* find out?"

I was immediately alarmed.

Seeing that I didn't outrightly respond she continued. "How did you know that I would be at the clinic? Meredith said she wasn't the one that told you but no one else in my circle apart from you is aware, so how did you know?" She hesitated. "Did she... tell you?"

I decided there were some things indeed we truly needed to straighten out otherwise it would be difficult for our relationship to survive. Love after all couldn't solve everything.

"Answer my question first," I said. "And then I'll answer yours." She gave me an incredulous look as though she couldn't believe that I wasn't joking.

She stared at me, long and hard and then I saw her shoulders slump in defeat.

"I wasn't going to do anything dra-" she stopped and looked at me and I could see her gaze soften. "I wasn't going to do anything drastic."

I waited for her to say more but when she didn't, I knew she was holding back.

I could read the guilt in her eyes in the way she couldn't quite meet mine as confidently as she had just mere moments earlier.

"But?" I asked and this time around her gaze met mine. She looked at me hard and said nothing.

"But?" I repeated and began to move around the counter with my hands in my pockets.

"I have nothing else to say," she said, however before I reached her, she started to retreat.

I eventually stood before her... close enough I could see the slight redness in a corner of her eyes.

I was instantly concerned, even though I knew there was

no reason to be. However, I couldn't help it. If she had kept such a big secret from me, I could only wonder how many other things and difficulties she had been through within the past two weeks that I was unaware about.

"It's your turn," she said. "How did *you* find out?"

I watched her, trying my best to completely understand her. My plan had been to hold out on telling her the truth, or to once again find a way to divert her attention, but it was clear now I was no longer going to get away with this. She was adamant that I be fair, and I couldn't blame her.

I truly hoped she wouldn't walk away. But as I watched the scorn in her eyes, it became too much of a risk to take so I leaned down, but she immediately moved away from me in alarm. Her back connected to the wall and her eyes flashed wide.

"What are you doing?"

"It's been two weeks," I said, my voice losing its harshness. Instead, it was breathless and buttery soft, and I was amazed.

The moment I had shifted my thoughts away from the response I needed from her, I suddenly needed to have her. It had been too long and in our absence from each other I had been tortured.

However, since my contact with her had been limited, my desire had been controllable but now... and with how fiery she currently was, I wanted that energy applied instead to her passion for me. If it even still existed.

"Kiss me," I said, and she immediately refused.

"No."

"Why?"

"Gideon," she called... confused.

"We can fight after," I said. "It's been too long."

"No!" her hands shot out to hold my chest at bay. But

then her gaze lowered from mine as she tried to catch her breath. Either this or she was trying to control her temper.

Suddenly she lifted her gaze and then to my surprise, her hand was curving around the back of my head. She yanked me closer to her, the heels of her feet lifting off the floor. And then she took my mouth.

I instantly submitted.

There was no better word for it because it was exactly what I did.

And it was jarring because it was a word I had never ascribed to myself before any person or circumstance. But before her, my spine weakened, or perhaps it was her kiss that made it so... effortless... instantly.

My arms wrapped around her waist so I could hold her as tightly to me as possible. Her body was crushed to mine and it wasn't enough.

I needed to be inside her but even this felt too inadequate.

I missed her so much more than I had thought, and as the sweet taste of her wrought through me like a storm, leaving me a complete mess internally, as well as the reminder she was pregnant with my child, I suddenly felt too overwhelmed. I didn't know what to do or how to process any of this, and I imagined now I could understand to an extent why she had chosen to keep this from me. It was too easy to have my head screwed off when I was with her, and at the lifting of a leg along the side of mine so she could grind as intensely as she could against my crotch, I was certain this was the case for her.

Her hand fisted the front of my shirt as her tongue slid passionately against mine. She sucked on my lips, and I grabbed onto her ass.

"Stop," she eventually rasped... out of breath. I was in

the same state, however I couldn't pull away even as she managed to wrench her lips from mine. I buried my face in the crook of her neck and embraced her hard, unable to let go.

"Gideon," she called but I didn't move. I considered pulling away but not until she grabbed onto my biceps and started to move me did I respond. The moment I got the inkling of her rejection, I came back to my senses and turned my face away so she wouldn't see whatever was reflected in my eyes. Even I wasn't sure what it was, but I knew it was soft and vulnerable and completely susceptible to her.

With a harsh exhale she leaned against the wall and didn't say another word until I turned and met her gaze.

We watched each other for a long moment and then she came forward to hold my face in her hands.

"What are we doing?" she asked. "We're supposed to be pissed at each other."

"Aren't we still pissed at each other?" I asked and she tightened her grip on my hair.

"Ow," I said calmly, and she stared even harder into my eyes. Then she leaned forward and gave me another kiss. This time round it was slow and intent and soothing... in the best possible way that could exist.

"Why were you mad at me?" I asked, my heart calmed.

Her eyebrows drew together in a frown, but she didn't pull away.

"There were many reasons," she said, and I pressed on.

"Name them."

She hesitated but eventually she spoke.

"Are we together?" she asked, and as my expression darkened she quickly hurried to explain.

"You can't blame me for asking," she said. "You didn't speak to me for almost two weeks."

"You didn't speak to me either," I pointed out.

"Because of the way you treated..." she caught herself. Then she restarted, but this time around in a calmer tone. "Because of the way things turned out with my dad."

I went silent as I waited for her to explain, and she did. "I appreciated that you helped us out, but you were so reluctant about it and unwilling to, that it would have been much better if you hadn't even bothered. It made us feel like hell that we didn't have a choice but to accept it. It was in exchange for our pride and dignity."

I watched her, and although I felt my temper slightly rising, I chose to remain calm for her sake because as I was beginning to realize I loved her beyond what should have been ordinarily acceptable for me.

"Are you the one who feels this way?" I asked. "Or is he the one?"

"It's all of us," she said sternly but I wasn't intimidated.

"I'd like to implore you not to feel that way because none of my antagonism is directed towards you. It was all directed at him and so if he does feel that way, then I don't have any plans to feel remorseful about it."

It was no surprise this greatly upset her.

"Let me go," she said and immediately started to pull away from me, but I hung on tight.

"Gideon!" she called angrily, but I held her gaze until she took up the challenge not to timidly turn away from me.

"You have to be on my side," I told her and at my words she stilled. "I understand he's your father but you're mine now. So, you have to be on my side. When I tell you his actions truly hurt me in ways that up till today, I am still trying to let go of for the sake of moving on, you shouldn't take it lightly. I'm not telling you to abandon him because he is your dad, but you cannot be against me either. You cannot consider his plight and ignore mine."

She watched me. "I'm yours?" she asked. "You could have fooled me."

I didn't respond.

"Anyway," she said. "I understand what you're saying but I also hope you can also see things from my perspective. As the man I lov-" She quickly caught herself but this time around it was impossible for her to conceal what she wanted to say.

"What I mean is that he's my family and you can't treat my family that way. For my sake at least. He did damage to both of our families and although I can't confidently say he has atoned for it, I can say I can't watch him die either. It will break my heart. I'd rather he be alive and estranged from me than... not here. Do you understand?" Her eyes were huge and when she lifted her hand to the side of my face, I couldn't find it in me to reject the affectionate touch. "Please say you understand me."

"Even if I don't?" I asked and she pouted.

My hand lifted then to brush her hair out of her face. It had been so long since I had done this, and I couldn't believe how intensely I missed such a simple act.

"Let's leave things at that for now. As you've asked, I'll give you some time to consider what I've said."

I continued brushing her hair in thought especially as my father's words came to mind.

'Have you ever considered that she would feel equally as furious to learn her father cheated with your mother? Then you'd want her to be lenient right? Then you'd want her to accept you regardless. Or would you want her to hate you because of it?'

"Why aren't you angry at my mom?" I asked.

It took a few seconds for her to process the question, and then she turned her face up to look at me.

"Who says I'm not angry at her?"

I waited for her to give me a proper response.

With a sigh, she rested her head against my chest.

"I can feel your heartbeat," she said. "I don't think I ever have before. We've never really slowed down enough to enjoy each other's company. Or rather we've not been allowed to slow down enough to enjoy each other's company."

I listened, wanting to redirect her back to the question she was completely avoiding but waiting because I enjoyed hearing her speak even if she was just currently rambling. Regardless, her words went straight to my heart.

"First it was James and then my dad and-" she stopped then and I almost shook my head.

Her pregnancy was the next thing we still hadn't spoken about. I suddenly no longer wanted to remain standing. I wanted to slow down, just as she had suggested and spend the time the both of us needed with each other. It was clear enough now that regardless of how mad we got at each other, neither of us was going anywhere. So, I pulled away and held onto her shoulders so she would focus on me.

"Let's go to bed," I said, and her eyes slightly widened in response.

"In the middle of the day?"

"It's late evening," I replied as I took her hand in mine. "And we don't have to sleep. I just want us to spend some time together."

I started to pull her along with me, but she didn't move eagerly.

When I glanced back, I saw the mistrust in her eyes.

"C'mon," I said and was finally able to get her to move.

We went straight to my bedroom and in no time, she was sliding up the covers to lie next to me.

She rested her head against my chest just as she had desired, and for the seconds that followed we simply basked in the other's presence. And then she spoke.

"There's too much to process right now," she said, and I listened. "Maybe later down the line, maybe when I see her, I'll feel angry. For the longest time I put a face to the woman that had pulled my family apart and given the fact my mother never really made a fuss about their separation, at least to me, I didn't take it to heart. Plus, when it all happened, I recall thinking my mother felt relieved rather than upset. I just never felt like she was too affected by it plus I was never really close to my dad. All in all, things remained pretty calm."

She stopped.

"Were you close to your mom?'

I considered this. "Not really."

She lifted her gaze then to look at me. "I would have expected you were given how you know... it's the opposite for you."

I understood what she was saying. "I'm close to my dad," I replied. "And I saw how he doted on her. He worked a lot but still he made the maximum effort he could to be with her but I guess he wasn't enough. I don't know. He's just always been quite sensitive to me. I couldn't understand it properly back then, but all I knew was he always honestly and almost innocently reacted to things so I guess in this case I was worried about what it would do to him."

"It pained me especially that I caught them and even though I wasn't too close to my mom I still loved her... and respected her. They broke that... they broke a lot of things, and I don't know... I'm trying to completely get over it. My dad has... so maybe I haven't because I've refused to see her but maybe eventually it will all resolve itself on its own."

Her hand stroked against my chest. I allowed the seconds to pass peacefully between us but was aware that other more urgent matters needed to be addressed. But still, I couldn't help but cradle my hand on the side of her face. She lifted her gaze and an unspoken truce passed between us.

"When did you find out?" I asked and she didn't look away. Her gaze however softened, and for a moment she seemed helpless. I held her even tighter.

"I think the day I saw you last at the hospital."

"You've known for two weeks?" I asked and she nodded.

I didn't know what to say after that so all I could do was stroke her hair and think.

"I'm sorry," I eventually heard her soft voice. "I wasn't careful enough."

This made me sigh. "You mean *I* wasn't careful enough."

"I took my pills... consistently so I really don't understand."

"I guess we're that 0.001%" I said and at the amusement in my tone she chased my gaze.

"You're really not mad?"

This made me frown. "Why would I be? What I'm concerned about is how this will affect you. I'll do everything to ensure you get all the help you need but ultimately and for at least a year or two you'll have to be out of school."

She went quiet again and truly I would have given anything to be able to read her mind. However, I couldn't help but recall where I had found her, and I knew if we also didn't address that, a part of me would always wonder if I had imposed and encroached on her will beyond what she desired.

I hoped she would address it herself but when she didn't bring it up, I had no choice. I tried to be as delicate as I could.

"Today I-"

"Can you -"

We both stopped and shared a laugh.

"Go first," I said, and she looked at me.

"What were you about to say?" she asked.

I replied. "The clinic."

She sat up then, crossed her legs and faced me. I also sat up and leaned against the headboard.

"I just wanted to confirm how I felt... to have some clarity. It's your baby Gideon... and I think I've wanted to have your babies since the first time I set my eyes on you."

My heart warmed.

"You were eleven," I reminded her.

"Exactly," she said, and I laughed.

"Still," she continued. "Something right done at the wrong time can leave a sour taste rather than a sweet one and for a while that's how I felt. Given the issues with my dad and school... and us... I didn't know how to feel so I wanted to consider all options and at least eliminate what I didn't want. Anyway, I got there today and knew instantly that I couldn't do it. Because it's yours. If it was anyone else, then maybe... but not yours. I love him or her already and even though it wasn't in my plan at all, the next option I was considering was doing it all by myself and in the future letting you know."

"How could-" I began but she interrupted me.

"Please let me finish," she entreated. "You must understand that I... I love you. I'm in love with you and I won't accept anything less from you. I either have that from you or nothing else at all. And at the time we were on much too shaky ground. We've been on shaky ground, and I was just preparing myself for the worst."

I sighed and nodded in understanding.

She reached forward then to settle on my lap.

"We're fine," she said as she ran her fingers through my hair. "I'm fine. I can take the year off or two. Besides I wasn't exactly having a blast anyway. I still believe I'm in the wrong major and do you recall what we discussed about interior design and creating products?"

I nodded.

"Well, I've had the time over the last two weeks to think about it and I really think I could make it work. I could use the time off to study and explore it as much as I want to, so..."

She looked deeply into my eyes, trying to gauge my reaction and I didn't hide anything from her because what I was now was calm.

I had listened to what she had to say and was on the same page with her, but I also had some things of my own to relay.

55

PAMELA

My nerves were tied up in knots.

I watched him and wondered what he was thinking.

He was back to being the Gideon I knew, calm and watchful and fucking indecipherable.

Uncomfortable, I started to get off his lap, but his arm came around and held me in place.

For once I was glad I had gone for a skirt today, a long linen one that I had never worn before. It was the only thing I could gravitate too when I wanted to head out earlier to the clinic.

Now it was allowing me all the access I needed to ground my sex against the hard bulge of him straining against his pants.

"Say something," I eventually pleaded, unable to take his silence any longer.

He smiled and complied. "I love you," he said and for a second, I felt my heart stop.

A little while earlier, I had hesitated when telling him the same but, in the end, I had decided not to make a bigger deal of it than was needed. After all, it was the truth and I figured if he couldn't handle it now, he would ever be able to. However, at his words... I wasn't ready.

"Yeah," was all I could say in response and his beautiful smile hit me. His hand moved to stroke the back of my head.

"This is why I want you to believe every word I'm going to say now," he said.

"Okay," I noted and listened carefully.

"I will be there with you every step of the way, but we have to agree on one thing from now on."

"What?" I asked.

"That even though we fight, we won't shut each other out like we did the last two weeks. You've known me for a long time Pamela and so have I you. We're family and given your stubbornness-"

"Hey-" I immediately protested more to mask the emotions that were rising in my throat.

He smiled and went on, "We'll definitely fight again... I'm sure of it, but let's not hurt each other in the process of trying to resolve things."

Tears stung my eyes without warning, so I immediately had to look away.

He embraced me even harder, so I was able to hide.

"I'm still not worthy?" He asked and for a moment I was unsure of what he was talking about. But then the statement I had made to him on the night we had officially gotten together in the first place came back.

"You're more than worthy," I mumbled and could hear his smile. However, something else occurred to me so I quickly pulled away to stare straight into his eyes.

"There's one more thing we need to talk about," I said, and he seemed to be aware of exactly what I was referring to because his expression remained unchanged.

I continued, undaunted. “How did you know where I was?”

After a long moment he started to look away, but I turned his gaze back to mine. Then I gave him a stern look which did nothing, but certainly alerted him that I needed his response. And that I wasn't going to let this go or sweep it under the rug. I was so curious about it that my mind kept going around in circles, wondering and speculating, because the only person it pointed to as the culprit had already earnestly denied it.

“Gideon," I called, and he sighed.

“You know what I do for a living right?” he asked, and I stared at him, wondering how this connected.

It soon dawned on me and the moment it did my eyes nearly popped out of my head.

My mouth fell open and for the longest time I could do nothing but stare in shock at him and then confusion.

“You hacked into my phone?”

“Putting it that way does sound terrible,” he said.

I frowned at this, furious and near shaking from it.

He noticed this and released a heavy breath.

“I was worried about you, and I was still racking up excuses to keep myself away from you, so I had to find a way to ensure that you were alright. It was driving me crazy.”

Despite my spilling emotions ranging from feeling everything to absolutely nothing all at once, I did try my best to consider his previous words and act accordingly.

“That’s unacceptable Gideon,” I said, and he nodded although he didn’t necessarily show any remorse and that bothered me.

“How many times did you do it?” I asked.

“A handful,” he mentioned. “I didn’t dwell though. I just

checked after we had separated the first time to be sure all was well.'"

I considered this and more atrocities came to mind. "So, you knew about James from the first moment I contacted him?"

"Well, I didn't know who he was at the time," he replied.

I could do nothing but stare at him, mortified.

"Gideon, that is extremely inappropriate."

"I know," he replied. "I'm sorry."

"And this time around?"

He looked into my eyes however, I looked away and tried not to give him an easy pass.

"I missed you," he said, and I shut my eyes. I hated that he could make me melt so easily but at the same time I couldn't help but be endeared by his words.

His voice softened even further.

"I just... needed to check that you were okay."

At this I sighed and got off him. However, I didn't get out of bed. Instead, I went to his side and leaned against the headboard.

Then I folded my arms across my chest.

"This will be the end of it right?" I asked, however, he didn't respond.

"Gideon!" I turned to him.

He sighed and nodded. "It will, unless there's an emergency and I can't find you."

"That's an extreme case," I said, and he nodded. Then he turned to me, and I met his gaze.

"I won't do it again. Now that I've admitted it to you... I won't do it again."

"Is this a promise?" I asked and he gave a nod. "It is."

"Can I trust you?"

"I'll make sure that you can, but then again only time will be able to tell."

I was satisfied with this. Still a little bit shocked and annoyed but I didn't want to keep fighting with him. I unfolded my arms and went to him and this time around he caught me in his.

He gave me a desperate embrace, kissed the side of my head and my cheek and then whispered the most beautiful words I had ever heard.

"I love you," he said, and my heart melted into a puddle.

"I love you." I said in return.

EPILOGUE

GIDEON

"I got accepted! I got accepted!"

She jumped into my arms before I could hear any more of the news and I could do nothing but catch her. A few of our guests turned at the scene and laughed out in amusement.

"Stop making us jealous," a woman from Pamela's circles called out and received other sounds of jolly agreement.

I turned to my beautiful fiancée and looked down into her eyes.

"You got accepted?" I asked.

Her eyes sparkled. "Yes, at the design firm. It's just an internship but it's a great start for me learning all the ropes."

"That's great, really great," I said, and hugged her once again.

"Gideon," I heard my father's voice behind me.

I turned around and saw him walking over, dressed in a brand-new suit that I didn't recognize. He never liked to attend these kinds of functions or dress up. So for years, he usually had only one go to set that he had kept. Today however it wasn't the usual black suit but a fitted, more luxurious striped, navy-blue suit.

His eyes were solely on Pam as he approached, and I could tell she was incredibly excited to see him.

He embraced her and then they went into pleasantries and discussions that I was not invited to join. Amused, I took my leave so I could say hello to the other guests. I soon got lost in conversation with Michael and a few of the executives from the company when my phone began to ring. I pulled it out of my pocket, scanned the room for Pamela and saw her sitting with my father at the bar and enjoying her freshly squeezed orange juice.

"Hello?" I answered.

"Hi Gideon," Pamela's mom's voice came through the phone.

"Hi," I replied. "You're not here yet."

"Just a bit delayed but we'll be there in a few minutes."

"Alright," I said but before the call came to an end, she stopped me. "Um... will you be able to meet us outside first?"

And it was then I realized what she was saying. "You're not coming alone?"

"I was hoping I wouldn't have to," she said. "It's his daughter's engagement party too. But if it will be uncomfortable for you then I understand."

I lifted my eyes then and gazed once again towards Pamela and my father. To my surprise they were playing a game of seeing who could throw almonds in their mouths and I couldn't help but shake my head with amazement at how effortlessly she brought out the playful, child-like side in my dad. She nearly fell off the stool, and my heart jumped at the thought of her falling and hurting not just herself, but also our growing baby, but he caught her and as her laugh rang out across the room, I sighed with relief.

"It's alright," I said slowly into the phone. "He can come. I'm sure she'd love to see him."

"Thank you," she replied gratefully, and the call came to an end.

Pam turned and caught my eyes then, hers were watering from laughing so hard. With an indulgent smile I headed towards them.

"You're teaching her terrible habits, Dad," I said as I curved my arm around her waist.

"I've been doing that since she was younger," he said. "Just back then we used to do this with candy."

"I don't remember that," I said, loving the way Pamela leaned into me.

"Of course, you don't," he said as he picked up his tumbler of whiskey. "You were too busy being a grown up and focusing on your work."

I leaned down towards Pam, a deep love filling my heart.

Thankfully, my father read the mood and took his leave with a slap on my shoulder.

I leaned down to kiss my bride-to-be, deeply and passionately and by the time I broke it off, she was left in wonder.

"Oh," she said, her eyes wide. "What was that for?" Her voice was a hoarse whisper.

"Nothing," I said as I wrapped my arms around her waist. "I'm just thankful you're mine."

She snaked her arms around me in a crushing hug.

I was on edge although I tried my best not to be, but it was quite hard not to look towards the entrance in wonder at when they would be coming in.

Eventually I was able to see them as they appeared at

the door but before I could go over, Pamela did. She was in a hurry, and I understood that she was probably nervous at the sudden sight of her father in his wheelchair. Her mother was behind him, and she caught my eye for a moment.

Pamela spoke to her, and it was impossible to hear anything given the music and crowd, but in no time, she turned to me, and I knew she had been informed. With a deep breath, I emptied my glass, my gaze locked on her father's and went over. Her eyes softened on me as I approached but I could clearly see and feel the worry in them. So, I sent her a smile and linked her hands with mine as I arrived. She leaned in and held onto me with both hands.

"Hello," I greeted, and her father looked at me.

"I heard you're marrying my daughter without permission," he said.

"Dad!" she complained.

"It's the least I can do," I replied and for a moment we were all silent and then he burst out laughing.

I had done my best. "Enjoy the party," I called and sent a warm smile to her mom and was on my way.

Pamela came along with me and when next I turned, her mouth was on mine.

"Thank you, I love you," she said simply. Her eyes widened. "I just felt the baby kick."

"Yeah?"

"Yeah," she confirmed softly.

"Keep him company for a bit," I said. "Don't hold back because of me."

She beamed and her smile was blinding. "I won't," she said excitedly and then whispered in my ear. "but I'll be saying my thanks properly tonight."

I laughed and couldn't take my eyes away from her as she began to back away. "I'll wait for it."

"You better," she warned, in a fake militant voice.

I'll always be waiting for you, Pamela. Always.

The End

COMING SOON - SAMPLE CHAPTERS

FLIRTING WITH THE CEO

Chapter One
Summer

The club is just starting to get busy.

Rebecca, Jess, Olivia and I have been here for almost an hour now, and while I'm glad it's starting to liven up a bit, I'm also already feeling the temperature going up and I know the heat will get to me sooner rather than later. The windows are already starting to steam up. I fan my hand in front of my face and Rebecca nods her head in sympathy with me.

"Should we go and get a drink?" Rebecca shouts over the thump, thump, thump of the music. I nod and follow her through the small groups of people clustered around the place towards the bar. The bar is the most crowded part of the club, but we duck, wiggle, and push our way to the front.

The bartender catches Rebecca's eye.

"Two gin and tonics please," she shouts.

"Four shots of red Aftershock please," I yell.

The bartender returns with our drinks, and since it my

turn, I pay for them. Then I pick my shots up, two in each hand and follow Rebecca through the throng. I make my way slowly and carefully, but I still feel little trickles of the sticky liquid running down my fingers. There's not much I can do about it. I wasn't going to ask for a tray for four shots but passing by people dancing, it's hard to avoid little knocks.

We make our way back to the little nook where we were originally standing. We come to this club regularly and this is our spot. It's right on the edge of the dance floor, which means we can rush to the dance floor easily whenever one of our favorite songs comes on. It also has a handy little ledge we can stand our drinks on.

I put the shots down on the ledge and Rebecca looks at me, a questioning frown on her face.

"Four shots? Really?" she asks.

"For the four of us, no?" I reply.

She looks at me with a confused expression.

"Remember Jess and Olivia?" I remind. "They went to the Ladies' room?"

Rebecca bursts out laughing and it's my turn to look confused.

"That was like an hour ago. They are long gone now."

"Oh," I say. I laugh too when I realize how long it's been since I saw either of them and somehow still didn't really register the fact that they had clearly left. I grin at Rebecca. "Oh well. I guess that means two shots each for us then."

Rebecca groans, but she picks up the first of her two shots. I pick mine up and we raise them in the air and down them in unison. Heat floods through me as I swallow. The peppery, cinnamon taste tingles on my tongue. Together we reach for our second shot. I throw mine down my throat and quickly I take a long drink of my gin and tonic to mask the taste of the shot.

I'm starting to feel more than just a little bit tipsy now and I like it since I'm not worried about a hangover. Today is Friday so I have two full days to get over any hangover before I'm back at work on Monday. Tonight, I'm free to do whatever the hell I like, and it feels good knowing that. I smile at that thought. At the moment my favorite song begins to play and I grab Rebecca's hand and pull her onto the dance floor.

We start to dance, our arms up, our hips swaying. Lost to the music.

We dance and drink, and drink and dance for the next couple of hours. Throughout it all, we laugh and feel high on life. Tonight was one of those spur of the moment nights that always ends up being the best nights.

It's getting towards closing time now at Sound Bound. There's only about an hour left before, but the club is still in full swing. We're dancing and my feet are throbbing, but Rebecca loves this song, and we never walk away from each other.

A blonde guy moves towards us and puts his hand on Rebecca's hip from behind, swaying in time with her. Rebecca catches my eye and gives me a look – what's he like? – and I give her a barely perceptible nod back – yeah, he's cute.

She exaggerates the movement of her hips and then she turns around and she smiles at the blonde guy. He says something close to her ear and she laughs and the next moment, she's turned towards him. I'm relieved because that means I can slip away and rest my feet for a moment.

I do just that, moving back towards our spot and plonking myself down on one of the tall stools that line the edges of the club. They're mostly empty except for the odd couple and one poor girl who looks like she's got the weight of the whole world on her thin shoulders.

I massage my feet and look around, content to people watch. The crowd of people seem to move as one, a happy, sweaty undulating mass of dancers. Part of me wants to go and join the mass once more, but part of me, the part with the sore feet, is glad to be free of it. If I'd worn slightly more comfortable shoes, but then I don't feel like my dress would have looked as good.

I check my watch.

There's half an hour to go now before the club starts to kick people out and I hop down off my stool to go towards the ladies' room. I move across the club, going around the dance floor rather than across it. I join the line for a cubicle and wait. The wait time isn't too bad and I'm soon in a cubicle. It's a typical club toilet – there's no lock on the door and no toilet paper and a seat I wouldn't want to sit on if I was paid to. I hover over the seat and then pull some tissues out of my purse. I finish up, go and wash my hands and then I head back out into the main body of the club. The heat hits me as I leave the ladies' room and I decide I've had enough for one night.

I move back across the club, looking for Rebecca and I soon spot her – it wasn't that hard, she hasn't moved from where I left her. She's still on the dance floor with the blonde guy. It's clear they are into each other. Their eyes are locked on each other's faces and their movements are very suggestive.

I smile. It's about time Rebecca let her hair down and had some fun with someone.

Generally speaking, Rebecca is a relationship girl. She doesn't go to clubs to pick up random men and she only dates guys she thinks are in a place where they are ready for something serious. In other words, she's my polar opposite. I'm not interested in a relationship. I'm at a point where I'm finally making a name for myself in my career, and I don't want anything getting in the way of that. That doesn't mean I'm against a hook up if a really, really, really hot guy shows up, but that scenario is as rare as a hen's tooth.

I move through the crowd and touch Rebecca on the shoulder. She looks around and grins when she sees me and then she hugs me tightly.

"Summer," she shouts excitedly. "This is Mark."

The blonde guy gives me a smile and I smile back and do a little wave.

"Listen, I'm going to take off before the line for a cab gets too ridiculous," I say.

"Oh," Rebecca mouth.

She looks deflated looking between me and Mark and I realize she thinks I'm expecting her to come with me. I'm expecting no such thing. The only reason I told her instead of just sneaking off is because I don't want her to worry and spend any time looking for me after I've gone. I would be so mad if she did that to me so I won't do it to her.

Not that getting home is ever a problem for Rebecca. She lives in an apartment above a deli on the next block over from the club. She can literally fall over twice outside of the club and she's as good as home.

I lean towards her and whisper. "Hey, you don't have to come with me. I'll be all right."

"Really?" she asks.

"Really," I confirm. "It's not like we're going in the same direction even if we leave together, is it?"

Rebecca's grin is back, and she hugs me again.

"Thank you," she says in my ear and then she releases me. "See you soon?"

"Yeah definitely," I say. I wink at her. "Enjoy the rest of your night."

"Oh, I will," she laughs.

I give her upper arm a final squeeze and then I give Mark another little wave and head for the exit. The cool night air is refreshing for about a minute and then it makes goosebumps appear on my arms and legs. I start to regret the short dress I'm wearing as I head to the curb to hail a cab.

I reach the line and join it. It's not too bad yet but I know I got here just in time before the massive influx of people at closing time descend on the line at once. I cross my arms and rub my upper arms with the opposite hands. It warms me slightly but not enough to stop me from stamping my feet up and down on the ground.

"Chilly?" an amused sounding male voice asks from behind me.

I half-turn ready to give a cheeky retort, but I find myself speechless when I see the owner of the voice. The voice is sexy – low and husky and I'm expecting someone who is pretty, good looking. What I'm not expecting is the most gorgeous man I have ever seen in my life outside of a movie screen. He's tall, around six feet I'm guessing, and his body is lean and in a nice proportion. No like one of those beefy bodybuilder types but he's no slouch and I can see the defined muscles of his arms beneath his white t-shirt sleeves. I also see what looks like a tattoo of a dragon's head poking out of one sleeve.

I look up at his face for the second time. The first time in my life, I was so taken aback by how good looking a man was, I shamelessly and openly drink him in. He must be a bit older than me – maybe in his mid-thirties to my twenty-nine. His silky black hair is brushed across his forehead and I have to stop myself from reaching out and running my hand through it. He has a strong jawline and well-defined cheekbones that makes him look almost like a Roman statue.

But all that pales into insignificance when I look into his eyes. They are, I suppose, gray, although to me, in the light of the streetlamp, they look silvery and shine like the precious metal. As I stare into those truly mesmerizing eyes, he looks back into mine and I see his irises begin to dilate, and I know he's reacting to me.

Whoa! Somehow, this gorgeous man is attracted to me! And his eyes are betraying his lust for me.

"Go on, speak. I promise I won't bite," he drawls with a wolfish smile.

His smile widens and shows a row of straight, white teeth. I stare at the tiny dimple that appear on his right cheek. To my amazement I feel myself getting wet just looking at him. I give my head a small shake as I remember – I'm being rude. He asked me a question and I can't find the words to answer it.

It wasn't even a difficult question. He only asked me if I'm chilly. The answer is: Yes, I was until I looked into his eyes and heat consumed my body. But I'm not about to say that to him so instead I just give him a half nod.

"I'd give you my jacket but as you can see, I don't have one," he says with an apologetic smile.

"It's okay. You probably wore the fitting T-shirt for the same reason I wore a mini dress," I croak.

He laughs at that, and I feel myself relaxing. Despite the heat between us, he seems like a pretty chilled out guy.

"I don't remember seeing you in Radium," he says. "And I'm damn sure wouldn't have forgotten you if I had."

I smile at his compliment even as I feel my cheeks flushing slightly. I tell myself to stop it. It was just a line and a cheesy as hell one at that. This thought does nothing to stop me from feeling warm inside though.

"That's because I was in Sound Bound," I say, nodding my head in the direction of the club I have just left.

"I sure picked the wrong club tonight," he says.

"You did," I agree. "It was bouncing in there.

"That's not what I..." he starts, then shakes his head slightly and smiles. "You knew exactly what I meant."

I can't help but laugh and he laughs with me.

"So, you had a good night then?" he asks after a moment.

"Yeah," I say. "I really did. What about you?"

"Nothing special, but it wasn't awful or anything." He pauses. "But it's certainly looking up now."

"Is that so?" I murmur with a raised eyebrow.

I'm almost at the front of the cab line and I don't want the time with this man to end. "Shall we share a club?" I hear myself asking.

"Come home with me," he says, his eyes darkening and his voice intense.

I blink at how confident and forward he is. That wasn't a question or a suggestion. It was a command. He didn't ask if I wanted to go home with him, he just told me that I should. I like that. I like a man who knows what he wants and isn't afraid to say so.

For a few seconds I silently debate playing hard to get, make him work for the yes, but what's the point? He's old enough to have had his share of women and he must know when someone is into him. And I'm definitely into him. He would make the perfect one night stand. Playing hard to get at this point will just make me look like I'm craving attention.

"Ok," I say.

I feel that heat swirl around my body as I agree to his command.

If he is taken aback by my willingness to oblige him, he doesn't show it. He just smiles slowly at me. Fucking hell, look at him I can't imagine he gets many 'no thank yous'.

The couple in front of us get into the cab that pulls up and we're next. We shuffle forward as a large group of men join the back of the line. They are a fair distance away from us, but they're shouting and laughing, and they are so loud it still almost drowns out what he says next, although I do manage to catch it.

"I'm Len by the way," he says.

"Pleasure to meet you Len," I smile.

Then another cab pulls up and he opens the door and gestures for me to get in. I clamber in and shuffle across the seat. Len follows me in and pulls the door closed behind him.

"Ten ninety-three Miller Square please," he says to the driver and the cab pulls away.

I stay quiet, trying to hide my surprise. Miller Square is in one of the most desirable zip codes in the city. It's the home of investment bankers and traders and several B list celebrities. I peer at Len out of the corner of my eye. Is he a model or something that I haven't recognized yet? I'm sure he isn't although he is most definitely hot enough to be.

"What do you do for a living?" I ask after a moment.

"You really want to talk about work right now?"

I shake my head. Truth is I don't. I don't care if Len is some sort of celebrity or if he is a trust fund kid. Tonight is all about finding a hen's tooth. I don't need to spoil it with mundane reality.

"I know what you're doing now," he murmurs softly. "You heard my address and now you're trying to work out if I'm the face of some fancy cologne or something aren't you?"

I debate saying no but he must be able to read the truth on my face and instead I shrug.

"Just wondering if you're not going to be on Oprah or something and tell her about the time you took a girl home that was so clueless she didn't even know who you were?"

Len laughs. "Nope you're definitely safe from that. I have a normal job that pays well."

The cab reaches Len's house and I get out as he pays the cab driver . I look at the house we're stopped outside and my jaw kinda drops. The house isn't just a house. It's more of a mansion. Like something out of a movie. I'm not exactly poor and my apartment is in a nice neighborhood, but this place is in another league altogether.

Len joins me and then he opens the gate and gestures for me to follow him. I follow him up the impressive driveway and to the front door. He pulls out a key, unlocks it and we go inside.

"Would you like a drink or anything?" Len asks, his breath feels warm and close to my head. I feel a shiver go through me.

"No thank you," I whisper.

I've drunk enough already, and I know my limits.

He holds his hand out to me. "Your wish is my command."

I take his hand and he leads me towards a wide staircase. We start to climb it and I feel myself blushing when I realize he took my refusal of a drink to mean I wanted to go straight to bed with him. I debate explaining that's not quite what I meant but what's the point? I do want to get into his bed with him and it's not like I'm going to see him again so what does it matter if I seem a little eager? It's better than having to make awkward small talk.

Lights come on as we walk, lighting up the stairway in front of us. We reach what I think is the top of the stairs, but Len turns and leads me up another flight of stairs. I keep following him and we step off this flight and into a long, cream hallway with deep pile carpet. It's painted cream, a fluffy white carpet finishing it off. Every few feet there is a modern painting displayed.

"So you like modern art?" I ask as I follow Len along the hallway.

"Yes. Do you like them?"

"Yeah," I say. "I'm no art critic but I like the bright colors. They work really well in this space."

He nods, seemingly pleased I like his choice of artwork. Finally, we reach a door. He opens it and pulls me into his bedroom. The room is huge. The wall opposite is all glass. Outside lights show me a stunning view of Len's back yard, including a large swimming pool, and countryside for miles.

I look away from the view and around the room. In the center is a huge bed, the sheets and comforter black satin. The floor is covered in the same plush white carpet as the hallway, and it offsets the black bedding and the black wood furniture perfectly. The wardrobe and chest of drawers and the nightstands are all black wood and although the room is very masculine, it also feels inviting. I suppose this moment should be kind of awkward, it really isn't.

Len moves behind me and closes the bedroom door. He turns to light down so its cast enough of a glow to see by. Then he puts his hand on the small of my back and guides me towards the bed.

"You never did tell me your name," he notes cordially.

We are almost at his bed, and I grin at him over my shoulder.

"No, I didn't," I agree.

"Ohhh little Miss Mysterious, huh," he taunts

I shrug and grin back. He pulls me into his arms, and he looks at me, his face serious, and his gaze so intense that I feel as though he's looking down into my very soul.

"There are more important things to know about you than your name," he says, his voice deep and lust filled. I feel a rush of warmth between my legs. He leans in and brushes his lips against mine, the touch so light it's almost as though I imagined it. His teasing touch sets my body on fire, and I want him so badly it's like a physical ache inside of me.

"More important things like how you taste," he whispers.

He leans in again and this time, when his lips touch mine, he doesn't keep his touch light, and he doesn't pull away. Our lips move together, our tongues colliding and mashing together as we hungrily explore each other's mouths. Len tastes of beer and something kind of spicy and exotic. I love the taste of him.

I want to consume him.

I press my body against his and wrap my arms around him, moving them beneath his t-shirt and over the naked skin of his back. I grab the hem of his t-shirt and lift it up. Our mouths pull apart long enough for the t-shirt to go over Len's head and then they come together again, more hungry than before if that's even possible.

I run my hands over Len's back and up and down his sides. I push my hands into his jeans' pockets and caress his ass through the rough denim. He runs his hands over my body too and one settles on my right breast, rubbing it through the fabric of my dress. I'm not wearing a bra and the friction of the dress rubbing over me brings my nipple to life. It springs up, hard and sensitive, and Len gently pinches it, rolling it between his finger and his thumb and I moan into his mouth.

I press myself even harder against him and I can feel his hard cock pressing against my belly. I want to feel him inside of me and I move my hands from his ass around to the front of his body where I push them between us and open his jeans. I push them down and I run my hand over the outside of his boxer shorts, feeling the length of his cock. I start to push my hand into his boxer shorts, but he grabs my wrist, his mouth coming away from mine.

"Not so fast," he says.

Before I can wonder if I've done something wrong, he pushes me backwards and my legs hit the bed and I tumble down onto it and I realize what he meant – not so fast to touch him because he doesn't want to climax too early and end our fun.

He stands looking down at me on his bed and I look back. His body is every bit as toned as it looked through his clothes and I see now that his dragon tattoo doesn't just sit on his arm – the body of the beast covers part of his chest too. There's something sexy about the tattoo and I keep looking back at it as Len leans down, still looking at me as he takes off his shoes and socks and kicks his jeans off his legs. He reaches down to me and tugs at my dress. It has already worked its way over my hips and so I lift my upper body from the mattress and lift my arms up and Len slips it off over my head and drops it on the ground with his jeans.

He grabs the sides of my panties, I lift my ass and he removes those too, pulling my shoes off while he's down there, his gaze lingering on my glistening slit as he pulls the panties down my legs. When they join the other clothes on the ground, I expect Len to get on top of me, but he doesn't. Instead, he kneels down at the side of the bed. He takes my ankles in his hands and pulls me roughly towards him. He throws my legs over his shoulders and his face comes towards me.

I gasp as his warm, rough tongue finds my slick clit and begins to work it. This is a man who knows how to pleasure a woman and he doesn't mess around. He moves his tongue from side to side, lapping at my clit and pressing down on my most sensitive nerve endings. I writhe beneath him, and I tighten my thighs, bringing them together and holding Len's head in place.

I move my hips in time with his tongue, enjoying the double movement sensation. I can feel my clit tingling deliciously, spreading pleasure outwards and up into my stomach. My pussy aches to be filled and it clenches as another wave of pleasure spreads through my body.

As I hurtle towards a climax, I grab his comforter in both hands, turning them into fists, twisting the cool fabric in my grip. My head goes back and my back arches as he hits the spot one more time and sends me headlong into an orgasm.

I close my eyes and let myself feel the tingling pleasure all the way through my body. My stomach contracts and my pussy tightens. Fireworks explode on my skin sending pleasurable little sparks rolling over me. I call out Len's name as I hit the peak of my orgasm and then I'm silent, gasping for breath as I coast gently back down.

I get no reprieve. The second my muscles turn to jelly, and I lose the hold on Len I had with my thighs, he stands up, my legs falling to either side of him. He smirks at me, a look that is all sex. It's such an intense look that I feel my already desperate pussy clench again.

I start to sit up, but Len has other ideas. He reaches down and takes hold of my knees and then he flips me onto my belly. I don't resist him as he pulls me closer to him by my legs. When I can feel his skin against mine, I push myself up onto all fours.

I hear the rustle of fabric and I figure Len is taking his boxer shorts off. I try to see over my shoulder, but he's standing just out of my line of sight. I'm eagerly awaiting his touch and the anticipation of it is making me crazy with desire.

When his touch finally comes, it comes in the form of a short, sharp slap across my ass cheeks. It's not something I've ever experienced before and I cry out, a mix of, not pain exactly, but surprised indignation and of course, pleasure. I'm not quite sure if I like it but I find myself wanting him to do it again all the same and he doesn't disappoint.

Another sharp slap in the same spot leaves my skin hot and smarting but as the nerve endings register the slight stinging pain of the slap, they send pulses of pleasure through me, and I moan and press my ass backward towards Len.

He slaps me again and I cry out, a sound filled entirely with pleasure now not pain, and I feel myself teetering on the edge of another orgasm, something I would have said was impossible from being spanked.

I wait for the next slap, but it doesn't come. Instead, Len plunges inside of me. There is no warning, no gentle pushing against my opening. He slams in hard and fast, and he fills me right to the top. I cry out again and Len begins to thrust in and out of me. My pussy is wet and slick and Len's huge cock thrusting in and out of me feels absolutely amazing. With each thrust, his tip hits my g-spot on the way back in and that feeling along with the tingling in the skin of my ass sends me over the edge within moments.

I hurtle into an orgasm that seems to consume my full body. Of course, my clit feels it, and it's pulsing with ecstasy, and my pussy tightens around Len's cock as he moves inside of me. But it's more than that. Every nerve in my whole body is thrumming, every bit of me is tingling and when I climax, I climax so hard that I lose consciousness for a second. It's long enough for my elbows to give way and I find myself on my knees, my cheek on the bed.

Len doesn't stop moving inside of me despite the state of me and I love that. I love that he knows I can take this even if my body has betrayed me in the worst possible way. When my orgasm has mostly faded away, I try to push myself back up onto my hands but the muscles in my arms are too weak to move and I stay on my face, but I pump my hips in time with Len's thrusts. His hands are on my hips now, moving me harder and faster as he hurtles towards his own climax.

With one final, hard thrust that makes me scream out, Len climaxes. I feel him spurting inside of me, his cock releasing his pleasure along with his seed. His hands stay on my hips, and he holds me in place as he makes a low, growling sound in the back of his throat.

He holds me until his orgasm is done and then he slips out of me, and he flops down on his back beside me on the mattress. I pull my legs out from under me, staying on my front, my head turned to face Len. He is gasping and panting and it's clear that he felt his own orgasm as strongly as I felt mine.

For a second, I almost regret the fact that I will never see Len again, but I remind myself that it was that knowledge that allowed me to fully let go and enjoy what Len had to offer.

I fold my arms beneath my face and sigh contentedly as I wait for Len to recover. I'm wondering if maybe we're going to do that again and my pussy is aching for Len's cock once more, but a glance at his face tells me it's probably not going to happen. Len's breathing has pretty much reached a normal pace again, but his eyes are already closing. He opens them again and turns his head slightly towards me and gives a sleepy smile and then his eyes close again. He's clearly spent and even if I can keep him awake, I don't think he's going to have it in him to do that again right now.

He reaches across his body, his arm slow and sluggish. He picks my hand up and puts it on his flat stomach and covers it with his own. It's an intimate gesture, something that would normally freak me out, but I tell myself it's only my hand and it's only for a little while. It's not like he's telling me he wants us to fall asleep in each other's arms and wake up together every morning.

I lay beside Len waiting for his breathing to even out. It doesn't take that long, and I'm soon confident that he's asleep but I wait. I need him to be deeply asleep so I can get up and grab my stuff and get out of here without waking him up.

I jerk awake and look around wondering where the hell I am. I see Len beside me, and I remember. I check my watch wondering how long I've been asleep for. I'm shocked to see that it hasn't been more than half an hour. I feel like I've been out for ages. Me falling asleep was never part of the plan but it passed the time quickly and Len must be in a deeper sleep by now.

I push myself up onto my knees and turn so I'm sitting up. He doesn't stir. I take my hand off his stomach, pulling it out from underneath his hand. His hand slides down his side and onto the mattress beside him and he makes a half snoring sound, but he doesn't wake up and I breathe a sigh of relief. Having a conversation at this point would just be awkward.

I scramble off the bed as quietly as I can and grab my panties and slip them on. I pull my dress over my head and pick my purse and shoes up. I creep to the door and open it. I look back once.

Len is still sound asleep and even laid there with his mouth slightly open he is still gorgeous. I'm wondering if I'm making a mistake sneaking away like this, but I know deep down inside of myself that the mistake would be me staying.

I slip out of the bedroom, then run down the corridor, down the stairs, and out of the front door. I wait till I'm out of sight of the house before I pull my cellphone out and call myself a cab.

As I wait for the cab, I can't help but keep thinking of Len.

It's hard not to when I can smell him on my skin and taste him on my lips. It doesn't matter how much I like him though or how good he was in bed. I'm not looking for a relationship right now, not even a casual one. I got what I was looking for; good, no strings sex. I wonder if I should feel bad about sneaking away like this, but I think it's for the best for both of us.

I hate the awkward, morning after conversation where we would both pretend we were going to see each other again, even though we both would know we really had no intentions of it. This way is just easier. Cleaner. More honest. And let's face it, Len was looking for a hookup every bit as much as I was.

You don't just ask someone at the cab line to come home with you if you're looking for more than a one-night stand.

As wonderful as it was, it's over, I told myself, but for some strange reason, I couldn't help feeling slightly sad about it.

Pre-order here:
Flirting With The CEO

ABOUT THE AUTHOR

Thank you so much for reading!
If you have enjoyed the book and would like to leave a precious review for me, please kindly do so here:

Hot Professor

Please click on the link below to receive info about my latest releases and giveaways.
NEVER MISS A THING

Or
come and say hello here:

ALSO BY IONA ROSE

Nanny Wanted

CEO's Secret Baby

New Boss, Old Enemy

Craving The CEO

Forbidden Touch

Crushing On My Doctor

Reckless Entanglement

Untangle My Heart

Tangled With The CEO

Tempted By The CEO

CEO's Assistant

Trouble With The CEO

It's Only Temporary

Charming The Enemy

Keeping Secrets

On His Terms

CEO Grump

Surprise CEO

The Fire Between Us

The Forgotten Pact

Taming The CEO Beast

Printed in Great Britain
by Amazon